If Carly was as squeaky clean as the PI reported, then Mitch would have to find another way to get custody of the boy. But how could he win her over?

Seduction? The idea shot across his mind like a comet. He weighed the possibility, and his pulse quickened and his palms tingled the way they did whenever he had a winning plan.

Guilt punched him a time or two, but he ignored it. Mitch had to carry out his father's last wishes or lose his and his siblings' inheritance. If that meant he had to blur the lines of decency, then so be it.

Sharing her bed wouldn't be a hardship. But how far would he have to go?

As far as it takes.

The Millionaire's Miracle
by Cathleen Galitz

ᗩ ᗩᕁᗩ ᗹ

"This will be the last favour I ever ask of you."

Gillian reminded herself that the pure animal magnetism she felt for him could not overshadow the fact that Bryce was the most infuriating creature God had ever put on this earth. And that she could never forgive him for letting her down when she'd needed him the most.

He cut her to pieces with a look of disdain. "I don't suppose you remember the last favour I asked of you."

Gillian shrugged her shoulders. "You'll have to refresh my memory."

Instead of honouring her request, he said, "I've got to hand it to you. You've got gall waltzing into my life after all this time, acting like a little girl lost and playing on my sympathies."

"Sympathy isn't a word anyone associates with you."

Bound by the Kincaid Baby
EMILIE ROSE

The Millionaire's Miracle
CATHLEEN GALITZ

MILLS & BOON®
Pure reading pleasure™

*First published in Great Britain 2009
by Harlequin Mills & Boon Limited,
Eton House, 18-24 Paradise Road, Richmond, Surrey TW9 1SR*

The publisher acknowledges the copyright holders of the individual works as follows:

Bound by the Kincaid Baby © Emilie Rose Cunningham 2008
The Millionaire's Miracle © Cathleen Galitz 2007

ISBN: 978 0 263 87097 8

51-0409

*Printed and bound in Spain
by Litografía Rosés S.A., Barcelona*

BOUND BY THE KINCAID BABY

by
Emilie Rose

Dear Reader,

I think most of us have lived the old adage "Life is what happens when you're busy making other plans." If not, look out. Your turn's coming. And trust me, being forced out of a rut is not a bad thing – once you get over the initial shock.

What I like about romance novels is that after a little squirming, the characters jump off the hook and swim right into the current of change rather than crawl to shore and hide in the shade the way most of us would.

Mitch Kincaid and Carly Corbin's lives are cruising along happily and then wham! Life happens. In trying to fulfil their loved ones' dying wishes, Mitch and Carly are forced to face their greatest fears and weaknesses, but in the process they're able to forge something better together than either one began with.

I'm raising my mug of chocolate coffee and hoping we'll all be as brave and as lucky if change comes a'knocking at our doors.

Happy reading!

Emilie Rose

EMILIE ROSE

lives in North Carolina with her college sweetheart husband and four sons. Writing is Emilie's third (and hopefully last) career. She's managed a medical office and run a home day-care, neither of which offers half as much satisfaction as plotting happy endings. Her hobbies include quilting, gardening and cooking (especially cheesecake). Her favourite TV shows include *ER, CSI* and Discovery Channel's medical programmes. Emilie's a country music fan because she can find an entire book in almost any song.

Letters can be mailed to:
Emilie Rose
PO Box 20145,
Raleigh, NC 27619, USA
E-mail: EmilieRoseC@aol.com

To friends found when we're not looking.
Sometimes they are the ones who show us
a new and better perspective.

Prologue

"Consider it done," Mitch Kincaid said Sunday afternoon to the trio gathered around the Kincaid Manor dining-room table for the reading of his father's will.

"Don't make it sound easy. Nothing involving a woman ever is," his older brother, Rand, warned.

"Hey!" their younger sister, Nadia, protested.

Richards, the attorney, looked over his half-glasses at Mitch. "The child is your half brother and stands to inherit one quarter of your father's estate. When billions of dollars are involved, unforeseen complications often arise."

"Let me get this straight. I'm supposed to bring my father's illegitimate son home to Kincaid Manor and keep him here for one year," Mitch summarized the absurd scenario Richards had read moments ago. It didn't sound any better now than it had then.

"That is correct. And if you fail to complete your task, you will also fail to inherit your share of Everett's estate." Richards paused to scan the three legitimate Kincaid offspring. "You all will. And everything Everett possessed will be sold to Kincaid Cruise Line's chief rival for one dollar."

Billions in assets and investments down the toilet. Fifty ships. Five more on order. Eight branded cruise lines under the Kincaid umbrella. Sixty thousand employees. All resting on Mitch's shoulders.

He tried to shrug off the crushing weight. Kincaid Cruise Lines wasn't just his job; it was his life, his wife, his mistress, his child. He wasn't like his brother, who, if not for their father's unexpected death three days ago, wouldn't be in Miami now. Rand had walked away from the family and the business five years ago without looking back.

Mitch wouldn't let KCL go without a fight. That meant not only did he have to accomplish his assigned task, but also he had to make damned sure each of his siblings held up their end of the inheritance obligations, too. Or lose everything.

Not gonna happen. Not on my watch.

He made a conscious effort to relax the hands he'd fisted. "What happens to the kid when the year is up?"

"That depends on who you want controlling his fortune until he reaches twenty-one. You or his aunt," Richards replied.

"Not the aunt," Mitch replied without hesitation and turned to his brother and sister. They hadn't been privy to the latest complication of their father's life or the cleanup detail Mitch had screwed up. No doubt that was why their father had assigned him babysitting duty. Punishment.

"The boy's mother is dead and her twin sister is the kid's guardian. I'm betting Carly Corbin is identical to her greedy, conniving twin in more than looks. She's young and single. She'll want to dump the kid. If she doesn't, I'll convince her."

"How?" Rand asked.

"Money. I've never met a woman who didn't have a price." His comment elicited another indignant squawk from Nadia.

"Dad instructed me to pay the boy's mother a hundred grand to have an abortion—an abortion she obviously never had and managed to conceal from us or we wouldn't be having this conversation."

Mitch's first mistake had been to trust the woman when she'd accepted the money. He should have ensured she'd done what she'd been paid to do whether or not he'd approved of his father's plan.

Rand's eyes narrowed. "You're sure the little bastard is Dad's?"

Mitch nodded. "A DNA test confirmed it."

A familiar hard knot returned to Mitch's chest. Their father had received the test results just days before the child's mother had been killed in a hit-and-run accident while crossing the street. The driver and car responsible hadn't been found.

He hoped like hell his father hadn't had a part in the woman's death. But Everett Kincaid had never liked playing by any rules other than his own. No one knew that better than Mitch—his father's right-hand man.

Nadia nervously tapped her nails on the table, anxious no doubt to hear her inheritance requirement. "Ignoring your incredibly sexist remarks and assuming Ms. Corbin hands over—what is our brother's name?" She glanced at her copy of the will. "Rhett. Oh, I get it. Ever-*Rhett*. After Dad. Cute. What do you know about taking care of a one-year-old?"

Mitch knew more than Nadia thought. But he wasn't going there. Ever again. "I don't need to know anything. I'll hire a nanny. The manor's large enough I'll never have to see the brat."

He aligned his pen beside the thick pile of pages constituting the will. "I'll have him installed in the nursery by the end of the month. Before year's end, I'll have guardianship and the aunt will be history. Bank on it."

One

A pricey pewter-colored SUV blocked Carly's driveway Monday evening.

She maneuvered the stroller around the big bumper and glanced at her house. The setting sun's slanted rays revealed an equally expensive-looking man on her porch swing. If he was the dishwasher repairman she'd called this morning, then she seriously needed to consider changing occupations because appliance repair paid better than physical therapy.

He rose as she turned up the walk, unfolding a tall and broad-shouldered frame beneath a black suit and pale yellow shirt and knotted black patterned tie. Short dark hair swept back from his forehead, and as she drew nearer she noticed the intense green eyes set beneath thick eyebrows in a gorgeous face. The kind of face that could launch a thousand sexual fantasies.

Despite the oppressive June heat and Miami humidity, he looked fresh from the boardroom while she dripped with sweat. And he had the successful and affluent thing going for him which meant he was probably one of Marlene's men.

Sadness slammed Carly like a rogue wave and sucked at her footsteps, tugging her into a riptide of grief. Maybe he didn't know Marlene was…

Carly swallowed the lump rising in her throat.

Gone. Her twin was *gone*. Forever. And all Carly had left of Marlene was her sister's precious baby boy.

She blinked at the sting of tears. When her vision cleared, she registered that this guy was young. Early thirties. Her sister had preferred wealthy men, specifically wealthy *older* men. Like Everett Kincaid. Rhett's daddy.

As if her nephew knew Carly was thinking about the father he'd never met and now never would meet, Rhett let loose a string of one-year-old babble.

God, she loved him. He was so darned adorable she wanted to snatch him up and hug him until he squealed. Hug him like she'd never hugged her own daughter. She tamped down that disturbing thought.

Rhett would get his cuddle, but first she had to deal with her visitor. "Can I help you?"

"Carly Corbin?" His voice was deep, polished, clipped. He descended the porch stairs to join her on the sidewalk and his eyes raked over her, making her conscious of her faded, skimpy running shorts, sweat-dampened T-shirt and stringy ponytail.

She had to tip her head back to look into his face. "Who's asking?"

"I'm Mitch Kincaid."

Anger flashed through Carly. So this was the jerk who'd done everything he could to break up her sister and Everett and who'd later tried to bully Marlene into having an abortion. It was because of his pestering that Marlene had given up her luxury apartment and moved in with Carly.

She'd heard about Everett's older children from Marlene.

Fear expanded in her chest, crowding out the anger. God help her if the Kincaids ever found out about Marlene's plot to snare Everett. Carly was terrified they would use it to take Rhett from her.

But they won't find out. You burned Marlene's journal. Nobody but you knows and you're not telling.

She dampened her suddenly dry lips. "And?"

"I'm here to meet…my brother. Is that him?" His narrowed gaze swept Rhett from his shock of baby-fine dark hair to his drool-covered grinning face to his chubby knees and double-knotted sneakers.

"Half brother," she corrected. "And, yes. This is Rhett."

Mitch's surprise-widened eyes found hers. "He looks like a Kincaid."

"Did you think Marlene lied?"

"DNA proved she didn't." His bitter tone indicated displeasure over that circumstance. "May I come in?"

Carly truly believed in close-knit family ties and wanted those for Rhett, but something was off here. Rhett's handsome half brother hadn't squatted down to the child's level or even spoken to him directly. That made her uneasy.

"Maybe another time. I need to feed Rhett, give him his bath and get him ready for bed."

"It's about Rhett's inheritance."

She bit her lip. Marlene hadn't had life insurance. At twenty-eight, she hadn't believed she needed it. Neither of them had. Carly made a decent salary, but the burial costs, child care and car and house payments consumed most of her income. She didn't know how she'd sock money away for Rhett's college education. "Everett provided for him?"

Kincaid's sexy full lips flattened and his eyes hardened. "Conditionally."

"Up. Up." Rhett held up his arms and squirmed to get out of the stroller.

Carly unbuckled him and lifted his warm, wiggly little body against hers. She held him tight and savored his sweet baby smell. "What do you mean conditionally?"

"Perhaps we could discuss my father's will while you feed the boy."

The boy. Kincaid hadn't even made eye contact with *the boy.*

Carly wanted Rhett to have everything a growing child needed, and she'd like for him to get to know his half siblings—just in case something ever happened to her. Marlene's death had been a shocking and sudden reminder that bad and unexpected things did happen. That meant she had to deal with Rhett's handsome half brother sooner or later. Might as well get it over with.

"Okay. But I'm warning you now that you need to shuck your designer suit jacket."

"*I'm* not going to feed him."

She ought to make him. Just for fun. She fought a smile and lost. "If you're in the same room, you need to be dressed for feeding time. It gets messy."

The intense green gaze locked on her face for several seconds, and his eyes met and held hers. Something deep inside Carly tingled. She squashed the fizzy feeling, pivoted quickly and jogged up the stairs. Her hand wasn't quite steady as she unlocked the front door, then gestured for him to follow her inside.

He'd removed his coat while she wasn't looking, and even though she'd told him to, now she wished he hadn't. Those wide shoulders hadn't been an illusion created by an excellent tailor. She'd bet he had washboard abs under that shirt and long, corded muscles beneath his knife-edged creased trousers. She worked with enough athletes to recognize and admire peak physical conditioning when she saw it.

She led the way through the house, leaving her unwanted guest to shut the door and follow. Or not. In the kitchen she washed Rhett's hands, strapped him into his high chair and poured a sprinkling of Cheerios on his tray to keep him occupied while she prepared his dinner.

She retrieved a sippy cup of milk and a couple of bottles of water from the fridge. Politeness demanded she offer her "guest" a drink and she did so ungraciously by plunking a bottle down on the counter in silent offering to the man who took up far too much space in her kitchen. She twisted the cap off her own. After chugging half the icy liquid, she pulled out a cutting board and started Rhett's dinner.

"So talk." She kept a wary eye on Kincaid.

He transferred the unopened water bottle from one long-fingered hand to the other and back again like a metronome. "Rhett will inherit one-quarter share of my—our—father's estate."

The knife slipped from her grip and hit the stainless sink with a loud clank. Everett Kincaid had been a billionaire. Anyone who read the newspaper knew that. Kincaid Cruise Lines was a huge firm that for years had been voted one of the top five places in the country to work.

"You're kidding me."

"No." That bitten out word carried hidden nuances Carly couldn't begin to decipher.

Maybe Everett wasn't the lecherous miser Carly thought him to be if he'd made arrangements for his son. She retrieved the knife, rinsed it and then focused on cutting bite-size pieces of bananas, grapes and cheese without severing a digit. "Go on."

"The condition is that Rhett must reside in Kincaid Manor for one full year to claim his share."

It took a second for that to sink in. And when it did, her heart slammed against her chest and her nerves snarled.

Feeling as if she'd swallowed a bucket of wet sand, she swung around to face Mitch Kincaid. "You want to take him from me."

"I'll make it worth your while."

She blinked and shook her head. "I don't understand."

"I'll pay you one hundred thousand dollars for your trouble. The same amount my father paid your sister to have an abortion."

No. Carly sucked a quick breath. Marlene had done a few questionable things over the years, but Carly couldn't believe her sister would stoop so low as to accept money for an abortion and then not have one. Besides, Marlene had been thrilled about her pregnancy and overjoyed at Rhett's birth. She would never have considered ending it.

But then Carly remembered Marlene's plan to coerce Everett into marriage and she wasn't as certain Mitch was lying as she'd like to be. That notebook had revealed an unattractive side of her sister that Carly hadn't known existed.

"Marlene didn't have that kind of money."

"I have proof she did. She lived with you for the last fifteen months of her life. You had to have seen evidence of her windfall." The last word dripped sarcasm. "You probably even benefited from it."

Indignant, she snapped erect. "I did not. And I don't know about any money."

Rhett pounded on his tray, jerking Carly back to the present. She numbly carried him his food.

Mitch Kincaid had to be lying. If Marlene had taken the money, then what had she done with it? She certainly hadn't spent it. Her living expenses after she quit her job as an air hostess for a corporate jet service had been negligible because, as Mitch pointed out, Marlene had moved in with Carly. Afterward the formerly sociable Corbin sister had rarely left the house until after Rhett's birth. She'd claimed it was because she was heartbroken over Everett's betrayal and his refusal to acknowledge his child.

Could Marlene have taken the money and used it for

hospital bills? Carly made a mental note to ask the attorney how one went about tracing things like that.

"I don't believe you, and I'm not loaning this child to you."

"I'm not asking to borrow him. I'm offering to take over as his guardian. You'll be free to go about your life unencumbered."

Déjà vu. Her heart clenched in horror and a chill enveloped her. The words sounded eerily similar to those she'd heard twelve years ago. She fought the urge to pull Rhett from his chair and hold him close.

"I love Rhett. I don't consider him an encumbrance. And my sister wanted *me* to raise him."

"As a struggling single parent?"

"If necessary."

"C'mon, Carly, you're young, single and attractive. Why would you want to be saddled with someone else's brat?"

Her brain snagged on *attractive,* but repudiated *brat.* Then she recalled how scraggly she looked after a five-mile run. Clearly Kincaid was willing to say whatever it took to get what he wanted.

"I was there when Rhett was born, when he cut his first tooth, said his first word and took his first step. God willing, I'll be there for every other milestone. I'm not giving him up."

"I can offer the boy more than you can." His supercilious gaze encompassed her outdated kitchen.

"My house may not be up to Kincaid standards, but it's safe and childproofed and full of love. I have a huge fenced backyard." She hated that she sounded defensive. She had nothing to prove to this jerk.

"What does a physical therapist make these days? Sixty, seventy grand a year?"

He knew what she did and how much she made. The knowledge sent a prickle of apprehension over her. How did he know? "None of your busin—"

"That's nothing compared to the roughly one point two-five billion Rhett will inherit if he comes with me."

"Billion?" she squeaked.

"Not in cash. Most of the assets aren't liquid," he clarified. "Either he moves in with me or he gets nothing."

Light-headed and growing queasier by the second, Carly sank into a chair. How could she deprive her nephew of the inheritance he so rightly deserved, one that would set him up so that he'd never want for anything?

But how could she let him go?

She couldn't. Carly had promised Marlene that if anything happened to her, she'd raise Rhett and love him—love him the way she'd never been allowed to love her own daughter.

Mitch Kincaid wasn't offering love. Other than that first searching glance, he'd barely looked at Rhett and had yet to touch him.

She took a deep breath and tried to think logically. Marlene had yearned for Everett to acknowledge his son, and now, better late than never, he had. Maybe there was a way to make this work. "I need to speak to my attorney. And I'll need a copy of the will."

Kincaid's mouth tightened with impatience. "We have a limited amount of time to implement my father's terms, Ms. Corbin. What will it take? Five hundred thousand for your trouble?"

At first she thought he was joking, then realized from the hard glint in his eyes and the harsh angle of his jaw that he was serious. Carly gaped at him. He honestly wanted to buy her nephew. Worse, he thought she'd sell Rhett. The idea infuriated her.

No wonder Marlene had called Everett's son a dirty, conniving rat bastard.

"You're out of your mind. You can't buy and sell people."

"A million?" He ignored her comment and extracted a

checkbook and pen from the jacket draped over his arm as if writing a million-dollar check was no big deal.

She rose on shaky legs. "Rhett isn't for sale, Mr. Kincaid. You need to leave."

Rhett chose that moment to cackle with glee and squish bananas through his fingers. And then the little urchin clutched fistfuls of his hair, moussing the silky strands with the banana mush. "Unless you'd like to help with cleanup."

Kincaid backed away as if a sewage spill threatened his polished shoes. He reached into his coat pocket again and this time withdrew a business card that he laid on the counter next to his unopened water. "I'll have a copy of the will couriered over immediately. Talk to your lawyer tomorrow and call me."

He turned on his heel. Brisk footsteps retreated, then the front door opened and closed.

Carly looked at her adorable nephew and her chest ached. "Oh, Rhett. What are we going to do? I can't lose you."

She dampened a washcloth and attacked his messy hands and face. "But you deserve a share of your daddy's estate. And I'm going to see that you get it."

"I'm sorry to interrupt," Marie, Mitch's personal assistant, said from the boardroom entrance, "but there's a Carly Corbin downstairs insisting on seeing you. She doesn't have an appointment."

About time.

"Show her to my office." After Marie left, Mitch stood and looked down the table at his brother. "Three days. It took her three days to cave. The question is how much is this little bastard going to cost us? I'll be back."

Rand waved him on. "Take your time. I'll handle the next applicant for Nadia's position and then grab lunch."

The damned will had left Mitch with an interminable number of complications. His sister had been banished to

Dallas to house-sit as required by her inheritance clause. Her sudden absence only increased his workload. He had to find her temporary replacement, and he had his brother's help whether he wanted it or not, thanks to dear ol' dad making Rand CEO instead of Mitch. That irritated Mitch like a sliver of glass stuck in his foot.

Rand had abandoned the business. Hell, his brother hadn't even spoken to anyone in the family in five years. Five years during which Mitch had busted his ass to prove he was worthy of taking the reins of KCL when his father retired.

But Dad had wanted Rand back and in charge.

Mitch entered his office through the connecting door to the boardroom. Before he could sit down Marie showed in his guest.

Carly barely acknowledged his presence with a brief nod before her wide brown eyes gazed past him to scan the thirty-foot wall of windows and the view of Biscayne Bay behind him.

He stiffened. Women didn't overlook him. It wasn't conceit to admit that his wealth wasn't his only asset. But Carly didn't seem interested in his face or body. Ignoring the jab to his pride, he took advantage of her inattention to assess her.

Her features weren't classically beautiful. But close enough. Her breasts were decent. Neither too big nor too small. Probably real. She wore a bubble gum-pink tracksuit with black stripes down the length of her legs. Killer legs, he recalled from their last meeting. Too bad she'd covered them today. Getting another look would have been a nice bonus to closing the deal.

Overall, Carly was nice-looking. Not traffic-stopping. But interesting. Until she smiled. That smile of hers could melt bricks. She wasn't smiling today.

Since she was an identical twin, he could see why his father had been attracted to her sister. But damnation, couldn't the man have practiced safe sex after preaching about it for decades? Or had Marlene Corbin had something to do with the birth control failure? Mitch would bet money on it. His father had made a number of mistakes, but he hadn't been stupid.

Carly's gaze finally returned to Mitch. A weird paralysis seized his lungs. He fought it off. "Do we have a deal, Ms. Corbin?"

"Rhett can move into Kincaid Manor," she stated matter-of-factly.

Victory surged through him. He pulled his checkbook from his interior coat pocket. "Excell—"

"But only if I come with him."

His fingers contracted around his pen. "Excuse me?"

"You exude about as much warmth as dry ice, Kincaid. Children need more than that."

His spine went rigid at the insult. "I know how to handle kids."

"Really? Because I didn't see evidence of that the other day. You didn't even try to make a connection with your brother."

"Half brother, as you pointed out. There wasn't time."

"Eye contact and a smile only take a second."

She had him there. "And your price?"

"I don't want your money."

Yeah, like he believed that. What game was she playing? "What of your home? You'll leave it vacant?"

"I can rent it for enough to cover the mortgage."

Her plan shouldn't have surprised him. In his experience, women were always looking for a free ride. In Carly's case, Kincaid Manor would be like a spa vacation compared to the in-need-of-renovation structure she inhabited. "Your presence isn't required."

"Rhett stays with me, his guardian. And since my attorney says you only had thirty days from the reading of the will to begin fulfilling your part of your father's demands or forfeit your inheritance, you're going to have to come to terms with the package deal sooner rather than later."

Nineteen of those days had passed. Days during which Mitch had employed two teams of lawyers to try to find a loophole in the will. When they'd failed, he'd spent more time hiring a nanny and trying to find out what he could about Carly Corbin. If Carly hadn't come to him by tomorrow, he would have gone after her.

"I would imagine you have my number since you have everything else." She backed toward the door.

"Carly, how much do you want?" He signed a blank check and then slid it and his pen across the desk. "You fill in the amount. Whatever you feel is fair."

Without even glancing at the pen and check, she observed him as if he were three-day-old July roadkill. "You just don't get it, do you, Kincaid?"

He linked his hands behind his back, hoping to appear casual instead of frustrated and irritated and damn near desperate. "Then perhaps you'll enlighten me."

"This isn't about money. It's about a little boy and what's best for him. It's always about doing what's best for the child. *Always*. In this case, you're not it."

"The boy will lack for nothing."

"Materially. And his name is Rhett."

Mitch struggled to rein in his temper, but his entire head grew hot. "*Rhett* will have the best of care."

Angry color stained Carly's cheeks and sparked in her eyes, making her look even more attractive. She approached his desk, planted her hands on the polished surface and leaned toward him. "Who will hold him when he's cranky? Who'll kiss his boo-boos and rock him when he has a nightmare? Who will tell him about his mother? And who will make sure he knows he was loved and w-wanted?"

The slight crack in her voice nailed him in the gut. She'd just lost her sister, and even if Marlene had been a mercenary, manipulative bitch, apparently Carly had cared for her. Maybe giving up the boy wouldn't be completely painless. But like ripping off a bandage, the discomfort wouldn't last long.

Being the middle child meant Mitch had learned the art of negotiation in the cradle. If he didn't compromise, he'd lose the brat. "I have employed a highly qualified nanny. I'm not trying to cut you out of his life completely. We'll arrange visitation."

"A nanny? You're going to *pay* someone to love him?" Her indignant tone and humorless laugh didn't bode well. Gold fragments glinted in her dark irises. "Is money your answer to everything?"

"There's nothing wrong with nannies. My siblings and I were raised by a series of competent—"

Her snort cut him off. "Now I get it. No wonder you're such a robot."

He flinched at her insult.

Leaving the check untouched on his desk, she marched to the door and paused with her hand on the knob. "That's my offer, Kincaid. Take it or leave it. You get both of us or neither of us. You can pursue this in court with a whole platoon of lawyers if you want, but considering your father allegedly paid my sister an obscene amount of money to abort, and you and your siblings are driven by potential monetary gains, no judge in his right mind will ever award you custody of Rhett even if you are an almighty Kincaid. And that's *if* you can get the case heard before your thirty days are up. Because rest assured, if you sue for custody, I will delay you in every way possible."

Her ponytail swung out parallel to the floor as she pivoted abruptly and slammed the door behind her.

Mitch swore. It didn't help that she was right. His attorneys had told him the same thing. He'd counted on her being as greedy as her sister and wanting fast cash.

Instead, he had no doubt Carly Corbin was in it to milk him for the long haul. And he had no choice but to accede to her absurd demands.

But he had every intention of winning this battle and he'd do whatever it took to come out on top.

"There's no place like home," Carly muttered under her breath. "There's certainly no place like this one."

She stood in the circular driveway Saturday morning staring up at the expansive ivory-stone facade of Kincaid Manor. The place looked like a castle that had been yanked out of the English countryside and dropped into a Miami gated community.

She'd had to stop and give her name at a guardhouse to get into the neighborhood, and then talk to a disembodied voice at a second set of elaborate iron gates. Those gates had glided shut behind her, locking her inside the Kincaid compound the moment her car had passed through.

Sunlight glinted off a multitude of windows on a steeply roofed two-story structure the length of your average strip mall. Shrubbery pruned to the nth degree surrounded the foundation and fenced the sidewalk as if intended to keep visitors from straying onto the perfectly manicured emerald lawn.

Not exactly ideal for a growing boy whose only speeds were asleep and wide open, but Carly's attorney had instructed her to make nice and play along while they explored their legal options. For Rhett's sake, she could put up with just about anything.

Hours after she'd left the KCL offices, Mitch had called, "invited" her to stay and given her directions to Kincaid Manor. Carly had immediately sat down and developed a step-by-step plan to bond the Kincaid offspring. She'd work on Mitch first, then she'd tackle his brother, Rand.

"Let's hope the palace is childproofed, buddy."

Rhett squirmed in her arms and babbled a reply. She set him down and herded him toward the porch. He toddled away with a childish giggle.

The imposing lead-glass front door opened, framing Mitch Kincaid. How appropriate. The lord of the manor had deigned to oversee their arrival. But he didn't step out to greet them. He waited, arms folded, while she helped Rhett scramble up the stairs on his hands and knees.

Even though it was the weekend, Mitch wore a suit—this one stark black with a blinding white shirt and a ruby tie. Did the man ever unwind?

Mitch barely glanced at Rhett. "You brought your things?"

Before she could stop him, Rhett bolted across the porch and wrapped his little arms around his half brother's thigh. Her nephew never met a stranger.

Mitch stiffened.

Was that a flash of panic Carly detected in his eyes? Of course not. Who would be scared of an adorable child? She must have mistaken annoyance for fear.

Rhett grasped two chubby fists in the immaculate fabric of Mitch's trousers and bounced, demanding, "Up. Up. Pig me up."

Step one in getting these two to know each other: Mitch might as well learn from the get-go that once Rhett started that song and dance, it wouldn't end until he got what he wanted.

"My minivan's loaded. I wanted to get Rhett settled before I started schlepping our luggage."

"Ingrid," Mitch spoke over his shoulder. "Take the boy to the nursery while I show Ms. Corbin to her suite."

A stacked and stunning blonde in snug hipster jeans and an even tighter, belly-showing T-shirt appeared behind him. The hand she placed on Mitch's lean waist as she ducked around him in the wide doorway was far too familiar for an employee, and her long acrylic nails were likely to put some-one's eye out. "Come on, little Brett."

"Rhett," Carly corrected automatically and stepped be-tween the woman and Rhett at the same time Mitch shifted.

Carly and Mitch collided. Her hip ended up aligned with

his rock-hard thigh and her shoulder pressed the equally firm wall of his chest. She inhaled sharply, and Mitch's cologne filled her nose. A flood of warmth and awareness swept through her. She stomped on the unwanted response and focused on the problem. *The other problem.* "Who are you?"

The blonde tossed her long hair over her shoulder and smiled intimately at Mitch before replying, "I'm Rhett's nanny."

With a face and body like that, I'll just bet you are.

Carly glared at Mitch, then bent to pry Rhett's stubby fingers from the lord of the manor's pants. Mitch's muscles contracted beneath her touch as she maneuvered. She could feel body heat radiating through the summer-weight fabric, and it almost scorched her. And being at eye level with his crotch was…distracting to say the least.

She finally freed her wiggly nephew and scooped him up. "I told you Rhett didn't a nanny."

"Who will watch him while you're working? Or do you intend to quit your job and live off my largesse?" The superior way he intoned the words and looked down at her, as if he expected her to freeload off him, set her teeth on edge.

"I'm not quitting my job. I'll watch Rhett when I'm here, and when I'm at work Lucy, his regular day-care provider, will watch him."

"And when you go out in the evening?"

Carly blinked. "You mean on a date?"

He lowered that square chin a fraction of an inch.

"I don't date."

Mitch's eyes narrowed. "You mean you're not seeing anyone at the moment. But that will change."

She hadn't dated since Marlene died and she had no inclination to wade back into the muddy dating waters again anytime soon. But she wasn't admitting that to Mitch and his playmate.

"If I want to go out, I'll hire a babysitter."

"Unnecessary. Ingrid will take over."

"Don't be ridiculous. Even if I went out every night of the week—which I won't—that wouldn't justify a full-time nanny's salary." She turned to the bottled, navel-ringed blonde. "Sorry, Ingrid. Nothing personal. But Rhett just lost his mother, and he's moving into a strange house. That's enough changes for one little guy to make right now."

"He'll adapt," Mitch snarled quietly.

Carly tipped her head back and held his gaze without blinking. "The way I see it, Kincaid, I hold all the cards. I have nothing to gain by moving in here and you have everything to lose if we don't."

Of course, Rhett would lose, too. But his safety was her primary concern. Not even a billion-plus bucks would make her overlook his well-being. She wasn't going to leave him in the care of Mitch's horny, dragon-clawed girlfriend.

She felt a bit unfair for judging the woman by her looks, but after interviewing dozens of day-care providers with Marlene, Carly had learned to tell almost instantly which ones had a rapport with children. Ingrid did not. She was almost as cold and detached as her boss—until she looked at Mitch. Then she looked ready to get XXX-rated hot.

Mitch's nostrils flared and his lips flatlined. He looked angry enough to bend horseshoes with his bare hands or maybe his clenched teeth. "Ingrid, please wait for me in the living room. I'll join you after Ms. Corbin and I have discussed your qualifications."

38-24-34. Oh yeah, those were serious qualifications.

But not for child care.

"I'll show you to your room." Mitch turned and stalked across an Italian marble foyer almost as large as the entire first floor of Carly's house.

He hadn't agreed to her terms, but Carly, curious to see more of the mansion and where Mitch intended to put them, followed him anyway. The staircase rose from the center of the polished flagstone floor like a water fountain arching in opposite directions at the top. Carly's gaze stuck to the flexing muscles of his butt like a fly to flypaper as he climbed.

No way. She couldn't find him attractive. Not after all Marlene had told her. She was merely one athlete admiring another's well-toned physique. *Right?*

Shifting her gaze from the glutei maximi ahead of her, she trailed her host. The walk through the gallery, past antique furniture and paintings that looked as if they belonged in a museum, seemed to take forever. "Good grief, how big is this place?"

"Fifteen thousand square feet," he replied, turning down a long hall. A set of double doors marked the end, but he stopped short of them and pushed open a door on the right.

"Your suite."

Carly brushed past him. Her shoulder grazed his chest. She cursed the frisson of goose bumps the small contact caused.

Surprised, she turned a slow circle, taking in the tasteful lavender, white and mint decor that included a curtained four-poster bed, ornate French furniture and plum-colored rugs. The room looked like a decorating magazine snapshot. Perfect down to the last detail. As much as Kincaid seemed to resent her presence, she'd expected to be stuck in a closet somewhere or maybe the servants' quarters.

"Me down," Rhett demanded and squirmed in her arms.

"Not yet, buddy." Not until she'd moved the expensive-looking breakables out of his reach.

She crossed to the bay window and knelt on its cushioned window seat to look into the backyard. Her mouth dropped open. People actually lived like this?

The formal gardens between her window and the opposite side of the U-shaped house looked elaborate enough for a government monument or a movie set, and whoever had designed them had been fond of rulers. All straight lines. Not one single curve. The roses probably even grew square petals.

An expansive tiled patio stretched across the base of the U, complete with a square water fountain and spouting Poseidon statue. The grassy area immediately off the patio contained, of all things, a koi pond. Beyond the fish, rigid rows of shrubs flanked an Olympic-length pool that reached all the way to a seawall, boat dock, yacht and what looked like two hundred feet of waterfront.

"We're going to have to keep Rhett away from all that water."

"I'll order fencing and safety locks immediately."

Crossing to a door, she pushed it open to reveal a luxurious bathroom straight out of a hedonist's fantasies. A glass shower. A tub big enough to accommodate four. A marble-topped vanity as long as a bed. Shaking her head at the opulence, she returned to the bedroom and opened a second door to reveal a closet the size of her bedroom back home. But she didn't see a crib or connecting door to a nursery.

She rejoined Mitch. "Where's Rhett's room?"

He nodded toward the window, indicating the opposite wing of the house. "In the east wing."

"I won't be able to hear him from here."

"That's why we have Ingrid."

"*We* don't have Ingrid. *You* have Ingrid."

His eyes narrowed to green slits. "What are you implying?"

"Your girlfriend is not looking after Rhett."

"She's not my girlfriend."

"Oh please. She almost slipped her hand in your pocket for a quick grope downstairs."

His chin jacked up. He closed the distance between them in three long strides and stared down at her with what would have been intimidating ferocity if she didn't work with professional athletes on a regular basis. She'd become immune to the psyche-out glare.

"I don't keep mistresses in my home."

"But you do keep them. Or in this case, her."

Before he could argue, Rhett launched himself at Mitch, startling Carly so much she almost dropped the imp. Kincaid's only choice was too catch him. Rhett clamped his hands around his half brother's neck and planted a slobbery kiss on his cheek.

The horror in the lord of the manor's eyes made Carly snort with laughter. Okay, so that had been a wet kiss. A little disgust was warranted. She released Rhett's lower half and her nephew shimmied up his brother like a monkey does a tree.

Mitch closed his eyes. The muscles in his jaw knotted—along with every other muscle group she could see. What was going on? He acted as if he couldn't bear to hold the child.

"Take him." He ground out the words.

Confused by his weird behavior, Carly hesitated. Rhett couldn't possibly be more adorable. And he was clean. He didn't even have a dirty diaper.

Mitch thrust Rhett back at her. Frowning, Carly took him. "You want to be his guardian? How are you going to do that when you can't even handle holding him? What is your problem, Kincaid?"

Boy, did she have her work cut out for her in bringing these two together.

Mitch scowled. "I don't have a problem other than a stubborn guest. I'll show you the nursery."

Carly shook her head and stood her ground. "Rhett and I are not sleeping a football field apart. Either you bring his crib in here or I'm staying in the nursery."

"Don't be ridiculous."

Carly held Mitch's gaze. After a moment's standoff, he huffed an aggravated breath, crossed the room to an intercom system imbedded in the wall and punched a button. "Mrs. Duncan, please have the nursery furniture transferred to the blue suite."

Mitch turned and scowled at Carly. "Satisfied?"

"That depends. Let's see the blue room."

He stalked across the hall and threw open the opposite door. Carly followed more slowly, making sure not to brush against him this time when she entered. Mitch made it easy by staying out of Rhett's reach.

Shades of blue from powder to midnight turned the room into a peaceful sanctuary. Like hers, the suite had a connecting bath and a closet large enough to be Rhett's playroom. "It's beautiful, and if I leave the doors open at night, I'll be able to hear him."

A look she couldn't identify flickered in Mitch's eyes. "Fine. Now if you'll hand the b—Rhett—over to Ingrid, we'll have lunch before moving your things inside."

"No Ingrid."

"She is not my lover."

"She wants to be."

A smug smile slanted his lips, and her stomach sank like a wet sandbag. He could charm the birds from the trees with that smile. She hoped he didn't aim it at her very often.

He tilted his head, his green gaze traveled down the length of Carly's body, then slowly returned. Her skin tingled and her nipples tightened in the wake of his inspection. "It disturbs you that she wants me?"

Carly stiffened at his implication that she might be jealous. "There's no accounting for tastes. You can sleep with her and each of the Miami Dolphins cheerleaders solely or en masse for all I care, but I'm not having the woman in charge of Rhett's safety concentrating on getting into your pants when she should be watching him."

The smile vanished. "Ingrid came highly recommended from a business associate."

"Then she won't have trouble finding another job." He opened his mouth—presumably to argue. She held up her hand to cut him off. "Mitch, this one's nonnegotiable."

"Apparently, many things are nonnegotiable with you."

"I'm not afraid to fight for what I want." She had been once, and she'd paid the price ever since.

"Like your sister." His tone made the comment an insult.

Fury, pain and panic hit her like a barrage of arrows. She gritted her teeth and blinked away the sting in her eyes, but she refused to engage in this particular war of words. He couldn't know about Marlene's plan. Her sister hadn't been the type to broadcast her secrets. Not even to her twin. And Carly had no intention of giving Mitch Kincaid ammunition by sharing what she knew.

"Deal or no deal, Kincaid?"

After a few tense moments Mitch nodded once. "No Ingrid."

Carly exhaled. She'd won the battle, but she had a feeling she'd unintentionally declared war against a man her sister had claimed didn't fight fair.

Two

Carly's plan to turn Mitch into a family man wasn't going to be as easy as she'd hoped. She hadn't expected to have to start with a man who couldn't bear to touch the child.

Tomorrow she'd have to reassess the stages of Mitch's conversion and possibly break the process down into smaller achievable increments. As if she were training an athlete for a marathon she'd set daily and weekly goals toward attaining the ultimate objective by the end of the year. She wanted Mitch to love Rhett as much as she did. Nothing less would do.

She yanked on her nightie and pulled open the bathroom door. Steam wafted into the bedroom from behind her. Glancing at the big four-poster bed, she anticipated sinking into the thick mattress, but first she needed to check on Rhett one last time. She crossed the hall.

This morning, a team of employees had removed the furniture from the blue room and replaced it with obviously new nursery furniture. After lunch, Mitch had surprised her by dismissing them and helping her unload her car himself during Rhett's nap.

So he wasn't a complete jerk and he wasn't afraid of hard work. But not once had she seen him try to connect with Rhett, and that annoyed her like a festering splinter. A child needed the love and support of his family. All of his family. And he needed to know he was loved and that the one in charge would do the right thing. No matter how difficult.

Rhett had been overwound after a day full of changes, but had finally gone out like a light thirty minutes ago. Carly straightened the lightweight blanket covering him and bent to kiss his forehead. She couldn't possibly love him any more if he were her own.

A sound behind her made her straighten and turn. Mitch stood in the open doorway silhouetted by the light she'd left burning in her bedroom.

"He finally settled?" His low rumbling voice raised the hairs on Carly's arms and reminded her she was naked except for her worn thigh-length nightshirt. She hadn't bothered with a robe because she'd thought Mitch would be off in his own wing of the monstrous ten-bedroom house.

Wrapping her arms around her middle, she crossed the lush carpet and stopped in front of him before whispering, "Yes. He's not usually so cranky. Today was a bit much for him, I think."

Mitch's slow head-to-toe appraisal set her pulse aflutter. Dark evening beard shadowed his jaw and upper lip, and his slightly rumpled hair looked as if he'd run his hands through the thick strands a few times. He'd removed his suit coat and tie and rolled back the sleeves of his shirt to reveal muscular forearms dusted with dark whorls.

In a word, he looked sexy. And he smelled great. The crisp aroma of his cologne had faded and a more masculine, more alluring scent had taken its place. Mitch's scent.

Forget it. He's not your type.

"Well...good night." She stepped forward and he moved aside.

"Good night." He turned and walked toward the double doors at the end of the hall. One stood open, revealing the bottom end of a king-size bed covered in a dark green damask spread.

Alarm bells clamored in Carly's head. "That's your room?"

"Yes."

How could she sleep with her door open to listen out for Rhett when she knew Mitch could stroll past at any moment?

Mitch's gaze turned arctic. "And don't bother sleepwalking. My door will be locked."

Anger shrieked through her like steam through a boiling teakettle. Before she could think of an appropriate comeback, Mitch entered his room and shut his door. The lock clicked.

Carly's short nails bit into her palms and fury chewed her insides. Marlene had been too kind in labeling Mitch Kincaid a rat bastard.

So much for sweet dreams.

Laughter pulled Mitch from the dining room to the kitchen. Surprise halted him in the doorway.

Mrs. Duncan had been a fixture at Kincaid Manor since before Mitch's birth, but he'd never heard the woman laugh. He wasn't even sure he'd ever seen her smile.

Making airplane noises, the head housekeeper bent over the brat's high chair with a spoon in her hand and a twinkle in her eyes. *Mrs. Duncan could twinkle?* She caught sight of Mitch and abruptly stopped buzzing. Her amusement vanished and her lined face settled back into a familiar expressionless cast. She snapped upright.

"I'm sorry, sir. I didn't realize you were waiting for your breakfast. I'll bring it right through." She set the spoon and bowl she held in front of Carly.

Mitch's gaze shifted to his unwanted guest. Instead of her usual ponytail, Carly's hair draped her shoulders in a silky smooth curtain of mink brown. The sunlight streaming through the window behind her glinted on a few golden strands.

"Morning, Mitch." She flashed him one of her brick-melting smiles and a shot of adrenaline negated his need for coffee. Apparently, *this* Corbin didn't hold grudges. Or did she merely conceal her vindictiveness better than her sister had?

"Good morning, Carly." She wore another tracksuit—this one in blinding tangerine with white stripes on the sleeves. He focused on her obnoxiously bright clothing in a failed attempt to wipe the image of last night's attire from his mind. Her shapeless, oversize T-shirt had been worn almost to the point of transparency. The shadows of her nipples, navel and the dark curls between her legs had been obvious through the faded fabric.

He'd resented the hell out of his instantaneous response. He didn't like the woman. How could he possibly desire her?

Because you need to get laid.

But not by her.

She had a bowl in front of her and a glass of orange juice. "Della treated me to her secret recipe apple-cinnamon-raisin oatmeal. You should try it."

Della? Who was Della?

"Mr. Kincaid prefers bacon and eggs," Mrs. Duncan said in her usual monotone.

Della was Mrs. Duncan? And Carly was on a first-name basis with her in less than twenty-four hours? As far as he knew, no one in the Kincaid household had ever called the formidable sixty-something woman by her first name.

Carly grimaced. "They're your arteries. But you'd think after your father's heart attack you'd be more careful."

"I am perfectly healthy, thank you." His cool tone dimmed her smile. "Why aren't you eating in the dining room?"

"Mr. Messy." Her nod indicated the slimy child.

"Which is why we should have kept the nanny. You could have eaten in peace." Yesterday she'd waited until the boy napped to eat lunch.

"Breakfast is one of our favorite times of the day. Isn't it, munchkin?" She tweaked the child's nose—the only clean part of his face as far as Mitch could tell. The brat cackled infectiously, stabbing Mitch with a reminder of other children and another time. An old ache invaded his chest.

"Besides, the view from the breakfast nook is gorgeous. But I told Della that you should add a bird feeder or two to the patio. Rhett loves to watch the birds—especially hummingbirds. We'll pick up some feeders this afternoon after church."

She attended church?

Probably to confess her fortune-hunting sins. She might try a different brand of ammunition than her twin, but he knew why she'd been prancing around in her nightshirt last night.

Carly's brown eyes took on a challenging glint. "So…are you going to eat in the dining room by yourself or are you brave enough to join us? Rhett's almost finished. You and your Armani should be safe from soggy cereal bombs."

"I'll join you." If for no other reason than to keep an eye on his unwanted houseguest—the same reason he'd put her in the suite beside his. He chose the chair farthest away from the alleged cereal-bomb thrower.

"Not a morning person, eh?" Carly asked as she scraped the last of her oatmeal from a bowl and tucked it between her pink lips.

"I prefer to gather my thoughts for the upcoming day and read the business section. Are you?"

"Absolutely. On really hot days, we take our run before we eat." She leaned over to wipe the boy's face with a cloth and her jacket and the top she wore beneath it gaped, revealing a glimpse of scalloped white lace on the pale curve of her breast.

The sight hit Mitch with an unexpected surge of hunger—and not for bacon and eggs.

No. He would *not* be attracted to Carly Corbin. Her sister had taken his father for a ride. This twin wasn't going to get the chance to do the same with Mitch. He made a mental note to call one of his usual dates—women who knew good sex was all he'd give them.

"Perhaps one day I'll join you on your run." Again, if only to keep an eye on her. The majority of his neighbors were wealthy and older—prime pickings for attractive gold diggers on the make. Like the Corbin sisters.

"If you can keep up, you'd be welcome. Rhett would love the company."

Another challenge. She seemed to enjoy issuing them. "I can keep up."

Mrs. Duncan placed a plate in front of him. Was that a smirk on her lined face?

"What's with the suit?" Carly asked, recapturing his attention. "Going to church?"

"No. To the office."

"It's Sunday," she enunciated as if he were lacking fifty IQ points.

"I have work to do."

Carly shook her head and made a face at Mrs. Duncan. "A workaholic and a diet disaster. Just like his father."

True, but his spine straightened regardless. "How would you know?"

Sadness shadowed her eyes. "Marlene told me."

"And yet she didn't tell you about the hundred grand she accepted to have an abortion."

Carly glared with enough fire to make a lesser man duck for cover. "If you want to talk trash, then you do it when we're alone. I will not tolerate you making Rhett feel unwanted. And I think you're lying about the money."

"I made the transaction myself. And I have a copy of the check with Marlene's signature on the back."

"I want to see it."

The Corbin women were identical in looks and yet not. Marlene had dressed in designer clothing. Her makeup had been flawless, and he'd never seen one single hair out of place. Beautiful, but hard, he'd concluded within seconds of making her acquaintance. And he hadn't been attracted to her. Nonetheless he'd tried seduction and later threats, but neither had swayed her toward breaking it off with his father. And when he'd finally convinced his father to end the relationship, she'd turned up pregnant a month later.

A calculating woman with an eye out for number one, he'd concluded. He hadn't seen that side of Carly. Yet. But he would. She camouflaged her mercenary streak well. But sooner or later the facade would crack.

Carly sipped her juice. Without the red gloss her twin had worn, Carly's mouth looked softer than Marlene's. Thus far, the only time Carly had shown her hard side was when butting heads with him over the boy. That was to be expected, since the kid was her ticket to Easy Street. Mitch hadn't figured out her MO yet, but she and Marlene were genetically identical twins— one egg separated in the womb. Carly's altruistic pretense had to be exactly that. A pretense to cover a mercenary heart.

And once she realized he was onto her, her mouth would twist the way her sister's had and her eyes would glint like flint. In the meantime, he'd watch Carly Corbin like a hawk does its prey, waiting for the perfect opportunity to swoop in and steal the child from her.

The boy slammed his hands on the high chair tray, startling Mitch. His eggs fell from his fork.

"Man. Man. Man."

Carly righted the sippy cup. "That's Mitch. Your brother."

"Bub. Bub. Bub."

"That's right. Your bubba."

Mitch's spine fused into a rigid line. He opened his mouth to protest he was no one's *bubba*, but the sparkle in Carly's eyes and something about the angle of her chin, dared him. The witch was trying to provoke him, he realized.

Too bad he refused to be her source of entertainment.

He flicked open his newspaper, concentrated on the financial section and tried to ignore the boy's chorus of "Bubbas" and the smirks on Carly's and Mrs. Duncan's faces.

He wasn't going to let Carly disrupt his life. In a matter of days—a month at the most—she'd realize she was fighting a losing battle. And then she'd turn over guardianship of the kid.

Peace and a nanny would return to the Kincaid household the day Carly Corbin moved out.

Carly's body reacted like a Geiger counter nearing radioactive material.

The hairs on her arms rose and her pulse stuttered erratically. By the sound of his step and the scent of his cologne she knew who had entered the living room behind her without looking over her shoulder.

Despite its predominantly white decor, the room wasn't cold or uncomfortable due to the plush rugs on the marble floor, overstuffed upholstery and surprising colorful accents scattered about. She preferred this space to the darker, more masculine den.

"Rhett looks like you," she said, keeping her gaze on the Kincaid family portrait hanging above the mantel. "How old were you when this was painted?"

"Eleven," Mitch replied.

"Everyone looks so happy. The all-American family success story." Her family had been happy...until she'd made an unforgettable mistake.

"Appearances can be deceiving."

That brought her around abruptly. Exhaustion dragged Mitch's features, not surprising since he'd left for work before eight this morning, and it was after 10:00 p.m. now. His suit coat was draped on his forearm and his loosened burgundy tie hung askew.

So much for Sunday being a day of rest. "What do you mean?"

He shook his head. "Nothing. Did you and Rhett get settled in today?"

"We did. Mrs. Duncan and I have babyproofed most of the rooms. So when you notice some of your priceless collectibles missing, I didn't hock them. They've been put away."

As a physical therapist, Carly spent a lot of her day encouraging people to go a little farther than they wanted to go. She saw no reason not to continue that practice with Mitch. "Why is the picture deceptive?"

"Let it go, Carly." If his voice dropped any lower he'd be growling. He turned away.

She reached out and grabbed his bicep to stop him. The muscle bunched beneath her fingers and his heat burned her hand through the thin fabric of his sleeve. "If you expect me to let Rhett live here, then you need to level with me, Mitch. Are there skeletons in the Kincaid closet that I should worry about?"

He stabbed a hand through his hair, effectively dislodging her grasp, and lifted his gaze to the oil painting. "As far as I can remember, my mother wasn't the contented person you see depicted there. She died in a car accident shortly after that portrait was painted. But I was a kid. So what do I know?"

"I'm sorry. Going through your teens without the steadying influence of your mother must have been difficult."

A familiar ache welled in her chest. Her daughter would be twelve now and entering what Carly's mother had always called the testing years. Was her daughter asking the same questions Carly had asked about her birthmother? Did she wonder why she'd been given up and if she was too flawed for even a mother to love? Carly prayed her daughter's adoptive parents were as supportive and loving as Eileen and Dan Corbin had been.

Carly pushed the questions and regrets aside, the way she always did, and focused on the present. But the ache didn't abate. It never did. The pain rested just behind her breastbone like a hole in her heart.

Mitch grunted a nonanswer and headed toward the wet bar built into the cabinetry flanking the fireplace. But instead of liquor, he splashed bottled water over his ice cubes.

"I'm sure you can see why I want to make certain Rhett doesn't suffer from Marlene's absence."

Studying his reflection in the mirror above the marble countertop, she noted the groove in his brow. For a moment, he looked tired and very much like a man who'd just lost his father and had to take over a multi-billion-dollar corporation despite the grief he must dealing with. "Rough day?"

He stared into his glass, then met her reflected gaze. "I've spent the past week reacquainting my brother with KCL. He's been working for our west coast competitor for the past five years. And we had to hire my sister's replacement. Rand and I spent the day training her."

Carly had been disappointed when she'd read in the will that Nadia would be out of state. She'd hoped the female Kincaid would have some maternal instincts and side with Carly on Rhett's care. "Training on Sunday?"

"The cruising industry runs 24/7, three hundred and sixty-five days per year. Good night." He headed for the foyer.

Tonight for the first time since she'd met him, Mitch looked anything but invincible and nothing like the overconfident rat bastard Marlene had described. For some foolish reason, Carly was reluctant to let this approachable mood pass. "Have you had dinner? Mrs. Duncan left a plate for you in the refrigerator. Want me to heat it up?"

His eyes returned to hers and narrowed suspiciously. "I'm capable of operating a microwave."

His terse reply raised her hackles, but for Rhett's sake, she'd be polite. She had to be if she wanted to make a place for the youngest Kincaid in this family. "I'm sure you can, but I'm offering help and company."

The long stretch of silence spoke volumes. "I could eat."

Carly headed for the kitchen despite the lack of warm fuzzies his reply elicited. And this time she didn't get lost. She'd taken more than a few wrong turns today in the enormous house.

She removed the plate from the refrigerator, slid it into the microwave and punched the buttons. "Your home gym is pretty amazing. Would you mind if I used it?"

"Go ahead."

She leaned back against the counter and observed Mitch. "If you like, I can check your form when you work out to make sure you're not doing yourself any harm."

His shoulders squared. "What are you doing?"

"Heating your dinner? Trying to make conversation? Offering professional advice?"

"Don't."

"Don't what? Don't be polite?"

"Don't try your wiles on me."

Carly's temper ballooned like the plastic wrap covering the plate rotating on the microwave's turntable. She gestured to her tracksuit, which had taken a beating during Rhett's dinner and bath. "That's the second time you've accused me of putting the moves on you. Open your freaking eyes, Kincaid. Am I dressed to seduce you?"

She realized her mistake immediately. Her question invited him to inspect her from her ponytail to her running shoes. He did so slowly and thoroughly, lingering over her breasts and legs before returning to her face. It annoyed her immensely that his appraisal left her breathless and agitated.

"It won't work, Carly. I'm not a sap like my father, nor am I so hard up for a woman that I'll fall into bed with the first attractive female who offers."

His rudeness shocked and infuriated her. If this were a cartoon, steam would shoot from her ears. "Hello! I'm not offering anything except leftovers."

"Precisely." From his tone she didn't think he referred to the leftover orange roasted chicken and vegetables.

The timer beeped. Mitch reached past her and retrieved the plate. She could feel both his warmth and, conversely, the chill emanating from him. He crossed the room and plunked his plate down on the kitchen table. His body language made it clear he didn't want her company.

Carly resisted the urge to stab him with the fork she retrieved from the drawer and settled for slapping the utensil down on the table beside his plate. "If your father was half the conceited jackass you are, then I can't see what Marlene ever saw in him."

"She saw a billionaire sugar daddy and a meal ticket."

Carly glared at him and prepared to blister him with one of the many insults she'd learned from the professional athletes she worked with. But doubt stilled her tongue.

Marlene had confessed in her notebook that she found Everett's fortune quite attractive. But surely her sister had cared about more than the man's finances? And what about the times Marlene had told her she loved Everett? Her sister wouldn't have lied to her, would she?

Yes, she would.

Carly broke eye contact and retrieved the pitcher of iced tea from the fridge. She set it down beside Mitch's plate.

"Go screw yourself, Kincaid. That's the only way a jerk like you will ever have a partner you consider your equal."

With that she pivoted and stomped out of the kitchen, leaving the lord of the manor to his solitary dinner.

She hoped he choked on it.

Three

Kill him with kindness.

As opposed to just killing him—a notion that had enter-
tained Carly far more than it should have for the past few
days. Okay, so she couldn't *really* off Mitch Kincaid. But
making him run a marathon on a treadmill with no change in
scenery could be fun. Or maybe five hundred sit-ups on a cold
tile floor...

But none of those would get her closer to her goal of
bonding Mitch and Rhett. She sighed and rolled the ball across
the emerald lawn to Rhett Wednesday evening.

It had taken her three days to cool off, three days of not
seeing the middle Kincaid, of Rhett not spending a single
moment with his half brother, for Carly to realize Mitch had
deliberately antagonized her Sunday night.

Why?

She didn't think for one minute he honestly believed she
was chasing him, because she hadn't flirted even once. Sure,

she'd appreciated his physique a time or two. Who wouldn't? But unless he had eyes in the back of his head, he hadn't caught her looking, so that didn't count.

He had to have been trying to avoid Rhett, and since she and Rhett were practically joined at the hip…annoying her meant avoiding his half brother.

She'd decided she'd have to follow through with her plan—regardless of Mitch's irritating comments—if she wanted the males to get to know each other better. With a thirty-something-year age gap between them, Mitch and Rhett would never have the close bond Carly had shared with Marlene. But the brothers had to start somewhere.

A salt-scented breeze blowing in from the water lifted the skirt of the simple peach sundress she'd donned for dinner. She smoothed the fabric back in place. Dresses. Ick. Give her a tracksuit or running shorts and a tank any day. Carly had been the jock in their family. Marlene had been the girly girl.

A wave of sadness swamped her. Carly lifted her chin and inhaled deeply, trying to alleviate the emptiness. The mouth-watering aromas of grilling swordfish with citrus salsa and marinated vegetables filled her nostrils. Her stomach growled with hunger. Mitch would be home soon and they'd have their first family dinner.

She dug her bare toes into the thick grass. So she'd dressed up. Big deal. The evening sun burned down on them, and her outfit would be cooler than pants. If Mitch wanted to make something out of it, fine. Time would prove him wrong. She wasn't looking for a lover, or a sugar daddy or anything remotely resembling either one. Her broken engagement had left her too raw to think about another romantic entanglement.

She caught the ball and rolled it back to Rhett. Rhett needed her. Sure, having someone depend on her for everything both frightened and overwhelmed her, but she wouldn't let down

Rhett or Marlene. Or herself. This time she wouldn't let anyone convince her to take the easy way out. This time she would be the parent she should have been twelve years ago.

The sound of the back door gliding open drew her gaze to the house. Mitch stepped onto the patio. With his eyes narrowed against the setting sun and his hands parked on his hips, he scanned the backyard like a lord surveying his property. He zeroed in on them and her pulse did something wonky. What was up with that?

She touched Rhett's shoulder. "Look who's here."

Rhett beamed and shouted, "Bubba. Ball."

Mitch grimaced and Carly didn't even bother to smother her grin as her nephew chugged forward. Mitch clearly hated the nickname—which is probably why Carly had practiced it with Rhett since she'd picked him up from day care.

"Evening, Mitch."

Mitch's lips flatlined and his attention returned to her. A breeze off the water lifted his glossy dark hair. "Where is Mrs. Duncan?"

"I gave her the day off."

His scowl deepened. "Carly, that wasn't your decision."

"Ball, bubba," Rhett said before hurling the red sphere.

Mitch caught it and tossed it back—gently, Carly was surprised to see. He fisted his hands by his sides. "I won't tolerate you interfering with the household staff."

"Why shouldn't the woman have time off?"

"She has scheduled days off."

"Sorry, but her younger sister didn't conveniently need emergency gallbladder surgery on Della's scheduled day off. Della wanted to be there and I thought she should. They need to spend time together while they can." Because you never knew how much time you had left with a loved one.

The stiffness eased from his rigid face and shoulders. "Why didn't you say her sister was ill?"

"You didn't ask." She transferred the fish and vegetables from the top rack of the grill to a platter, then covered it.

"What is that?"

"Our dinner. We're eating outside. The weather is too gorgeous to be cooped up inside."

"It's eighty-five."

"But the humidity is low for a change and there's a great breeze blowing in off the water. Shed your jacket and you'll be comfortable." She set the platter in the center of the wrought-iron and glass table and pulled the shrimp cocktails from the cooler she'd tucked underneath.

She'd never known there were special bowls or forks to serve the appetizer. This morning when Mrs. Duncan had produced the stemless martini-ish glasses that rested inside crystal globes filled with ice, Carly had had to ask what they were. The special dishes were just one of the many contrasts between the Kincaid's überrich world and her working-class ways. When she had shrimp cocktail, it came on a black plastic deli tray from the grocery store.

"Have a seat and help yourself." She flicked a hand toward a chair.

Mitch laid the folded newspaper he carried beside the plate on the opposite side of the rectangular table from Rhett and hung his suit coat over the back of his chair. "You cooked?"

"Yes. But don't worry. That's parsley on the squash and zucchini, not arsenic. There's wine if you want it."

Mitch lifted a dark eyebrow. "You're not drinking?"

She shook her head. "We're going running later."

He didn't open the bottle, but instead filled his and her water goblets from the insulated pitcher on the table.

She buckled Rhett into his high chair, wiped his hands and then served his diced grilled cheese sandwich. She added a spoonful of green peas and some of the grilled veggies so he could practice his fine motor skills.

Rhett attacked his food as if he hadn't eaten in a week.

Mitch eyed his half brother and then pulled out her chair, showing he did have some manners. "You shouldn't have waited."

She shrugged and sat. "Rhett only looks like he's starving. He had a snack two hours ago. And for him to get a sense of family, we should eat together whenever possible."

Mitch's expression closed like a slamming door.

"No matter how hectic things were when Marlene and I were growing up, my mother insisted on family dinners. It's a great way to unwind and catch up on what everyone else is doing."

Suspicion entered Mitch's eyes. "Carly—"

"Shut up and eat, Mitch, before the ice under your shrimp melts. Contrary to your high opinion of yourself, this is not a date."

Wincing, she reached for her napkin. So much for maintaining peace. She'd just bonked him over the head with the olive branch she'd hoped to extend. But his distrustful glares really rubbed her the wrong way.

"I'm sorry. There's no excuse for me being rude. But it's just dinner. Della already had most of the meal prepared before her sister called. Cooking it was no big deal."

Mitch stared at her in silence as if weighing the truth of her words, and then he nodded and started on his shrimp. Carly dug into hers, savoring the citrus tang of Mrs. Duncan's marinade. She caught herself watching the absurdly sensual sight of Mitch's straight white teeth biting into the shrimp and his lips surrounding the meat.

Get a grip. Kincaid is not on tonight's or any other night's menu. Remember how he treated Marlene?

She polished off her appetizer and reached for the main course. Mitch followed suit, piling large helpings of fish and vegetables on his plate. He devoured his meal almost as ravenously as Rhett had, but with the perfect form of one who'd had etiquette lessons. She wondered who'd taught him the fine art of eating politely. One of his nannies?

"Did you eat lunch today?" she asked to break the silence.

"There wasn't time. Where are your parents now?"

She gave him points for making conversation. "Arizona. Dad needed the drier climate for his health."

"With all your talk of family, why don't you move out there with them?"

"I've thought about it. But my parents' lives are filled with retirement community activities. I'd have to apply for a new license in a different state, and that could mean months without income. My parents can't afford to support us, but they'd feel obligated to try. Add in that children aren't allowed to stay overnight in their complex, and things get even more complicated."

"Leave Rhett with me."

She sighed and wiped her mouth. "Give it up, Mitch. That's not going to happen."

"It could. Say the word and you're a free woman."

She'd been footloose and fancy-free before and she hadn't liked it. How could anyone expect her to go back to normal knowing she'd given up something precious? Twice.

"You act as if caring for Rhett is a burden. It isn't."

"You say that now, but give it time."

"I'll say the same thing next week, next year and ten years from now."

He snorted a sound of disbelief, but she decided not to waste her breath arguing. Talk was cheap. He'd soon see by her actions that she meant what she said.

"You're only twenty-eight. Aren't your parents too young to retire?"

"Mom was forty and Dad forty-five when they adopted Marlene and me." And because Carly had been adopted, she knew exactly what kinds of questions her baby girl would be asking.

Silence returned, broken only by Rhett's babble and the chink of silverware.

"Does Mrs. Duncan need more than one day?"

Surprised, Carly searched Mitch's face. Good to know the rat bastard had a human side after all. "It would be nice if you'd call and offer it. I have her sister's phone number."

"I'll get someone from the temp agency in to cook our meals and oversee the remaining staff if Mrs. Duncan needs more time."

"Oh please. We're adults. We can feed ourselves. I know my way around the kitchen if you don't. And I think your staff can muddle through pushing a vacuum and making beds for a couple of days." His eyes narrowed to slits, pinning her like a butterfly on a collector's board. "What?"

"You intend to work all day and then come home and cook for me. Why?" Suspicion laced his voice.

"For us. And don't take it personally. I'm not after your heart via your stomach. Rhett and I have to eat, too. And I like to cook. I used to prepare all the meals for Marlene and me."

He looked ready to argue, but instead consumed the last bites of his swordfish. He sat back, still wearing the skeptical, guarded expression. "That was good."

"Thank you. And it's healthier than your usual dinners."

His eyebrows slammed down. So much for the truce. "Don't try to change me, Carly. Don't interfere in my life."

"Wouldn't dream of it," she denied and knew she fibbed. By the end of the year she'd have his bachelor lifestyle turned upside down. Priorities changed when a child entered the picture. He'd discover that sooner or later.

He studied her as if she were a puzzle he couldn't figure out—and one he didn't trust.

"Down. Ball," Rhett demanded.

Mitch stood. "I'll clear the table. You get the boy."

Carly blinked. A man in Hugo Boss who wasn't afraid to

do dishes? Nice. Too bad she wasn't looking. "Thanks, but he'd rather play with you."

"No." Swift. Harsh. Unequivocal. Mitch stacked their plates and strode into the house.

Carly stared after him. Mitch Kincaid was going to be a tough nut to crack—even harder than her most difficult client.

But just like she did with her more pigheaded patients, she would find a way to motivate him.

Carly Corbin was a sneaky, devious woman.

Mitch opened the tap in the sink to drown out the squeals of laughter penetrating the kitchen windows. Turning his back on the woman and child racing through the gardens, he bent to load the dishwasher.

Carly was determined to drag him somewhere he would never go again with her home-cooked meals and let's-play-family games. He still had the scars from his last round of playing house. He wouldn't give his heart to a child only to have it ripped out when the mother—or in this case, the guardian—had a change of heart. Once he could guarantee Rhett wouldn't be leaving would be soon enough for Mitch to befriend him. Until then, he'd keep his distance.

Carly had clearly given the idea of moving across the country to be closer to her parents careful consideration. Unless she left the boy behind, that put the terms of the will and everything Mitch held dear in jeopardy.

He had to get custody of his father's little bastard.

Soon.

He closed the dishwasher and straightened. The stillness of the backyard grabbed his attention. He scanned the garden and spotted a splash of peach and Carly's bare legs sprawled on the lawn between the fountain and the koi pond.

Alarm flooded his veins with adrenaline. Had the boy fallen in? Dammit, he'd ordered the gardener to fence the shallow pond and pool, but the custom-made materials hadn't arrived yet.

Or had Carly hurt herself dashing across the grass with her hair and her dress streaming behind her.

Mitch slammed through the back door, leaped from the porch and sprinted past Poseidon and across the grass. He rounded the roses and jerked to a halt.

Rhett lay stretched out on his belly beside Carly with his dark head near hers. Her bare arm encircled the boy's waist.

"Orange. That one's orange," Carly said, pointing at the water.

"Orange. Big," the boy warbled.

"Yes, the orange fish is big. The white one is small."

Mitch's heart jackhammered against his ribs and his lungs burned. Relief over finding them safe segued into awareness of Carly's long legs. Runner's legs. Lean, but muscled. Smooth and tanned. A charge of sexual awareness flooded him and that pissed him off. "What are you doing?"

The duo startled at his harsh tone. Keeping one hand on Rhett's waistband, Carly rolled to her side. "Looking at the fish."

Barefooted and bare-legged, with apparently no concern for the grass clippings clinging to her dress, calves and feet, Carly attracted him far more than was safe. Despite her denials, he knew damned well she was out to hook him. The way her sister had his father. The way countless other women had tried to work their way into the Kincaid beds and coffers.

Sure, Carly was more subtle and she brought a unique angle to the table. She might deny the attraction, but he'd seen the interest in her eyes when she looked at him. Like now. With her sun-streaked hair pooling like silk on the grass, her chin tilted up to expose the long line of her neck and her gaze slowly climbing his body.

Oh yeah, she wanted him.

But even without her mercenary genetics, he couldn't get

involved with her. He'd learned the hard way through both his and his father's affairs that running a business the size of KCL left no room for anything more than temporary liaisons. He'd forget to call, or miss a date, and then there would be hell to pay from the neglected woman. Too much hassle.

He'd stick with women like him who were too committed to their careers to want more than physical satisfaction now and then. The women he called didn't expect romance. They expected hot, sweaty sex. And nothing more. But even that wasn't safe with Carly Corbin.

She rolled to her feet as graceful as a cat and brushed the grass fragments from her clothing. She missed the blade stuck in her hair. Mitch fisted his hands against the urge to reach for it. For her.

"Up. Up. Pig me up," Rhett demanded. Mitch ignored him.

Carly frowned at Mitch, shook her head and bent to lift the boy. Her top gaped as she did, revealing the curves of her breasts and the dusky hint of her nipples. She wasn't wearing a bra. Need kicked Mitch in the gut.

"Want to help me give Rhett his bath?" Carly asked as she straightened.

He forced his gaze from her chest to her face. "No."

But he wouldn't mind bathing Carly, cupping her flesh with soap-slick hands and sinking into her.

Not gonna happen.

He was not like his old man who'd never learned from his mistakes. Mitch thought with the head on his shoulders and not with the one in his pants.

A woman had made a fool of him once.

It wouldn't happen again.

No matter how much he wanted this one.

"Settle him, Carly," Mitch muttered and struggled to ignore Rhett's cries as he paced his room. "C'mon, settle the boy."

Mitch's heart hammered against his ribs and his nerves stretched tight. He didn't want to get involved, but the noise from the blue suite continued to rise.

Where in the hell was Carly?

He yanked open his door and stalked down the hall. Her bedroom door stood open, but the room and bed were empty. Had she gone downstairs? Snuck out of the house for a date?

Bolted like he wanted her to?

At any other time he'd rejoice at the prospect, but not when he was alone in the house with the kid. He forced himself to turn and scan Rhett's darkened room. The glow of the new night-light illuminated the unhappy, red-faced child.

Short arms extended toward Mitch. "Bubba."

"It's okay, kid. Go back to sleep."

Rhett whimpered in response, ripping Mitch in two.

He strode into Carly's room to check the status of her clothes. If they were here, she was coming back. Before he reached the closet another sound registered. Running water. The shower. Relief mingled with disappointment. She hadn't left.

He crossed the plum carpet to the closed bathroom door and lifted his hand to pound on the panel and order her to get her ass out here and take care of the kid. An off-key voice belting out a country ballad stilled his fist and an image of Carly's wet, bare golden skin seized his mind and sent a jolt of arousal through him. The slam of his heart reverberated in his groin.

Down, boy. You can be attracted to any woman but her.

He looked over his shoulder and through the open door at the crying child. Which was the lesser of two evils?

Normally Mitch enjoyed naked women, especially wet naked women, but the genetically identical version of the Machiavellian bitch who'd screwed his father over with the oldest trick in the book was off-limits.

His life would be easier if his feelings for Carly were identical to his feelings for her twin. Marlene had left him cold and not just the day she'd calmly accepted cash to get rid of her baby as easily as she would lunch money. She'd never flipped his switch. She was a liar and a con artist who'd set out to nail herself a rich husband and pulled out all stops to achieve her goal. The boy was better off without Marlene Corbin in his life.

"Mama, Mama," Rhett wailed and Mitch winced. The kid already called Carly Mama. Would Rhett also be better off without Carly? Didn't matter. Carly Corbin's days as Rhett's guardian were numbered.

Being in the same room with Carly when she was undressed and living under his roof could open the door to all kinds of lawsuits and legal complications—if she was looking for a free ride, as he suspected. The last thing he wanted to do was give another Corbin grounds to extort more Kincaid money.

He backed away from the door, heading for the lesser of two evils. The crying child.

Rhett's breath hitched when Mitch entered the room. The boy stood in his crib and held his arms out, opening and closing his tiny hands. "Pig me up."

Mitch fisted his hands by his sides. "Hey, buddy. Carly's in the shower. She'll be here in a few minutes."

The kid's face scrunched up and his bottom lip quivered. Fresh tears oozed from his big brown eyes. Eyes the same shape and color as Carly's. "Up. Up."

Mitch remained a yard from the crib. "You have a bad dream?"

The whimper turned into a cry. The boy grasped the railing and bounced. "Up. Up."

Letting the kid get close even once would be the beginning of nothing good. But he had no choice since Carly wasn't here doing the job she'd committed to do. He shouldn't have let her talk him out of the nanny.

Wishing he could avoid it, but knowing he couldn't, Mitch

gritted his teeth and moved closer. Rhett immediately latched his arms around Mitch's neck, crushing Mitch's windpipe. Or maybe it was the memories choking him. He lifted the sturdy little body and automatically patted the diaper, checking for soggy overload. It felt dry.

The kid hiccupped and burrowed his wet face against Mitch's neck. Mitch awkwardly thumped the narrow little back, and when that didn't settle the boy, he crossed to the rocking chair and sat. Toeing the rocker into motion, Mitch tried to remain detached, tried to shut down the memories. Memories of nights with a colicky child. But he couldn't. His chest tightened with each sway of the rocker.

Soothing nonsense poured from his lips as if it had only been yesterday when he'd performed this same task for another little boy.

A boy he'd planned to adopt and claim as his own.

Rhett felt like Travis, smelled like Travis, cuddled like Travis. Same weight. Same size. Same desperate need for a father's love.

Rhett quieted and grew heavy, telling Mitch he'd drifted back to sleep. But as reluctant as Mitch had been to pick up the boy, now he didn't want to let him go.

He'd missed this. And the only way to ensure he wouldn't have to let Rhett go was to get rid of Carly Corbin.

The sooner the better.

Carly halted outside Rhett's bedroom door and blinked.

As if it weren't shocking enough to find Mitch cradling Rhett and gently stroking his back, a quiet baritone filled the room. Humming? Mitch Kincaid *humming?*

The image didn't fit the arrogant executive she'd seen over the past week and a half.

Eyes closed and with a sad expression on his face, he rested his dark head against the back of the rocker. Rhett sagged on

Mitch's bare chest with his head tucked beneath Mitch's jaw, clearly sound asleep.

Something inside Carly twisted at the sight of the big, strong man gently holding the small boy.

Why was Mitch here? Had he come in on other nights without her knowledge? Was his jerk act just that? An act? Which was the real Mitch Kincaid? The picture in front of her certainly didn't mesh with the description Marlene had provided of Everett's henchman or the emotionless robot Carly had seen so far.

Carly entered the room, and Mitch's eyes flew open.

"Is something wrong?" she whispered.

"He woke up crying. You didn't come." The accusatory tone raised her hackles.

He rose quickly and laid Rhett back in the crib. Carly pried her gaze off the bare, broad V of his back to note the care Mitch took not to jostle the child. He handled Rhett with experienced hands and tucked the blanket around him.

Interesting.

"I didn't hear him. I was showering off the stench of our evening run. I forgot to take the baby monitor into the bathroom with me."

When Mitch turned, the sight of his naked chest made her catch her breath. Oh yeah, he had a fine physique above the low waistband of his pants. Wide shoulders. Muscled arms. Washboard abs. Dark swirls of curls circled his flat nipples and painted a silky line down the center of his lean abdomen.

Dampening her suddenly dry lips, she hoped the lust percolating through her didn't show on her face.

"Don't forget next time." His sandpaper voice sounded harsh in the quiet room. He brushed past her, heading toward the door.

"You've done this before."

Mitch stopped in the hallway and slowly turned. "I told you I knew how to handle kids."

"This is the first evidence I've seen of that. Do you have children of your own who live with their mother?"

"No."

"Then where did you get your experience?"

"Leave it, Carly."

She advanced on him in the dimly lit hall. "You expect me to trust you with Rhett. Tell me why I should."

A nerve in his jaw twitched. "I was engaged to a single parent once."

"What happened?"

"She went back to her famous ex-husband." His blank expression couldn't completely mask the pain in his eyes or the husky edge to his words.

"I'm sorry." Carly reached out and gave his forearm a comforting squeeze. His skin scorched her, but she couldn't seem to pull away.

Mitch's muscles shifted beneath her palm and his chest expanded on a long, slow inhalation. His gaze met hers and desire widened his pupils. The same hunger flooded her veins.

Carly gulped. This could so not happen. Not with *him*.

"What are you doing, Carly?"

Playing with fire, that's what. But she could only shake her head and lower her hand. Too late. Electricity arced between them unbroken.

The dark green gaze dropped from her eyes to her mouth. "Is this what you want?"

Mitch hooked an arm around her waist and yanked her forward. The thin cotton of her sleep shirt and robe weren't nearly enough protection from his searing flesh. Her torso fused to his.

Mitch took her mouth roughly, the initial contact slamming his teeth against hers. She squeaked a protest, but he didn't release her. He merely changed the angle of the kiss.

Every cell in her body screamed with alarm. With arousal.

This wasn't supposed to happen. Mitch Kincaid had hurt and insulted her sister. Carly didn't even like him. How could she when he made no secret of his desire to dump her and keep Rhett locked up like a dog in quarantine?

She had every intention of shoving him away when she dug her fingers into his arm and pressed her free hand against his waist. But the moment his bare, supple skin melded to her palm her body seemed to come up with a different plan. It burned and ached and *needed,* reminding her that she hadn't been with a man in a while. And even then, making love with Sam hadn't felt like this—like a swarm of fireflies taking flight, flickering and sparking nerve endings that had previously lain dormant.

Mitch's lips parted and his tongue traced the outline of her mouth, caressing, stroking. She gasped, and he swept the inside of her bottom lip, tempting her against her will into settling against him and relaxing her jaw. Their tongues touched, intertwined.

She shouldn't be kissing him back. But his flavor filled her mouth and his musky scent invaded her lungs. Dizziness rocked her. She grappled for steady ground.

One hand mapped an upward path along his bicep to grasp his shoulder. The other spread over his back. Hard muscles flexed beneath his smooth skin.

Mitch's big hands raked her back, her waist. He cupped her buttocks and pressed her against his thickening flesh. Her internal muscles clenched and wept in appreciation of the length pressing her belly. A moan snaked up her throat.

He shoved her robe from her shoulders. It snagged at her waist. His frustrated growl filled her mouth. A quick tug and the belt gave way. Her robe parted. His hot hands found her waist through the thin fabric and raked upward. He traced the underside of her breasts with his thumbs and the air thinned.

She ought to protest, but she couldn't seem to put the

words together. She could barely think. All she could do was feel. His heat. His strength. His ravenous mouth. Lust, unlike anything she'd experienced before, rose within her. Her short nails dug into firm tissue and held on.

He palmed her breast and unerringly found her nipple, stroked it, then rolled it between his fingers. A lightning storm of desire shot straight to her core, melting her, making her heart race and her thighs quiver.

A snuffle from the crib penetrated her sensual high and shocked her back to awareness of where she was and with whom.

She ripped herself out of Mitch's arms. Gasping for air, she backed away, righted her clothing and cinched her robe around her waist like a tourniquet.

How could she be turned on by Mitch Kincaid? She knew too much about him. None of it good.

She swiped the back of her hand across her damp and still tingling lips. "That shouldn't have happened."

Mitch's nostrils flared on a sharply indrawn breath. The passion in his eyes turned to frost and his mouth twisted in derision. "Oh, c'mon, Carly. Don't act like it wasn't your plan to soften me with dinner and a sexy sundress. Screwing me is only the next step on your agenda."

"What agenda?" She had one. But it had nothing to do with sex.

"Did you and your sister have a contest going to see who could land the richest sugar daddy?"

Shock and fury and grief ripped through Carly like an explosion. She dug her nails into her palms to keep from slapping his face. "I was engaged, you moron, to an intern with student loans to rival the national debt. Not a sugar daddy. And don't blame that kiss on me. I've done nothing to attract your attention."

"Haven't you? What would you call the curve-hugging clothes, the braless sundress and the hypnotic walk?"

She had a hypnotic walk? "I don't dress suggestively."

"Give me a break. You have a damned good body and you display it like a trophy. Men probably fall at your feet."

Flattering, in an insulting kind of way. But wrong. "Are you deluded?"

"Not deluded enough to fall into your trap. Cast your line somewhere else. Because you're not landing this Kincaid." He stalked toward the stairs.

"If I landed you, Kincaid, I'd throw you back or use you for shark bait. Go to hell, you conceited jerk."

"I've already been there," Mitch growled to the empty foyer. "And you're not taking me back."

He strode down the hall, heading straight to the book-lined study—formerly his father's, but now Mitch's domain. He dragged his father's old Rolodex out of the drawer and flipped through the cards until he found the one he needed. The cool leather chair against his back did nothing to soothe his overheated skin as he punched out the cell phone number.

"Lewis Investigations," a man's voice answered on the second ring despite the late hour.

"Frank, this is Mitch Kincaid."

"Sorry to hear about your father, Mitch. Everett and I went way back."

"That's why I know I can trust you with this job." He briefly summarized the situation, and then said, "I need you to dig up dirt on Carly Corbin. I want anything that could discredit her or prove her an unfit guardian. And I need it yesterday."

The P.I. laughed. "You're definitely Everett's son. I'll get right on it. Any chance you can get me a set of fingerprints?"

He remembered the dinner dishes. "I'll get them tonight and have them couriered to you first thing tomorrow. While you're checking into Carly I want you to look into her sister, too."

"Anything in particular I'm looking for?"

"I want to know what Marlene Corbin did with the hundred grand we paid her. And I want you to see what you can find out about the hit-and-run that killed her three months ago. The police have moved the investigation to the back burner."

Mitch's fingers tightened around the receiver. He had to know the truth, and his father had sworn Frank Lewis was the soul of discretion.

"I need to know if my father was involved in her death."

Four

The rat bastard could kiss.

Carly did *not* want to know that.

She increased her speed, trying to outrun her disturbing thoughts and banish the grogginess left over from a restless night. Rhett cackled in his stroller ahead of her, loving the faster pace and the wind in his face. He pounded the squeaky horn on his toy steering wheel, shattering the stillness of the morning.

Rebound romance.

That's the only way she could explain her reaction to Kincaid's kisses. It had been three months since Sam had dumped her. When he'd learned Carly had been appointed as Rhett's guardian, her fiancé had claimed he wasn't ready for an instant family, and he'd added that he didn't want to raise someone else's brat anyway. Sam had given Carly an ultimatum, him or Rhett.

After the brat comment Carly hadn't had a choice. She couldn't love a man who refused to even try to bond with a child simply because he hadn't genetically contributed to its DNA or one who'd ask her to make that kind of sacrifice a second time. Although to his credit, Sam hadn't known about the daughter she'd given up for adoption at sixteen. She hadn't told him for fear he'd find that decision as unforgivable as her college boyfriend had.

She'd chosen her nephew over fiancé and that had been the end of her engagement. And her sex life.

Okay, so chalk up last night's fiasco to neglected hormones. But still…it was one thing to acknowledge Mitch Kincaid was good-looking and sexy. It was another to have locked lips with him and thought even for one second about jumping his bones.

But she had.

And that's why she'd taken the coward's way out this morning and gone for an early run rather than face the rat ba— Mitch—over breakfast. She couldn't look in his eyes and know he'd made her as antsy as a dog in heat. Not until she had her hormones locked back in their kennel.

Maybe she should go out on one of those dates Mitch had mentioned. She weighed the idea and discarded it. Sex with some guy she picked up in a bar or with one of the blind dates her coworker seemed determined to arrange for her just didn't appeal. She preferred a steady, monogamous relationship with her sex. And love. Or at least exceptionally strong and optimistic like.

The distant scruff of footsteps behind her pulled her out of her funk. Safety wasn't an issue here since the gated community had only one entrance, but company on her run would be surprising. She glanced over her shoulder, but a curve in the road and a lush oleander hedge blocked her view. Funny how many of the mansions were surrounded by the toxic plant. She made a point to keep Rhett's curious fingers out of reach.

If there was one thing she could count on in this very exclusive section of Miami, it was the solitude she needed to get her head together. Rich folks, she'd learned since moving into Kincaid Manor, stayed behind their tall fences. They didn't jog or stroll through the meandering, tree- and shrub-lined streets. The pricey peninsula couldn't be more different from her friendly neighborhood of culs-de-sac and block parties. She knew all of her neighbors.

She jogged in place at a hand-carved wooden Stop sign and waited for a banana-yellow Lamborghini to pass. She waved a greeting, but couldn't see through the darkly tinted windows whether or not the occupant waved back.

The nearing footsteps told her the other runner was gaining on her. She glanced back again. *Mitch*. A nearly naked Mitch. Her heart rate shot up.

He wore skimpy running shorts and shoes. Nothing else. And the view of his torso in the bright sunlight was a hundred times better than it had been in Rhett's shadowy room last night. A fitness model would envy that body, those legs, those abs, and oh, mama, those mile-wide shoulders. There wasn't an ounce of surplus fat on him. Corded muscles wrapped in tight, tanned, glistening skin, bunched and flexed with each long stride and pump of his arms as he closed the distance between them and drew up alongside her.

If not for her tight grip on the stroller handle, Carly would have fallen flat on her face—after tripping over her tongue.

"Good morning, Carly." Like her, he jogged in place. Unlike her, he wasn't winded. Or drooling. His gaze raked over her, lingering on her breasts encased in a sports bra tank before traveling to her shorts and her legs.

So much for avoiding him for a few days. She hoped he'd attribute the heat in her face to exertion and not lust—which had hit her like a hurricane the second she spotted him. His kisses had been that good.

"Morning, Mitch." Carly snapped her attention back to the road and resumed her run. He kept pace beside her.

"Don't let us keep you." *Not exactly subtle, Carly.*

"I've decided to join you and the kid when you run."

Why did she doubt it was for the pleasure of their company? "His name is Rhett."

"Bubba, bubba, bubba," Rhett singsonged.

Mitch shot ahead and turned. Jogging backward, he said, "Mitch. Not bubba. *Mitch.*"

"Mitt. Mitt. Mitt."

"Close enough." Mitch nodded and fell back in line beside her.

They covered a block in silence broken only by the slap of their shoes and the bleats of Rhett's horn. "Did your sister leave a will?"

Carly's steps faltered. "Yes. Why?"

"I'd like to see it."

"I repeat, why?"

"Because anything that concerns Rhett concerns me. I am, after all, his brother. You're only his aunt."

Worry twisted her stomach. The attorney had promised the hastily scribbled will was valid. But he was a small-time attorney and not one of the high-profile types the Kincaids probably kept on retainer. "Half brother. Marlene's will was handwritten, but notarized and completely legal."

"Then you have no reason not to share it."

She couldn't stop him from getting a copy. Cooperating would probably be for the best. "I'll tell my lawyer you want a copy."

"I'd prefer to see the original."

Her nerves snarled tighter. "Why?"

"To make sure the document is valid."

He was going to challenge her right to Rhett. It was all she could do to keep putting one foot in front of the other. "It is."

"Find a renter for your house yet?" he asked before she could get past her panic.

"No."

"Are you comfortable leaving it vacant?"

If his goal was to ruin her run, he'd succeeded. "My neighbors will keep an eye on it for me."

"You trust them that much?"

"I do."

"You might want to consider a security system."

"I can't afford one."

"You could. Just say the word."

"If I moved back home, I wouldn't need a security system." Carly usually ran farther, but she couldn't stomach more of Mitch's company this morning. She took a sharp right at the intersection without warning and headed back toward the manor.

Mitch's steps echoed hers, and he tracked her back toward the house. "Running from something, Carly?"

Yes. You. She glanced at him. "I need to go into work early this morning."

A lone dark eyebrow hiked as if he recognized the lie for what it was. But she didn't care. Mitch wasn't interested in his half brother's well-being. All he cared about was the billions of bucks Rhett represented.

Carly needed to call her attorney and find out if Mitch had any chance at all of stealing her precious nephew. If he did, then renting her house wasn't going to be an issue, because she'd have to sell it and use the equity to pay the legal fees.

Mitch Kincaid seemed determined to screw up hers and Rhett's lives. And Carly was just as determined to stop him.

No matter what the cost.

"Fax coming through," Frank Lewis's voice said through the cell phone line. "You're not going to like it."

Mitch tossed his keys into the porcelain bowl on the credenza. "Why?"

"Because Carlene Corbin is squeaky-clean."

"Nobody's that clean. How far back did you go?"

"Eighteen. Want me to look further? Check for a juvenile record?"

"Yes."

"It'll take some time to crack sealed records."

"I'll wait. What about the other matter?"

"I used my connections to get what the police had on the sister's accident. Nothing of interest so far. No flags on your father."

Mitch exhaled in relief. "Good. Keep looking."

"Everett wasn't Mafia, Mitch."

Mitch entered the study and closed the door. As predicted, the fax machine spewed pages. "No, but we both know you didn't cross him. Marlene Corbin backed Dad into a corner. He would have come out swinging. And he wouldn't plan to lose the fight."

"I hear you. I'm on it. Read the fax. Give me a call if anything rings your chimes."

"Will do. Thanks, Frank." He disconnected, retrieved the report and scanned the pages, noting Carly's University of Florida, Gainesville, education, her steady work history and her broken engagement. Something niggled at him as he settled in his leather desk chair. He reread until he nailed the odd part.

She'd graduated from high school at nineteen when many kids did so at seventeen or eighteen. That wasn't too unusual. Had she missed the age cutoff for entering school? Repeated a grade? He double-checked her birth date. July 9. She hadn't missed the age cutoff. Probably nothing, but he'd get Frank on it.

She'd had a long-term relationship with one man in college, and she'd been engaged until recently to another. What had happened to the college boyfriend and the ex-fiancé?

A knock on the door yanked him away from those intriguing questions. He opened a drawer and shoved the fax inside. "Yes?"

The knob turned and the oak panel opened. Carly filled the gap. She had Rhett on her hip and judging by her purple tracksuit had just returned from work.

"Mitt," the kid screamed and beamed and waved.

A stab of something, probably a hunger pain, jabbed Mitch in the midsection. He jerked a nod. "Hi, kid."

Carly stepped into the study. "Della needed another day. I can have dinner ready in about an hour. Will that work for you?"

"That makes three days off."

"Get over yourself, Kincaid. She's trying to take care of her sister, not going out of her way to inconvenience you. And I told her to take as long as she needed."

He gritted his teeth over Carly interfering with household matters. *Keep your eye on the goal. Get the kid. Get rid of the aunt.* "We'll go out to dinner."

Refusal tightened Carly's features and stung Mitch's pride. Women didn't turn down his invitations. "I just picked up Rhett from day care. Lucy said he was teething and cranky today. I'm not going to leave him with a sitter."

"We'll take him with us."

Carly's brown eyes narrowed suspiciously. "You want to eat out with Mr. Messy even knowing he's likely to be fussy?"

He'd rather have a vasectomy without anesthetic. "We have to eat, Carly. And you've worked all day. You shouldn't have to cook."

Most women would fall all over themselves to be accommodating. Carly deliberated for nearly sixty seconds, and the lack of enthusiasm on her face wasn't flattering.

"Give me ten minutes. And don't make reservations for some swanky place. Make sure it's family-friendly. Rhett will need a high chair." She left, closing the door behind her.

Mitch steepled his fingers and tapped his chin. Earlier today his lawyer had informed him Marlene's will was airtight. Not only had the document been written in her handwriting, the writing of the one-line testament had been witnessed by two bank employees who knew her well.

I leave everything I hold dear, my possessions, my assets and my beloved son, Rhett, to my sister, Carlene Leah Corbin, because she'll be a better mother to my son than even I could be.

In an overkill move, Marlene had had the thing notarized. Had she taken such drastic moves because she'd feared Everett's rage?

Mitch had never seen his father as livid as he'd been that day in late January when Marlene Corbin had brought her eight-month-old son to the house to meet his daddy. Everett's fury hadn't abated during the month of February while they'd awaited the DNA test results. And then on the first of March Marlene was dead. His father's only comment, "Good riddance," had been heartfelt.

Had his father stooped to murder? Mitch shrugged to ease the knot of tension cramping between his shoulder blades. He'd know soon enough. And then he'd deal with it.

But for now, contesting Marlene's will was out.

He retrieved the fax and resumed reading, but found nothing else of value. True to her word, Carly returned ten minutes later. She'd changed into a short white denim skirt that displayed the length of her legs and a sleeveless wrap-around red knit top that clung to her breasts and narrow waist.

She looked good. Good enough to momentarily distract him from his plan. Forcing his head back into the game, Mitch rose and escorted her outside. She headed for her car, he for his.

She stopped in the driveway. "The car seat's in my car."

He eyed the minivan without anticipation and held out his hand for her keys. "I'll drive."

"My car? I don't think so." She turned away and leaned into the backseat to strap the boy in.

Mitch's eyes zeroed in on the curve of her butt, and he almost said to hell with dinner. He didn't like being attracted to his unwanted houseguest. But eating alone wouldn't get him anywhere. After the way she'd kissed him two nights ago, he needed to get her out of the picture. Fast. Or he'd end up no better than his father. Hooked by a Corbin.

Biting back his objections, he pried his gaze from her rear end, rounded the hood and climbed into the front passenger seat. It had been seven days since she'd moved in. He'd expected to see some sign of discontent by now. When would the craving for her single lifestyle kick in? When would she start feeling tied down by her sister's kid?

Waiting for Carly to grow tired of caring for the boy was moving too slowly. He needed faster results.

She settled in the driver's seat, buckled up and turned the key. Mitch checked her ring finger and noted a faint pale indentation he hadn't noticed before. He waited until she'd cleared the guardhouse before asking, "What happened to your engagement?"

Carly braked a little too hard at the stoplight, jolting him forward. He braced a hand on the dash. "It ended. Where are we going?"

"Head toward the bay side of South Beach. Why did your engagement end?"

She shot him a guarded glance. "Sam wasn't ready for a family."

And she came with one. Unless she dumped the kid. "That's a circumstance easily remedied, Carly."

Her fingers strangled the steering wheel and her glare made it clear she'd rather wrap them around his neck. The light turned green and she punched the gas. "Oh for pity's sake. Would you get off that horse? I'm not giving up Rhett."

"You must have loved Sam. You were engaged for two years."

Her throat worked as she swallowed. She kept her eyes straight ahead. "I'm not going to ask how you know that. But, yes, I did. I stopped the day he asked me to walk away from Rhett."

Mitch bit back a curse as another avenue closed. But when faced with a roadblock, he'd learned to search for an alternate route.

If Carly was as squeaky-clean as the P.I. reported, then he'd have to find another way to get custody of the boy. But how could he win her over? How could he gain her trust?

Seduction? The idea shot across his mind like a comet.

He weighed the possibility, and his pulse quickened and his palms tingled the way they did whenever he had a winning plan.

Could he deliberately seduce Carly and win her trust, then stab her in the back by taking the kid?

Guilt punched him a time or two, but he ignored it. It would be nothing more than doing to Carly what her sister had done to his father. Marlene had set up his father, then taken something from him.

Mitch had to carry out his father's last wishes or lose his and his siblings' inheritance. If that meant he had to blur the lines of decency, then so be it. The boy would be well cared for, and no one would be hurt in the long run.

The kiss had proved he and Carly were physically compatible. He studied the curve of her breasts, her narrow waist and the length of her toned legs, and arousal buzzed through his veins.

Sharing her bed wouldn't be a hardship. But how far would he have to go?

As far as it takes.

He'd even marry her if he had to and adopt the child. When the marriage ended, he'd have custody of the kid and Carly would have a healthy bank account.

A win-win situation.

* * *

"He looks just like you, Mitch, except he has Carly's eyes."

Carly opened her mouth to correct the woman Mitch had introduced as a member of his yacht club, but Mitch cut her off.

"Rhett definitely has his mother's eyes."

"Don't tell me Miami's most eligible bachelor is finally going to settle down?" the anorexic, overly tanned, forty-something blonde asked.

Mitch gave her an enigmatic smile and a slight shrug.

Carly wanted to kick him under the table. What was he trying to pull?

To Carly she said, "Kudos, my dear. You have accomplished a miracle."

Carly stiffened at the implication that she'd landed Mitch. Or that she'd even want to. "I—"

"Thanks for stopping by, Sandra," Mitch interrupted. "Tell William I said hello."

"I will. And again, I am sorry about Everett. It's great seeing you, Mitch, and meeting you and your adorable little one, Carly. Ta ta." The skinny body slinked away.

Ta ta? Who said *ta ta* these days? But Carly had bigger fish to fry. "What on earth were you thinking? You let her believe Rhett was yours. And mine."

The idea of having Mitch's baby made her stomach churn.

Mitch glanced at Rhett, who had almost finished smearing and eating his dinner. "You said the kid had a short attention span. Do you really want to waste time explaining this convoluted mess my father and your sister left behind when we could be finishing our meal before he has the meltdown you predicted?"

"No. But—"

"Forget it, Carly. Sandra isn't worth the worry."

"But you lied."

"Replay every word I said. I never lied. She assumed. I

didn't correct her, nor did I confirm her speculations. Give it a rest. The media frenzy my father's death created is just beginning to die down. I'd rather not jump-start it with the kind of scandal his illegitimate child will create. That'll happen soon enough."

Media frenzy. She suppressed a shudder.

She hated that Mitch was right almost as much as she hated that he'd chosen the perfect restaurant and been completely charming and polite throughout the meal. He'd even smiled at Rhett a couple of times.

But he'd been nothing but distrustful and acerbic before tonight, and that made her wary. "Why the chameleon act?"

A dark eyebrow lifted. "I beg your pardon?"

"Why are you being nice?"

"You've stated your case. You're not going to give up the bo—Rhett. That means we will be sharing a roof for the next fifty-plus weeks. No reason why we can't do so amicably."

"I stated my case the day we met. Nothing's changed."

"I thought you'd change your mind. Now I realize you won't. We'll make the best of our alliance." He wiped his mouth and laid his napkin beside his plate. "Would you care for dessert?"

She blinked at the sudden switch in topic. An inkling of suspicion wiggled like an earthworm inside her. Leopards didn't change their spots. Or so the cliché said. And clichés were clichés for a reason. They were usually true.

Mitch had to be up to something. The question was what?

But even more worrisome, Carly had actually enjoyed Mitch's company tonight. She'd better watch herself, because he was still the same rat bastard who'd hurt her sister and had recently threatened Carly's custody of Rhett.

Letting her guard down around Mitch Kincaid wouldn't be a smart move.

Five

Wooing a woman he didn't like but wanted to sleep with was a unique experience for Mitch.

Carly was too smart to fall for the usual bought-without-a-thought generic bouquet or jewelry trinket. Lucky for him, his personal assistant, Marie, knew where to find the right ammo.

Mitch rounded the house with Carlos, the Kincaid Manor groundskeeper, and two large potted plants on hand trucks. Carly looked up from Rhett on his new riding toy. She said something and the kid looked Mitch's way, then abandoned his wheels to scamper over.

The huge grin on the boy's face hit Mitch in the solar plexus with memories of other grins, other kids who'd been happy to see him back in the days when he used to rush home from KCL in time for dinner instead of working until the cleaning crew ran him out of his office. Kids who'd moved from Miami to Los Angeles and out of reach when their father had been traded to a west coast basketball team.

"What's up, little man?" He released the hand truck and extended a hand for a high five, but Rhett bypassed it and twined himself around Mitch's pant leg and stuck like a thorny vine.

Carly followed at a slower pace. Today's tracksuit matched the blue sky above. She'd shed the jacket, and her white tank top hugged the curve of her breasts. Her hair had been released from its usual ponytail to drape her bare shoulders, and a breeze lifted the strands away from her face. How had he never noticed that she didn't wear earrings? Her lobes weren't even pierced, and he found the naked, virgin flesh unusually alluring. Did he even know another woman who didn't have at least one hole in each ear?

Carly nodded to Carlos as she joined them. "What are those?"

"Bud-something. To attract hummingbirds." Odd how tight his throat was this afternoon. He patted the head bumping his thigh.

"Buddleia. That's not what I meant. I know what a butter-fly bush is. I have three in my yard. Why do *you* have them?"

"You said the—Rhett liked to watch hummingbirds. These should draw them, since the feeders alone didn't do the trick."

"Up. Up. Pig me up."

Mitch couldn't shake the kid off and he lost a few leg hairs trying. Admitting defeat, he bent and scooped the boy into one arm, and earned himself a slobbery kiss on the chin.

"Mitt."

Mitch swallowed. Hard. He wasn't ready yet to let Rhett squeeze his heart with those stubby little fingers.

Hands on hips, Carly stared at him through narrowed eyes. "Why?"

"I gave you the reason." He passed the kid to Carly and turned to the other man. "Carlos, set one pot on each corner of the patio."

Carly persisted, "And I might believe that was your only motive if you hadn't bought Rhett a wading pool yesterday and the riding toy the day before that."

"The plastic pool is to keep him away from the big pool. And he loves that blue train."

Carly cocked her head. "Have any Greeks in your ancestry?"

"As in, 'Beware of Greeks bearing gifts'?"

"Yes."

"Haven't you ever heard, 'Don't look a gift horse in the mouth'?"

"I also know that one end of the horse bites and the other one kicks. I'm still trying to figure out which end you are. I'll tell Della you're home for dinner. She wasn't expecting you." She turned on her heel and marched through the French doors.

Shot down. Again. He'd known Carly would be a tough nut to crack. He even admired her intelligence in not accepting the gifts at face value because he did have an ulterior motive.

He shoved his hand truck into motion. What would it take to get through to her? And why did it suddenly matter so much?

"Buy you a drink?"

The quietly rumbled question broke the hard-won silence. Carly pivoted away from the crib and jerked a finger to her lips. "Shh."

Mitch leaned against the doorjamb of Rhett's room. Since they'd eaten out together last Friday, Mitch had shown up for breakfast and dinner each of the past seven days. Given Della said Mitch had rarely made it home for evening meals before Carly and Rhett had moved in, Carly had to question the sudden change. And while she was suspicious, she didn't want to rock the boat because dining with him furthered her goal of bonding the brothers. Rhett loved "Mitt's" company.

Unfortunately, so did she.

She joined Mitch in the hall. Once her eyes adjusted to the brighter light, she noticed he'd exchanged his suit for a black polo shirt, a pair of worn jeans that fit him like a designer glove and leather deck shoes. It might be the Fourth of July and a national holiday, but Mitch had gone to work.

"Rough night." The low midnight pitch of his voice made the hairs on her arms lift.

"Rhett's new molar is giving him fits. I gave him Tylenol hoping that'll help him sleep through the night." Rhett had been exceptionally fussy during dinner. Mitch had stuck out the entire miserable hour which had a) earned him points with her, and b) proved they'd made progress. And then her nephew had been nearly impossible to settle for bed.

"A glass of wine might help you unwind enough to sleep. Join me on the patio." Mitch pointed to the baby monitor in her hand. "We'll take that with us."

The wine sounded good, but a voice in her head shouted, "Not wise." She nibbled the inside of her bottom lip in indecision. Just because she'd begun to enjoy their shared meals and verbal sparring, and just because she'd learned to tell the difference between Armani, Brooks Brothers and Hugo Boss, and just because Mitch looked mouthwateringly gorgeous in all three didn't mean she'd do something stupid like fall for him. Thanks to Marlene, she knew too much about him to ever do that.

Which meant she could safely join him for a drink.

"Okay, sure." She hooked the monitor on her waistband and walked beside him down the hall, the stairs and into the kitchen. He snagged a bottle, a couple of glasses and the corkscrew from the counter and tilted his head toward the back door.

Carly opened it and stepped outside. The flagstones radiated remnants of the day's warmth against her bare feet. The patio glowed in the flickering light of the dozen pewter pole torches surrounding the area, and the scents of citronella oil and the sweet aroma of the butterfly bushes mingled in the humid night air.

"You must have been pretty confident I'd join you to light all these."

"I know I needed a drink after dinner. I assumed you would, as well."

She sighed. "You assumed right. Rhett's not usually like that."

"I know." He guided her toward a plushly cushioned seating arrangement where a candle's flame reflected off a small gift-wrapped box resting on the rectangular coffee table.

Carly stared at the package while the man who'd lured her into the moonlight opened and poured the wine. She didn't sit. The setting was far too romantic. Second thoughts crept over her. She shouldn't have come out here with him. Standing awkwardly beside the love seat, she wondered how quickly she could guzzle her wine and make her escape.

He offered a filled goblet. "To two successful weeks as housemates."

She accepted the glass and chinked the rim against his. "May there be fifty more."

For Rhett's sake.

Did she imagine Mitch's eyes narrowing slightly as he drank? He lowered his glass and inclined his head to indicate the gift on the table. "It's for you."

Stalling, she sipped the reddish-colored beverage and shifted on her feet. She'd never been much of a wine drinker, and she certainly wasn't a connoisseur, but this vintage could become a habit.

Wine, moonlight, gifts. Watch it.

"It's not my birthday." Not yet. But soon. And she dreaded waking up Wednesday and knowing Marlene wouldn't be here to share their special day.

"Doesn't matter. Open it." When she made no move to do so he picked up the box, offered it to her and repeated, "Open it, Carly."

Presents meant nothing to him, she reminded herself. So

why did her heart quicken and her body flush over finding a golden-wrapped package for her? Stupid, really.

He had money to burn and he burned it. He'd come home with something for Rhett each day this week. Not that he was spoiling his half brother. Each gift had been something so appropriate and well thought out she'd begun to suspect Mitch might be a decent guy under his expensively tailored wolf's clothing. He'd even bought a car seat for his SUV, claiming that he could get away from the office more easily than she could cancel her appointments if Rhett should ever need an emergency pickup from day care.

She took another healthy swig of the wine, letting the fruity liquid roll around on her tongue before swallowing. She accepted the package, weighed it in her palm and debated the intelligence of accepting a present from a man she had previously considered the enemy. But she wanted to maintain the recent goodwill between them. If the gift was inappropriate, she'd simply refuse to accept it.

She set down her goblet and slipped a fingernail under the tape. Hyperconscious of Mitch's unwavering gaze on her trembling hands, she carefully loosened the foil paper to reveal a square blue velvet box and then flipped open the hinged lid.

Resting on a bed of white velvet, an inch-long golden charm in the shape of a boy hung from a delicate rope chain. Mitch reached out and flipped the charm over. RHETT had been engraved down the center of the back.

Her resistance melted. She could have refused just about anything else. But this...this was perfect. "It's lovely. I— thank you, Mitch."

He took the box from her, removed the necklace and opened the clasp, but instead of walking behind her the way most people would to assist, he stepped closer and raised the ends of the chain to her shoulders.

The warmth of his fingertips brushed her jaw and tunneled beneath her ponytail. She shivered at the featherlight scrape of his short nails on her nape, and then the cool metal settled on her skin.

His palms rested on her shoulders as he studied the jewelry he'd hung around her neck. Electricity flowed from his flesh to hers. "You're good with him."

She shrugged, but the movement didn't dislodge his hands. "It's easy to be."

"Even tonight?"

Carly wrinkled her nose and tilted her head back to look up into that too handsome face. "Tonight wasn't as easy as most, but it's not his fault his gums hurt, and it's not hard to forgive someone when you love them."

Several miles away, the dark sky exploded with color. Seconds later, a muffled series of booms reached her. Fireworks to celebrate the holiday.

Mitch didn't even glance at the light show. He dragged a fingertip down the chain to where the charm rested between her breasts just above the scooped neck of her tank top. Desire arched through her, igniting her skin and tightening her lungs. She tried to tamp down the unexpected and unwanted response, but instead, the memory of how he'd kissed her last week and how he'd touched her made her mouth water and her nipples peak.

Sexual tension hung between them as hot and heavy as the damp night air, and sensation exploded within her like the distant pyrotechnics. The muffled reverberations vibrated along her spine.

Move away, Carly.

But her feet remained planted. Her toes curled on the flagstones. Mitch's grip on her shoulder tightened, and that lone finger trailed back up the chain. He brushed a stray lock of hair out of the way and traced the shape of her ear, fingering the lobe. Carly shuddered. She'd never realized how sensitive her ears could be. Her pulse ba-ba-boomed. Hard. Fast. Insistent.

"You feel it, too," he murmured huskily.

She played stupid, because it was the smart thing to do. "Feel what?"

He lowered his chin and gave her the kind of don't-mess-with-me look that probably sent his employees running for cover. "You know what. The desire. The pull. The connection."

She didn't like knowing she wasn't alone in her insanity. "That doesn't mean we have to act on it."

Another volley of lights and bangs lit the cloudless night sky.

"Why shouldn't we?" His deep voice rippled across her nerve endings, and he lowered his head. His lips feathered over hers, lifted and returned once, twice, each caress as gentle as a butterfly touching down on a blossom.

Carly's muscles locked and her breath lodged in her chest. Awareness ignited below her navel like a lit fuse. She balled her hands against the urge to yank him closer and deepen the kiss.

The big hand on her shoulder shifted to cradle her face and angle her head, and like a mannequin, she let him move her any way he pleased. His mouth opened over hers. He sucked her bottom lip between his. The sharp nip of his teeth sent a bolt of desire through her and surprised a gasp from her.

C'mon, Carly, move away.

And still she couldn't seem to break the connection. Her lips parted and his tongue sought hers. Slick, hot, seductive. She tasted wine and Mitch and a hunger so intense she could barely stand.

Oh, this was a mistake. A big one. No doubt about it.

Mitch's fingers speared through her hair, releasing and discarding her clip, holding her captive. The cool, loosened strands rained down on her shoulders. His other arm banded around her waist, bringing her body into hot, searing contact with his from the knees up. She tried to save herself by leaning back, but that only pressed their pelvises tighter together. His arousal swelled and lengthened against her hip bone, and an answering need swirled inside her.

Oh, mama. Another barrage of booms came across the water and bounced off the stone walls of Kincaid Manor to seemingly pound her from both directions. Or maybe it was her reaction to Mitch hammering her senses.

Getting physically involved with him was wrong on so many levels. But it—*he*—felt so right. His kisses consumed her. His touch inflamed her. Her fingers found his hair, twining in the thick, soft strands. She kissed him back with everything she had. A vibration of approval slid up his throat and down hers to settle low in her belly.

She'd stop in a minute. Before this got out of hand.

But for the moment he made her feel wanted and feminine and desirable in a way that Sam's desertion had stolen from her. Mitch's mouth worked magic on hers. One big hand swept the length of her back and then molded the curve of her bottom.

She finally admitted something her grief over losing Marlene hadn't allowed her to acknowledge. Her broken engagement had battered her ego; Mitch's attention was not only arousing, it was healing to her wounded spirit.

The steam of Mitch's breath on her cheek drew her out of her dark thoughts. She splayed a hand over his pounding heart and lost herself in the baby-soft cotton fabric of his shirt, in the strength of the muscle-packed body against hers and in the flood of his scent, his heat, his flavor.

Boom. Boom. Boom. Her heart echoed the fireworks.

She knew enough about herself to understand this rush of hormones was temporary. As temporary as it was unwise to let herself trust Mitch Kincaid. Once before, she'd allowed herself to get swept away on a whirlwind of desire, and she'd regretted it ever since.

Pulse racing, she reluctantly eased back and wiggled

free of his embrace. From the safer distance of several feet away, she locked gazes with him and took a moment to catch her breath.

His pupils had expanded to almost obliterate the green of his irises, and in the flickering torchlight, dark swipes of color painted his cheekbones. His chest rose and fell as rapidly as hers, and he fisted and released his hands by his side. The hunger on his face sent concussions of want through her. But she resisted throwing herself back into his arms. Barely.

She licked her lips, savoring his taste one last time, and endeavored to shut down this runaway train. "We should forget that ever happened."

His damp lips parted and his eyebrows shot up. "Forget it?"

"It shouldn't have happened, Mitch. Our lives are complicated enough without this." She fluttered a hand to indicate the two of them.

"What's complicated? We share a house, a child and some phenomenal chemistry. Why not share a bed?"

He made it sound so logical. So tempting. "I'm not ready for another relationship."

Mitch's shoulders squared, and his lips compressed. He closed the distance between them, stalking her like a predator does prey. Carly backed up until the wrought-iron chair against her calves stopped her.

"You're the one who forced your way into my house and insinuated yourself into my life."

Before she could escape, his hands lifted and captured her face. He took her mouth roughly, all aggravated, aroused and determined male.

At first, she was too stunned by the barely leashed violence she felt in him to react. And then she flattened her palms against his chest, intending to push him away, but despite the untamed plunder of her mouth, his hands remained gentle on her face. The gentleness got to her. She'd never experienced this kind of pure, unadulterated need. And in that moment of hesitation, the raw hunger of his kiss weakened her resistance.

His hands caressed her face, her hair, her back, her waist. And against caution and common sense, her body responded. Her muscles weakened, her head tipped back allowing him deeper access. Her skin grew hypersensitive to his touch, and her panties moistened. When his thumb found her nipple her breath hitched and arrows of desire hit a target deep inside her.

Instead of shoving him away her fingers fisted in his shirt, then her grip slid upward and clung to the broad beam of his shoulders. She shouldn't be doing this, but at the moment she couldn't remember why and didn't care.

Mitch abruptly released her and set her away almost roughly. Chest heaving, nostrils flaring, he glared at her. "Forget the passion between us if you can, Carly. I sure as hell won't."

And then he stormed inside, leaving Carly alone with her hunger and her doubts and her self-recriminations. A shrill whistle of sound and light split the sky followed by the grand finale of the fireworks exhibition. Carly watched without awe or excitement. Her mind was occupied elsewhere.

What had happened to her vow to keep her distance?

What about Marlene? It seemed disloyal to want the man who'd been so cruel to her sister. And yet Mitch had had Carly clinging and all but begging.

If he'd truly been the untrustworthy rat bastard Marlene described, wouldn't Mitch have taken what he wanted?

Was it possible her sister had exaggerated...or lied?

Six

Forget his kiss? Like hell she would. He wouldn't let her.

Mitch charged downstairs Saturday morning determined to stick to Carly like barnacles on a ship's bottom. If she refused his company, he'd simply insist on spending time with the kid. Where Rhett went, Carly followed.

The sounds of laughter and high-pitched childish gibberish reached him as he neared the kitchen. It had been three and a half years since he'd said goodbye to Travis and Ashley. Would the haunting memories of what he'd lost ever go away? He stopped on the threshold.

The kid spotted him and smiled around a mouthful of food. "Mitt."

A pain clutched Mitch's stomach. *A hunger pain*. He entered the room and paused behind Carly's chair. "Hello, squirt. Mrs. Duncan. Carly."

He rested a hand on Carly's shoulder. She stiffened and her

silky ponytail twitched and swished across his knuckles, but she kept her eyes on her oatmeal. "Morning, Mitch."

"Good morning, sir. I'll have your breakfast in a jiffy."

"Thank you." He circled the table, entering Carly's field of vision and catching a glimpse of desire in her chocolate eyes before she quickly averted her face. His pulse revved in response. "Sleep well?"

Her throat worked as she swallowed. "Yes. Thank you."

"Liar." He lowered his voice so Mrs. Duncan couldn't hear him and earned himself a scowl. The faint circles under Carly's eyes told the truth.

At least he wasn't the only one who'd been miserable. He was still kicking himself for almost losing control last night. He'd never had a problem reining in his hunger before. No meant no. The fact that he'd come so close to overriding Carly's objections and taking what he wanted—what he'd made her want—right there on the patio alarmed him.

Bulldozing over others had been his father's MO. Not Mitch's. Everett Kincaid may have been a brilliant businessman, but he'd been a hurricane in his personal life, leaving a trail of destruction wherever he passed. The Kincaid money broom had always managed to sweep up the debris.

Until Marlene Corbin had come along. And now Mitch had to deal with her twin. Identical DNA. Identical risk.

Still, there was a fine line between seduction and coercion—a line Mitch had no intention of crossing. Morning-after regrets and recriminations were hell to deal with. He'd leave Carly no recourse to cry foul. When she came to him she would do so willingly, and not in a passing bout of insane passion. He'd keep this affair, their marriage and their eventual divorce strictly legal.

His father hadn't always cared on which side of the law he walked, but Mitch cared.

"I didn't hear Rhett get up last night," he said to force her to look at him, but paused before adding, "Despite the fireworks."

The flush on her cheeks told him she hadn't missed the double entendre. They'd definitely set off their own personal pyrotechnics. She blinked, hiked her chin and took in his casual clothing. "He slept through the night. You're not going to the office today?"

"I'm spending the entire day with my brother." He lowered himself into the chair directly across from her.

"Will he be around later? I'd like for Rhett to meet Rand."

"I meant Rhett."

Her lips parted and her breasts lifted when she inhaled. Her expression turned guarded. "Rhett and I have plans."

He wouldn't let her shake him off that easily. "Change them."

"I can't."

"Then you'll have company."

"I don't think—"

"To borrow your phrase, Carly, this one's nonnegotiable. You haven't been reticent about your desire for me to spend time with Rhett. I've cleared my schedule for the weekend. He's my priority."

A mix of emotions crossed her face, but the last one, a mischievous twitch of her delectable lips, made him uneasy.

"Okay. We're leaving at eight-thirty." She rose to refill the kid's sippy cup, giving Mitch an opportunity to appreciate the shape of her breasts in a red tank top and her incredible legs below the hem of her blue running shorts.

"You've already had your run?"

"Yes."

"Tomorrow I'll join you."

"We go at six." Her tone implied she hoped that was too early for him.

"I'll be ready."

Mrs. Duncan set his breakfast in front of him. He nodded his thanks, then checked his watch and refocused on Carly.

"If you're going to take a shower before we leave, you'd better get started."

"Rhett hasn't finished eating."

"We'll feed the rug rat."

She looked from him to Mrs. Duncan. "You're sure?"

"Got it covered," Mitch replied before the housekeeper could respond.

Carly looked ready to argue, but instead shrugged. "I won't be long."

She left the kitchen. Mitch looked at Mrs. Duncan. "Do you have a spare apron?"

If his question surprised her, she hid it well. "Yes, sir. I'll get it."

The kid had been fed and hosed off by the time Carly returned with the diaper bag on her shoulder twenty-five minutes later. Her hair draped her shoulders like damp sun-streaked silk, and makeup covered the evidence of her lack of sleep. She'd changed into a lemon-yellow T-shirt and a midthigh-length khaki skirt and white sandals. She looked good. Damned good.

She scooped up Rhett from the living-room floor where Mitch had parked him with a toy truck. "Let me change him and then we can go."

"Done." Mitch never went into any battle without a winning strategy. Diaper duty always scored big points with women.

She stopped in her tracks. "Della changed him?"

"I did. We'll take my car." He led the way to the foyer.

"How old were your fiancée's children?"

Not a conversation he wanted to pursue. "One and four when we moved in together. What's on the agenda for today?"

"And what age when you split?" She ignored his question.

"Two and a half years older. Where are we headed?" He opened the front door and changed the subject.

"Hialeah. Wow. That must have been hard. What were their names?"

He gritted his teeth. "Travis and Ashley. What's in Hialeah?"

"Tina, one of my coworkers, lives there."

The sun shone in a cloudless blue sky. It was early, but the day promised to be a July scorcher. He opened the front and back passenger-side doors and then circled to the driver's side to prevent more questions. By the time Carly strapped Rhett into his new car seat and joined Mitch up front, he had the radio on and the sunroof open. The combination of music and wind noise guaranteed to make conversation difficult.

"Address?"

She recited the info. He typed it into his GPS, which eliminated the need for directions, and set the car in motion. Sure, he'd have to endure a visit with one of Carly's coworkers, but then he'd have her to himself for the rest of the day.

His confidence lasted until he saw half-dozen minivans lining the street and the Mylar balloons attached to the mailbox bearing the street address she'd given him.

"It's a birthday party," he said flatly.

The mischievous twinkle returned to Carly's eyes and the corners of her lips curled up, revealing her enjoyment of his predicament. Her smile had the usual effect of hitting him in the solar plexus.

"For Tina's five-year-old twin sons. Don't say I didn't try to warn you."

Damn. Not the day of seduction he had in mind, but he could roll with the change in plans. The party would last an hour or two, and then he'd be back on schedule. He parked his SUV between two mom-mobiles and tried to conceal his lack of enthusiasm. He'd endured kids' parties before. Hell, he'd planned them. The only guarantees were noise and mess.

Carly ignored the concrete walk leading to the front door of the modest two-story structure and carried Rhett around the side of the house. She pushed open a tall wooden gate, revealing a backyard filled with a couple dozen kids of various ages and half as many moms and set the boy on his feet. Rhett toddled into the melee full steam ahead. Not a shy bone in that boy's stubby body.

Balls of every size, shape and color dotted the patchy lawn and kids raced and swarmed like insects. A wooden swing set with a tree house on one end took up one back corner of the lot. An inflatable bounce castle had been set up in another. Mitch scanned the area for a father, but there wasn't a single male over seven in sight.

"Hey, mister, catch." A football came hurtling toward his head from the left. He caught it one-handed and passed it back.

The gathering of women on the back deck turned in unison. Eyebrows rose, mouths dropped open. Mitch followed Carly across the grass and forced a smile to his lips.

Carly would soon discover that, compliments of his father, Mitch detested being set up to fail.

But he'd have his revenge.

Carly's plan had backfired.

She'd allowed Mitch to horn in on her outing to teach him a lesson. Instead, she'd been the one who'd learned something. For someone she'd believed didn't like children, he'd handled himself and the rambunctious boys very well.

Oh sure, the look of horror on his face when he'd realized they were attending a children's birthday party had been priceless. But his dismay hadn't lasted long.

Within minutes Mitch had charmed the mothers in the group, and then he'd gone to work on the younger set. He'd taken charge of the older boys and organized them into one game right after another for the past ninety minutes, earning him a never-ending stream of accolades from the other women present.

Carly just wanted to go home and get away from the sight of Mitch having fun and the rumble of his voice and his laughter. The combination was doing a number on her concentration. A fact her hostess hadn't missed, if the curious glances were any indication.

Speak of the devil…

Tina plopped down on the picnic bench beside Carly. "You should have told me you were dating again. I would have quit throwing men at you."

Carly looked up from the small pop-up tent where Rhett played beside Tina's two-year-old daughter. Carly had known Tina for six years, and if there was anyone she could trust with the story of Rhett's parentage, it was the coworker who'd taken Carly under her wing on Carly's first day on the job at the sports medicine practice. Tina was ten years older but a hundred years wiser.

"I'm not dating. Mitch is Rhett's half brother."

Tina's blue eyes went wide.

"But keep their relationship to yourself, okay? The press would make a big deal of it. I'm sorry for springing him on you, but he wanted to spend the day with Rhett, and he wouldn't take no for an answer. I tried to call—"

"But one of the twins knocked the phone off the hook and I wasn't carrying my cell phone. It's okay, Carly. Mitch is dessert for those of us who can't have cake and ice cream." Tina glanced over her shoulders to make sure none of the other mothers were within hearing range. "I can't believe it. Rhett's one of the more-money-than-God Kincaids?"

Carly nodded. "I didn't tell you because Marlene asked me to keep it quiet until after Rhett was born and she'd worked things out with Everett. But she died before she and Everett could come to an agreement, and then three months later Everett died. I've been a little crazy trying to sort out everything."

"But you did, right? Renting your house isn't an attempt to clear up a financial mess Marlene left behind, is it? I mean, it was one thing when she moved in and started mooching off you, but—"

"She didn't mooch off me," Carly defended her twin automatically and out of habit. She had to turn away from Tina's give-me-a-break expression. Carly's gaze found Mitch on the far side of the yard. He had the twins and their friends involved in a game of touch football. The man was a work of art, all ropey muscles and athletic grace. A spurt of something wild pulsed through her. She ignored the unwanted feeling and returned her attention to her friend.

"There is no financial mess." Well, other than that missing hundred thousand Mitch claimed he'd given Marlene, but her attorney was looking into that. "The terms of Everett Kincaid's will require Rhett to live in Kincaid Manor for a year if he's to inherit his share of the estate."

"So that's why you were so stingy with your new address."

Carly shrugged. "I don't think I'll be hosting any mothers' mornings out while I live there."

"Mitch invited you to stay?"

Carly grimaced. "Not exactly. He just wanted Rhett."

"Without you? Carly, we both know you'd never give up Rhett. How did Mitch expect to pull that off?"

She hesitated, but after last night's kiss she needed to say the words out loud to remind herself of how low Mitch would go. And Tina knew the truth—the whole ugly truth—of Carly's past. "He offered me money—a *lot* of money—to relinquish guardianship of Rhett."

"The bastard." Tina slapped her fingers over her mouth and glanced at the toddlers in the tent. "He didn't?"

Carly nodded. "Between that and what Marlene told me about him trying to break up her and Everett, I'm afraid to trust him. No matter how charming and sexy he might be."

"He's being charming and sexy?"

"He is now, but in the beginning…" She shook her head and shuddered.

Tina tapped her chin and then a wily smile slid over her

lips. "First, remember your sister tended to be a drama queen. She might have—*probably*—exaggerated. And second, Mitch might be Rhett's kin, but he looks at you like you're the corner piece of cake and he can't wait to dive into all that rich, creamy icing."

Carly jerked around and her gaze slammed into Mitch's. She sucked a sharp breath at the hunger he telecast over the five-year-olds' heads.

"Oh, baby, I want some of that," Tina whimpered.

Cheeks hot, Carly whirled back to her friend. "Stop it."

"Admit it, you want some, too. And when we close up shop in ten minutes you can go home and get some while Rhett naps."

"Didn't you hear a word I said? Besides, even if Marlene exaggerated—and I don't think she did—the last thing I need is a rebound romance. Even if I am tempted." She muttered the last under her breath.

"Honey, you'd have to be dead not to be tempted. And nobody says you have to take an affair seriously." Tina studied her nails with faked nonchalance. "I'd do him just for the memories."

Carly's skin burned like a blowtorch. "Your husband should hear you talk."

"Hey, my husband loves it when I talk dirty." Tina winked and then turned pensive. "Maybe Mitch wants more than just Rhett. Maybe you could have your cake and eat it, too."

"You have got to stop dieting. I can't follow your starvation logic."

"All I'm saying is, why can't you have a few nibbles of Rhett's big brother while you're sharing his house? At the end of the year you'll return to your home and your real life…unless you land yourself a shipping tycoon in the meantime."

"Remind me why we're friends again? Because you're encouraging me to embark on certain disaster."

Tina grasped Carly's hands and squeezed. "No, honey, I'm trying to bring you back to the land of the living. Sam's gone. Good riddance, I might add. And Marlene's gone. Until today, I thought you had, too. This is the first time in months I've seen you excited about anything or anyone besides Rhett. Go for it."

Carly planted her elbows on her knees and her head in her hands. "Tina, that is *so* not the advice I needed to hear."

"You handled the children well today," Carly said as she joined Mitch in the living room just before noon.

"I spent every summer since high school working on Kincaid cruise ships. Corralling and controlling kids was part of the job." He waggled his water glass and raised a dark eyebrow, silently asking if she'd like a drink.

"A glass of Della's lemonade would be great."

He turned to the wet bar to fulfill her request.

"What kinds of jobs?" She placed the baby monitor on the coffee table and sank into the overstuffed sofa cushions. Her sleepless night was catching up with her. She probably should have requested something with caffeine.

"Have you ever been on a cruise?" He passed her the glass, and their fingers touched.

She fought a shiver and shook her head. "Thanks."

Instead of taking the high-backed wing chair he'd been using since she moved in, Mitch sat beside her. His weight tipped the cushion and Carly toward him, and even though their bodies didn't touch, he settled near enough that she could feel the heat radiating off him and smell the potent combination of his cologne mixed with fresh sweat and grass from running around Tina's yard with the boys. Heady stuff. The subsequent squeezing of her stomach had nothing to do with hunger due to the approaching lunch hour.

Her gaze fixed on his muscular legs below the hem of his shorts. A spattering of dark curls covered his tanned skin. She yearned to test the texture, but tightened her grip on her cold glass instead and gulped her drink, hoping the bite of the tart lemonade would shock her hormones back into line.

"There are a variety of activities on board, from day-care-type settings to swimming and rock climbing lessons. When we dock at Crescent Key, KCL's private island, there are scuba lessons, parasailing, kayaking, wind surfing, Jet Ski rentals and an inflatable kids' water park."

"The Kincaids *own* an island?"

"The company does."

She digested that and the slight chill in his voice, and then backtracked to the rest of what he'd said. "So you don't hate children?"

He frowned, leaned back against the cushions and stretched an arm along the sofa behind her. The shift of his body caused his knee to nudge hers. Atoms of awareness coalesced at the contact point. She inched her leg back, but he moved to fill the tiny gap she'd created. Her pulse sped up. "What gave you the impression I did?"

"Besides the snowman act?"

He lifted his water glass and took a sip. "I don't get attached to the ones who are only passing through. I've done that before and I didn't enjoy the aftermath."

"Your fiancée's children?"

If she hadn't been only inches from him, she would have missed his slight flinch. He nodded. Once.

Her heart ached for him. "Do you keep in touch with Travis and Ashley?"

He sat forward, braced his elbows on his knees and studied the contents of his glass. "I tried at first. But it confused them. So I stopped."

He wasn't a heartless bastard after all. He'd done what he thought best for the children. The stiffness of his shoulders and the rigid line of his jaw revealed more than words about the pain he'd suffered. No wonder he'd tried to keep his distance from Rhett.

The fragile shell of her resistance cracked and the need to reach out and offer comfort almost overwhelmed her. "Then you understand why I'll never willingly walk away from Rhett. He wouldn't understand how both his mother and I could leave him."

"He's young. He probably won't remember…her."

Did she imagine that pause? Did Mitch understand how much it still hurt to say her sister's name?

"I hope you're wrong. I hope a child never forgets feeling loved and wanted, even if the ones who loved them are only a part of their lives for a brief time."

She prayed that was the case and that one day her daughter would understand how much love it had taken to make the painful, unselfish decision to relinquish. Because Carly had so desperately wanted to be selfish and keep her. But she'd been sixteen and her baby's father had wanted nothing to do with her or their child. What kind of mother could she have been? She'd had no job and no high-school diploma. What kind of future could she have given her daughter? All the love in the world wasn't enough to put food on the table.

Mitch's green gaze probed hers. He had a way of looking at her that made her feel as if he could see her secrets. She struggled to camouflage her pain.

"What happens when you fall in love again and your future husband, like your ex, doesn't want to raise someone else's kid?"

"Then he won't be my husband. Loving means accepting the entirety of a person. The good and the bad." The men in her life hadn't been able to do that.

"You'll have to find someone who shares your interest in Rhett's future." He paused for several heavy heartbeats. "Someone like me."

Everything inside her went still, but the sudden tinkling of the ice cubes in her glass revealed her hands weren't as steady. "Wh-what are you saying, Mitch?"

He set his glass on the coffee table and then took hers and did the same. "Perhaps we should explore this attraction between us. For Rhett's sake as well as our own. We could have something here, Carly."

He lifted his hand and dragged the back of his knuckles along her cheek. Her reaction to the gentle caress mushroomed through her like an atomic blast.

"I don't think that's a good idea." She dampened her lips, and his eyes tracked the movement.

"Why?"

"Because you tried to persuade my sister not to have Rhett."

His long fingers curved over her shoulder. "As my father's right-hand man, it was my job to carry out his wishes. He asked me to make sure Marlene understood he was too old to raise another child—especially with a woman he didn't love."

Carly winced. "Marlene loved him."

Or at least she'd told Carly she did. And she'd been very convincing.

But what about Marlene's notebook? What about her plan to force Everett to marry her?

"Then I'm sorry for her. His not wanting to share his life or parenthood with her must have hurt." His thumb circled with mesmerizing, breath-snatching effect beneath her clavicle. "Is Rhett down for the count?"

"Yes. I'm glad you were driving so I could keep him awake on the ride home. If he takes a five-minute nap in the car then he won't go back to sleep when we get to his crib, and he'd be seriously cranky by dinnertime." She was babbling, but that was because if she quit talking she'd start moaning.

She couldn't do this again. Another one of his kisses and she'd be a goner.

Get up. Get out of here. At least until you're certain Marlene fibbed about him being a jerk.

Mitch's other hand settled on her opposite shoulder. His long fingers dug into the tense muscles in the back of her neck and massaged with mind- and willpower-melting results. By the time his thumbs traced the sensitive underside of her jaw, her reasons for resisting the intense attraction between them were getting pretty darn fuzzy. Her head and eyelids grew heavy.

"Give us a chance, Carly."

Before she could dredge up an answer from the sludge he'd made of her brain, he leaned forward and kissed her.

Seven

Carly made a decision she was almost certain she'd regret.

She kissed Mitch back.

But she couldn't help herself. Today, this entire week actually, she'd seen a different side of him. One she liked. A lot. One that, when combined with the shocking contents of Marlene's journal, made her wonder if her twin hadn't altered the facts to suit her purposes. It wouldn't have been the first time.

Mitch didn't touch her anywhere except for his lips and the thigh pressed against hers. It wasn't enough. She lifted a hand and cradled his face, loving the prickly warmth in her palm. She stroked his jaw. The slight roughness of his beard abraded her fingertips in a delicious way.

His growl of approval filled her mouth, and the echoes resounded deep inside her. His lips parted and his tongue sought and tangled with hers. The pressure of his mouth increased, tilting her head back for a deeper kiss. She adored his taste, his slick, wet heat, his scent.

But still, he didn't take her into his arms.

Carly moved her other hand to his knee below the hem of his shorts. The crisp curls tickled her palm. She kneaded the hot skin of his thigh and hunger seeped over her like a rising tide, pulling her deeper under his spell.

Mitch's hands flattened over both of hers, halting her movements. He lifted his head. Desire burned in his eyes and darkened his face. His fingers threaded through hers and returned her hands to her lap.

"We need to take this upstairs. But before we do, you need to be damned sure you know where this is headed."

She bit her lip and tasted him. "Where is it headed?"

"I want you, Carly. I think we have a shot at something good together. But I can't make guarantees of forever."

Her heart raced and her palms moistened. Did she want something long-term with him? Maybe. She'd certainly never experienced passion this strong before.

Getting involved again—and so soon—was a gamble. She'd taken several of those in her life and lost everything. But Mitch understood how much walking away from a child hurt. He'd been there. And he'd made the unselfish choice for the children. That fact alone made him more appealing than either of the men she'd thought she'd loved. Surely Mitch could understand and pardon her decision to give her daughter up for adoption?

And then there was Rhett. As Mitch had pointed out, they both had the child's best interest at heart.

She took a deep breath and slowly exhaled. "I'm willing to risk it."

Mitch's nostrils flared. He rose, pulling Carly to her feet. With their fingers still intertwined, he yanked her forward and their bodies slammed together, soft against hard in shocking, exhilarating contact. He pressed a quick, firm kiss on her lips, then released one hand and led her out of the room and into the foyer. He ascended the stairs without haste.

She wanted him to race. To do this before second thoughts overtook her. She hadn't known him long, and it wasn't like her to tumble into bed so quickly, so impetuously.

As if he sensed her encroaching doubts, he stopped on the first landing, backed her against the banister and lowered his head. Hot and hungry and slightly rough, his mouth devoured hers, stealing her breath, her defenses and her doubts.

Her back arched over the rail. The potential danger of falling to the hard marble floor below only intensified the adrenaline rush. She clung to his lean waist.

Just as quickly as he had begun the kiss, he ended it and resumed climbing, but faster this time. His long stride rushed her down the hall—not that she minded—past hers and Rhett's rooms and into Mitch's suite. He shut the doors and backed her against them. She had a brief impression of the bedroom behind him as huge, painted in the palest sage and flooded with sunlight from windows on both the front and back sides of the house.

"Last chance to change your mind." But already his hands reached for the hem of her shirt. The yellow cotton swished over her head in a blur and landed on the floor.

She answered by mimicking his movements and tugging his shirttail up and over his head to reveal those barbell-wide shoulders, the dark hair spattering in a Y across his torso and his amazing, muscle-ripped physique. For a moment she stood motionless, surveying the territory she had revealed. He did the same. His jaw muscles clenched and his pectorals rose on a deep inhalation.

His hands moved to the button and zip of her skirt. The rasp of his knuckles from her navel to her mound weakened her knees and sent a swirl of want to her abdomen. The skirt fell to her ankles, leaving her in a white bra, matching bikini panties and her sandals. For an instant she wished she'd worn something sexier than plain cotton, but the rapid expansion of his pupils smote the thought.

She kicked off her shoes and reached for the waistband of his shorts. The fastening gave way and the khaki fabric dropped down the length of his legs. She had a scant second to appreciate the long, thick bulge tenting his black boxers. The minute his pants hit the floor he kicked them and his shoes aside and swept her into his arms. The radiator warmth of his body pressed her side. She tangled her arms around his neck and scanned the room as his long stride ate up the floor between the entry and his bed.

A sea of glossy hardwood floors surrounded an island-size bed draped in a dark green spread. Matching tall stainless floor lamps arched like palm fronds over each side of the mattress, and pillows piled high against the tall scrolled wooden headboard. She didn't need to see the hardback thriller on the nightstand to know Mitch spent time reading in bed. Something else they had in common.

He set her on her feet and flipped back the covers, revealing sheets in the same sage as the walls. And then his thumbs hooked in his boxers and he bent to shove the silk to his ankles. He straightened, and her lungs and her womb contracted.

Oh, mama! Her fingers curled in anticipation of touching him, stroking him, taking him deep inside. She reached for her prize, but he brushed her hands aside to flick open the front catch of her bra. He caught her breasts as they spilled out, enclosing her sensitive flesh in the warmth of his hands. He thumbed the tips and a moan bubbled in her throat.

Briskly, with sudden impatience, he released her, rushed her bra over her arms and her panties down her legs and then backed her onto the bed. Her bottom bounced on the firm mattress and cool sheets met her back. He turned away briefly, yanked open the bedside drawer, retrieved and swiftly donned a condom and then returned to her. The mattress dipped beneath his weight, and his thighs separated hers. He planted his palms on the pillow beside her head.

She pressed her hands to his chest, halting his descent. She wanted to savor this, to make it last. "Wait. Slow down."

Even his eyebrows went rigid. He squeezed his eyes shut, inhaled. The veins in his throat and one in his temple pulsed wildly. When he lifted his lids she could see he'd reined himself in. As if in slow motion, his elbows bent and he lowered himself, stopping short of full body contact. His lips touched down, hovered and touched hers again, like a hummingbird on a feeder.

His kisses traced her cheekbone, her jaw, the cords of her neck, sipping and laving. His teeth scraped ever so lightly on her skin, and she shivered with need. The mattress quaked beneath her, telecasting the depth with which Mitch fought for control. She slid her hands from the supple skin of his chest to the bunched muscles of his shoulders and then into his soft hair. Cradling his head, she brought his mouth back to hers. His ravenous kiss slayed her. She thought her lungs would burst. The rest of her wasn't far behind.

He lifted his head, stretched out beside her and propped himself up on his elbow. The scalding length of him, of his torso, his erection, his legs, blanketed her from shoulder to ankle. His gaze greedily gorged on her nakedness. His hand stroked and caressed, plucked and glided over her breasts, her waist and her belly, sweeping her into a tornado of sensation. And then his lips followed the same path.

His mouth found her center, and an approaching orgasm coalesced deep inside her. Hunger and passion consumed her, making her forget all about going slow. Her hips arched off the bed. She wound her arms around him, urging him on. "Now."

He lifted his head and leaned back, leaving her hanging on the verge of release. She whimpered in disappointment. He grasped her knee and hiked it over his hip, rolling her to her side, leaving her most intimate parts opened and exposed. His gaze held hers as he kneaded the curve of her bottom and then slipped his hand between them to her slick center.

She loved the dark, passionate look in his eyes, as if he were as close to losing control as her. His fingers slid deep and then withdrew. That single thrust pushed her back to the edge, but left her aching and empty and yearning for more. He cut short her frustrated groan by painting a mind-twisting circular pattern over her flesh. Her lids fluttered closed as intense pleasure arrowed through her. She forced them back open to watch the intense concentration on his face.

Her thoughts, her senses centered on those dexterous digits and on the intense green eyes holding hers captive. Pressure built until it bordered on pain. Once again, he let it subside. Wanting, needing more, she lifted her hips in invitation, pressing against the heel of his hand. "Mitch, please."

His breath hissed. "Not yet."

She was so close her back arched in anticipation and tremors racked her body. She dug her nails into his shoulders and clung, teetering on the brink. She nipped his jaw, his neck, his collarbone because she couldn't reach his mouth. Mitch removed his hand, and she sobbed in frustration. Before she could voice her complaint, he pushed her onto her back and rose above her.

"Now." He took her mouth and her body in duel of simultaneous thrusts. His growl filled her lungs and vibrated to her core.

The shock of his sudden penetration stretched her, filled her and sent a Niagara of release rushing over her. She twisted her mouth free to gasp for breath and held him tight as the cataclysm overtook her to the beat of his hard, deep, rapid thrusts.

He bowed his back, bent and sucked her earlobe between his lips. She'd never felt anything more erotic in her life than the swirl of his tongue combined with the steam of his breath on her neck, the swivel of his hips and the powerful surge of his body into hers. His tempo increased, and her tension renewed. Another climax gathered so swiftly she had no chance of holding back, no chance of prolonging the moment, and then it rained over her like a sudden, violent cloud burst.

Mitch's groan echoed her cry in the big room and then his body collapsed onto hers. Panting for breath, she twined her arms around him and held him close, relishing his weight and the hammering of his heart against hers. She ran her fingertips along his sweat-slicked spine. His shudder made her smile.

She'd had good sex before. She'd even had what she'd considered great sex. Until now. But she'd never experienced anything like this.

Mitch Kincaid had marked her for life.

And she wasn't sure if that was a good thing or merely the promise of another disaster in her future. One far more devastating than any of its predecessors.

Mitch stared at the ceiling and tried to figure out where he'd miscalculated.

Carly was simply another woman he'd slept with. With wealth came women—plenty of women—who'd do whatever a man wanted. A fact his father had taken advantage of too many times to count. Only the last time, it had blown up in his face.

Which brought Mitch back to his present predicament.

He had a plan to execute. Emotion played no part in it.

He wasn't supposed to lose control.

But he had.

He was screwing Carly both literally and figuratively. How twisted did it make him to have enjoyed the process so much that he'd momentarily lost sight of his goal?

Seduce her. Propose. Get custody of Rhett.

His marriage to Carly would be a good one. Short. But good. One he intended to dissolve as soon as the ink dried on the adoption papers.

A twinge of guilt made him want to slide out from under the woman dozing so trustingly on his shoulder and hit the shower. He dismissed the feeling. He wasn't breaking any laws. And in this case, Carly and Rhett would be better off once the dust settled.

Despite Carly's protests, Mitch still believed she'd tire of the mommy game. Not that she'd shown any signs of doing so yet. But she would. He'd bet his share of KCL on it.

Why wouldn't she prefer her freedom when she could have all the benefits of Kincaid money via a generous divorce settlement and none of the obligations?

His mother had done something very similar. She may have stayed in the marriage, but she'd been an indifferent mother at best, one who'd turned their care over to a series of nannies, and Mrs. Duncan, then gone about her life as unfettered by parenthood as possible despite her middle child's attempts to gain her attention.

No. Getting rid of Carly was the right thing to do, and he doubted he'd need whatever Frank Lewis dug up to convince her to move on. If the P.I. found anything.

Carly snuffled in her sleep. Her breath tickled the hair on his chest and the fingers she'd rested just below his navel contracted. The ankle hooked over his calf slid languorously down to his foot and then back up to his knee.

His body tensed and responded as if he hadn't just been sated out of his skull. Would they have time for round two before the rug rat awoke from his nap? Before he could lift his wrist to check his watch, Rhett's cry penetrated the closed door.

Carly stiffened. Eager to escape the awkward postmortem—at least until he got his head screwed on straight—Mitch buried his mouth in the silky, coconut-scented hair next to her ear. "Go back to sleep. I'll get him."

He eased Carly onto the pillow beside him.

"You're sure?" Her drowsy, throaty voice and heavy-lidded eyes hit a bull's-eye on his libido. He wouldn't have to worry about the physical side of their marriage. If today was any indication, the sex would be phenomenal. Not that he intended to cheat, but it was nice to know he wouldn't want to.

"Got it covered." He climbed from the bed and took a good look at her. Once he had his game face back on, he'd take the time to enjoy every inch of her lithe, curvy body. He pulled the sheet over her before he said to hell with the crying kid and took what he wanted. The way he would have done earlier if Carly hadn't slowed him down.

Where in the hell had his restraint gone? The slow seduction he'd planned had taken a NASA rocket out of sight.

Another squawk from the blue room grabbed his attention. He knew from experience the kid started quietly but then opened up to full-throttle screaming.

Mitch yanked on his clothes and strode down the hall.

Rhett stood in his crib, sleepily scrubbing his eyes with his little fists. He spotted Mitch and stretched out his stubby arms. "Mitt. *My* Mitt."

Mitch's heart clenched. Something stuck in his throat. He cleared it. Rhett copied him and then beamed and chortled. Mitch gritted his teeth against a flood of emotion.

Okay, so maybe he was getting attached to the squirt. But that was okay. Soon Rhett would be a permanent member of the Kincaid household.

And Carly would be gone.

He shoved that thought aside and reached for Rhett. The kid latched on with a strangling grip. Mitch pried him loose and shoved a stuffed alligator in the kid's paws. He made quick work of the diaper change and then hefted the kid over his head. Rhett rewarded him with a gurgling laugh.

"What do you say we have lunch, kid?"

He jogged down the stairs, jostling the little baggage, and Rhett giggled. Mitch caught himself grinning back. He marched into the kitchen. Mrs. Duncan turned. Her penciled eyebrows rose and her mouth thinned, reminding Mitch he hadn't bothered to check the mirror. With the way Carly had run her fingers through his hair, he probably looked like an unruly hedge. And then he noticed his polo shirt was wrong-side out. Busted.

"Carly's napping. We need lunch."

"Yes, sir." There was a bite to her words he hadn't heard before. If she'd guessed what went on upstairs, she didn't approve.

Tough. She worked for him. He didn't need her approval.

He strapped Rhett into his high chair and dumped some of the diced fruit and cheese Carly kept in the refrigerator onto the tray and filled the kid's cup. It might have been years since he'd done this routine task for Travis, but his memory hadn't failed.

Mrs. Duncan prepared his meal in silence. She'd never been the talkative type, but this silence screamed disapproval.

"Would you keep an eye on Rhett while I wash up?"

"Yes, sir."

Mitch strode to his study, closed the door and righted his shirt. The red light blinking on the answering machine to his—formerly his father's—private line caught his attention. He rarely used this phone and had intended to have the line disconnected, but hadn't made the call to the utility company yet. He crossed the room and punched the Play button.

"Kincaid, I hit the mother lode on Carly Corbin." Frank Lewis's voice filled the room. Mitch's heart pumped faster, and lava settled in the pit of his stomach. "I need more time to follow up. I'll get back with you when I've filled in the blanks."

What could Carly possibly have in her past to put that note of excitement in the P.I.'s voice?

Part of him wanted to know.

But part of him didn't. And that part concerned him most. Weakness led to defeat. Or so his father always claimed.

He hit the Erase button and then paced into the adjoining

bathroom where he mechanically combed his hair and washed his face. He braced his hands on the counter. The man in the mirror staring back at him looked the same.

But where was the get-the-job-done edge?

He'd wanted dirt on Carly, hadn't he?

So why wasn't he pleased to know he might not have to marry her to get the boy?

Mitch's green gaze crashed into Carly's the minute she entered the kitchen. Her cheeks flushed, and her face wasn't the only part of her warming up. Every area he'd touched made its presence known and his scent still clung to her skin, filling her nose with each breath.

Like a true gentleman he rose and pulled out a chair for her beside a happily babbling, food-stuffing Rhett. She crossed the room, hyperconscious of Mitch's visual caress of her breasts, hips and legs. When his gaze returned to hers the knowledge of the intimacy they'd shared flashed in his eyes. Her pulse tripped wildly and her palms moistened.

But other than that fleeting reaction which passed so quickly she could have imagined it, he offered no cue on how to handle their status change in front of the housekeeper.

"Hi." A crazy shyness stole the rest of her words.

Mitch nodded, but there was no secret smile or even a softening of his stoic features. He didn't lean down to kiss her cheek as she slid into her seat or even touch her shoulder. He returned to his end of the table and picked up the thick toasted sandwich on the table in front of him. He ate with one hand and sorted through the mail stacked beside his plate with the other.

Okay, this was awkward. She'd had morning afters before, but never midday and she'd never shared one with an audience. She wasn't sure how to proceed. She felt as if she'd been dismissed and that stung far more than it should have.

You're falling for him.

Could it be true? Did she more than just like and desire Mitch Kincaid? The leaden sensation in the pit of her stomach delivered the answer.

Desperate for a distraction Carly abruptly diverted her attention to Rhett. She blew him a kiss and received a messy grin in return. As it so often did, her heart swelled with love for this precious child and it ached with sadness that her sister wouldn't be around to see her son grow up. Mitch would, and if Carly had anything to say about it, Rhett's other siblings would also be a part of his life. Because of the terms of the will, he'd have to wait a year to meet his half sister, but that was twelve months during which he could bond with his brothers.

Twelve months in which Carly could get her heart broken. Again.

Was this a rebound romance or something more? Could she and Mitch give Rhett a stable home and maybe even brothers and sisters? Where did they go from here?

Her gaze strayed back to the man at the opposite end of the table. His expressionless face gave no clue. Uneasiness stirred inside her and tension invaded her muscles. Did he expect her to act as if nothing had happened?

Did he regret making love with her? Did the intimacy mean nothing to him? Did he think it meant nothing to her?

Did he think she was easy?

Old taunts and accusations drifted through her mind like ghosts, chilling her, haunting her.

"Is turkey salad okay with you, Carly?" Della's question rescued Carly from her painful past.

"Yes, thank you, Della."

Della brought her a plate. Carly forked a bite of salad into her mouth and glanced at Della. She'd really come to like the housekeeper, but her presence kept Carly from asking the questions burning and churning inside her.

She needed to know the prognosis for this relationship. Good or bad.

One silent minute stretched into five. The only sounds in the room were Rhett's occasional chatter, the crunch of Mitch's teeth biting into his sandwich and the shuffle of papers as he dealt with his correspondence.

Carly's appetite died. She pushed her salad around on her dish and focused her attention on Rhett, but for once her nephew had decided to feed himself relatively neatly and without any assistance from her.

When she couldn't bear the tension any longer she laid down her fork and cleared her throat. "I had a call about my house before I came downstairs."

Mitch's hand stopped halfway to his glass. One dark eyebrow lifted.

"A prospective renter wants to see it this afternoon. I agreed to meet them at three…unless you have other plans."

Hint, hint, big guy. Tell me you want to spend the afternoon together.

"You plan to meet strangers in your house? Alone?"

"They're not strangers. They're a married couple who are good friends with Tina's sister."

He nodded. "Leave the rug rat with me."

The knot of tension between her shoulder blades eased only slightly. She would have preferred he offer to come with her, but she wanted Mitch and Rhett to bond, and this was a step forward. She'd take what she could get, and when she returned from showing her house, she'd corner Mitch and find out exactly what was going on. And then she'd develop a new strategy from what she learned.

"I should only be gone a couple of hours."

"Take your time."

Her gaze searched his. There was a reserve in his eyes that she hadn't seen since the early days in their relationship.

What had changed in the thirty minutes from when he'd left her in his bed until she'd joined him? Because whatever it was, she could feel Mitch pulling back.

Eight

"You ready to tell me what's going on? Or do I need to kick your ass again?"

Mitch flipped a rude hand gesture at Rand while treading water in the deep end of the pool and trying to catch his breath. "You only beat me by two body lengths after ten laps. That's pathetic, considering *I* wasn't on my high school and college swim teams and you were."

Apparently, his brother hadn't slacked off in his training.

"Yeah, yeah, save face any way you can."

Joking with Rand again felt good. It had been a long time. Too long. Once, they'd been close, competitive, too—their father had ensured that—but close. "You're in decent shape for an old man."

"Only two years older than you, brat. And two years wiser."

Shaking his head at Rand's need to get the last word, Mitch swam to the side and, ignoring the ladder a few yards away, hauled himself out of the water. He turned on the stone surround, offered Rand a hand and hoisted him onto the deck.

Rand scooped two towels out of a nearby chair and tossed one to Mitch. "What's up with the unexpected invitation?"

Unexpected because their relationship had been strained since Rand's return to Miami. Mitch hadn't exactly offered his brother an olive branch for stepping up to the plate instead of walking away from the challenge to fill their father's shoes. Maybe he should now that he knew the reason. Rand had left because their father had allegedly slept with the woman his brother loved. A woman currently putting Rand through the wringer, thanks to big brother's portion of the inheritance clause.

"It's good to have you back. I wasn't sure it would be at first, but it's good to be a team again." His brother was holding up his end of KCL and doing a damned fine job of it.

"It's good to be back." Surprise laced Rand's voice. "Now quit stalling. Why am I here?"

"Carly wanted Rhett to meet you." And Mitch wasn't ready for a quiet, intimate evening with his potential bride-to-be. Not until he wrapped his head around the brain-frying sex and the P.I.'s phone call. Mixing business with pleasure had never been an issue for him before. Why did it bother him now?

"Where is Dad's little bastard?"

A sharp rebuke sprang to Mitch's lips. He clamped his jaw shut to contain the words and briskly scrubbed the towel over his body. Not too long ago he'd referred to Rhett the same way, but for some reason he found the words offensive when Rand used them.

"Mrs. Duncan has him. She wanted to do a Web cam chat with her sister, so her sister could see Rhett. You'll meet him at dinner. I'll even let you sit beside him." He barely held his smile in check. His brother had no idea what he was in for.

"Our old guard dog is computer savvy?"

Rand sounded as shocked as Mitch had been. But then Mrs.

Duncan had always remained in the background, more like a fixture of the house than a person. If she'd had personality or interests beyond Kincaid walls, she'd kept them to herself for thirty-plus years.

Until Carly.

Within a week of moving in, Carly had learned the names, hobbies and family history of every Kincaid Manor employee, the neighborhood security guards, the mail carrier and the delivery men, for godsakes. Mitch only knew the names of those whose paychecks he signed or the ones who weren't doing their jobs and needed to be fired. He didn't want or need to know more.

His father hadn't been that way. Everett Kincaid had thrived on knowing every intimate detail about anyone who touched his sphere—primarily so he could use it against them.

"Mrs. Duncan has a top-of-the-line laptop."

"Has she said anything about retiring with the half million Dad left her?"

"She hasn't mentioned it. But she might stick around. She's getting pretty attached to Carly and the little guy."

"Sounds like you are, too."

Deliberately ignoring the first half of that equation, Mitch shrugged. "He's a cute kid. Hard not to like him."

"And the aunt? Any luck getting rid of her?"

Buying time while he debated how much of his plan to reveal, Mitch ambled to the built-in patio bar and plucked a couple of bottles of imported beer out of the minirefrigerator.

Better to keep his idea to himself rather than risk Rand throwing a wrench in his plans. His big brother had always been a rule follower, and while Mitch's plan wasn't illegal, it wasn't exactly kosher, either, even if he believed everyone would end up satisfied in the end.

"Not yet." He offered his brother a drink.

Rand accepted the bottle and popped the cap. "Five weeks

ago you thought this job would be easy, but you haven't sealed the deal. Are you having trouble meeting the Corbin woman's price?"

Mitch took a swig of his beer. The cool liquid did nothing to relieve his parched throat. "I offered her a million to sign over guardianship. She turned me down."

Rand's face hardened. "The bitch wants more?"

Mitch's fingers contracted so tightly it was a miracle the bottle didn't shatter. He reminded himself again that he'd used those same words before he'd gotten to know Carly, back when he'd expected her to be identical to her twin in temperament and greed, as well as looks.

Feigning calm when he was anything but, he eased into a chair and propped his feet on the tabletop. "Carly claims she doesn't want any Kincaid money."

Rand sat in the opposite chair. "You were always a decent judge of character. Either she's not as mercenary as you expected or she's angling for more than cash. Which is it?"

Mitch studied the sweat already condensing on the green glass in the late afternoon heat. A droplet snaked down the side of the neck and over the black label.

As the middle kid, he'd learned to read people pretty well, but his record wasn't flawless. He'd never expected Trish to go back to her cheating ex or Marlene to take the money and run. He sure as hell hadn't expected his father to knock off Marlene Corbin. If he had.

There was always a chance Mitch had the wrong bead on Carly. The future of KCL depended on him being on target. But Carly was…

He didn't even begin to know how to explain Carly Corbin to Rand. She had the bullheaded determination of a Fortune 500 executive, and yet she'd thrown herself in where needed at Kincaid Manor without being asked. Was she selfish or selfless?

"I don't think Carly is as greedy as her sister. She appears more interested in making sure Rhett's future is secure. Once I convince her it is, she'll go." If he was wrong, he'd pay dearly. Especially if he married her. He was counting on her being willing to walk away.

The back door opened. Instead of Mrs. Duncan, Carly waltzed out with a shirtless Rhett on her hip. Mitch nearly fell out of his chair when he saw the amount of skin she had on display. His feet slapped on the tiles and he shot upright. He wanted to wrap his towel around her and conceal her from his brother's close scrutiny.

"Are we too late to join you for a swim?" she called out.

Carly's black bikini wasn't brief by Miami Beach standards, but it framed every curve to full, mouthwatering advantage.

She strolled toward them with a fluid, athletic grace that sent his blood racing for his swim trunks. The woman made her living getting others in shape. She didn't skimp on herself.

Rand whistled under his breath and muttered almost inaudibly, "I'd offer to pull a dad for you, but—"

"No." The word exploded from Mitch's mouth. Their father had stolen more than one woman from Rand. Taking what others wanted—personally and professionally—had been one of Everett Kincaid's favorite sicko games. Mitch had learned early on to hide his emotions and his ambitions.

"I'm glad. Rhett loves the water." Carly had obviously mistaken his no as a response to her question.

Rand rose and extended his hand before Mitch could make introductions. "Rand Kincaid. You must be Carly. And this has to be Rhett. He has Kincaid written all over him."

His brother had turned on the charm and the lady-killer smile. Mitch wanted to clock him with his beer bottle.

"It's nice to meet you, Rand. I've been eager for Rhett to get to know all of his siblings. It's a shame he can't meet Nadia until this year's over."

The handshake lasted too long.

"Mitt," Rhett squealed and dove for Mitch. Mitch caught him, and in the transfer, his forearm brushed Carly's breast. The brief contact sent a jolt of electricity through him. But the best part of the kid's dive was that it severed the handshake.

A tiny hand fisted in Mitch's chest hair. Pain radiated outward and Mitch had to smother a howl. He detached the persistent fingers and pointed to Rand. "Brother."

"Bubba," Rhett replied just as Mitch had hoped he would. This time, it was funny.

Rand grimaced. "Rand. I'm Rand."

"Did you rent your house?" Mitch asked, to draw Carly's brick-melting, mischievous grin away from his brother.

"Yes, the couple signed the lease my attorney prepared. They're moving in Friday. So you're stuck with me for a while."

He ignored the question in her voice. He wouldn't lie and tell her she was welcome here. She wasn't. She was merely a necessary evil. A necessary evil that just happened to light his fuse.

She stared at him and when he remained silent, tension slowly invaded her features. A flush crept up her cheeks and then her chin lifted. Her gaze dropped to Rhett.

"Let's go for a swim, munchkin." Carly reached for Rhett. Her fingernails lightly grazed Mitch's bare chest from his underarm to his nipple as she took the boy. Goose bumps prickled his skin. Deliberate?

Mitch looked into her chocolate-brown eyes and the heat he saw there incinerated him on the spot. Oh yeah, definitely deliberate. What was she trying to pull? The action had been subtle. Rand couldn't have seen it. But Mitch's reaction to her touch and to the memory of how uninhibited Carly had been in bed wasn't going to be as easy to miss. He'd be tenting his trunks if he didn't break her spell.

He wanted her. Now. To hell with his brother—brother*s*, plural. The strength of his craving didn't bode well for his plan to kick her out at the end of the year. But he would. Even if he wasn't right about Carly eventually bailing on mom patrol, Mitch was already married. To his job. It was the only mistress that didn't ask for more than he was willing to give. And the only one that wouldn't betray him.

Carly strolled toward the pool. Mitch's gaze zeroed in on the sway of her delectable butt.

"Nice," his brother said.

Mitch scowled at Rand.

His brother gave him a pitying look.

Damn. He'd invited Rand over for a swim and cocktails because he wasn't in the mood for one of those angsty chats women preferred about what sex really meant. And he knew from Carly's searching glances both at lunch and a minute ago that she had one brewing in her brain.

But instead of his brother being a buffer, Mitch had discovered a possessive streak he hadn't known himself capable of, and he'd played his cards like an amateur.

If he wasn't careful, he could wind up broke.

If his brother smiled at Carly one more time, Rand wasn't going to have any teeth left to smile with.

Mitch set his wineglass on the coffee table and stood. "It's late. Carly and I have to get up early to run before church."

"Church? You?"

He ought to say yes just to wipe the wiseass smirk off his brother's face, but then he'd have to attend the service and Rand would really have something to yank his chain over. Except for weddings and funerals, the Kincaid offspring hadn't seen the inside of a church since their mother's funeral, after she'd nailed their father's favorite sports car to a tree when Mitch was twelve. Their father had always refused to acknowledge a higher power than himself.

"Carly and Rhett go. I have to work."

Rand leaned forward to deposit his glass beside Mitch's, but not fast enough to hide his amusement. "Then I'll get out of your way."

The SOB knew exactly why Mitch wanted him gone. Mitch didn't like being laughed at. He was the CFO of a multibillion-dollar company, respected in his field and damned good at his job. No one laughed at him.

"Thank you for inviting me to dinner, Carly." Rand stood and extended his arm.

Carly unfolded the long legs she'd tucked beneath her in the chair and rose to shake hands. Rand held hers for too damned long. "You're welcome. Please stop by again. I'm so glad to have finally met you."

Mitch ground his teeth. He'd had to compete for his mother's attention and then his father's and then Trish's. He'd be damned if he'd compete for Carly's. She was *his* part of the will fulfillment. Rand could worry about fulfilling the requirements of his own inheritance clause, which, from all reports, wasn't going well.

"I'll show you out."

Rand's lips twitched again and he shook his head. "I know the way."

Mitch stormed to the front door and held it open anyway because Rand wasn't moving fast enough. He waited and tried to rein in the possessive streak burning through him like a lit trail of gunpowder as his brother and Carly ambled toward the foyer at a slug's pace.

What in the hell had happened? When had he lost control of the evening? And why did he care that his brother could make Carly laugh?

He shook with the effort required to restrain his temper and quietly close the door behind Rand.

"I like your brother," Carly said behind him. "He's funny."

The words made Mitch see red. He pivoted. "He's taken."

Carly looked at him strangely. Probably because he'd spit out his reply like chewing tobacco. "He said he lives alone and hasn't bothered to furnish his apartment. He didn't mention being involved with anyone."

"That's because he's on the verge of screwing this inheritance up for all of us. Tara, his personal assistant, is part of it." He advanced on her. "You flirted with him."

Carly parked her fists on her hips, right beside the baby monitor she'd been wearing clipped to the waistband of her low-rider jeans since returning from tucking Rhett into bed an hour ago. Anger slapped her cheeks with color.

"Oh please. You set him up by sitting him next to the kamikaze kid. At least he had a sense of humor about getting bombed. Unlike someone I know."

She charged forward until they were toe to toe. "I didn't flirt. But what if I had? It's not as if you care. For all the warmth you've shown tonight, we could be strangers who met on the street this afternoon, not two people who shared a bed and our bodies ten hours ago."

He'd never liked pushy, temperamental women, but strangely, Carly's anger and aggression aroused him. And he couldn't help but admire that she wasn't intimidated by him. If anything, she leaned into him as if she were trying to bully him. Impossible. He'd been bullied by the best—his father— without success.

"You want warmth? I'll give you warmth." He snaked an arm around her waist and yanked her close. Her body crashed against his, jarring the air from his lungs. He took her mouth almost violently in a kiss that was more combat than caress. Lips and hips ground.

Instead of flinching, Carly gave as good as she got. Her nails dug into his biceps, holding him, not pushing him away.

He grabbed her waist, swung her around and backed her up against the wall beside the front door. She landed with a soft thud and an *oomph*. But she didn't break the kiss. Her palms shifted to cup his face and hold it there.

He forced open her lips and invaded her mouth. Their tongues clashed and dueled, fighting for supremacy. He didn't give an inch in the skirmish, but neither did she. His hands fisted in the fabric of her shirt. He wanted to rip it off. Only their location stopped him. Any of the staff could barge in. Being a Kincaid meant being tabloid fodder. Everyone had a price, and even the most dedicated employee could be bought.

Carly hasn't been bought.

Yes, she has. But by living in luxury instead of with cash.

And still he wanted her. It pissed him off.

Without freeing her mouth, he tangoed her backward down the hall and into his study. One slap slammed the door. A flick of his wrist locked it. He didn't stop until he had her pressed against his desk. Furious with her for the laughs and smiles she'd shared with his brother and even more disgusted with himself for his loss of control, Mitch didn't try to be gentle. He tore her shirt over her head and shoved her jeans down her legs. The monitor landed with a thump. Batteries spilled out and rolled across the rug. He didn't care. Her bra and panties sailed over his shoulder.

But instead of being naked and cowed, Carly attacked. She mimicked his actions, pulling, yanking, popping buttons, and within seconds they were both down to their birthday suits and breathing heavily. His hands chaffed her skin, hurriedly, impatiently, greedily. He wanted to touch all of her. Now.

Her nails raked his chest, his back, his ass. She dug in and pulled him close. Hot skin smelt hot skin. He tasted her naked lobes, her neck, and then bent her over the desk to sample the tight tips of her breasts.

It wasn't enough to sate his savage hunger.

He lifted her onto the dark, glossy surface, pushed her knees apart and stepped between her legs. His muscles clenched in anticipation of sinking deep and then locked in screaming protest. Her slick flesh cradled his erection, tempting him to break every rule ever drilled into his head. "Damn."

"What? Don't stop *now.*"

"No condom," he forced between gritted teeth.

"I'm healthy. If you are, then it's okay. I'm on the Pill."

For an unforgivable second he wanted to believe her, to trust her. That infuriated him. Those were probably the same words her sister had used to entrap his father.

"Not good enough."

She whacked his shoulder with an open palm. He barely noticed the sting. "Jerk."

He spewed a four-letter word—one he never used in the presence of a female.

"Please do." The hunger and frustration darkening her eyes slashed right through his restraint. But he didn't see cunning or avarice.

To hell with it. If there were consequences, his attorney would deal with them. Mitch grabbed her hips and yanked her forward, impaling her. A hot, wet inferno enfolded him and his spine caught fire.

He withdrew and slammed home again and again and again, harder and faster with each return. His name rushed across his shoulder in a scalding breath. Her teeth bit into his flesh and her nails scored his back. He'd never come close to experiencing anything like the fierce, animalistic claiming.

Fighting for dominance and control, he forced her back onto the desk. A pen cup fell over. The phone crashed to the floor. He didn't care. He took and took some more—sucking, nipping—and Carly did the same. Her hands and mouth burned over him. They'd both be marked tomorrow.

"Faster." Her heels hooked behind his butt, urging him on. She quivered beneath him. And then her back bowed and her head tilted back, spilling silky hair across the desktop and baring her throat. He sank his teeth into the exposed tendon on the side of her neck, no better than a damned vampire, hungry, so damned hungry for her.

She convulsed beneath him, clenching him with her arms, legs and internal muscles. And he lost it. Shudder after shudder racked him, draining him of everything including his strength.

The arms he had braced on the desk beside her head folded and he collapsed on top of her. His sweat-dampened torso fused to hers and their chests billowed in unison. But as the sweat dried on his skin and his body cooled, so did his fevered brain.

Bowing his head, he silently cursed his stupidity. He'd taken a chance he shouldn't have taken, made the one dumb-assed mistake he'd never made before. Sex without a condom. He couldn't risk the fallout. Couldn't risk her going to ground the way her sister had done, disappearing and showing up fourteen months later with an eight-month-old Kincaid.

He couldn't risk the hell Trish had put him through when she'd become pregnant despite his religious use of protection. The betrayal of finding out the woman he'd worshipped had slept with her ex-husband while she and Mitch were talking marriage had been a living hell. And then he'd had to endure nine agonizing months of wondering if the baby was his or her ex's, and the disappointment of finding out the child wasn't his. Not a good time.

He forced his arms to support him and levered his upper body off the pillow of Carly's breasts. "You'll have to marry me."

She stiffened beneath him. Her legs fell from his thighs and she rose to her elbows. "What?"

"For Rhett's sake." And in case she'd lied about being on the Pill. He wasn't going to wait for the P.I. report or risk her disappearing or face another nine-month wait for a DNA test. He'd push this deal through ASAP. "He needs two parents."

He separated from her physically and attempted to do so

mentally, but the sight of her draped across the desk, of her curves and the damp dark curls between her legs, knocked his willpower sideways. He turned his back, reached for his pants and stepped into them, zipping up before he could repeat his mistake.

He'd never considered having kids before Travis and Ashley had come into his life. After Trish's pregnancy, he'd decided he never would. If there was one thing he'd learned from his relationship with Trish, it was that the mother held all the cards. Even if the baby had been his, Trish would have returned to her ex and Mitch would have been powerless. He might have been granted joint custody. But in majority of the cases the mother was granted primary custody, and the father was turned into a visitor. That was tough on the kids but even tougher on the parent who'd become an outsider in his kid's life.

He wasn't going to be that parent.

And now, thanks to his idiocy and lack of control, more than the Kincaid inheritance was at stake.

Nine

"Are you crazy? You don't get married just because you've had sex."

Carly had once been naive enough to believe otherwise. She'd lost her heart, her virginity and her baby in the process of learning that painful lesson.

She scrambled off the desk, snatched up her shirt and scanned the room for her bra. She didn't see a hint of lace anywhere. Forget it. She stuffed her arms inside her sleeves and towed the fabric over her head.

Mitch's hard, direct stare pinned her in place. "You want to ensure Rhett's future is secure. So do I. This is the best way to do it. We'll marry and adopt him."

Rhett would be her son.

Too good to be true.

Holding her jeans and panties in front of her like a shield, she searched Mitch's face, looking for something—*anything*—to clue her in to his emotional state.

Nada.

And yet she was tempted by his proposal. She liked Mitch more with each exposure and was only a nudge away from falling for him. This evening, watching him verbally spar with his brother had reminded her of what she'd never have with Marlene again. That empty, aching void, one very similar to the one left by giving up her daughter, seemed impossible to fill.

Rebound romance, the voice in her head screamed a now familiar warning.

"Why would you want to marry *me?*"

Mitch finished tucking in his shirt and then fastened his leather belt with much more dexterity than she'd fumbled it open earlier. "We're good together. Explosive."

Amen. She'd never had sex like that before. Wild. Unrestrained. And oh so wonderful. All right, maybe she and Mitch had some pretty powerful chemistry between them.

But marriage?

She couldn't ignore the caution lights illuminating her brain like the Vegas strip. "We've known each other less than three weeks. I don't think it's a good idea, Mitch."

"Besides the timing, give me one good reason why we shouldn't."

Feeling exposed in more ways than one, she stepped into her pants and fastened them.

"Love?" Or lack thereof.

"You've been in love before. How'd that work for you?"

She grimaced. "Not so well."

All three of the men she'd loved had let her down, betrayed her in one way or another and left her. Was it better to go into a relationship with something less fragile than love as the glue to hold it together? With her track record, it was beginning to look that way.

And with the way she felt, wasn't love right around the

corner? But she didn't want a one-sided affair. She wanted to be loved back. Was Mitch Kincaid capable?

He might have started out as a jerk, but she and he shared a strong sense of family. If not, they wouldn't be butting heads over a determination to do the right thing by Rhett. And if she lived here as Mitch's wife and a permanent part of Rhett's upbringing, she could do her best to ensure her sister's precious son wouldn't be exposed to the world of nannies or turn into some spoiled, rich brat who snorted his life away.

"I like and respect you, Carly, and I admire your dedication to your nephew. It's enough to build on."

Nephew. A reminder that Rhett wasn't hers.

But he could be.

"You said earlier today that you couldn't promise forever," she reminded him.

"I said I couldn't guarantee it. How many marriages starting with that pledge actually last 'til death do us part?"

Less than fifty percent.

We could be a family.

And Carly could give Rhett what her sister had so desperately wanted for him but hadn't been able to achieve—the right to grow up in Kincaid Manor, his father's home.

She was tempted. Very tempted. And not just for Rhett's sake.

Marlene hated Mitch. She'd called him a conniving rat bastard.

But Marlene had called everyone who gave her a hard time names, Carly reminded herself. Her twin had been hot-tempered…and devious, if the notebook was to be believed.

Mitch tried to convince Marlene to abort.

But he'd done so on his father's orders.

Mitch cupped her shoulders, interrupting her private debate. "We could have this—" a nod indicated the desk "—every day for as long as the passion lasts."

Need twisted through her abdomen, wreaking havoc with her reservations. But Mitch had a thing about women having a price. "I'm not looking for a sugar daddy."

"I don't intend to be one."

"I would never abandon Rhett."

"I won't force you to."

Indecision rocked her like a buoy in a tropical storm. "We'd always discuss what's best for him?"

"Absolutely."

"What about brothers and sisters for him sometime in the future? I'd—I'd really like to have a...a baby one day."

Mitch's nostrils flared. "One child at a time. Let's get through the adoption first."

"But you like children?"

He expelled a slow breath. "I like kids."

"And you'd—we'd—be...exclusive?"

"When I make a commitment, I see it through."

Her heart pounded so hard she could barely think. Her resistance wavered.

Do what's best for Rhett.

All she had to do was say yes and Rhett would have a home, family and security, and she'd have the possibility of another baby in her future.

It wouldn't be a storybook marriage, and she wasn't deluded enough to believe she could ever fill the hole in her heart left from relinquishing her daughter. But she wanted a baby and another chance to be the mother she'd always dreamed she could have been. And despite being burned three times, she still wanted a chance at love.

She closed her eyes, inhaled deeply and exhaled slowly, trying to buy calm and time and to gather her courage.

It's the right thing to do.

She met Mitch's gaze. "I'll marry you."

Mitch's fingers contracted, and then he released her. "I'll

have my lawyer draw up a prenup. As soon as it's done and yours has looked it over, we'll do this."

The caution lights flashed. "A prenup?"

"Standard protocol when there's so much inequity in each partner's net worth."

Understandable. If she were him, she'd want one, too. But a small nagging part of her wished he trusted her without legal backup. "You're in a hurry to do this?"

"Why wait?"

"I'd, um…like my parents to be here."

"I'll charter a jet."

"I'll need to see how soon we can reserve the church."

"I'd prefer a private ceremony here."

She'd always dreamed of a church wedding. "But—"

"Your sister has been dead three months, my father just over one. An elaborate ceremony would be inappropriate."

He had a point. "Okay. But I want my preacher to preside."

"A judge will work just as well."

"Not negotiable, Mitch. I want the church's blessing."

His jaw shifted into the stubborn angle with which she'd become so familiar. "If he can do it by the end of the week. I'll make it worth his while to be available."

Her head spun at the speed with which he made life-changing decisions. "I'll talk to him tomorrow after the service. He's not going to be happy about the rush. He usually requires some kind of premarital counseling. Perhaps you'd like to come with me and persuade him to skip that part."

His shoulders stiffened. Mitch's green eyes darkened and drilled into hers. "I'll be there."

Even her preacher had his price.

Carly would become Mrs. Mitch Kincaid Friday evening.

Shocked and a little disillusioned by how easily money had trumped faith and principle this morning, Carly followed

Mitch toward the hundred-foot-long yacht docked at the back of the Kincaid property after church. All it had taken was a generous donation and her pastor had fallen all over himself to accommodate Mitch's wishes. If he'd had other plans for Friday evening, he hadn't mentioned them.

"It's Rhett's nap time. Can't we go boating later?"

"He can sleep on board. I had a nursery set up in one of the cabins while we were out this morning. We have a two o'clock appointment."

"With?"

He paused and turned on the sidewalk. The brisk breeze blowing off the water ruffled his nearly black hair and fluttered the lapels of the navy suit he'd worn to church. She couldn't see his eyes because of his dark sunglasses. "The jeweler."

Her mind shrieked and her feet skidded to a stop. Rings. She hadn't even thought about rings. He was moving too fast. "Can't we drive there?"

"Yes, if we want our engagement to be front-page news tomorrow. I'm trying to avoid having cameras shoved in our faces each time we leave the house."

Front-page news? A shiver racked her despite the ninety-degree heat. She hugged Rhett closer. "That's going to happen?"

"Our marriage will make news. But the attention will pass. Eventually. Lunch is waiting on board."

Carlos, the gardener, and Tomas, a general handyman who helped wherever needed, waited on the dock. Mitch greeted them, stepped on board and turned to offer Carly a hand across the gangplank. The hot seal of their palms quickened her pulse. They'd made love four times in the past twenty-six hours, the most recent just before church this morning, and yet her heart still tripped when he touched her.

From the moment she stepped into the main cabin, she realized the Kincaids took luxury with them wherever they went. She'd been on boats before, but never one as opulent as this. This floating living room with its hardwood floors, white leather sofas and beveled glass and teak tables could have been in anyone's home. China, crystal and a silver ice bucket holding a bottle of something waited on a full-size dining-room table beneath a sparkling chandelier. The plastic high chair looked as out of place as Carly felt.

The engines rumbled to life beneath her feet, but the boat barely rocked as Carlos and Tomas cast off. Mitch led her to the table, took Rhett from her and competently strapped him into the high chair. Mitch had come a long way and no longer froze when Rhett touched him. In fact, he often initiated contact and this morning he'd had Rhett dressed and fed before Carly emerged from the shower. He'd be a good father.

Mitch pulled out her chair. Carly sat. His fingertips dragged along her neckline as he lifted her hair away from the high back of her chair, and she shivered. He bent down and pressed a kiss in the curve of her neck and shoulder and then his teeth grazed her skin. Her breath hitched and heat blossomed in her abdomen.

He straightened, circled to the opposite side of the table and sat directly across from her. She couldn't look away from his handsome face, his tanned skin and his intensely green eyes.

Hers. The possessive statement echoed through her as she briefly shifted her gaze to his mouth. The contrast between his hard jaw and soft lips sent arousal prickling through her. The things he'd done with those lips last night had devastated her inhibitions.

As if he could read her mind, hunger flared in his eyes and arousal darkened his cheekbones. A corresponding flush swept over her. She broke his gaze and focused on Rhett, who was busy examining the dog stamped onto the back of his hand in the church nursery this morning. The church stamped parents and children with the same figure at drop-off time to keep anyone from taking home the wrong child. Both she and Mitch wore blue dogs to match Rhett's.

Bonded by a blue dog. Marked as a family.

Mitch had surprised her by not only allowing himself to be stamped, but also by not washing away the ink as soon as possible.

He'd surprised her in a lot of ways this morning. First, he'd been so attentive at church that anyone watching them would believe this was a real romance. Second, he'd incited very impious thoughts each time his thumbnail grazed her palm or his thigh pressed hers during the sermon. And third, he'd played her preacher like the powerbroker she suspected Mitch Kincaid might be behind his KCL desk.

It bothered her that he believed money could buy anything. But in his experience, it probably had.

She wanted to trust that their marriage would work and wanted to have faith that mutual passion and concern for Rhett would be enough to sustain the relationship. And if she were lucky, love would grow. She was already heading down that path. How could she not? Mitch was tall, dark, handsome, confident, intelligent and fair. His employees respected and trusted him—much more than they had his father, apparently.

And he did nice things. She fingered the boy charm pendant.

Despite the haunting invasion of her sister's warnings that kept seeping into her brain, Carly kept finding more to like about Mitch every day.

Elena, Carlos's wife, entered with a tray. She served Carly and Mitch skewers of large grilled shrimp atop beds of rice and sautéed vegetables. Rhett's plastic plate held his favorite diced foods. Elena left them.

Mitch reached for the bottle and corkscrew. The dark hairs on his wrist beneath his snowy shirt fascinated Carly as he worked the cork free. "After we finish with the jeweler, you need to call your parents. I've arranged for the jet to pick them up Thursday morning and carry them back Sunday. Since we can't leave town until the end of the year unless it's business-related, we won't have a honeymoon."

A honeymoon. Time devoted to nothing but discovering each other's minds and bodies. She hadn't given it a thought, but now that he'd planted the seed she realized she'd love a week of Mitch's undivided attention. Desire made her shift in her seat. "That's okay. I wouldn't want to leave Rhett anyway."

He popped the cork without spilling a drop—the sign of experience—and then filled the flutes with bubbly gold champagne. After wedging the bottle back in the ice, he lifted his flute. "To us. May our marriage be everything we expect it to be."

"To us," she echoed and *tink*ed her rim against his.

The chilled liquid slid down her throat like nectar. "Mmm. You know your wines. I'll grant you that."

Carly found an appetite that had been AWOL since yesterday morning. She set down her glass and attacked her lunch. The shrimp and crisp veggies tasted divine. She'd been too nervous to eat breakfast today. She had no trouble replacing the calories they'd burned now.

"Rand will be my witness. You can invite one of your own or use your parents," Mitch said fifteen minutes later after she'd practically inhaled her meal.

"Only one?"

"The fewer people who are a part of this, the less likely it'll turn into a circus. And unless you intend to quit your job you'll need to warn them at work that they might need to beef up security until the media storm blows over."

"What? No, I'm not going to quit. I love my job."

"Paparazzi enjoy exploiting the rich and famous."

Paparazzi. A warning prickled her skin. "I'm neither."

"You will be."

She chewed over the disturbing news. It wouldn't be the same as before. She wasn't young and naive, and Mitch wasn't going to hang her out to dry to save his own reputation.

Was she making a mistake to bring Rhett into a world where the media watched and waited for fodder?

No. She was giving him what Marlene had wanted—his birthright.

"We'll apply for the marriage license first thing in the morning."

"What about my clients?"

"Reschedule an hour or two. And while you're at it, take Thursday and Friday off."

"Mitch, I can't. People are counting on me."

"Your parents will be here and you have a wedding to plan."

Right again. She mentally pictured her schedule, trying to guess who could be shuffled and who couldn't. "I'll see what I can do."

Rhett finished his lunch and his eyes grew droopy. Carly was glad of the excuse to escape. Mitch showed her below deck to a stateroom as posh as the one in the manor. He'd taken care of every detail from diapers to Rhett's favorite stuffed gator.

She changed Rhett and tucked him into the crib. He immediately went to sleep, taking away her excuse for hiding out. It was almost two o'clock, so she made her way back upstairs.

The engines quieted as she returned to the living area. "Why are we stopping?"

"We have company."

Before she could ask who, she spotted another boat bumping alongside. But it wasn't the harbor patrol, which often stopped boats to check for safety issues. The crew of the other yacht linked the boats, and a distinguished-looking older gentleman wearing a goatee and carrying a briefcase came aboard. Mitch greeted him at the door and gestured for him to enter.

"Carly, this is Mr. Belmonté, our jeweler. He has a selection of rings for you to look over."

Surprised once again, she glanced out the windows on

either side of the room. The closest landmass was at least a mile away. "We're in the middle of the bay."

"It's the best way to ensure privacy," Mitch said as if he shopped in such odd places on a regular basis.

She'd assumed they'd dock at the back door of the jewelry store…or something.

"Good afternoon, Ms. Corbin. I have chosen a number of designs based on Mr. Kincaid's description, but if none of them pleases you I have more back at the shop."

After shaking her hand, Belmonté placed his briefcase on the coffee table and flipped it open. Carly nearly fell over backward. The glittering display of fifty or more rings on black velvet had to be worth bazillions. She couldn't catch her breath, and someone had glued her feet to the floor. Surreal.

Mitch slipped an arm around her waist and guided her to the sofa. Carly collapsed onto the cushion because her legs had started shaking. And then Mitch sat beside her, as close as a postage stamp. The heat of his body seeped into hers.

"Do you see anything you like, sweetheart?"

Sweetheart? Her head swiveled his way. Their gazes collided. "I—I—"

Mitch looked at her steadily. His hand covered the fist she'd curled on her thigh. *He's playing a part.* He'd said everyone had a price. Did he think the jeweler did, too?

Play along. It will be better for Rhett in the long run.

"Which do you prefer? Yellow gold, white gold or platinum?"

Carly turned her attention back to the tray. "They're all so beautiful…and so…" Huge. There couldn't be anything in the tray that cost less than her car. She'd bet some of the pieces cost as much as her house.

She blinked and tried again. "I can't wear anything too large. I work with my hands."

"May I make a suggestion?" The jeweler selected a ring. "This is a flawless three-carat Asscher cut stone. When the platinum bands are added—" he paused to flank the ring with a pair of matching bands "—the stone is protected."

The wedding bands cupped the stone's edges in a swirl of gleaming metal. "It's beautiful."

"Try it on," Mitch urged her. "Here. Let me."

He took the rings from Belmonté, lifted her hand and slid the cool metal down her finger. Warm hands. Cold rings. The contrast overwhelmed her nervous system. But the rings fit as if made for her. A sign? Or a coincidence?

"Like it?" Mitch asked in that low rumble that made her skin tingle.

A knot formed halfway down her throat. Her fingers convulsed around Mitch's. She nodded, and garbled, "Yes."

"We'll take it."

"And your ring, sir?" The jeweler flipped a lever and another velvet layer dropped to cover the solitaires and display a selection of men's rings. "You suggested something simple."

She doubted she could afford anything in the tray, but tradition stated the bride buy the groom's ring. "Mitch—"

"This one." Quick and decisive, the Mitch she'd come to know, selected a wide band and slipped it on.

"Very good choice, sir. Also platinum and it complements Ms. Corbin's ring nicely."

She nudged Mitch's thigh. "Could I speak to you a moment?"

"Certainly. Excuse us." He rose and escorted her toward the bow of the ship. Carly glanced through a doorway and gaped. The kitchen or galley or whatever it was called was roomier than the one in her house. Mitch stopped in a stateroom that put her Kincaid Manor suite to shame.

"I'm not sure I can afford that ring."

"I'm paying for it and the rest of the wedding."

"But the bride is supposed—"

"Supposed to let the groom take care of her."

"But, Mitch—"

His mouth covered hers. He parted her lips and swept the protests from her tongue with his. Leaning closer, he sandwiched her body between inflexible wall and immovable muscle. His strength and his weight held her captive, freeing his hands to caress her waist, her hips and the outsides of her breasts. Overwhelmed by his flavor, his possession, Carly's senses rioted. The strength seeped from her frame until only the thigh he'd wedged between hers held her upright.

By the time he lifted his head, she couldn't find her breath or gather her protests to argue her point. She now knew what kissed into submission meant. In a minute she'd work up a protest over such manhandling.

"Let's get rid of Belmonté," his rough voice scraped over her already heightened senses.

Protesting could wait. "Good idea."

They returned to the salon. Within minutes, the deal was done and Belmonté had left on his boat. Carly stared numbly at the rings weighting her hand like concrete blocks.

She was doing the right thing.

She was certain of it. Almost.

Anxiety gnawed at her stomach, but then Mitch laced his fingers through hers and led her toward the stateroom.

She'd worry about worrying later. Because anything that felt this good had to be right.

Ten

"**B**oons! Boons!"

Rhett's excited squeal drilled Carly's eardrum and jerked her out of her inattentive funk. She looked up and stopped midshuffle.

Helium-filled balloons in every color of the rainbow filled the breakfast nook. "Yes. Balloons."

Rhett kicked and squirmed. She set him down and he scampered across the tile to the curling ribbon streamers tied to the back of the chair Carly always used.

Who? Della? And how had she known it was Carly's birthday? The housekeeper wasn't in the kitchen, but she'd been here because the coffee was on. The scent of Mitch's favorite gourmet brew filled the air.

Mitch stepped up behind her. He didn't make a sound, but Carly's personal Mitch detection system kicked in and she knew he was there before his chest nudged her shoulder and his arm encircled her waist.

He pulled her against him. "Happy birthday."

The balloons were from Mitch? She gasped in surprise and then promptly choked up. Not just because this was a totally unexpected and frivolous gift coming from a no-nonsense man like him, but because she couldn't share it with Marlene. Her sister had loved over-the-top gestures like this.

As if he understood, his arm tightened. He rubbed his smooth, freshly shaven jaw against her temple and his cologne teased her nose. "Nadia says there comes a time in a woman's life when adding more candles to a cake becomes annoying. But she says you can never have too many balloons or flowers. I don't know your favorite color, so I covered the bases."

"Blue. I love blue." Boring, conservative blue. What did that say about her?

"Boons, Mitt. Boons!" Rhett trilled and jumped up and down on the tile by Carly's chair.

"I take it he likes balloons?"

"Oh yes." A crinkling sound caught her attention. She twisted to face Mitch.

He pulled a massive bouquet of long-stemmed roses in every shade from the purest white to the deepest burgundy from behind his back and offered them to her. "Twenty-eight buds for twenty-eight years. But no blue. Sorry."

"They're beautiful, Mitch. Thank you." She accepted them and buried her nose in the fragrant blooms. Marlene would have adored this, too. Carly's indrawn breath stuttered across each rib. She was not going to lose it. Not in front of Mitch. Not in front of Rhett.

"How did you know? About our—my birthday, I mean." She had to force the words through her tight throat.

His gaze shifted briefly to the excited child before returning to hers and then he shrugged. "Tina must have mentioned it."

"Well, thank you. This is a wonderful surprise and a great way to start the day." She forced a smile.

He took the bouquet from her and laid it the on the table and then cupped her face in his warm hands. His thumbs lifted her chin. "You okay?"

No. How was it possible to be so happy and sad simultaneously? She squared her shoulders. "Of course. Why wouldn't I be?"

"Because you're thinking about your sister."

She snatched a breath at his perceptiveness. The fact that he could mention her sister without the usual sneer in his voice doubled her surprise. "How did you know?"

His fingertips grazed her cheek, her neck, and then his palms skimmed down her arms to catch her hands and squeeze. The gesture of comfort and support nearly made her bawl.

"Could be the way you slinked out of my bed this morning and crept back to your room to hole up in the dark instead of letting me be your wake-up call."

Desire burned through her like a blown gas main. Since Sunday, he'd awoken her every morning with his hands and mouth and passion.

At the risk of ruining the mood, she decided to be honest. "Marlene and I usually spent our birthdays together. When we couldn't we talked on the phone early in the morning. This is the first time we w-won't. I—" She paused to swallow an immovable lump. His grip tightened around her fingers. "I didn't expect it to be so h-hard."

Their gazes held and the understanding softening Mitch's eyes made hers sting. "I didn't always like my father, but that doesn't mean I don't miss him every single day or think of things I want to tell him or show him." His gaze shifted over her shoulder to the child still enthralled with the *boons.*

"I'm sorry he missed out on Rhett." Raw grief roughened his voice.

She loved him.

The emotion didn't sneak up on her as it had with her past

loves. It hit like a head-on collision, winding her and making her adrenaline race and her heart thump wildly. In that instant Carly knew without a doubt that she'd fallen *hard* for Mitch Kincaid.

Hoping her discovery wasn't written all over her face, she searched his eyes, looking for reciprocity. But, as usual, Mitch hid his emotions well. That's why the rare glimpses into his head like the revelation about his father meant so much to her.

He blinked, breaking the spell, and then a wicked smile slanted his lips. "Call in sick today. We'll play hooky, hang out at the beach or laze by the pool. Spend the day in bed. We'll do whatever you want."

She was tempted. "I can't. I've already had to shuffle too many patients because of the wedding...and it's better to keep busy, I think."

"I can keep you busy." The sensual promise in his words threatened to hijack her brain on a hormone express train.

"If I didn't have people counting on me to help them get their lives and bodies back together, then I'd jump on your offer...and you." Her face burned. She'd never made such a forward statement before.

His nostrils flared and his chest and pupils expanded. "I like the sound of that. And I'll hold you to it. Tonight."

He brushed a kiss over her lips, a kiss that tasted like a promise. A kiss that upped the stakes.

Because now she not only had to make Mitch love Rhett, she had to make him fall in love with her.

"Where are you racing off to?"

Rand's question cut Mitch off midwhistle. He stopped in the hall outside his brother's office.

Whistle? Had he been whistling? He had. "I'm headed home."

"You've left early every night this week."

"Six isn't early."

"It is for you."

Couldn't argue with facts. He stepped into Rand's—formerly their father's—office. Strange how the anger and resentment he'd experienced upon hearing the terms of the will had faded. But Rand had proved his worth, so maybe not so surprising after all. "I want to have dinner with Carly and Rhett."

And not just because he knew he'd have Carly naked seconds after Rhett crashed for the night. Anticipation kicked his pulse up a notch.

"Didn't you and the kid take Carly to lunch today?"

"I thought she needed the pick-me-up of lunch with Rhett. It's her birthday. Her first without her twin."

Rand's eyes narrowed. His leather chair creaked as he leaned back. "You have a thing for her. Got her in the sack yet?"

"That's none of your business. But, yeah, I have a thing for her. We're getting married Friday night. Be my best man?"

Rand's jaw dropped and his eyebrows shot up. "You're getting married in two days and you haven't mentioned it?"

He'd intended to ask Rand sooner, but they'd spent the past three days in confidential meetings trying to unravel some issues their father had left behind. By the end of each day, Mitch wanted nothing more than to leave the stress of his father's sloppy management behind and go home to the warmth and the laughter that now embodied Kincaid Manor. The current atmosphere was a big change from the meat-locker chill of the past.

"I'm telling you now." He'd delayed informing Rand about the wedding because he knew his brother would want explanations—explanations that would delay his departure.

"Are you out of your mind? What happened to your conviction that Carly is a mercenary bitch identical to her twin in more than looks?"

"I told you I'd misread her."

"You told me you *might* have misread her and that she'd rejected the million-dollar offer to hand over Rhett."

"She also declined the five million I offered in the prenup."

Carly's attorney had nearly had a heart attack at the conference table when Carly had refused to sign until the settlement clause was struck from the document.

Rand's eyes narrowed suspiciously. "Why?"

"She said the money wasn't hers and she didn't want it."

And surprisingly, Mitch believed her. Carly's stubborn insistence had initially shocked the hell out of him, but then he started replaying details in his mind. She'd lived modestly even since moving into the manor, and the house she'd left behind was no showcase. She budgeted her expenses and paid Rhett's day-care bills without asking Mitch to pitch in. In fact, she hadn't asked him for anything that came with a price tag other than fencing around the water features to keep Rhett safe.

Maybe she was the real deal. He'd seen so few altruistic women in his lifetime he probably wouldn't recognize one if she bit him on the ass. Which Carly had. Several times. And he'd liked it.

He wiped off his grin and focused on Rand's scowling face. "Looks like identical DNA doesn't produce identical personalities."

These past few weeks of playing house had made him question his "everybody has a price" mantra. And he'd begun to believe Carly would never tire of Rhett and responsibility, and run.

Rand stared at him as if he'd sprouted horns. "You think marrying her will put a lock on the kid."

He should have known big brother would figure out his plan. "It won't hurt. But that's not why I'm marrying her."

"You telling me you love her?"

Did he love Carly? No. But could he?

"Your silence is screaming, little brother."

Mitch glanced at his watch. A knot of tension snarled at

the base of his skull. "I know what I'm doing. So are you going to be there Friday night at eight or not?"

"I'll be there. But I hope to hell you're not making as big a mistake as Dad did when he became entangled with the other Corbin."

So did Mitch. Because Carly made him want to try something he didn't believe existed—an honest, committed relationship based on something besides his bottom line.

He could get used to this.

Mitch stared at the moonlight dancing on his ceiling and waited for his heart rate to drop back into double digits. But that wasn't going to happen if Carly pressed her lips to his chest one more time.

He tangled his fingers in her hair and tugged her head back. She smiled up at him and tenderness filled him—an emotion that had nothing to do with ringing the bell to start round two of astronomical sex.

This marriage to Carly would be good. And perhaps he wouldn't rush to end it immediately after the adoption went through.

"Thank you for everything you did today, Mitch. It helped…a lot."

"I'm glad." The approval in her eyes made him want to pound his chest like some damned caveman. He settled for pulling her flush against his body and tucking her head into the crook of his shoulder. The air-conditioning kicked on, cooling his sweat-dampened skin.

She took a shuddery breath and tensed against him. "I woke up this morning thinking about Marlene's last moments. That's why I sneaked out. I needed to call the police detective and check the status on the investigation. I need to know the bastard who hit her will be held accountable for what he did."

Mitch fought the tension invading his limbs and robbing

his peace. He couldn't tell Carly he suspected his father had either been driving the car or had paid someone else to take out her sister. "What did the detective say?"

She rolled up onto her elbow. "He says the case has been put on the back burner due to more pressing issues. You're an almighty Kincaid. Can't you light a fire under them? I want someone punished for leaving Marlene to die."

"Carly—"

"Please, Mitch. I don't want your money and I couldn't care less about the Kincaid fortune. But I would really, really like for you to use your influence on this."

He didn't know what to say to her plea. Finding her sister's killer could destroy his family and KCL.

"I'll see what I can do."

But he wouldn't be calling the police.

Carly's parents were due in a matter of hours, and she still hadn't found her missing bra.

Mitch had whisked her straight upstairs to bed after she'd accepted his proposal, and then life had intervened and she hadn't had time to return to the study and search again. Her days had been an exhausting crush of caring for Rhett, working in rescheduled patients, looking for a wedding dress and squeezing in lawyer visits. Her nights had been filled with Mitch.

She plucked at her shirt, fanned her overheated body and expelled a long, slow breath.

She'd expected one of the cleaning ladies to find her bra, and then it would turn up in her laundry. But they hadn't. With her luck, her father would find it. She knew how much he liked libraries, and the Kincaids' book collection was impressive. He'd probably locate her Playtex between Plato and Poe…or wherever Mitch had thrown it.

She headed straight for Mitch's study the minute she

handed Rhett off to Della who had begged to borrow the child for another Web cam chat. The widowed Duncan sisters had declared themselves honorary grandmothers, and with her parents living all the way across the country, Carly couldn't be happier for Rhett to have a makeshift extended family.

The study smelled of lemon polish and eucalyptus. Every surface gleamed—even the desk where she and Mitch had savaged each other five nights ago. Carly scanned the furniture and the tall cherry shelves. Nada.

She dropped to the floor and looked under furniture. No bra. Wait! A white fragment caught her eye. The fax rang as she scrambled to her feet. She ignored it and headed for the floor-length curtains. She whipped back the heavy drapes. Jackpot!

She snatched up her bra and stuffed it in her pocket. The fax spewed pages. There had been a bit of back and forth conversation between her lawyer and Mitch's over the prenuptial agreement and Rhett's adoption. Was this more of the same?

She crossed the room as the last sheet slid onto the tray and lifted the report. Her name jumped out at her from the cover sheet. But this wasn't from an attorney's office. The header said Lewis Investigations, Discreet Private Detective Agency.

A sense of foreboding invaded her, chilled her, and made her hands tremble as she turned to page two.

Kincaid, I promised you a mother lode of info to discredit Carly Corbin as guardian of your father's kid. Here it is. You'll have to consult your attorney to see if Corbin's juvenile records will be admissible in court. If so, then you should have a good shot at gaining sole custody.

Her knees buckled. She sank into the leather chair behind the desk. Mitch didn't want to adopt Rhett and become a family. He wanted to rip her precious nephew right out of her arms. And he was willing to marry her to accomplish his goal.

The gifts, the lovemaking, the proposal had all been ways to win her trust and cover his duplicitous tracks.

Her eyes and throat burned. She blinked and turned the page.

You were right about Carly graduating high school a year later than her twin. Good catch. That clue led to the break I needed.

At age sixteen Carly Corbin had an affair with her twenty-four-year-old volleyball coach. She became pregnant. The coach stated publicly that he wanted nothing to do with Carly or her child—which he doubted was his because Corbin was promiscuous. He accused her of seduction and trying to break up his family. He returned to the wife and kids after receiving no more than a slap on the wrist for screwing an underage kid. His wife not only stood by him, she filed an "Alienation of Affection" suit against C. Corbin, which was later dismissed.

C. Corbin spent six months in a home for unwed mothers and gave the baby up for adoption.

See attached copies of court documents, newspaper articles from Nashville paper, etc.

Carly numbly sifted through the pages and her past came rushing back. She'd been crucified in the papers, deemed the Locker Room Lolita, abandoned by her friends and asked to leave school. She'd disappointed her parents and herself. She'd lost her heart, her innocence and her baby. Her family had moved to another state while she was in the home for girls, to escape the shame she'd caused.

An elephant-size weight settled on her chest. Like every other man she'd fallen for, Mitch had betrayed her. She couldn't believe how much more it hurt this time than the others.

She forced herself to read on.

C. L. Corbin opened an offshore account eighteen months ago with a single one-hundred-thousand-dollar deposit. The beneficiary of that account is Rhett Kincaid Corbin.

She squeezed her eyes shut and groaned. Mitch hadn't lied. Marlene had taken the money to abort Rhett and then not gone through with the procedure.

Questions tumbled like an avalanche through Carly's brain. Why hadn't Marlene aborted after taking the money? Why had she continued the pregnancy but kept it a secret? Why had she practically gone into seclusion in Carly's house and waited until Rhett was eight months old to introduce him to his father?

Had she felt guilty because she knew taking the money was wrong? Or had she been afraid?

Why had her sister opened the account in Carly's name? It wasn't as if Marlene hadn't pretended to be Carly before, but…this made no sense. If the money was for Rhett, then why not list the account in his name?

"Marlene, what have you done?"

Acid burned a path up her esophagus, but she was determined to finish the last paragraph of the damning report.

I have yet to find evidence linking your father to Marlene Corbin's "accident," but will continue to investigate if you are convinced of his involvement.

Shock stole her breath. Mitch suspected his father had been involved in Marlene's death.

Slowly the gears in her brain turned. That was why he'd silenced her with a kiss last night. He didn't want to discuss Marlene's death or his father's part in it. The Kincaids certainly had enough money to cover up something of this magnitude.

She had to do something. But what?

She heard Mitch's voice in the hall and wanted to run. She couldn't face him now. Not while she felt raw and exposed and too hurt to be logical. But short of diving beneath the desk, escape wasn't possible.

He entered the office with his cell phone to his ear. "I'm getting it now."

And then he spotted her. His gaze dropped to the papers in her hand, then bounced to the now empty fax tray and back to her.

"I'll call you back." He snapped the phone closed. "Carly."

It hurt to look at him. Hurt to know she'd been such a fool. No better than she'd been at a young, naive, stupid sixteen. Now she couldn't use young or naive as excuses.

This time she'd just been stupid. But now she was hurting and angry. She pushed to her feet. "You think your father killed Marlene. How could you keep it from the police? How could you keep that from *me*—especially after last night?"

"There is no proof he's responsible, but I needed to know— for my sake—that he wasn't."

"And if he was?" A tremor overtook her. Not even wrapping her arms around her middle could stop it.

Mitch shoved a hand through his hair. "I don't know. He's already dead, Carly. He can't be held accountable. But if this leaked, the press would take the family and KCL down. People who had nothing to do with Marlene's death would suffer. Nadia, Rand, Rhett and sixty thousand employees."

The way Rhett would suffer if the Kincaids found out Marlene had deliberately trapped their father. Both of them had secrets they'd rather not share. "And you."

"And me."

"Cleaning up Everett's mess is all you care about."

"It's not all I care about, but it is my job."

And she, Marlene and Rhett had been just another cleanup

detail. She understood Mitch's logic for withholding his suspicions, but she didn't like it.

"You could have asked about my past, Mitch. You didn't have to sneak around behind my back."

"I instigated the investigation before I got to know you."

"I don't want to hear your excuses." Because she'd want to believe him. And for her sake, *for Rhett's sake,* that wasn't wise.

"I'm not making excuses. I'm stating facts."

"Hiring a P.I. to smear my reputation shows how low you're willing to go to get what you want. You want Rhett. You don't want me. But I won't be a part of that plan, and I won't let Rhett be raised by a mean bastard who would intentionally hurt others."

Tugging off the engagement ring and placing it on the leather blotter hurt more than it should. "I'm not marrying you. And if you try to take Rhett from me I will go straight to the press with everything. I survived being flayed by them once. I will again.

"I made a youthful mistake of trusting the wrong person. But you, you're deliberately and willfully trying to cover up a possible murder and take a child from the one person who loves him most."

She forced her feet to carry her around the desk. Mitch stood between her and the exit. "Marlene was right. You are a cold, conniving rat bastard."

Mitch didn't even blink. "Carly, you can't take Rhett and leave. We'll—he'll lose everything."

"Maybe you should have thought of that before. Integrity is worth so much more than money. And you apparently have none of one and too much of the other.

"Here's your fax." She shoved the papers into his hand, stepped around him and headed for the door. But she paused in the threshold. Mitch needed to hear the truth, even though he probably wouldn't believe it. No one had. Except Marlene. Carly didn't know why his knowing mattered, but it did. She faced him.

"The newspaper was wrong. Wes seduced me. He convinced me that I had a chance at a college scholarship if I perfected my volleyball skills. At first I only stayed a few minutes after practice. And then we met longer and on weekends. I thought I was in love. And when he kissed me and held me, I thought he was, too." Her voice broke, but she soldiered on.

"I didn't know he was married until I turned up pregnant. He told me then he'd never leave his wife for me and he offered to help me take care of my problem. *My* problem. As if he'd had nothing to do with the baby we'd made. He took my heart, my virginity and my trust, and threw them away as if they meant nothing.

"I had nowhere else to go but to my parents who went to the police. Wes went to the papers."

She sucked in a slow, painful breath. "He told the reporters I was a tramp hell-bent on destroying his marriage and a hazard to all the innocent boys in my school. I denied it, but nobody listened because Marlene…"

She wheezed in another burning lungful of air. She'd loved her sister, but Marlene hadn't always made the best decisions.

"Marlene got into sex early on. But when she slept with a guy, she always pretended to be m-me. I had a reputation for being loose even though I'd never slept with anyone before Wes. So when he said I seduced him, everyone believed it."

Her nails dented the wooden door frame. "I lost everything. My friends. My home. My parents' trust."

A tear burned a trail down her cheek. She swiped it away. Tears solved nothing. She'd cried an ocean of them twelve years ago to no avail.

"But more than that, I lost the right to watch my precious baby girl grow up. I don't know her name. I'll never see her smile or hear her laugh. I won't get to brush her hair or dry her tears. I can't be there if she n-needs me, and I can never tell her how much I loved her even before she was born or how much it hurt to give her away. But it was the right thing to do. So I did it."

A sob clawed its way up in her throat. She swallowed it back. "So, yeah, if you want ammunition to take Rhett away from me, you probably have it. But the man I thought you were, the man I fell in love with, couldn't be that heartless."

He flinched, and that flinch told her what she needed to know. He didn't love her and probably never would.

"Now you know the facts. Tell your private investigator he got it wrong." She bolted down the hall and up the stairs.

Mitch didn't call her back.

Once in her room, she locked the door, backed against it and slid down the wooden surface until her butt hit the floor. She tilted her head back and blinked furiously to keep her tears at bay. When her vision cleared, she saw the wedding dress she'd fallen in love with but couldn't afford hanging from the canopy bed frame. Mitch must have bought it.

But the beautiful hand-beaded silk gown would never be worn. Not by her.

What was she going to do?

Rhett deserved his share of the Kincaid estate now more than ever before. But Carly didn't think she could bear to stay at Kincaid Manor. Mitch's betrayal had demolished her respect for him and for herself.

Worse, his P.I. might be right. Her past might very well cost her the child she adored.

Eleven

A tap on the door froze Carly's muscles and set her heart racing.

She didn't want to talk to Mitch.

"Mama," Rhett's treble penetrated the closed bedroom door.

Rhett. She'd been in such a panic to pack her belongings that she'd left him with Della too long.

Della. Another casualty of Mitch's deviousness. Carly was going to hate losing the older woman's friendship.

"Carly?" Her mother's voice.

And suddenly Carly needed her mother more than she needed anyone. She dumped her armload of clothes on the bed, rushed to the door and flung it open.

How was she going to explain there wouldn't be a wedding?

She didn't have to say a word. Her mother set Rhett down inside the room, closed the door and opened her arms. Carly fell against her and took strength from her hug.

After a few moments, her mother leaned back to look into

Carly's eyes. "Mitch says you're not going to marry him. Tell me what I can do to help you."

The whole story tumbled out in fits and spurts. The will and Rhett's inheritance. Falling in love with Mitch. The P.I.'s report. Getting her heart broken. Again. Her mother waited until Carly ran out of steam.

"First off, Mitch is right. If his father is responsible for Marlene's…end, then a higher power has already dealt out the consequences. That doesn't mean I don't want to know what happened. I won't rest easy until I do.

"Second, you are my daughter. I know you're hurting now, but I also know you have the most generous heart of any woman I've ever met. You're going to make the right decision." She cradled Carly's cheek. The love and approval in her mother's eyes and words brought tears to Carly's eyes.

"Whatever your decision is, your father and I will support you. If you need to leave, we'll help you. But if you want to stay here for Rhett, then your father and I will move to Miami to be your backup."

"But you love your life in Arizona."

"We love you more. And just like we moved to give you a fresh start after you relinquished your baby, we'd move for you again in a heartbeat."

"I thought you moved because I'd embarrassed you."

"No, dear. We told you we left Nashville because we didn't want you to be continually reminded of painful things and because the press wouldn't let you forget. I know you didn't believe us then, but that's the gospel truth. And with the dangerous path Marlene was headed down, it was a good time for us all to start over somewhere else."

Carly's breath snagged. "You knew about Marlene?"

"Of course I did. And your father and I tried to help her, but she wouldn't let us. She derived something from those boys' attention, as inappropriate as it might have been, that we couldn't give her."

"But the home for unwed mothers…I thought you wanted me out of the house and out of your sight. I thought I'd disgusted you."

"Oh, Carly, I'm sorry I didn't communicate my concerns better. I tried, but I was afraid to harp on and sway you into making a choice you'd regret, one you might hate me for later, so perhaps I didn't say enough. Baby, letting you go through that alone was like tearing off a limb, but we did it anyway because we wanted you to have counselors who would help you make a decision *you* could live with. The home promised me their specialists could do that."

Tears streamed hot paths down Carly's cheeks. "They did. And I know in my heart that I did the right thing. I couldn't have been the mother my daughter deserved."

She studied her finger, the one that for a few hours had worn Mitch's ring. "Mom, for Rhett to inherit his share of Everett's estate he has to live here for the rest of the year. I don't know if I can handle that, but I won't abandon him. He deserves this. It's the only thing his father will ever give him. I need to find a way to make it work."

"Why am I not surprised that you would put Rhett's concerns ahead of your own? Running away has never been your style. And I have no doubt that if you choose to stay, you will find a way to manage it. You're strong, Carly. You can handle anything."

Her mother sat silently for a moment and then tilted her head. "Is there a way to share this monstrosity of a house without having to cross paths with Mitch too frequently?"

"Pish! Orange pish. Big," Rhett cried out.

Carly's glanced over to where he knelt on the window seat pointing toward the koi pond. The evening sun glinted off the windows across the yard and an idea took root.

"The nursery is on the opposite side of the house."

Her mother stood and offered a hand. "Then I think we need to see the nursery, don't you? And if it's suitable, then we're going to lay some ground rules for Mr. Kincaid. He's going to learn he can't mess with the Corbins. We are a formidable team."

"I don't need you tonight," Mitch said Friday afternoon from the door of Rand's office, and then immediately turned and left. He didn't want to discuss his aborted plans.

"Whoa," his brother called out and chased him into the hall. "You can't drop a bomb like that and keep walking. You're supposed to get married in a matter of hours. What happened to the wedding? You come to your senses?"

Rand shadowed him past his PA's desk and into his office. "Spill it, Mitch."

"I had Dad's P.I. do a little checking into Carly's past and her sister's death."

"Marie, hold his calls," Rand told Mitch's PA and then shut the office door. "What did he find? She's already married? A black widow? A transvestite?"

Mitch scowled. He wasn't in the mood for Rand's twisted humor.

"There's nothing in Carly's past to change my mind." If anything, he wanted to hunt down an ex-volleyball coach and remove the guy's nuts with a rusty knife.

He'd been his father's axman for years. He should be able to handle this situation without breaking a sweat. He wiped his brow, trying to clear the vision of Carly's pain-filled eyes from his mind. No such luck.

She loved him.

The idea energized him, but at the same time filled him with panic.

"Then what's the problem?"

"She found Frank Lewis's report."

Rand whistled silently. "The guy is thorough and he doesn't pull his punches."

Rand would know. He'd dealt with Frank before moving to California. "No. He doesn't."

"And? C'mon, Mitch, don't make me drag this out of you word by word."

"I also had Frank investigate Marlene Corbin's death. I was concerned that Dad might have had something to do with the hit-and-run that killed her."

Rand swore. Viciously. "You think he did it?"

"Or paid someone to. I have no proof and no reason other than he was more pissed off at Marlene for having Rhett than I've ever seen him about anything before. Not even Nadia's marr—" No need to bring that up. Not speaking about his sister's early and tragic marriage had become a habit. "You know you didn't cross our old man."

"No. Not without repercussions." Rand and their father had a serious load of issues. His brother's part of the will requirement involved one of them. Rand had been forced to return from his self-imposed exile, take over as KCL's CEO and work side by side with the woman their father had stolen from him. The only woman his brother had ever loved, in Mitch's opinion.

He focused on his own problems. "If Dad was involved, I wanted to know before some reporter ambushed us with evidence and used it to take KCL down."

"Understandable. What did Frank find?"

"Nothing to incriminate Dad. But the fact that I'd suspected him and had Carly investigated was enough to send her into orbit."

"Understandable. Wouldn't you have been pissed?"

"Why? I was dealing with facts, not slander."

Rand stared at him with an odd look on his face.

"What?"

"The end justifies the means. You've become Dad."

Mitch reeled back in disgust. "No, the hell I haven't."

Folding his arms, Rand remained silent.

"I didn't break any laws," Mitch defended.

"What about a violation of her privacy? Withholding evidence from the cops?"

"There is no evidence. That's what I'm telling you. Whose side are you on? I'm trying to protect our inheritance and this company."

"We all are, Mitch. But at what cost? Is Dad going to make us stoop to his level to keep what's rightfully ours? And is holding on to Kincaid Cruise Lines worth sacrificing our self-respect?"

Carly had called him a conniving bastard who would intentionally hurt others. Cold, sobering realization crept over him. She was right, and so was Rand.

He'd become his father.

The idea horrified him. He staggered to the window and stared out at the bay thirty stories below. Everett Kincaid had been a mean, bitter SOB. Not openly. He was too clever for that. No, to your face he was charming, caring, and a benevolent CEO of a company voted best to work for five years in a row. He could charm confidential information out of you and you'd never even notice you were handing him the nails to your own coffin.

And then he'd stab you in the back and bury you without hesitation or second thought if it served his purpose.

Mitch did not want to be his father.

"Did she and the kid move out?"

Rand's words yanked him out of an arctic well of discovery. "They've moved into the nursery."

Yesterday afternoon she'd ordered *his* staff to move her and Rhett's belongings, and afterward Carly and Rhett had gone out to dinner with her parents. Last night, his wing of the house had echoed with silence. Silence he'd once relished. Silence that had kept him up most of the night.

This morning, Mrs. Duncan had appointed herself their guard dog. She'd been cold and abrupt—the housekeeper he remembered from the pre-Carly days. He hadn't even caught a glimpse of Carly and Rhett, and damn it, he'd missed the racket and the cereal bombs at breakfast.

"So we're still in this fight to fulfill the terms of the will," Rand said. "I hope to hell Nadia isn't having as tough a time as we are."

"Yeah." Their father's demands might have brought Rand home, but they'd also kicked Nadia out of the only home she'd ever known.

"What are you going to do?"

Mitch looked up and met his brother's gaze. He didn't have it in him to bluff. "I don't know."

Mutiny.

There was no other word to describe the situation at Kincaid Manor this past week, Mitch decided. His entire staff had turned against him and sided with Carly. They spoke to him respectfully and followed his orders, but otherwise stayed out of his way. Mrs. Duncan served his meals in silence.

He'd become an outcast in his own damned home. And he had no one to blame but himself. He'd hurt someone every member of his staff cared about.

Carly and Rhett were within the walls each evening, but managed to completely avoid him. They ate and played in the nursery. If Carly went running, then it wasn't in the gated community. The jogging stroller stayed in the back of her minivan, which led Mitch to believe if she ran she did so elsewhere.

If he wanted to see her, he'd have to hunt her down.

He hiked up the back stairs Thursday evening after dinner. He'd always avoided the nursery. Sealed off from the rest of the house by thick soundproof walls, the place had been his prison as a kid. He, Rand and Nadia had only been allowed out when they were clean and well-behaved. One screwup and back to prison he'd go. He'd learned early on to listen and not draw attention to himself.

The sound of Rhett's squeals and laughter reached him as soon as his feet hit the landing and he caught himself smiling. His step lightened. He quickened his pace and pushed open the nursery door. Carly knelt on the floor beside Rhett in the large main room. Judging by the towel she held, his brother had just finished his bath. There were three bedrooms off this play area, four if you counted the nanny's suite. Which had she chosen for Rhett? For herself?

"Mitt," Rhett screeched. His naked little body streaked across the room.

Mitch dropped to his knees and held open his arms. The boy hit his chest like a torpedo, winding him, making him ache for what he'd thrown away. Mitch hugged him.

Over the top of the fuzzy dark hair, Mitch's eyes sought Carly's. She rose, clutching the towel in front of her. Her damp T-shirt and low-rider jeans clung in all the right places. His pulse drummed out an appreciative beat.

"You'd better diaper him fast unless you want to use a mop." She tossed a disposable diaper in his direction. Mitch caught it, gently tumbled the boy onto the rug. Rhett rewarded him with cackles and wiggles as he taped the diaper on. And then he lifted his little brother and held him tight.

His fool of a father had missed this. And the boy's mother would, too.

Mitch wasn't going to. But how could he convince Carly to let him back into their lives? He stood, holding Rhett against his heart. "You've been avoiding me."

"Rhett has been getting to know his grandparents. They're talking about moving here to be near him."

"They didn't take the jet back to Arizona on Sunday."

She shook her head and her ponytail swayed. "They preferred to get a commercial flight. They flew out this afternoon."

She'd been with her parents all week. That explained why she hadn't been here when he raced home from KCL each night to his silent, solo dinner. He stared at her and tried to prioritize the week's worth of thoughts he'd saved up to tell to her, but settled for, "I'm glad you stayed."

Her chin lifted. "I promised to see this year through for Rhett's sake. He deserves to know his family and to have something from his father besides DNA."

"I agree." Rhett squirmed. Mitch set him down. The child bolted for Mitch's old room and returned with a toy dump truck. He plopped down on the floor and *vroomed* the truck around the rug.

Carly watched him for a moment before turning back to Mitch. "I tried to return the wedding dress. The store wouldn't take it."

"Don't worry about it."

"It was expensive. I hate to see you waste your money. And it's a beautiful dress. Someone needs to wear it."

No, she definitely wasn't mercenary like her sister. How could he have ever believed otherwise?

"I miss your company, Carly. Yours and Rhett's."

Her gasp filled the silence. She blinked and averted her gaze.

"Come back to the other side of the house."

She shook her head again but didn't look at him. "I can't do that. I can't lo—live with a man who'd try to hurt us."

She walked away. The sight gutted him mainly because he knew his actions were the cause of the gulf between them. He wanted to call her back, to haul her back. Into his life. Into his arms. Into his bed. He'd settle for seeing her face across the breakfast table.

He loved her.

The realization crushed his chest and depleted the oxygen in the room. That's why his life had sucked since Carly had returned his ring. The staff hadn't mutinied. Their cold treatment was the same as it had been for years. Ditto the silent tomb of the house. Both were *exactly* the way he used to like them.

But that was before Carly and Rhett had shown him how different, how dynamic life at Kincaid Manor could be.

He missed the controlled chaos. He missed them.

The house and staff hadn't changed. *He* had.

Because of Carly. Because of Rhett.

"Carly." He waited until she cautiously looked at him. "I'm in love with you."

The color drained from her face and her eyes turned guarded. Tense, silent seconds dragged past. She licked her lips and then swallowed as if gulping down nasty medicine. "You're a man who says and does whatever it takes to get what he wants. But that was low, Mitch. Even for you."

A bowie knife under the ribs would hurt less. "I'm not that man anymore."

Disbelief twisted her mouth. "You're not the man you were seven days ago?"

"No."

"Forgive my skepticism. But no thanks to whatever you're offering. We're happy here."

She didn't look happy. She looked as if she wasn't sleeping any better than he was.

"I'll prove I've changed."

A parody of a smile revealed straight, white teeth. It couldn't distract him from the pain in her eyes. Pain he'd inflicted by acting like his father and taking what he wanted without regard to the casualties.

She picked up Rhett. "You do that, Mitch. Now please leave. I need to get Rhett into bed. Good night."

He'd never been one to walk away from a fight, but he

wouldn't get anywhere with Carly tonight. And if he forced the issue, he might run her out of the house. Now that he knew he loved her, he had to come up with a winning strategy.

But before he left, he wanted to remind her of what they'd had. He strolled toward her. Her expression turned wary. He stopped mere inches away and reached out to hug Rhett. If in the process his hand grazed Carly's rib cage and he made her breath catch, too bad. He planted a kiss on the kid's forehead and inhaled his fresh-from-the-bath scent. He caught a whiff of Carly's fragrance, as well. Hunger and need swelled within him. His throat closed up.

He would not lose them, damn it.

"Good night, kid," he choked out before pivoting on his heel and stalking from the nursery. When he reached the bottom of the stairs he sucked air as if he'd just climbed a mountain. His chest ached, reminding him of that video game he and Rand used to play back in their teens. One where the Ninja master punched into some poor sap's chest and ripped out his beating heart. Mitch was that sap.

Winning Carly back seemed impossible. He had to find a way to convince her he'd changed.

But how?

She didn't care about useless trinkets or money. He couldn't buy her love. A first for him, because he'd never met a woman he couldn't buy. Even Trish had liked to be shown affection via a shower of material goods.

Instead of returning to the emptiness of the house, he slipped out the back door, walked down to the waterfront and stared across the bay. The lights of the distant shore and a few passing boats only marginally distracted him, and the waves lapping against the bulkhead did nothing to soothe him.

What could he give Carly that she would never give herself?

An idea shot across his brain. His pulse quickened and his palms tingled. He knew he had a winning plan.

Flipping open his cell phone, he punched Frank Lewis's auto dial. The P.I. answered on the first ring.

"Lewis Investigations."

"Frank, Mitch Kincaid. I have another job for you."

She'd survived. Barely.

Carly leaned against the door she'd closed behind Mitch. She hadn't expected seeing him to hurt so much. But the fact that the old cliché "out of sight, out of mind" hadn't worked with him should have been a clue that getting over him wouldn't be easy.

And when he'd said he'd fallen in love with her, she'd wanted to believe him so badly she'd almost broken down.

"Mitt. My Mitt."

"Yes, munchkin. Your Mitt. Bedtime." She carried Rhett to bed and tucked him in. After a good-night kiss, she retreated to the nanny suite. Restless, she paced the confines of her room. There was no way she could sleep. Not now. She needed a run—a *l-o-n-g* one. But she couldn't leave Rhett alone.

The week had been both physically and mentally exhausting. Without her parents' help, she wasn't sure she could have endured the dragging time. She'd worked flat out every day, and in the evenings her parents had asked her to show them each of her favorite parts of Miami. In the process of visiting her old haunts, she'd managed to run into her ex-fiancé. Her first one.

Seeing Sam again had been one of those good news–bad news situations. On the positive side, she hadn't experienced even a twinge of jealousy when he'd introduced his new girlfriend. She'd honestly been able to wish them well with no ill will.

On the bad side, she was completely over Sam and not just trying to plug a hole his leaving had caused. That meant her feelings for Mitch weren't a rebound romance.

She blew out a slow breath, crossed to the window and

pushed back the curtains. Her eyes caught a movement down at the dock. Mitch. Those broad shoulders and erect carriage were impossible to mistake. Her heart clenched.

Her love for Mitch was the real deal. And that meant it would be around to haunt her for a very long time.

Twelve

A video conference call was a hell of a lousy way to have a family reunion. But given the terms of his father's will, with him and Rand stuck in Miami unless traveling for work and Nadia in Dallas, Mitch had no choice.

As uptight as he was about what he had to reveal to his siblings, he couldn't help noticing the stress of being exiled from her home and the job she adored was taking a toll on his sister. "You've lost weight, Nadia."

She grimaced into her Web cam. "Most women would take that as a compliment, but I'm not getting that vibe from you. What's going on, Mitch? You didn't have a video-equipped computer system delivered to my door at the crack of dawn so you could nag me about my diet."

He considered and discarded a dozen options for opening the dialogue. "I'm in love with Carly Corbin."

In his peripheral vision, he caught Rand's head whipping in his direction, but kept his focus on his sister.

"Isn't she's our little brother's guardian?" Nadia asked on the wide-screen monitor in front of him.

"Half brother," Rand corrected.

"Yes, Carly is Rhett's guardian."

"Love is a good thing. Why do you look like hell instead of happy to be sharing this news?"

"Because I screwed up." To bring Nadia up to speed he ran through the details, from trying to buy Rhett to his plan to seduce Carly, marry her and divorce her and ended with the investigation and falling in love.

Rand watched and listened without changing expression or saying a word.

Nadia winced a few times. "You've dug yourself a deep hole. How are you going to get out of it?"

He'd lain awake last night trying to come up with an alternative strategy. He'd found none and had finally rolled out of bed before dawn, skipped breakfast and come into KCL to walk the premises.

"Carly is convinced I'll do or say anything to get my hands on my inheritance. The only way I can prove her wrong—" they weren't going to like this "—is by walking away."

Rand bolted upright. "Are you out of your mind?"

Nadia nodded. "I see your point."

"Mitch, you can't make us lose KCL," Rand's carefully level tone all but shouted.

Mitch swiveled his chair toward his brother. "You're the one who said Dad was forcing us to get down on his level to hold on to the company. I don't want to be him, Rand. I don't want to be a cold SOB who uses people and destroys anyone in the way of my quest."

"He's right, Rand. After sitting here for almost six weeks with nothing to do but watch dust motes dance through the air, I'm ready to call it quits."

"What do you mean, nothing to do?" Rand asked. "I shipped you cases of books and videos."

"And I sent the container garden for your deck and a dozen cookbooks and videos and kitchen gadgets. You have time to learn now," Mitch added.

"And they're all great. Thanks. But I can only sit on my butt for so long. You know the will stated I'm not allowed to work, and I'm only allowed out of this building a few hours each day. It's like being in solitary confinement. I'm going crazy. I don't have any neighbors to talk to. The floors below me are commercial offices and the other penthouse apartment is empty."

Mitch detected a trace of hysteria in her voice. "Do you need me to come down there?"

She seemed to gather herself. "Dad is—was—intolerant of weakness, my need to keep busy. My guess is he set me up like this to make me deal with my baggage. I'm dealing. Let's find a solution for you."

"There isn't one."

"Mitch, love is a once-in-a-lifetime thing. Don't throw it away for money or for Dad. Or for us."

His brother shifted in his seat, drawing Mitch's attention. Rand had never been a squirmy one.

"If I do this, we'll lose everything."

"Do it," Rand barked abruptly. "Do what you have to do. To hell with Dad and his games."

"I agree. Mitch, this is your life. We're all smart, educated and experienced. Rand's already proven there are other companies out there that will hire us. We can find one that suits us without the strings attached or the hoops to jump through."

He looked from his brother's stoic, determined face to his sister's. "You wouldn't hate my guts for this? You wouldn't consider me a traitor?"

Rand shook his head. "You, more than any of us, have always taken one for the team. It's time to take what you need."

"He's right, Mitch. It's your turn. Call me as soon as you've done it. The minute you do, I'm out of here."

His siblings' support brought that damned recurring lump back to his throat. If it didn't clear up soon, he'd have to see a doctor. Mitch nodded. "I'll let you know when it's over."

"I can't wait to meet Carly. She has to be great if she's snagged you. Good luck," Nadia said.

"Thanks. But I'll need more than luck."

"You can do this," Carly told herself when she heard Mitch's key turn in the front door. "You've had a broken heart before."

Not like this.

No, she'd never hurt like this. But she had more at stake now. She had to think of Rhett, and for that precious boy's sake she would suck up her hurt feelings and ignore her broken heart and go back to sharing meals with Mitch.

It wouldn't be the most painful thing she'd ever done.

But it would come close.

Her heart beat faster with each tread of Mitch's firm steps across the marble foyer, and then, framed in the living-room archway, he stopped. His eyes found hers and she felt as if she'd caught a twenty-pound medicine ball in the stomach.

"Mitt. My Mitt." Rhett squirmed in her arms. Carly wheezed in a breath and set him down.

Mitch seemed surprised and pleased to find them waiting for him, but neither emotion could hide the stress tightening his features or erase the tired lines bracketing his eyes and mouth.

"Hey, buddy." Mitch knelt, dropped the papers he carried on the floor and swept his brother up into a hug. For precious seconds, he tucked his face into Rhett's baby-fine hair, closed his eyes and held tight.

Carly's heart turned over. Mitch's love for his brother showed plainly on his face.

Mission accomplished.

Anything she might suffer from her time with Mitch would be worth it because Rhett now had another adult in his corner. One Kincaid down. Two to go.

"We missed you at breakfast," she tendered an olive branch.

Mitch lifted his lids and looked directly at Carly. "I went into work early."

"Pig me up."

He scooped up his folders and rose with Rhett in his arms and then strode purposely toward her, not halting until he was only scant inches away. Determination firmed his jaw. "We need to talk."

His body heat and his scent engulfed her. She swallowed and fisted her hands against the need to smooth a hand over the lapel of his charcoal suit that Rhett had bunched and stroke the beard-stubbled line of his jaw.

"Dinner's waiting. Rhett's hungry."

"Eat. Eat. Eat," the imp chanted.

"Mrs. Duncan." Mitch barely raised his voice, but the housekeeper instantly came bustling through the door from the kitchen as if she'd been waiting for his signal. "Would you please feed Rhett and put him to bed? Carly and I will eat later. We'll serve ourselves."

"Yes, sir. My pleasure." Smiling, she took Rhett and returned to the kitchen.

Carly couldn't handle being alone with Mitch. "I don't th—"

He held up a hand to silence her. "We have a lot of ground to cover, beginning with Marlene's death."

Carly barely had time to grasp that info before Mitch continued.

"Frank Lewis located the car that hit Marlene. The driver,

a college kid, admitted he'd been switching CDs and not looking at the road. When he hit Marlene, he panicked and left the scene because he'd had a few beers. When he heard she died, he was afraid to come forward because he knew he'd face jail time. He stashed the car and only recently took it to a shop for repairs. Frank turned the evidence over to the police."

"Thank you. My parents and I needed answers. I'm sorry for the boy, but I'm also glad your father wasn't involved."

"So am I. Not just because of the legal hassle, but because I needed to know he wasn't such an unfeeling bastard that he'd murder someone—the mother of his child, for godsakes—for pissing him off."

He shoved a hand through his hair. Tension radiated from every abrupt, tight movement, but his unwavering gaze held hers. "I've racked my brain to find a way to prove that I love you and that I have no intention of using you to gain custody of Rhett or taking him away from you to get my hands on my inheritance. I'm ashamed to admit that was my original plan. It isn't anymore. I was selfishly thinking of what *I* wanted, what *I* needed, and I never considered who would be hurt in the process. Although I honestly believed you'd tire of playing mommy and want your freedom."

"I would never do that."

"I know that now." He dropped his files on the coffee table and closed his fingers around her upper arms. His warm grasp contrasted with the cold she felt inside.

"I don't want to lose you, Carly. I don't want to go back to being the ice man you so rightly accused me of being, and I don't want to be a heartless SOB like my father."

"Mitch—"

"Hear me out."

She had no choice unless she used her self-defense

training, kneed him in the groin, broke free and ran. But where would she go?

"The only way I can think of to prove that it's *you* I want and not this pile of rocks or a bunch of ships is to renounce my inheritance."

She gasped. That he wanted her more than this estate or the company he lived for made her eyes sting and her heart well with hope. "You can't do that."

He grimaced. "Right. I can't do that. Because I can't self-ishly walk away and screw my sister and brothers out of what they deserve. I won't cost them their inheritance."

He released her and picked up the top file. "You'll find the paperwork in here dividing my share of my father's estate between Rhett, Rand and Nadia, but that can't go into effect until this year is over and the terms of the will have been met."

He tried to thrust the documents into her hands, but she refused to accept them. "Take it."

"Mitch, you can't do this. I won't let you."

"I can do whatever the hell I want with my share. It's not against the law to give it away and no one will be hurt."

"*You'll* be hurt."

"If it proves my love for you, I'd happily give it all away."

He loved her. He'd said it before, but this time she believed he meant it. Her heart blipped irregularly.

"This is your legacy, Mitch. Your future. It's the last thing your father gave to you."

"Don't you get it? It doesn't matter. Not without you." Looking frustrated, he tossed the file back on the table and swiped that hand down his face. He paced a few steps away, pivoted and retraced his path. After huffing a deep breath, he picked up the manila envelope and offered it to her.

She kept her hands by her sides. "If that's more of the same, I don't want it."

"It's not. I can't give you your daughter back. I can't erase twelve years of second-guessing your decision. But I can tell you her name, show you her smile and let you hear a recording of her laughter. I can tell you her life story to date."

Carly had never fainted in her life. She came close now. Spots dotted her vision. She staggered back a step and took huge gulps of air. A tremor started in her legs and worked its way upward until her entire body shook.

She stared at the envelope Mitch held, torn between wanting to rip it open and greedily soak up every detail of her daughter's existence and terrified by what she'd discover.

She thrust her arms behind her back.

Mitch frowned. "I thought you'd want this."

Her breath hiccupped three times. "I do. But I—I don't."

She shook her head. "What if I made a mistake? What if she's unhappy or neglected or unloved? How could I live with myself knowing I'd ruined her life?"

"You didn't."

She clung to those words and searched his eyes for the truth. "How do you know?"

"I had Frank Lewis find her."

"I don't think that's legal."

He sighed. "Probably not. But giving her up has haunted you. I wanted to put your mind at ease."

As far as gifts went, this topped the necklace for being the most perfect thing she'd ever received. But she couldn't accept it. She grasped the golden Rhett charm in her fingers and brushed her thumb over the smooth surface.

"You did the right thing, Carly."

"You're sure?" Her eyes burned. She blinked them furiously and focused on Mitch's face instead of the envelope that could answer what felt like a lifetime of questions.

"I'm sure." He backed her toward the chair closest to the fireplace. "Sit."

She did, not because she liked following orders, but

because her knees were ready to buckle. Until her fingernails bit into her triceps she didn't realize she'd wrapped her arms around her chest and hugged herself.

Mitch opened the flap and extracted a single typed page.

She quickly averted her face and covered her eyes. "Wait. Stop. I can't contact her or see her. I would never disrupt her life like that."

"No. You can't and you won't. I had Frank delete any contact information from his records. So even if you wanted to go too far, you couldn't."

She sought Mitch's eyes again. "Just tell me one thing. Is she happy?"

Mitch looked inside the envelope. "Yes. Do you want to see her picture?"

"Yes. *No!*" She wrestled temptation. "No, it's better not to know, better not to search for her in every crowd. I do that enough already without knowing what she looks like."

"Would you like to know her name?"

The push-pull for answers continued. A name wouldn't hurt. She nodded. "Just her first name."

"Her name is Katherine. She goes by Katie."

"Katie." She rolled the name around on her tongue. Her little girl's name was Katie. A sob punched its way up her throat.

"She's not alone, Carly. She has parents who love her and a younger sister who's also adopted."

Maybe Katie's sister would be there for her the way Marlene had always been for Carly. For several moments, she was too choked up to speak. "Thank you."

"Do you want to see the rest?"

It took a minute to find the strength to do the right thing— the right thing for Katie. But she finally shook her head.

"Are you sure?"

"Yes. It's enough to know Katie's happy."

He extracted another sheet from the envelope and offered

it to her. Carly leaned back and squeezed her eyes shut. It wasn't easy when she wanted to know so much.

"It's a list of addresses of the agencies that help connect birth parents with the children they relinquished. I'll help you sign up. And then after Katie's eighteen, if she ever wants to find you, she can."

She opened her eyes and accepted the list. The page rattled in her hand. She hugged it to her chest and blurted, "Burn it."

Mitch stiffened. "The file?"

"Yes. Please, Mitch. I'm strong enough to do the right thing now. I might not always be."

After a moment's hesitation he crossed to the fireplace, extracted a match from the brass holder and struck it into flame. His gaze caught hers, waiting. Carly nodded, and Mitch set the match to the corner of the envelope.

Fire licked upward, consuming secrets best left untold. For Katie's sake.

Mitch dropped the burning pile onto the grate and returned to Carly's side. He knelt by the chair, rested one hand on Carly's knee and the other on her shoulder. Together they watched the last bits of paper curl into ash and the microcassette warp and melt.

When it was over, he cradled her face and wiped her wet cheeks with his thumbs. His eyes met hers, and the love and approval she saw in the deep green depths filled her with hope.

"You did the right thing, Carly," he repeated.

She couldn't hear those words often enough. And whether Mitch meant today or twelve years ago didn't matter. A smoldering ember of happiness flickered to life deep inside her.

"Marry me, Carly. Not for the inheritance. Not for Rhett. Marry me because you've taught me how to do the right thing. And let me love you. Because of you I finally know how."

Air stuttered from her lungs, forced out by the emotions

expanding inside her. She cupped his face and brushed her thumb over his mouth. He kissed the tip.

"You always knew how, Mitch. You've been putting your family first all along. I love you, too. Yes, I'll marry you. For Rhett's sake. But mostly for mine."

Epilogue

Ten months later

"What's that?" Carly asked as she approached the double lounger where Mitch reclined on the back deck of the island villa he'd rented for their honeymoon.

He tossed the envelope on the table and checked out Carly's curves in the tiny bikini he'd bought her this morning. Oh yeah. He wanted some of that.

Her knowing smile reminded him he hadn't answered her question. "It's a letter from my father. The attorney gave it to me before we left Miami. I'll read it later. Right now I have better things to do, like starting our honeymoon off with a bang. Literally. And for that I need you naked."

He winked and reached for the string tying her top at her nape. "This cottage is isolated enough that no one will see if you stay naked for the duration of our stay."

She grinned but swatted his hand away. "I will if you will, but first, the letter. We waited nine months for this honeymoon. I'm sure you're man enough to wait five more minutes."

Her challenge made him smile. The woman did love issuing challenges. Anticipation hummed through his veins. He and Carly had married in her church within two weeks of her accepting his proposal the second time, and he still couldn't get enough of her. The year required by the terms of his father's will had finally ended, and they'd wasted no time in turning Rhett over to his grandparents for some serious spoiling and jumping on a chartered jet. They'd officially kicked off their honeymoon an hour later—in the mile-high club.

He pulled her onto the chair beside him and against his chest before reaching for his father's last words. Part of him didn't want to let the old man intrude on what promised to be one hell of a great week.

Thanks to Carly, Mitch had his head on straight. KCL was thriving under Rand's leadership and Nadia had put her ghosts behind her and was finally happy.

"Mitch, read it. Whatever it says, we'll deal with it. Together."

He took strength from the love-filled brown eyes of the woman he adored more than he ever thought possible and reached for the envelope. His hands trembled as he broke the seal and unfolded the page.

Dear Son,
If you're reading this, then I've kicked it and you've done what I expected of you. You stuck out the year with your little brother. I always could count on you, Mitch. You were my right hand.

It saddened me to see you shut yourself off after you shed that faithless bitch you had the misfortune of hooking up with a few years back. Good riddance to her. She wasn't right for you.

If I played my cards right, being responsible for your brother might have thawed that heart of yours. Children have a way of doing that. Each and every one is a blessing. One that should be shared with someone you love. When you have some of your own, you'll know what I mean, and I hope that day comes while you're still young enough to enjoy them.

I put you in a difficult position with Rhett's momma and for that, I apologize. Marlene swore she loved me, and I think she honestly did. She showed it in a dozen ways. She wanted to be my wife and knew I was old-fashioned enough to want to be married to a woman carrying my child. And while I don't appreciate what she did, I do understand it. But I didn't have any love left in me to give her. Any tender, sappy emotions I might have been capable of died with your mother. And I wasn't about to desecrate her memory by bringing another woman into her house.

But that ended up being a decision I didn't have to make. With Marlene gone, I knew there was only one man who had the tenaciousness to bring the youngest Kincaid into the family if I wasn't around to do it. You.

From everything Marlene told me about her twin, I'm sure the past year hasn't been an easy one for you. From all accounts it sounds like Carly Corbin is as reliable and dedicated to family as you are. I never met her personally, but both Frank Lewis and my attorney tell me she's been a bulldog with that boy since her sister's death. Protective. Possessive. Loves him like a mother. That's all any child needs.

So if you've hooked up with Carly, I take full credit for throwing you two together. If she's made your life a living hell, then it's nothing your ol' man hasn't already done. You're strong enough to survive it.

Take care of Rhett, Mitch, and take care of y

I've never said it to your face, and now it's too late
but I'll tell you anyhow.

I love you, son. You've made me proud.

Your father,

Everett Kincaid

Carly laughed. "He takes credit for hooking us up?"

Mitch shook his head and tossed the letter back onto the
table. "That's my father. Take credit for what goes right.
Pass the buck when it goes wrong and send someone in—
usually me—to do cleanup detail. This time, cleanup detail
was pure pleasure."

"He believes Marlene loved him."

Something in Carly's tone sounded off. "There was a doubt?"

Carly sighed. "Yes. I never told you I found her journal
after she died. She had a step-by-step plan for marrying your
father. She'd always claimed she loved him, but after seeing
her pursuit diagramed in detail I wasn't sure. And then there
was the money she took to end the pregnancy."

He tucked a silky lock behind Carly's ear. "My guess is she
set that up for Rhett because she was afraid of my father.
When she told him she was pregnant, he went ballistic. Before
he had her thrown off KCL property, he vowed she'd live to
regret her actions. And then he sent me to buy her off. She
probably believed he'd do something drastic. He was livid
enough that I believed he would, too."

"It's sad that we suspected the worst of them."

"But loved them anyway." He stroked a finger along the curve
of her breasts. "I like the way this suit accentuates your assets."

"About that…" She blanched, licked her lips and glanced
away looking nervous all of a sudden, and nervousness wasn't
an emotion his confident wife often displayed.

Alarm prickled along his spine. "Carly?"

...t his gaze. "Your father might

...ce the, um…joys of parenthood? I'm

...ions hit him like a freight train. Joy. Excitemen... ...ou're pregnant?"

Car... ...ose crinkled with worry. "Yes. I know we didn't plan this, Mitch, but please…tell me you're okay with it. Because I want this baby and I don't think I could—"

"Okay with it?" he parroted back. Awestruck, he stroked a hand across her flat belly. Wonder filled him until he thought his lungs would burst. "We've made a baby."

"Yes. Probably after I caught Rhett's tummy bug last month. I did the test this morning."

He carefully pulled her on top of him until her knees straddle his hips. He cradled her face in his hands and locked gazes. "I love you, Carly Kincaid, and nothing would make me happier than for you to have our baby."

Mitch pulled her closer and sealed his words with a kiss, because Carly had taught him that actions spoke louder than words.

* * * * *

THE MILLIONAIRE'S MIRACLE

by
Cathleen Galitz

Dear Reader,

The characters in this book are very dear to my heart. I relate in a very personal way to what they are going through. My husband and I struggled to conceive children and had our fair share of heartache along the way. When the doctor informed me that I was pregnant again, following a life-threatening miscarriage, we were ecstatic. Nineteen years later, we feel deeply blessed to have two healthy, wonderful sons.

Their births were complicated, though, and both were Life Flight-ed out of our rural town to Denver Children's hospital where they fought valiantly with completely unrelated congenital issues. Those days had a profound impact on my life. Not every couple was as fortunate as we were to take our precious babies home.

My wish for Bryce and Gillian and you, dear friend, is to make every moment count and to take special care of each other and yourselves.

Best,

Cathleen Galitz

CATHLEEN GALITZ,

a Wyoming native, teaches English to students in a rural school. She feels blessed to have married a man who is both supportive and patient. When she's not busy writing, teaching or chauffeuring her sons to and from various activities, she can most likely be found indulging in her favourite pastime – reading.

This one is for Mom for showing us how to live
with faith, dignity and unwavering love.

One

Gillian Baron formed a fist, lifted it in the air and let it fall to her side—twice—before finally forcing herself to rap on the door of the upscale apartment.

Even then she had to fight the urge to run away like a naughty child, who'd pulled a prank on the neighbors.

Considering that this portal to the past had never been closed to her before, knocking on it now shouldn't feel so surreal.

Maybe he isn't home....

Gillian leaned forward on the balls of her feet and assumed the ready position.

Ready for what? To bolt again? To run away from

all that had once been good and true in her life? Back when life had been as close to perfect as humanly possible and she'd had the key to this man's home— and his heart.

Before everything went so terribly, irreparably wrong.

Before he'd come to hate her.

Sighing in relief at her good fortune to avoid the awkward encounter she'd been dreading, Gillian turned to go.

"I tried," she said, rehearsing what she would tell her sisters when they demanded why she'd failed to speak to him. "Really I tried."

The belated sound of footsteps from inside the apartment caught Gillian midstride.

"I'm coming," rumbled a deep voice.

How she hated being here, dredging up old memories and wallowing in a sea of what once was. Hated dragging Bryce back into the complicated mess that was her life. Hated feeling so terribly vulnerable and weak-kneed after coming to terms with her own solitude at long last.

She doubted he would believe that she was here only on behalf of her father. With typical arrogance, he would more than likely misconstrue her presence on his doorstep as a ploy to finagle a way back into his life. Her pride already sorely tested, Gillian prepared to have the door slammed in her face.

When it finally swung open, Bryce McFadden stood before her in just a pair of faded jeans. His heavy-lidded eyes snapped open in recognition. A flash of something tender streaked across those blue orbs before dark clouds shadowed them and the perfunctory greeting on his lips froze.

"Hell—"

"O?" Gillian finished, hoping that was the intended salutation rather than a deliberate invective. "I hope I didn't wake you."

Seeing him stand at the door half-dressed with his hair bed-tousled and wearing a look of confusion on his unshaven face, she hoped it was just his sleep she'd interrupted and nothing more intimate.

Not that it mattered to her one way or the other.

Still, her stomach rolled as all logic ceased. Dropping her gaze from the silver-blue eyes that were pinning her down, she trained her own on his bare chest, where a mass of curly blond hair dusted its smooth surface. It turned a darker shade just below the sternum before eventually disappearing under the band of his unbuttoned jeans. Heat infused her cheeks when she realized she'd been caught gawking.

Hooking a lazy thumb through a belt loop, Bryce leaned back against the door frame and proceeded to rake her from head to foot with an overtly masculine gaze, with which she was far too familiar. Gillian reminded herself that pure animal magnetism couldn't overshadow the fact that this was the singularly most infuriating creature God ever put on this earth. And that she could never forgive him for letting her down when she'd needed him most.

"May I come in?" she asked, feeling more like the Avon lady than someone with whom he'd once had a life-altering relationship.

"Of course."

As Bryce stepped aside to let her in, Gillian took in his home with a sweeping glance. A big-screen TV, roomy leather couch, matching recliner and exercise equipment saved the place from looking like an efficiency apartment, but the lack of decoration gave it a spartan feel nonetheless. Not a single painting or photograph graced the walls.

Idiot! Did you think he'd keep a photo of you enshrined in his bachelor pad just because you couldn't bring yourself to destroy your own pictures of him?

"Nice place," Gillian said, feigning a nonchalance that matched his own.

She noticed that he hadn't bothered with a Christmas tree this year; a cheerful holiday bouquet on the coffee table was the only acknowledgment that the holiday was only a week away. The arrangement seemed out of place in such masculine digs, but she had to admire his attempt to add color to the austere black-and-white decor that dominated the room. This luxury apartment was nothing like the quaint little Victorian they'd once shared. Squeezing her eyes shut, she fought to forget the images of well-tended flower beds, hand-stenciled accents, antique furniture, a cozy little room decorated with teddy bear wallpaper and—

Stop it!

She couldn't afford to let maudlin memories sidetrack her from the task at hand. Just breathing in and out was proving difficult enough without attempting to battle ghosts at the same time.

"Would you like a cup of coffee?" he asked.

Grateful for anything to keep her hands occupied, Gillian gave him a tight smile.

"That'd be nice."

Bryce helped her shrug off the heavy coat, which was more of a necessity in Cheyenne winters than any kind of fashion statement. The small act of courtesy seemed both familiar and unworldly. In spite of the snow falling outside the window, Gillian felt her temperature rise. Standing in this strange living room inhaling Bryce's familiar musky scent, she could easily recall why she'd loved this man once upon a time. When he left the room to get her coffee, she glanced at the bouquet again, admiring it, and noticed a card sticking out of the blooms. Although Bryce would be back in a minute, she couldn't resist sneaking a peek.

Yes, yes! A thousand times yes!
Love,
Vi

Who the hell was Vi?

Gillian's thoughts turned catty. Had she misread the name? Maybe it was the Roman numeral six and Bryce was into numbering his women now. Or was that hackneyed expression written in feminine scrawl an acceptance of a weekend getaway or something more permanent?

The possibility of Bryce actually asking someone to marry him caused the floor beneath Gillian's feet to undulate. Sternly telling herself that there was too much riding on this meeting to let her imagination get the best of her, she stuck the card back into its little plastic holder before he returned a moment later with two steaming cups of coffee. Her hands shook as she accepted one from him.

"It's instant," he apologized. "Not nearly as good as yours."

Gillian felt a stab of regret that lives once so rich

had been reduced in a single word to the state of a lousy cup of caffeine.

Instant coffee.

Instant messaging.

Instant gratification.

Instant heartache.

"Thanks," she said, taking both the proffered cup and a place on the couch.

She was relieved when Bryce chose a seat in a nearby recliner rather than the empty spot next to her. That way she could speak to him without the risk of physical contact.

Truth be told, it wasn't the current arcing between them that worried Gillian but the deep emotional response this man evoked in her. That Vi's note had the power to send a hot spurt of jealousy coursing through Gillian's veins was disconcerting to say the least.

Taking a sip of coffee, Gillian realized he wasn't lying—it was truly awful. Suddenly she felt inexorably sad to think of him drinking such tepid stuff out of his chipped mug every morning in this sterile place. Especially knowing how much he once savored starting his day with her special brew.

In bed with her.

Setting her cup on the table, she watched Bryce rub the stubble on his jaw. She couldn't help remembering how rough it had felt between the palms of her hands. Not the type to carry on small talk while ignoring the elephant in the room, he looked at her expectantly.

"Why don't I save us both the agony of trying to make small talk?" she offered, searching frantically for the right words to do just that.

"That'd be nice," he drawled.

Bristling at the sarcasm in his voice and unable to think of any way to soft-pedal what she'd come here to say, Gillian simply blurted out the reason for her unannounced visit.

"Stella and Rose want to have Dad declared incompetent."

Launching a grenade in the room would have caused a less appalled reaction on Bryce's face. A muscle twitched in his jaw, and his eyes turned the color of polished gunmetal.

"What's that got to do with me?"

It wasn't exactly the first question Gillian was expecting from him, but it was nonetheless a fair one. Who could blame him for not wanting to be sucked into the drama that was her family all over again?

"By all rights this really isn't your problem," she consented, "but it's not by choice that I'm here."

"Has something happened that I should know about?"

Bryce had always been close to her father, and

Gillian knew his concern was genuine. She struggled to explain the situation without somehow sounding as guilty as she felt. It hadn't been easy pulling her life back together the past two years, but just because her father lived clear across the state and she was keeping limitless hours at work didn't make her feel any better about neglecting the man who had raised her single-handedly after her mother had passed away.

"Stella says he's fallen a couple of times and has been spending money so frivolously and erratically that both of them think he might be suffering from early stages of A-Alzheimer's."

It was hard enough getting the word out of her mouth let alone wrapping her mind around all its awful implications.

Not having actually seen her father since the last holiday when he'd expressed his disappointment in her decision to leave Bryce, Gillian had to rely on her sisters' judgment of his current physical and mental state. And while she couldn't bring herself to believe that either one of them would commit their father to a nursing home just to gain access to his money, she was worried they might be overreacting. Unfortunately their threat to take the matter to court put the onus on her to do something before things got out of hand and irreparable damage was done to the entire family.

Nothing short of a full-blown emergency would have compelled Gillian to be here otherwise.

Bryce's features softened for an instant. "I'm sorry to hear that."

Sorely tempted to seek comfort in his strong arms as she once would have, Gillian instead focused her attention on a tiny run sneaking up the thigh of her black nylons. Self-consciously tugging at her tweed skirt to hide it, she wondered how, after all the trouble she'd taken to make herself look presentable today, she could have missed such a fashion faux pas. It was the kind of flaw that highlighted her own unraveling state of mind.

She cleared her throat and got down to business. "It turns out that Dad has given both of us equal durable powers of attorney in case he's ever unable to take care of himself."

There was no way Bryce could have faked the shocked look on his face, dispelling once and for all Rose and Stella's notion that he'd personally masterminded this whole thing a long time ago. The harsh words they'd exchanged during the bitter divorce proceedings created a rift Gillian doubted could ever be bridged. Only after the impact of her announcement sunk in did the irony of it register upon Bryce's features.

He coughed up a dry chuckle. "I get it. Your sisters can't commit the old man to the loony bin unless you and I do the dirty work for them."

Unwilling to be drawn into another "discussion" about family dynamics, Gillian tried to keep a defensive note from creeping into her voice.

"Nobody said anything about a 'loony bin.' They have some valid concerns that can't be ignored," she stated coolly. "And there are some lovely facilities in the area."

"Et tu, Brute?"

His words hung in the balance like a tightrope walker stranded in the wind between two opposing fortresses. As much as Gillian resented the Shakespearean implication that she would stab her own father in the back, she was worried that Bryce himself would take a similar view of the legal proceedings her sisters were considering.

Would he be able to separate her from their actions? *More importantly, would she?*

Bryce stabbed his fingers through his uncombed hair in exasperation.

"Just what in the hell is it you want from me, Gill?"

Her heart hammered in her chest as she looked straight into those unforgiving eyes of his. And momentarily lost herself there.

"I want you to go to the ranch with me. Dad won't budge from the house until he has a chance to talk to us both together, and my sisters are threatening to initiate proceedings if he doesn't. My father has promised to abide by our joint decision, which is the only way I see of keeping my entire family from falling apart."

Bryce snorted as he dropped his head back onto the cushion of his chair and closed his eyelids. Dark circles hung in half moons beneath them. That he was working too hard came as no surprise to Gillian. She regretted interrupting his sleep on a Sunday morning, but this was the only time she could count on him being home. Besides, as difficult as it was for her to see him, this wasn't a matter she cared to discuss on the phone.

When he finally opened his eyes, Bryce sounded every bit as tired as he looked.

"Suffice it to say I've got a lot going on in my life right now. Why don't I just sign off as executor or whatever the hell it is that John made me, and you and your sisters can divide your thirty pieces of silver however you want?"

Gillian flinched at his words.

"You'd really do that?" she asked, feeling strangely disappointed. Here he was offering to do the very thing for which her sisters were so desperately praying, but while *they* would be delighted with such a decision, this just didn't feel right to Gillian. She was bound more by her own conscience than the rules of a blind and binding legal system.

"I'd do anything to be rid of the Baron clan once

and for all," he snapped. "But I would have thought you at least would have the decency to wait until the old man was dead before laying claim to his estate. You know how much he loves that ranch—and how hurt he'll be by any claim that he's incapable of running it himself."

"You don't think I know that?" Gillian said. The thought of declaring the strongest man she'd ever known to be unfit seemed nothing short of sacrilegious.

"Your father won't take kindly to being caged up in a nursing home," Bryce told her flatly. "He'll never forgive you."

Gillian folded her arms over her chest as if to protect her aching heart and glared at him. "Regardless of what you might think, I'm not any more comfortable with this than you are. If, after seeing him, we're equally satisfied that he's capable of looking after his own affairs, that'll be the end of that. We can both go on with our lives without having to look back on today with regret."

Bryce's harrumph echoed off bare walls.

Fearing that her courage would fail her, Gillian continued on in a rush. "I know it's a lot to ask, but Dad considers you a friend. He trusts you. And despite our past history so do I. Any advice you can offer would be greatly appreciated. Not to mention that you're legally involved whether you want to be or not. As I understand it, I have to agree to your signing off, and I'm not willing to do that until we talk to my father in person and assess the situation ourselves. Considering this could drag on for years if my sisters decide to take the matter to court, it'll be the quickest way to get me out of your life permanently."

Something ugly and hard leaked into her voice as she couldn't resist adding, "I'm sure that's something Vi could appreciate."

Looking surprised that she was familiar with the name, Bryce nonetheless conceded the point.

"Considering that I've asked her to marry me, I'm sure she would."

A seasoned actress couldn't have held herself together any better than Gillian did upon hearing that newsflash. Her chest felt as if it were going to implode, and the difficulty she was having breathing had nothing whatsoever to do with the high altitude.

"Congratulations," she said with difficulty. Hoping not to come off sounding as pitiful or bitter as she felt, she added, "You deserve to be happy. Really."

On some level she really meant it, but her smile hurt.

"I promise this will be the absolute last favor I ever ask of you."

Bryce cut her to pieces with a look of sheer disdain. "I don't suppose you remember the last favor I asked of you."

Gillian gave him a blank look and shrugged her shoulders. "You'll have to refresh my memory."

"It was when I begged you not to divorce me."

Two

"That hardly qualifies as a 'favor,'" Gillian said angrily.

Bryce glowered at her. "No more than the one you're asking of me. I've got to hand it to you, baby. You've got some gall waltzing back into my life after all this time, acting like a little girl lost and playing on my sympathies."

"*Sympathy* isn't a word anyone associates with you," she retorted.

They glared at one another for what seemed forever before Gillian managed to pull herself together.

"I was hoping that you could put aside your

personal animosity for me to do what's best for my dad, a man I happen to know you respect more than your own biological father. A man who trusts you enough to put his fate in your hands—even if you're no longer officially part of the family."

While their father's decision to include Bryce merely annoyed her, it infuriated her sisters. Still, whatever they wanted to believe about Bryce, Gillian knew only John Baron himself was to blame for instigating this awful face-to-face meeting between his youngest daughter and the ex-son-in-law he loved like a son. Gillian hoped her father wasn't playing them all for rubes. God help him if she ever found out he was faking his condition in hopes of contriving a reconciliation between them! The thought filled her with sudden guilt. A *good* daughter wouldn't even entertain such a wicked notion when doctors had confirmed that her father was ill and in need of all the support she could give him.

Hoping a more philosophical approach would better advance her cause, Gillian posed a hypothetical question. "Can we at least agree that fate sometimes brings people together, even when they're doing their best to stay apart?"

"I don't think so."

An exasperated sigh ruffled an errant tendril that

had fallen over her forehead. Clearly she was going to have to appeal to this man's overdeveloped sense of duty if she were to stand any chance of enticing him back to the ranch over the holidays. She knew that severing his relationship with her father had been particularly hard on Bryce. Asking him to become emotionally involved all over again with her crazy family didn't seem fair, especially if her father's condition was truly as dire as her sisters would lead her to believe. Terrified by death's knock at her heart's door, she couldn't imagine anything more painful than watching a disease destroy someone she loved so dearly.

"I'll only admit that I hate leaving John to the mercy of Jekyll and Hyde," Bryce said. "I'm not surprised that they've grown tired of depending on your father's generosity. I'm sure they feel 'entitled' to their inheritance before he squanders it all away on something as unimportant as the ranch he's spent his entire life building."

Gillian bristled at the insult to her sisters. However, since it was a step up from what he used to call them—the "bitch brigade"—she let it pass.

"How I would love to return a measure of the misery those two caused me over the years. I wonder how they'd manage if they were suddenly cut off without a penny?" A smile played with the corners of Bryce's mouth as he mulled over the idea of karmic payback in his head.

Clearly he'd never forgiven them for encouraging Gillian to file for divorce when he could have used their support. Gillian's voice turned as cold as the sleet building up on his front window. "If you could just let go of your anger toward them for one second and focus on a less vindictive—"

Rolling his shoulders as if to shake off the heavy burden that had been placed there, Bryce interrupted, "You always did have a blind spot where Rose and Stella were concerned, and while it shouldn't make a damned bit of difference to me whether those two bitter old maids lock your father away or bamboozle you out of your rightful inheritance, I still consider myself a man of principle. Right is right, and wrong is wrong. So, as much as I resent it, if John has placed his trust in me, I won't let him down."

Gillian's heart stumbled over itself.

"You'll do it?" she asked, wanting to make sure she hadn't misunderstood.

Bryce spelled it out for her in no uncertain terms. "I'll do it for your father. Not out of any sense of misguided sentimentality or obligation to you."

There was little chance Gillian would get the wrong idea about his motives, not when he was looking at her as if she'd just slithered out from under a rock. Biting her lower lip to stop herself from saying what she really thought, Gillian simply nodded.

"Whatever your reasons, I appreciate it," she said. "Thank you."

Those two little words cost her dearly. They hung in the thick space between them as their cups of coffee grew cold and the pendulum of the chrome clock on the wall swung back and forth in a perfect rhythm belying the chaotic nature of life.

Having made up his mind, Bryce suddenly became all business. "How do you propose we coordinate this little adventure?" he asked. "It shouldn't be any problem for me to take time off work over the holidays, but I'd love to get this over with and be home in time for Christmas next week. How about you?"

The eyebrow Gillian raised in disbelief plunged them back into the same old argument that had plagued their marriage.

"I told you I'd eventually be able to spend less time at the office. If only you could have been a little more patient—"

"Patient!" she exploded. "What you called temporary was literally a lifetime."

Apparently unfazed by the intensity of her emotions, Bryce had the acumen to point out the facts coldly. "You weren't the only one who suffered over the course of our marriage. Why are you so certain that your feelings are so much more heartfelt than mine? Do all women assume they have cornered the market on emotion? Or just you?"

Gillian clenched her fists at her sides and wondered how they'd managed to live together as husband and wife for as long as they had without killing each other. At the moment there was nothing she would have loved more than to slap the smug expression right off his face.

"Can we get back on track?" she asked, wanting to appear the more mature of the two. "It's pointless rehashing things we can't change."

She remembered all too well the times she'd complained about him spending so much time on his career to the exclusion of their home life. As a newlywed she'd been stunned by how lonely she'd felt when he was at work. It wasn't as if his hours hadn't been bad before they were married, but a part of her had hoped he'd make her a priority once they'd said "I do." Since the divorce two years ago, however, Gillian had gained new empathy for what it took to make a living. It hadn't been easy earning her real estate license and trying to carve out a niche in a challenging market.

How ironic it was that since becoming a full-time working woman, she'd adopted Bryce's own over-the-top work ethic. Looking back, she wondered if she'd been too hard on him about investing so much energy into his fledgling software business, not that it excused him from neglecting his obligations to his family. It wasn't the need for money nearly as much as his masculine pride and driving sense of ambition that ultimately put such a wedge between them. After all, her father had been more than willing to help them out financially.

"Christmas is a slow time for selling houses," Gillian said, shoving to the back of her mind all the reshuffling she would have to do to keep her broker and clients happy. "Taking a couple of weeks off shouldn't be too difficult," she lied.

It was Bryce's turn to look surprised. "I'm impressed that you've managed to strike the perfect balance between your personal and professional life in such a short time. Or is it safe to assume that your daddy's money is supporting your little foray into the business world?"

"Go to hell." Gillian resented the implication that she was just dabbling in real estate as a hobby courtesy of her father's generosity.

"I've paid every penny back I've ever borrowed from my father—just like you did," she said, taking perverse pleasure in reminding him that he'd once been financially in debt to John Baron, too.

Bryce barely reacted to that jab. While they'd

been married, he'd taken his responsibility as bread winner seriously—much too seriously in Gillian's opinion. It had cost his ego greatly to finally accept help from his father-in-law at her persistent urging. She believed they would have been far better off if her stubborn husband had relied more on family rather than trying to do everything on his own.

"Glad to hear it," he said.

The lopsided grin he gave her had Gillian self-consciously smoothing out a wrinkle in her skirt. She hated to think she was still susceptible to his charms, but wasn't going to make eye contact just in case.

"Sometimes it's hard for me to remember that all you once wanted to be was a wife and a mother."

Gillian was surprised at the unexpected tenderness in his voice. It was true. Had fate not sent her blindly down such a cruel path, she probably would have still been deliriously happy with that humble dream. Struggling to overcome the pain that Bryce's simple observation evoked, she abruptly changed the subject.

"It's sure to be a challenge getting to the ranch this time of year. Flying out of Cheyenne to Jackson Hole shouldn't be much of a problem—except for the exorbitant holiday price they're sure to charge."

Mentally, Gillian clicked off the days remaining until Christmas. Eight total.

"The hard part will be getting from the airport to the ranch in the dead of winter," she added.

Since ten-foot snowdrifts made regular transportation impossible in the winter, Bryce suggested hiring a private helicopter or renting a snow coach.

"It would be easier just to pack in," she countered with the glib attitude of someone raised in the heart of some of the most challenging terrain in the country. "If you don't have any objections, I'll go ahead and make arrangements for Sid to have a couple of snowmobiles ready for us when we get to Jackson."

She wasn't surprised that the thought of strapping himself to a sleek six-hundred pounds of raw power appealed to Bryce's adventurous nature.

When he readily agreed, she asked, "Do you mind if I make a couple of phone calls before I leave to get the ball rolling? The battery on my cell phone died on my way here."

"I think I left the portable phone in my bedroom. It's down the hall and to the right."

Gillian headed in the direction he pointed. A moment later she stood transfixed and trembling in the doorway of his bedroom.

Hearing her gasp, Bryce rushed to her side. "What's wrong?"

Understanding dawned as he followed her gaze to the only picture in the apartment. Hanging above his bed the photo of an infant's foot was enlarged many times over so one could truly appreciate the proportions represented within its gild frame. Two thumbs—Bryce's and Gillian's—cradled and dwarfed the tiny foot. A diamond wedding ring glinted in the background.

The photograph had been taken shortly after Bonnie's premature birth, just a few short months before their daughter died of SIDS—while Bryce was at work.

Gillian stepped over the threshold and robotically made her way across the room to stand before the haunting representation of the fragility of life. On the bottom of the frame was a brass plaque upon which a single word was engraved.

Forever.

Bryce reached out to catch her as she stumbled.

Three

Steadying herself, Gillian shrugged off Bryce's helping hand. She'd never fainted before and wasn't about to start now, however shocked she might be. Righteous anger was as good as a shot of adrenaline for shoring up her rubbery muscles.

"What are you doing with that?" she demanded, pointing at the offending image.

The concern in Bryce's eyes vanished so quickly that it made Gillian wonder if she hadn't imagined it there in the first place.

"I'm so sorry," he drawled sarcastically. "I didn't

realize that I needed to check with you before hanging anything on my walls."

Reality trickled in with the light through the window, casting a supernatural glow on the photograph above his bed. She and Bryce were no longer husband and wife, and as such, Gillian had no business judging either his decorating decisions or his emotions.

"I would think such a poignant reminder would render you incapable of getting out of bed every day," she said, her tone wavering between an apology and an accusation.

"Such a poignant reminder of what a lousy husband and father I was, you mean," Bryce paraphrased.

Gillian's silence spoke for itself.

"Then I guess it's a good thing I was a stellar son-in-law," he added caustically. "Otherwise we'd be happily going our own ways like other divorced couples instead of dealing with complicated family matters that shouldn't involve me."

Gillian wouldn't be goaded into admitting how hurt she'd initially been by the discovery that her ex-husband was the co-executor of her father's estate. Choosing water over blood was a blatant betrayal on John Baron's part, especially considering that Bryce was no longer even tied to the family by marriage.

Her gaze drifted back to the touching image on the wall. She'd almost forgotten how tiny Bonnie had been. Swamped by an unstoppable wave of grief, Gillian regretted letting herself be coerced into coming to Bryce's apartment. Just as she had been afraid it would, this encounter only served to stir up painful memories.

Bryce's features softened. "Would you like me to have a copy made for you?" he asked.

Gillian was surprised by his thoughtfulness. For a fleeting instant, she seriously considered the offer. Certainly her own bare apartment could stand such a loving touch. Since moving in, she'd done little but use it as a place to eat and fall asleep after pouring all her energies into long days at the office. Meeting clients at all hours and strong sales were rapidly making her a rising star in her profession and giving her virtually no time to remember her old life. Which was, of course, the point.

"I don't think I could bear it," she explained, amazed that he could.

After Bonnie's death, he had been the one to encourage her to let go of the past and move on. Despite her needing him, Bryce had spent more and more time at work. Although a part of her had wanted to mend their marriage somehow, Gillian's sisters had made her realize that Bryce would never change.

When she presented the divorce papers, he refused at first, but eventually signed. Considering him cold-hearted for putting work ahead of her and Bonnie, Gillian was amazed now to see him immortalize their baby in such a sentimental, moving manner.

Swiping at her eyes with the back of her hand, she struggled to keep from crying. She blinked hard and forced herself to look away. The last thing she could afford to do was think Bryce had changed. A part of her still loved him despite their turbulent past, and she knew herself well enough that any weakness on her part could send her back to his arms.

Damn it!

Bryce had never wanted to make this woman cry, especially when her tears were like kryptonite to him. His reaction astonished him. In spite of all the painful things they'd gone through, he still felt a tug of protectiveness at the sight of her fighting back tears. He'd always had a soft spot where Gillian was concerned.

She was still just as beautiful as he remembered with her Snow White fair complexion, dark hair, amethyst eyes and those full, pouty lips that made all men thank God for making women. There was no denying that lust was what had initially attracted him to her, but that hadn't been the only element at play. The first time they met, he'd felt an aura of goodness surrounding Gillian that one often associated with fairy-tale heroines.

Bitterly Bryce reminded himself that real life didn't promise any magical happily-ever-afters, and that sometimes evil stepsisters triumphed over Prince Charming with poisoned words, not apples. By the time he finally signed the divorce papers with which he'd been served, he couldn't be sure whether Gillian wasn't a monster herself.

She'd averted her gaze from the picture of Bonnie to a photograph on his nightstand. In it, he had an arm draped affectionately around the shoulders of a pretty blonde who was in her mid-thirties. A little tow-headed boy standing next to him clutched Bryce's free hand and grinned into the camera.

"I presume that's Vi." Gillian's voice was flat and devoid of emotion.

Bryce nodded. "And her little boy, Robbie."

"He's adorable."

"He's a great kid."

Bryce went on to explain that in spite of losing his father in a tragic automobile accident, Robbie was an incredibly well-adjusted child, who desperately needed a father. Wanting more than anything to be an integral part of a loving family again, Bryce was ready and willing to step into that role. He felt no need to justify his decision to put his miserable divorce behind him finally and rejoin the land of the living.

"Vi's wonderful, too," he added.

Gillian gave him a wobbly little smile. "I just hope she understands why you're taking off over the holidays to help me."

Bryce steeled himself against the wounded look that smile failed to hide. As a red-blooded American male fired by the memory of making glorious love to this woman, he may have little control over the testosterone rushing through his veins, but he did have a good deal to say about committing to someone who'd once used his heart as a toothpick. He definitely needed to think about Vi's feelings and forced himself to concentrate on the logistics of this trip rather than the scent of the perfume wrapping around him in deceptively strong silken threads.

She had no right to begrudge him any measure of the comfort Vi brought to his life. Or the joy that her little boy shone into his lonely days.

"How soon can you book an available flight?" he wanted to know. "I'd like to get this over with as quickly as possible so I don't miss the look on Robbie's face when he opens his presents."

Bryce felt bad when Gillian's eyes clouded over with longing for all the Christmases they'd never have with Bonnie. To be kind, he neglected to add that he didn't want to miss Vi's response, either, when she unwrapped her present from him: a three-carat diamond engagement ring that was far more impressive than the one he'd barely been able to afford for Gillian once upon a time.

Back when he'd been struggling to make a go of his fledgling company, his starry-eyed bride had assured him she didn't care about the finer things in life like diamonds and fancy trips that he was so bent on buying for her. All Gillian wanted was for him to spend more time at home with her and the baby. Even now, Bryce wished there was some way he could have made her understand about a man's sense of pride. About his need to provide more than just the basic necessities for his family. About his desire to make something of himself that would make a wife proud.

Now that the company he'd started was about to turn his dream of becoming a millionaire into reality, Bryce wondered if Gillian would ever regret leaving him. Since she hadn't believed in him back when it meant so very much to him, he felt that crowing about his success now would be little more than a hollow victory.

Studying the emotions playing across his ex-wife's face, he hoped that Gillian wasn't going to try to make him feel guilty about moving on with his life, especially since he'd never wanted the divorce in the first place. But now that their marriage was over and he had finally come to terms with it, he resented her showing up on his doorstep unannounced, reminding him all over again how very much he'd once loved her.

"I'm happy for you," Gillian said sincerely.

While trying to say the right thing—or at least not the wrong thing—she prayed that the smile pasted on her face didn't look as strained as it felt.

She couldn't imagine anything worse than having to spend time with her ex-husband on a long, drawn-out trip down memory lane while he was in the process of planning his wedding. No matter what the emotional cost, Gillian vowed never to let Bryce know just how much power he still exercised over her battered heart. Nor to interfere in his new life with his picture-perfect, ready-made family.

Upholding her end of a polite conversation wasn't easy, though, when her thoughts kept wandering to his impending nuptials. Would Robbie be the ring bearer or the best man? Would the bride wear traditional white? Would Bryce look as handsome and completely sure of himself as he had on *their* wedding day? Shaking her head as if she could get rid of those unwanted images like an Etch-A-Sketch, Gillian made herself focus on the crisis at hand.

"Are you expecting your parents for the holidays?" she asked, hoping that wouldn't present yet another obstacle to her scheduling nightmare.

Bryce shook his head. "I gave them a cruise for Christmas this year."

"How generous of you," she murmured.

And smart...

Gillian knew the only way his parents would take such a lavish trip would be if someone else paid for it. It came as little surprise to her that his parents would prefer some exotic location to the tedium of decorating a tree, wrapping presents and squeezing in time with a son who never could do enough to please them. Besides, she was no longer around to wait on them hand and foot while Bryce was blissfully off at work. If her sisters were the bane of his life, she could claim the same about his parents. She'd always believed Bryce to be closer to her father than to his own because Sedrick McFadden was so innately selfish. And cheap. The only thing tighter than Sedrick's wallet was his wife's pocketbook, and Gillian was convinced that was because it was welded shut.

She imagined that Bryce's generosity was born of the fear of someday becoming as stingy as them. From the time he was just a kid working both a morning and evening paper route, he'd been expected to earn his keep. Growing up, he'd been on his own much of the time. Only after he married Gillian did Sedrick and Donna decide to make up for lost time by visiting often—always when it was most convenient for them regardless of how busy Bryce was or how exhausted their pregnant daughter-in-law was.

They treated each visit as their gift and her servitude as their just reward. Far more willing to share the good times than the bad with Bryce, they'd given Gillian the distinct impression that it had been a real sacrifice on their part to show up for Bonnie's funeral in lieu of simply sending their regrets.

Pushing aside those stale memories, Gillian tried to make herself present in the moment.

"I'll call you with all the details after I finalize our travel arrangements. I really do appreciate you doing this for me—for Dad, I mean," she amended quickly, feeling her neck redden.

She was growing more desperate by the minute to get out of this stifling place and was grateful when the phone rang, allowing her the opportunity to make a quick getaway. Only after she was safely outside Bryce's apartment did her heart rate start to slow.

Her hands trembled as she punched the buttons on the elevator. Try as she might, it was impossible to get the picture of Robbie's cherubic little face out of her head. She was overwhelmed by old feelings of somehow failing as a woman. They were immediately followed by a swell of bitterness at a God who would give one woman a perfectly healthy child while depriving another of the same joy.

Oddly enough, what cut most deeply wasn't that Bryce was moving on with his life.

With someone else.

And a little blond angel who looked like a custom-ordered replica of Bryce when he was a boy.

It was that, despite severing all ties to her old life, Gillian was permanently mired in the quicksand of the past, watching the rest of the world move on without her.

Four

Three short days later Gillian stood waiting in line at the airport, wondering if Bryce was going to bother showing up at all. Just as she had suspected, it had been a good deal easier obtaining tickets at inflated holiday rates than packing to accommodate the snowmobiles that would transport them on the final leg of their journey. Feeling like Charlie Brown so wrapped up in winter layers that she could barely move, she unzipped her coat to reveal a bulky sweater. Underneath her jeans she wore a pair of pink long johns.

Recognizing her customized ring tone, she

reached for the phone in her coat pocket and flipped it open. Even with all the background noise, Stella's voice was unmistakable. Gillian was relieved that it wasn't Bryce canceling at the last minute.

"No, he's not here yet," she reported.

As irritated as she was at the moment with Bryce, the last thing she wanted to do in a crowded airport was rehash the argument she'd had with her sister earlier about taking Bryce to see their father. Stella couldn't understand why her contrary ex-brother-in-law didn't just gracefully bow out of their private family affairs since he was no longer a member. If she ever found out that Gillian had been the one who actually talked him out of signing off as an executor, there was no telling what kind of protracted family squabble would erupt.

"Still the same old, selfish Bryce, expecting the universe to wait on his overloaded schedule," was her sister's cynical observation.

"He'll be here. Don't worry."

Gillian hoped she sounded more confident than she felt. One could never discount the possibility that Vi had decided at the last minute to keep Bryce at home because she didn't want him alone with his ex. Of course, Vi had nothing to worry about since both Gillian and Bryce hoped they could go their separate ways permanently once they returned.

"Little sister, when are you going to stop counting on men in general and Bryce in particular?" Stella demanded. "I don't understand why you would expect him to take any precious time off from work on such short notice when you're divorced. He certainly didn't bother when you were married, back when it really would have meant something to you."

It still meant something to her, but Gillian wasn't about to admit it. Stella might have good intentions, but her judgmental attitude did tend to grate on her nerves. She wished her sister would spare her the lecture and let her get on with the difficult task at hand. It was hard enough dealing with painful memories without having someone rub salt into old wounds. The strained silence on Gillian's end of the phone did little to discourage Stella. Bryce used to say that she could put a dog with a bone to shame.

"By the way, thanks for the birthday card," Gillian said, hoping to change the subject.

In spite of her sister's faults, she never doubted the sincerity of Stella's concern for her. Still, Gillian was relieved when their conversation was cut short by another call. It came as no surprise that it was from the office. Even though her co-workers had promised to cover for her while she was gone, Gillian was generally considered indispensable at work. Having spoiled her clients with the kind of conscientious, personal attention that was a rare commodity in the business world, it was far more difficult for her to take time off than she'd led Bryce to believe.

It wasn't that her job wasn't gratifying. Aside from the satisfaction of being a financially independent woman, Gillian truly enjoyed matching clients with houses that were perfect for them. She also took special pride in helping young couples purchase their first home; they greatly appreciated the decorating advice she threw in for free. Unfortunately all that talent was wasted on her own minimalist apartment, but Gillian was glad she didn't have to bother asking anybody to water her plants or watch a pet while she was away.

As much as her job served to numb the pain of losing a child and going through a divorce, Gillian was nonetheless ready for a break. It was just too bad that the plane she was boarding wasn't bound for a tropical vacation spot instead of the one place certain to make her feel like a little girl all over again.

"I left all the paperwork for the McVee contract with Becky," she assured her boss before hanging up. Their flighty secretary was certain to be in for a lecture for neglecting to mention the fact to the broker whose blood pressure was dangerously high even on rare days when everything went right at the office.

Stepping up to the boarding gate, she handed the attendant her ticket. "Any chance this flight will be delayed?" she asked, checking her watch for the millionth time.

"There's nothing to indicate that it won't leave according to schedule, but you know what they say about the weather in Wyoming—If you don't like it, just wait fifteen minutes for it to change."

Gillian thought the cheesy saying was just as applicable to Wyoming men as it was to its weather. Casting a final glance over her shoulder, she was relieved to see Bryce racing toward the boarding gate. Her pulse leaped, and she suddenly felt sixteen all over again. Hating the way her fickle body betrayed her, she supposed she should be glad to feel anything at all. For the longest time there had been nothing but pain beneath her skin, and she'd deliberately pushed away anyone who challenged her to feel anything else.

Gillian reminded herself that she had no right to the tingling possessiveness that surged through her veins as every woman in the general vicinity swiveled her head to get a better look at the handsome man who skidded to a stop beside her. She passed him his ticket without saying a word. Instead she gave him one of the aggravated looks she'd perfected in their marriage. That he didn't bother with an explanation—or an apology—only deepened her sense of irritation.

Once on the tiny prop jet, Gillian located her seat next to a window. Since it was far safer concentrating on the tarmac outside than the emotions tearing her up on the inside, she turned to look at a world as bleak as the task that lay before her. Outside, men in jumpsuits cleared ice from the underside of the plane's wings.

"Do you still get nervous about flying?" Bryce asked, sliding into the seat next to her.

She nodded, remembering how he used to hold her hand before the engines even wound up and didn't let go until they were safely in the air.

Feeling like a pebble about to be launched from a slingshot, Gillian told him, "Takeoffs are still the worst."

"Better than bumpy landings."

Digging her fingernails into the armrests, she wondered if he was referring to one that lay ahead of or behind them.

"Welcome aboard, ladies and gentlemen," a masculine voice announced over the intercom. "Today we'll be cruising at an altitude of twenty-six thousand feet. At the present time the weather in Jackson Hole is a chilly twelve degrees. Due to our short flight time, I would request that you keep your seat belts fastened until we arrive."

The fact that she was wrapped up like a Christmas

present made little difference to Gillian when Bryce's hand settled on her thigh after he reached over to fasten his seat belt. Even through layers of clothing, his touch had the power to make her flinch. Hoping he hadn't noticed, she didn't release her death grip on the armrest until she heard the landing gear retract.

"Thanks," she muttered.

"No problem." He grinned, making her wonder if she was the only one who felt the charge between them.

Determined not to dwell on it, she folded her hands demurely in her lap to hide their telltale tremors and studied the landscape below.

Intricate patterns of snow fences snaked across the Great Plains for miles in all directions. From this vantage point she thought she and Bryce may have just as well been crossing the arctic tundra of Alaska as the frozen prairie of Wyoming. It was hard to imagine the hardships that men like her great-grandfather had to endure in laying claim to this land through homestead laws intended to settle the rugged West.

When Bryce struck up a friendly conversation with another passenger, Gillian found herself resenting how much more easily he could talk to complete strangers than to her. By the end of their marriage it seemed they could barely manage to mumble simple courtesies to each other let alone hold real, meaningful conversations. Just as she feared when she first decided to contact Bryce, all the old horrible feelings associated with their divorce came tumbling back.

Gillian dreaded returning to the solitude of wide-open spaces where there was no way of ignoring the ghostly voices of the past echoing off the red canyon walls, but she was no longer so certain that running away was the best way to rebuild a shattered life. Studying the lay of the land with a bird's eye perspective, she couldn't help but wonder if she might have been happier had she stayed put rather than succumbing to the allure of geographical change.

When the Grand Tetons loomed into view, looking more like the Swiss Alps than anything belonging in North America, Bryce asked her permission to get a better look.

"By all means."

She instantly regretted those words.

The warmth of his breath against her cheek when he leaned across her seat was enough to make her light-headed. The smell of his favorite cinnamon gum took her back to a time when she'd felt free to kiss him whenever the urge took her—as it did now. She beat back that urge with a vengeance.

"Does your father have any idea how much the old homestead's gone up in value over the years?" Bryce asked, apparently unaffected by their close proximity.

"I doubt it."

Gillian didn't really want to talk about market values. It saddened her to think about selling the home where she'd grown up. No matter how much profit was involved, some things just couldn't be measured in dollars and cents.

From fifteen thousand feet up she was surprised to see Jackson Hole encroaching upon the wilderness that abutted the snowy valley lying at the foot of those majestic mountains. One fabulous mansion after another was being built in what was quickly becoming the Beverly Hills of the West. Perhaps it was too much to ask that the quaint mountain town of her childhood remain the same when she herself had undergone so many changes.

"With so many millionaires having two or three trophy homes, I wouldn't be surprised if most of those sprawling estates are vacant during the winter except for an occasional ski weekend or holiday," she offered in the way of polite conversation.

"I'd bet every cent of your next commission that both of your sisters know exactly how much the land is worth."

Gillian threw up her hands to ward off the attack. "Can't we just leave them out of this?"

"I would love nothing more than to leave them out of the rest of my life," Bryce rejoined, "but I have a sneaky suspicion they aren't about to let that happen any more than they could keep their noses out of our business when we were married."

"Why is it so hard for you to believe that they're as torn up about this as I am?" Gillian snapped, rushing as she always did to her sisters' defense.

"Maybe because you love that old man as much as I do. Or at least you once did."

Gillian felt her blood pressure soar. The man could provoke a saint to violence.

"Who are you to question my loyalty—"

Her response to his provocations was interrupted midsentence as they hit an air pocket and Gillian's stomach lurched into her throat.

The pilot's voice crackled over the intercom. "We're experiencing some turbulence and ask that you stow all unsecured items under the seats or in the overhead bins. Please fasten your seat belts and put your seat backs in the upright position."

Gillian hoped it was nothing serious. She had no desire to spill her guts to her ex-husband as her life flashed before her eyes and their plane crashed into the white abyss below. Still, when Bryce wrapped an arm reassuringly around her shoulder, she didn't pull away. Grateful to have something warm to hold on to, she knew better than to read anything more into the gesture than kindness inspired by the terrified expression on her face. Even so, a comforting squeeze flooded her mind with memories of intimate moments they once shared.

Looking at that big masculine hand on her shoulder, she remembered the simple gold wedding band she'd given him. Inside, she'd inscribed it with the same naive word that blindsided Gillian when she'd discovered it below that incredibly moving photograph in Bryce's bedroom.

Forever.

"Trust me," Bryce said in a voice that somehow managed to sound more authoritative than the captain's. "Everything's fine."

Gillian desperately wanted to believe him—just as she had when they'd made their vows to one another. Those words came back to her as clearly as the day they said them to each other in front of a crowded church.

In sickness and in health.

Until death do us part...

As the plane bounced through another air pocket, a collective groan filled the cabin. Gillian sought strength in Bryce's calm demeanor and steady gaze. Those eyes had seen their fair share of dreams both fulfilled and shattered without losing their shine.

"Hold on," Bryce said, wrapping his arms around her and pressing her tightly against his chest.

Gillian felt the strong beating of his heart against hers as they hit the runway.

Hard.

As the sound of brakes roared in her ears, she squeezed her eyes shut. The first thing she saw when she finally opened them was an amused expression on Bryce's face as the plane rolled to a safe, anticlimactic stop.

"How are you doing?" he asked.

Gillian hadn't seen such tenderness in his features for a long, long time. It was her undoing. Tears welled up in her eyes as she somehow managed a squeaky "fine" in response.

Fine. Except that being with you scares me more than the thought of hitting the ground at two hundred miles per hour....

Gillian told herself that it was ridiculous to get sucked back into any fantasy that involved reviving a dead relationship. A little turbulence shouldn't make her forget that not only were they divorced but that Bryce was engaged to another woman. One she assumed could give him even more children than the healthy little boy whom he already adored.

As the captain announced their safe arrival, Gillian struggled to regain a sense of composure. In the seat in front of her a young mother was busily reassuring her four-year-old that everything was all right. She wiped away the tears rolling down the girl's chubby little cheeks and gathered her into her arms.

Gillian's own arms ached at the sight.

"There's nothing to be afraid of, honey," the woman promised. "We're safe and sound on the ground now, and Daddy's waiting to take us home."

The toddler took solace in the thumb she stuck into her mouth and studied Gillian solemnly over her mother's shoulder. That she would have been a wonderful mother herself was of little consequence in the flickering shadows of dead dreams. Stepping off the plane into a subzero blast of air did nothing to lift the sense of depression that settled into Gillian's heart. Against the imposing background of the Tetons, the wind whistling through the valley was bitter and merciless. The dark bank of clouds building up in the distance predicted even colder weather to come.

In the short walk from the plane to the terminal, she felt the sting of the cold against her exposed face. She wasn't looking forward to traveling in such frigid weather. Making her way inside the airport, she welcomed the miracle of central heat. Since neither Bryce nor she had brought along more than carry-on baggage, there was little to do but wait for a taxi to take them to Sid's Outpost, where an old friend would outfit them with snowmobiles and all the latest gossip.

They'd barely pulled out of the airport before Bryce was on the phone to Vi. It wasn't so much his conversation as the loving tone with which he conveyed the routine details that made Gillian wish she could crawl out of the back of the taxi.

"I miss you, too," he said a moment later. "I'll call as soon as we get to the ranch so you don't worry."

Gillian heard him chuckle deeply.

"Robbie said that? What did the teacher say?"

He paused for her reply and then laughed again.

"Would you mind putting him on the phone? I'd really like to talk to him."

The loving expression on Bryce's face left little doubt that he had truly bonded to the boy. Gillian's stomach roiled as she pictured the two of them together doing all the things a father and son should. All the things he would never get to do with Bonnie.

"Hey, slugger, how're you doing? Your mom tells me you've been helping her wrap presents. I'm going to do my best to get back in time for Christmas. You stay off Santa's naughty list, and I'll be home before you know it. I'm also going to try to get a couple of tickets for that Nuggets game in Denver that we've been talking about."

Bryce probably would have chatted longer had the cell service in the mountains not been so spotty. Before saying his final goodbye, he told Robbie to "take good care of your mother. It's important to look out for those you love—no matter how old you are."

Gillian bristled at the implied censure she imagined to be directed at her.

"You have no right to judge me," she said as he put his phone away. "I don't need you to make me feel any guiltier than I already do."

"Who said I was judging you?" Bryce asked.

"Right!" she intoned sarcastically. Gillian didn't buy his innocent act for an instant.

Although the heater in the taxi was on full blast, it did little but push the cold air to the back of the vehicle. There was certainly no chance of it thawing the chill building up between the two passengers who would rather look out their respective windows than risk speaking to each other again. Gillian blew on her hands and rubbed a hole in the frost-covered window. An eagle flew across her line of sight. Farther down the road a bullet hole added unnecessary punctuation to a No Hunting sign posted on a buckboard fence.

Such familiar sights brought back memories of the times she'd spent riding the range with her father. He was the one who instilled in her an abiding love of nature. As miles passed without a word being spoken, they neared the town of Kelly, a community so small it barely warranted a dot on the map.

Bryce was the first to break the silence. "When we get to the ranch, do you think we could pretend this isn't as painful as it really is—if only for your father's sake?"

"Only if you can stop trying to make me feel like such a terrible daughter every chance you get."

"That's your conscience talking, not me."

It wasn't because Gillian found that nasty dig unworthy of a reply that she clamped her mouth shut and refused to dignify it with a response. But rather because, deep down inside, she suspected he was right.

Five

Some things never changed.

Gillian counted herself lucky that Sid Meridan was one of them. His grizzled features and rough manner were as famous around these parts as the bottomless cup of coffee featured on his limited menu. A person could spend hours catching up over one of those white cups feeling right at home. An unlikely looking Good Samaritan, Sid had been a fixture in Kelly for as long as Gillian could remember. His Outpost was a restaurant, gas station, snowmobile rental and sales office and community gathering hole.

Years ago he'd sold Gillian's father one of the first Kitty Cats ever made and had taught her how to drive the child-size snowmobile. He'd also been there to pull her out of a ditch when she'd had her first car accident. At seventeen she'd swerved to avoid a moose that had lumbered out of the woods in front of her one snowy evening. Sid had placed the call to her father and had assured him that his youngest daughter was safe and sound. He'd also been a pall-bearer at her mother's funeral.

"How the hell have you been?" Sid asked, pumping their hands simultaneously.

A wide smile revealed that he'd lost yet another tooth. Soon they were exchanging pleasantries about Gillian's father, the anticipated length of their stay, snow conditions and the weather forecast, as well as the perplexing state of the world in general.

"I've got two machines serviced and ready to go for you," he told them. "John's made arrangements to pay for whatever you need in the way of clothing, helmets and boots so go ahead and pick out whatever suits your fancy."

"I hope your sisters don't take your father's gene-rosity as another sign the old man's lost his mind," Bryce said.

Gillian struggled to maintain a polite smile if only for Sid's sake. A headache had settled in behind her right eye, and the thought of airing personal business in public didn't do much to lessen it. Swallowing the acrimonious response on the tip of her tongue, she headed for the nearest rack of snowmobiling attire. While she sorted through various styles and sizes, Bryce wandered over to look at the latest sled gleaming on the showroom floor. He'd always had a weakness for fast machines whether they were cars, jet skis or snowmobiles. With all the gadgets and the creature comforts available, combined with 185 horsepower, the model that captured his attention sported an eye-popping sales tag.

"SPP included," Sid said with a knowing wink.

Bryce chuckled at the local reference to the "small penis package" designed for egomaniacs who had more money than brains.

"In the old days, this baby'd be sitting here a good long time before anybody'd be willing to pay the sticker price," Sid explained. "Now I have trouble keeping 'em in stock."

While Gillian slipped into a changing booth to try on her bibs and matching coat, Sid filled Bryce in on the monumental changes affecting the valley.

"Traditional working ranches are selling for millions and being repackaged as 'ranchettes.'"

He gave the word as much respect as the wad of chew rolling around in his mouth. "I've heard rumblings that some big-time developer's been speculating about dividing up Moon Cussers, as well."

A muscle in Bryce's jaw vibrated. "Do you think John knows anything about it?"

"Doubt it."

The name of his ex-father-in-law's ranch evoked images of pirates rather than cowboys since, in days of old, the term was associated with scoundrels living near the New England coast who deliberately hung false lights out so that captains would mistake them for beacons and run their ships aground, allowing the brigands to pillage the disabled vessels. They cursed the moon because its glow would reveal their scheme to crews of passing ships.

A curious transplant from Maine, John's great-grandfather established himself as a respected cattle baron only after getting his start in the business by rustling mavericks from other herds. He, too, was rumored to swear at the moon on nights when there were no clouds to hide his activities from law-abiding cattlemen. Of course, none of this had ever been proven beyond local lore.

After indulging in a steaming cup of coffee and a cinnamon roll so huge it spilled over the edges of their respective plates, Gillian and Bryce set out for the ranch dressed more like a couple of explorers ready to conquer the North Pole than modern-day voyagers. Eighteen miles wasn't that long a distance, but Gillian knew such a venture could easily take thirty minutes to two hours depending on conditions. Sometimes inclement weather made the trip altogether impossible.

It had been a long time since she'd been on a snowmobile, and she enjoyed the feeling of being out in the wide-open spaces again. Her sisters could barely contain their contempt for such an inconvenient mode of transportation, but she enjoyed the sense of freedom that only a snowmobile could provide. She couldn't remember the last time she'd had such a feeling of power at her fingertips.

Bryce flew past her in a blur, stirring her competitive spirit. She pulled the throttle to the handle bar and held on tight. An instant later she was arching a rainbow of snow in his direction as she shot by him. Waggling the rear end of her snowmobile, she deliberately taunted him. Out of the corner of her eye, she caught a glimpse of his machine edging up beside her.

Fat chance! she thought to herself.

Gillian veered off the groomed trail toward the archway marking the edge of her father's property. Since the ranch abutted one of the largest elk refuges in North America, only an outsider might consider it odd that the arch itself was made of interlocking antlers. Unmarred by a single human track, the snow was a pristine blanket of white. She and Bryce crisscrossed open meadows, played cat and mouse with each other and reveled in a vast playground where there was nothing to catch the wind but an open heart.

A coyote ventured out from a nearby copse of bare aspens to chase a snowshoe hare that would have been impossible to see in its winter coat had it not been moving. Gillian turned her machine to dissect their path, purposely cutting the predator off from its prey. With a startled yip the coyote scurried in the other direction as she brought her sled to a halt.

"That was for Mr. Floppers," she said, recalling a morning many years ago when she'd awakened to the sight of an eagle feasting on her pet bunny outside her bedroom window.

Gillian's chest tightened at the sight of Bryce climbing the side of the mountain with determination written on his face. He looked tiny against the distant timber line. And uncharacteristically vulnerable.

At the top of his ascent, the snow began to give way like sugar. Any amusement Gillian might feel about his need to show off for her was overshadowed by the thought of him rolling that big machine down the mountainside. She shut off her own snowmobile and removed her helmet. When Bryce pulled up next to her a little while later covered in a layer of fine powder, Gillian couldn't help but feel relief that he was still in one piece.

He took his helmet off to reveal eyes the same color as the sky overhead. They were shining with exhilaration. Gillian squinted against the waning light. Bryce looked exactly like the young man she'd fallen in love with years ago.

"You've got something in your eye," he said, pulling off a glove and reaching out to remove a fat snowflake from the tip of her eyelashes.

When he trailed his index finger down the side of her face, Gillian's corresponding shiver went far beyond anything that the cold could induce.

"We'd better get going. I don't like the looks of those clouds in the distance," she said, replacing her helmet on her head.

The ominous rumbling they heard had nothing to do with the clouds, however. Such bitter cold weather didn't breed thunderstorms in the dead of winter. Only when the windshield on Gillian's snowmobile started vibrating did she grasp the precariousness of their situation.

"Avalanche!" Bryce screamed.

Directly above them a huge cornice broke loose from the cliff face. Careening down the mountainside in what looked like slow motion, the oncoming snow-slide appeared as harmless as a snowball.

Gillian knew better. As it gained speed, that little snowball could very well bring the entire mountain down upon them in less than a couple of minutes.

"Follow me!" Bryce yelled, pointing his machine in the opposite direction and giving it everything it had.

Wrapping her hand around the throttle, Gillian leaned forward as if to urge her machine onto the frozen lake that stretched in front of them. She didn't dare look back as boulders disappeared behind her and trees snapped in two as they vanished beneath a rolling wave of snow that churned up anything that got in its way. It was all she could do to keep ahead of the thunder. The roar drowned out the warning crack of ice beneath her sled. Roosterlike tails of water fanned out behind her runners. In less than five minutes she and Bryce managed to cross the half-frozen lake, which they should have never been on in the first place.

Once safely on the other side and away from imminent danger, Bryce slid to a stop in front of her.

"Gillian!" he cried.

Dropping his helmet into the snow, he attempted to run to her. In three and a half feet of fresh powder that was no easy feat. Sinking to his chest, he crawled toward Gillian on his belly.

The thin line separating love and hate dissolved in a blur of snowy landscape and tears as Gillian pulled off her own helmet, then dropped into the snow and reached out for Bryce. Their fingertips touched, and a moment later they were holding on to each other as tightly as if fate might make yet another attempt to snatch one from the other.

"Are you okay?" Bryce asked.

His words echoed in the deafening silence and lodged in the empty place inside Gillian's heart. She could only reassure him with a nod. It would be a while before words would come.

Anticipation thrummed through her entire being as Bryce lowered his face toward hers. An instant later his lips claimed hers with a ferocity that would have been frightening under any other circumstance. She responded in kind, deepening the kiss by slipping her tongue into the warmth of a sensual mouth that remembered every inch of her body. Closing her eyes, she willingly granted him access to her very soul.

Oblivious to snowflakes falling around them, they devoured one another. A primitive sound emanating from somewhere deep in Bryce's core evoked in her a mewling response that was nearly drowned out by the hammering of her heart. Gillian filled her lungs with the all too familiar scent of his cologne, which she had never been able to forget, no matter how hard she tried.

All of the things that she'd wanted to say to him but had never been able to put into words seemed magically conveyed in the power of that single devastating kiss.

Pulling away from her, Bryce cleared his throat. "I—I don't know why I did that. Um, what do you say we get you home before anything else can go wrong?" he asked with a strained smile.

Home!

Gillian liked the sound of that word. Her residence might be hundreds of miles away, but her real home lay somewhere beyond the next hill.

The question was which one?

As much as she hated to admit that she'd become disoriented by Bryce's kiss, the truth was Gillian had no idea where they were. Any sign of the groomed trail had been completely wiped out by the avalanche, effectively and indefinitely cutting them off from the rest of the world. Even if by some miracle they managed to find their way to the ranch, being near Bryce was every bit as frightening to Gillian as the avalanche itself.

Six

The look on Gillian's face must have told Bryce everything he needed to know about her unraveling state of mind.

"Everything's going to be okay," he promised. "We just got turned around trying to outrun the avalanche. All we have to do is skirt the edge of the lake and keep on going until we make our way back to where the trail used to be. The ranch should only be a couple of miles away from there."

Gillian donned a brave smile. He was right of course. They just needed to stay together and keep their wits about them.

"I'll break a trail for you. Stay in my tracks and keep your speed up so you don't get bogged down," Bryce said.

Gillian was not affronted by the directives. If something were to happen and they became stuck in the snow, it would take an inordinate amount of energy to dig out the machines. And if, for some reason, they couldn't break free, they'd have to spend the night in the middle of nowhere waiting for help to arrive.

"Let's get out of here," Bryce barked.

A little over an hour later, they emerged from a heavily wooded area into an open meadow where Gillian recognized a couple of familiar landmarks. She began to breathe more easily. Cresting a nearby hill soon after, she caught her first glimpse of the ranch and was flooded with love for a place she was convinced was the most special in the world. Through the falling snow, it looked more like a Currier and Ives engraving than an actual home where people lived. A curl of smoke coming out of the chimney reassured her that even if the avalanche had cut off all electricity and telephone service to the house, at least her father was warm and cozy.

She wished she could say the same about herself. No matter how advanced the technology, top-of-the-line equipment and thermal clothing were still no match for prolonged exposure to the piercing cold in this part of the country. She was pretty sure that her hands, which she had wrapped around the heated handlebars, were the only parts of her body that weren't chilled to the bone. Never had Gillian seen a sweeter sight than the Moon Cussers' sign marking the entrance to an estate that had been passed down from one Baron generation to the next. Constructed of ancient logs, the original house qualified for the National Historic Register. Numerous additions over the years remained true to the integrity of the structure and only added to its value and beauty.

Parking their snowmobiles by the hitching rack out front, Gillian was too cold to pay attention to the symbolic clash of past and present. She and Bryce tarried only long enough to drape their helmets on their handlebars before heading for the front door, which swung open before they could reach it.

"I'll be damned!" said the grizzled man who stood waiting for them in the doorway. A wide smile graced his weathered features. "You made it after all. I was just about to call Search and Rescue to go looking for you."

"That might not have been such a bad idea," Bryce said as he stomped the snow off his boots.

John Baron may have shrunken a little since the last time he'd embraced his daughter, but even at a gnarled six foot one he was still a big man with the spare frame of someone who'd worked hard all his life. Gillian's greeting was muffled in his shoulder as he enveloped her in one of his famous bear hugs. He smelled of flannel, pipe tobacco, Old Spice—and home.

"Dad!"

That little word was almost too big to fit through Gillian's throat. Brushing a kiss against the stubble of his cheek, she closed her eyes against the tears welling to the surface. Just stepping through the front door made her feel like daddy's little girl all over again. Safe and sound.

She was sorry that she'd let her own insecurities keep her away for so long. "Come on in. You're letting all the warm air out," he said, ushering them inside.

Gillian watched as he shook hands with Bryce. His father's eyes reflected the sincerity of the welcome as the two renewed their unique bond with the time-honored gesture of respect. In these parts, a firm handshake was still as good as a signed contract.

"You have no idea how much it means to me that you're here," John said. "It just doesn't feel like the holidays without family around."

The comment warmed Gillian in a way that no heater ever could. Frankly she'd been a little worried as to how she might be received. The last time she'd spoken to her father on the phone, they'd fought bitterly. John Baron never bothered hiding the fact that he thought Gillian had made a terrible mistake divorcing the man he considered a son.

"What took you so long?" he wanted to know.

"That's a story that will take some time to do justice to. Do you mind if we have something hot to drink before launching into it?" Bryce asked.

John was anxious to hear all about it. While he went into the other room to fix them a hot toddy, Gillian shed her layers of cold, wet clothing in front of the roaring fireplace. Bryce dug his cell phone out of a zippered pocket and speed dialed his fiancée before he even bothered to take off his boots.

Gillian didn't want to eavesdrop, but he practically had to shout to overcome the static on the line. He walked over to the front window in the hopes of improving the reception.

"Hey, baby, it's me," he said in the breezy way of a man in love. "The good news is that we made it to the ranch all in one piece. The bad news is that it might be awhile until I can get out of here. I hate to tell you this, but there's been an avalanche and I don't know if I'll be able to get back in time for Christmas. I'm sorry."

Gillian felt like taking the phone from him and apologizing to Vi herself as an image of Robbie's disappointed face flashed before her eyes. She really did feel terrible about taking Bryce away from his new family. She couldn't help but notice how careful he was to downplay the most upsetting details about their journey to spare his fiancée any unnecessary worry—details that included a kiss that Gillian could still feel.

"I'll do everything in my power to get home as soon as I can," he promised. "I want to make sure that everything is settled here before we leave John all alone here again. It may take a couple of days before the trail is safe to travel. I wouldn't be surprised if the Forest Service doesn't come in with some dynamite to try to knock the snow loose from the peaks to prevent other avalanches like the one we outran today."

The expression on his face gave no indication that the woman at the other end of the conversation was nothing but *Saint Vi*, Gillian thought.

"I love you, too," Bryce said before disconnecting.

Gillian turned away so he couldn't see what effect those words had upon her. She'd never been the jealous type, but it was hard not to resent the happiness that Bryce had found.

By the time her father returned with three steaming mugs, she was soaking up the heat from the fire and trying to rub some warmth back into her frozen derriere. Certain that Vi would never present herself in such a ridiculous fashion, she was glad that Bryce refrained from making any jokes about her unfeminine long johns.

While he filled John in on the details of their harrowing adventures, Gillian savored her drink. Staring out the front window, she watched as big, wet snowflakes covered the world with nature's lace. In the fading light of shortening winter days, the pine trees cast long shadows across the front yard.

And across her thoughts.

Rolling her cup between her palms, Gillian wondered how she could possibly broach her concerns about her father's well-being without getting him all riled up in the process. Although he'd agreed to talk to Bryce and her about his health, there was no guarantee he wouldn't put up a fight.

"You're lucky you weren't killed," was John's assessment when Bryce had finished the story.

Taking a deep breath, Gillian saw an opportunity to plunge into territory where even angels dared to tread.

"While we're on the subject of dangerous scenarios, it worries me to think about you all alone and cut off from the world," she said. "What if something awful were to happen when nobody was here to help you?"

"Then I'd die a happier man than I would as an invalid in some old folks' home," he said unequivocally.

Ignoring the warning glance her father slanted her

way, she continued. "That won't change the fact that your family is worried sick about you."

Her father bowed his neck. "Listen here, missy. I didn't ask you to come here to fret over me. I just want you and Bryce to help me put some matters to rest. That's all. Nobody's putting me out to pasture."

Gillian didn't appreciate his scolding tone. Why should she be made out to be the bad guy just because she had the audacity to express her concerns? Having already lost so much, she couldn't bear the thought of losing her father, as well.

"And don't forget that Dustin's still around," he added with a huff, referring to the ranch foreman who lived in a smaller house nearby on the property. "He and Bette check in on me just about every day."

Gillian was on the verge of saying that every other day wasn't good enough when Bryce jumped in with a question she presumed he asked simply to change the subject.

"How are the Nickelsons doing anyway?"

Although the tension in the room eased as the conversation took a less contentious path, Gillian wasn't sure she approved. The issue of how much longer her father could continue to live on his own in such a remote location would have to be addressed sooner or later. Bryce might very well think that she was borrowing trouble too readily by bringing it up so soon, but she'd never been much for putting off the inevitable, no matter how unpleasant it might be. Including filing for divorce so soon after Bonnie's death.

"Dustin and Bette dropped off a Christmas tree just this morning," John said, pointing to a massive blue spruce propped up in a corner of the room. "It's a little more than I'm up to this year so I'm hoping you two don't mind decorating it. It looks like we'll have plenty of time to enjoy it."

It was the first time Gillian had ever heard her father acknowledge any physical limitations, and she felt bad about secretly questioning his motives in bringing the two of them back here. The scent of Christmas in the air took her back to a time when she'd loved the holidays. Since Bonnie's death, she couldn't bring herself to buy a tree let alone decorate one. She'd thought about investing in an artificial tree, a little one that wouldn't demand much from her. Certainly nothing that would require digging through boxes of ornaments for fear of stumbling on any marked "Baby's First Christmas."

She pinned a bright smile on her face and said, "Sure, Dad. That sounds like fun."

"I'll bring the decorations down from the attic tomorrow if that's where you still keep them," Bryce offered.

Trimming a tree was the least they could do for a

man who had done so much for both of them, especially if this proved to be her father's last Christmas at the ranch. Gillian recoiled at the thought. As spry as ever, he looked better than she'd expected. From the way Stella talked, though, death was practically knocking at his door.

Was it possible that her sisters had misjudged his health?

Gillian didn't even want to entertain the possibility that Bryce was right about them exaggerating his condition simply to benefit their own personal agendas. If the chili he served for dinner that night was any indication, his stomach at least was holding up as well as those of men half his age. The food was just as hot and spicy as Gillian remembered. Being home seemed to sharpen all her senses; while she wasn't sure she wanted to awaken her appetite so completely, she didn't have much choice in the matter.

Sitting across the table from her in a pair of form-fitting jeans and a dark turtleneck, Bryce looked even more handsome than she remembered. The lines of experience that once eluded his youthful face had turned him into a ruggedly good-looking man. Gillian knew that most women would line up to offer him what she had once held so dear. An idealistic romantic, she'd asked him to wait until their wedding night to consummate their vows.

And had not been disappointed by what an amazing lover he'd proven to be.

Even if the kiss they shared in the woods was borne out of the relief of surviving a near-death experience, it still had the power to rekindle a passion she'd thought had died long ago. Gillian was afraid that such longings might well stir a blaze that, left untended, would burn with an intensity that knew no bounds— and had the power to destroy everything in its path.

"It's way past my bedtime," her father said, admitting to yet another sign of advancing age.

Gillian glanced at her watch. It was barely eight o'clock. As he struggled to get out of his chair, she cringed to hear his bones creak and was surprised when he headed in the opposite direction of his bedroom.

"I converted the downstairs den into my living quarters last month," he explained, "so I don't have to deal with the stairs. They were getting to be too much for me. You two take the rooms upstairs. Bryce can have mine, and you can sleep in your old room."

Those rooms were right next to each other, and Gillian would have liked a more respectable distance between the two of them for the duration of their stay. She dismissed the temptation to blame the sleeping arrangements on a misguided attempt by a romantic old fool to force a reconciliation between her and Bryce. Clearly, if her father moved downstairs because he was having trouble navigating the stairs, Stella and Rose weren't entirely mistaken in their assessment of his failing health.

When John stumbled suddenly, Gillian felt instant repentance for ever doubting his motives. She jumped to her feet and rushed to his side.

"Let me help you," she insisted.

He accepted her assistance with uncharacteristic meekness. "Did I mention how glad I am you're here?" he asked.

Gillian nodded.

"Me, too." She was a little surprised she meant it. "I'd forgotten how much I missed home."

John smiled. There was less censure than longing in his voice when he added, "There's a lot to be missed around here if you'll just give yourself permission to remember them."

Making their way down the relatively short hallway to a separate section of the house, Gillian couldn't help worrying what would happen should something befall her father out here all alone.

"I'd die a happier man than one locked up in an old folks' home...."

Remembering the conviction in those words, she wondered if there could be a finer gift than allowing someone you love to live life on his own terms. Gillian was relieved to see that her father's quarters were just as nice as the rest of the house. She also noticed that he'd ordered a new recliner, one with a lift kit built in to help him get in and out of it.

An old friend awaited John on his bed. A graying Irish setter lifted his head off the pillow and wagged a tired tail in acknowledgment of Gillian's presence.

"Padre!" She rushed over to embrace the beloved pet that had been part of their family for the better part of two decades.

The old dog barked without getting up and licked Gillian's hand in appreciation at the affection she lavished on him.

"I can remember when he was just a pup," she said, finding it hard to believe he was still with them.

"Poor old guy's just about blind," John told her. "He's losing his teeth, too. In fact, he's not much use around here anymore. Probably not worth that expensive soft food I buy him. I know I should probably put an end to his suffering, but I just can't bring myself to do it."

His voice quivered a little as he added, "I'd like to think somebody would do the same for me when the time comes that I'm no longer good for anything."

Tears sprang to Gillian's eyes. "Don't talk like that," she scolded. "And don't worry about Padre. It's no bother taking care of those we love."

She heard the echo of what Bryce told Robbie on

the phone back in the taxi. Although she shared her father's views on quality of life, she wanted him to understand that there was a good deal more to love than sentimentality alone.

"A person, or a dog's worth for that matter, can't be measured by how productive he is or how much trouble he becomes."

Gillian understood how important it was to protect those she loved from all the practical people who coldly devalued the contributions they made over the course of a lifetime.

When her father kissed her good-night, he passed on some words of advice. "I know life dealt you an unfair hand, honey, but remember, Bryce is a good man and time really does heal all wounds."

Too tired to expend the energy to argue, she quipped, "If only it would wound all heels."

She patted his hand lovingly and was surprised at its papery texture.

"Just don't go getting your hopes up for something that's not ever going to materialize, Dad."

Gillian headed back the same way she'd come, wondering all the while how she was going to manage being confined in close quarters with the only man she'd ever loved and hated with equal measure.

When she returned to the family room, she was grateful to find a fresh log on the fire and the room empty. All she had to do now was slip into bed without disturbing Bryce.

And letting him slip uninvited into her dreams.

Seven

Bryce saw little need to stoke the fire before turning in. Just thinking about how sexy Gillian looked in those ridiculous pink long johns made him hot all over. Frustrated by his lack of willpower, he figured the smartest thing he could do was to forget about his ex's luscious body, tuck himself into bed and fall sound asleep for the next ten or twelve hours. He doubted that would prove too difficult after a day in which he'd been more successful outrunning an avalanche than his emotions.

It didn't take him long to unpack the few things he'd brought along. Since he preferred sleeping in the nude, he hadn't minded that there wasn't room to pack pajamas. Slipping between the cold sheets of John's king-size bed, he was surprised when sleep eluded him in spite of his exhaustion. He'd hoped to be blissfully unconscious before Gillian returned to rattle his world through walls that were too thin to protect him from his own wicked imagination.

Moonlight filtered through the window, illuminating one of many pictures of Virginia Baron scattered throughout the house. A woman of striking good looks, she exuded the same aura of gentleness that first attracted Bryce to her daughter. Had she lived, Bryce wondered if she could have somehow managed to do for Gillian what he himself could not: coax her out of the same grave in which they'd buried Bonnie. Bryce thought it tragic that John never found anyone to take his beloved wife's place. What a terrible waste that such a vibrant man couldn't bring himself to remarry.

Bryce supposed it was different when the love of one's life preceded a spouse in death—as opposed to having her rip your heart out while she was still very much alive. Vi may not stir his blood the way Gillian did—and still could if his reaction to her in a pair of long johns was any indication—but she loved and appreciated him as he was. She didn't expect him to be in two places at once.

Or to be perfect.

Vi was the kind of woman who put her child's welfare above her own. The kind of woman who felt secure enough about their relationship to let him go on a cockamamy holiday pilgrimage without making a big deal about it. Bryce thought she might even forgive him for the kiss he'd shared with Gillian, considering it an impulsive act of a man just happy to be alive after outrunning an avalanche. Nevertheless, he had no intention of hurting Vi by divulging that particular bit of information.

She deserved better. Staring at the ceiling in the dark, Bryce promised himself that she would get it, too. That ill-advised kiss would be his one and only indiscretion.

The sound of drawers opening and closing next door tested that newly minted vow. Hearing Gillian reacquaint herself with her old room, Bryce couldn't help but wonder what she was wearing. Was she still filling out those long johns with enticing womanly curves? Or had she found some sexy nightie hanging in her closet? Was she sleeping in the nude like him?

Long after she'd turned off the lights next door, Bryce lay awake thinking. When sleep finally settled heavily on his eyelids, it was only to torment his dreams with a demon with amethyst-colored eyes.

* * *

Bryce wasn't the only one who had trouble sleeping that night. Gillian thrashed so wildly beneath her covers that she awoke shortly after falling asleep. Bathed in sweat, she emerged from her night terrors and sat up in bed, disoriented. She was shaking all over.

"So much blood…" she mumbled, reliving the nightmare all over again.

In her dream Virginia Baron had been young, beautiful and very much alive. And very excited about throwing her youngest daughter a baby shower. Surrounded by balloons and decorations, Gillian smiled as she opened present after present. One was a beautiful receiving blanket that her mother had painstakingly made by hand. When Gillian showed it to Bryce so he could get a better look at the unicorn so intricately embroidered on its satin cover, it ripped in two. That was when Gillian knew that something was wrong with her baby. She started screaming…and screaming….

Gillian covered her mouth with a pillow. The last thing she needed was for Bryce to hear her crying and rush in to see what was the matter. Fighting the urge to seek comfort in his arms, Gillian tried to calm herself down.

"There's nothing to be afraid of. It was just a bad dream," she whispered into the dark.

"You can always have more children. Remember?"

Although Gillian had disavowed motherhood altogether after Bonnie's death, time had a way of healing the spirit and renewing old dreams. Seeing Bryce in that snapshot with Vi and Robbie had awakened in her a longing that was even stronger than her grief. She admired his willingness to take on another man's child as his own and seriously allowed herself to consider adoption for the first time. Feeling somewhat hopeful, she slid back under the covers and fell into a deep sleep untroubled by anything more than the haunting memory of a kiss exchanged in the swirl of falling snowflakes.

Gillian awakened refreshed the next morning to the smell of fresh coffee, bacon and pancakes. She could think of only one better way to start the day, but since the prospects of a long, lovely bout of love-making were nil, she gave herself over to her growling stomach with excitement. It couldn't remember the last time she'd eaten anything for breakfast other than cold cereal or some lousy fast food grabbed on the way to work. Without pausing to do her makeup, Gillian donned a pair of jeans, pulled on a sweater the color of pink carnations, and headed downstairs.

Looking more like his old self after a good night's

sleep, John Baron greeted his daughter with a fork poised halfway between his plate and his lips.

"Good morning, sleepyhead," he said.

Gillian sniffed the air appreciatively. "Morning, Daddy."

She was surprised to see Bryce standing over the stove flipping flapjacks with an expertise that he must have mastered sometime after the divorce. She didn't remember him having any proclivity for cooking while they were married. Taking her seat at the table, she said as much.

"Good morning to you, too," he said, taking umbrage at her observation.

He approached her with a stack of pancakes hot from the griddle and waved them under her nose.

"Anybody hassling the cook can always forgo breakfast altogether," he suggested.

"I'll be quiet," Gillian assured him as she stuck a fork in the top pancake and dropped it onto her plate.

A moment later, she complimented him through a mouthful of melted butter and maple syrup.

"This is good. Delicious in fact."

Sunshine poured through the window filling the kitchen with a sense of holiday cheer. A feeling of déjà vu came over Gillian as she was transported to a point in her marriage when fresh coffee, good food, small talk and fond touches were the way she normally started the day. Imbued with a rare feeling that all was well with the world, she gave herself permission to enjoy the moment without second-guessing her feelings.

Only after everyone at the table enjoyed a second helping did Bryce broach the subject of why the two of them made the trip to the ranch.

"This seems as good a time as any to discuss whatever it is you wanted to talk to us about, John."

John agreed. "I don't suppose it's any secret that Rose and Stella want me to sell the ranch and move into town, presumably in an assisted-living community or old folks' home so they'll get their inheritance."

Gillian laid her fork down and opened her mouth to argue with him, but John didn't give her the chance to mince over his choice of words.

"Which I understand is pretty sizable if rumors about the value of this property hold true. As a realtor, that's something I'd expect you to check into, Gillian."

Nodding, she let him continue without interruption.

"Your sisters and I have already had words about what they consider my 'erratic behavior,' and they didn't like what I had to say on the matter. They're under the impression that I'm some doddering old fool who can be manipulated at will. That they're in such a dither about the two of you sharing durable power of attorney for me tells me that my suspicions about their motives aren't entirely unfounded."

"To be fair, I can understand how they might perceive an outsider like me as a threat," Bryce said. "I already told Gillian I'd be more than happy to take my name off any official documents and let you and your daughters handle your own affairs without any interference from me."

Gillian was taken aback when Bryce interjected on behalf of two people she knew he despised.

"You're no outsider!" John exploded. "Don't you know I think of you as a son?"

He wasn't saying anything that Gillian didn't already know. Still, as much as she once appreciated the closeness between these two men, it was hard not to resent it now that she was divorced. Didn't her father have any faith in *her* ability to handle such matters without Bryce looking over her shoulder? Didn't he realize what an awkward position he was putting her in, pitting sibling against sibling and ex-wife against ex-husband?

Bryce was clearly moved by the disclosure, but since neither man was one to linger over sentimental feelings, John simply cleared his throat before continuing.

"I want you two to take as much time as you need to look through my books and determine the state of my mental and physical health without any outside interference from anyone. And when you're done, I have a little proposition for you."

Gillian braced herself. Sharing a leery look with Bryce, she heard an old line from a movie playing in the back of her mind.

I'm gonna make you an offer you can't refuse....

Eight

It came as no surprise to Gillian that her father was less than forthcoming about his little "proposition." An expert horse trader, the man had mastered the art of suspense long ago. John Baron wouldn't be rushed. He flatly declined to explain himself any further other than to say he'd be glad to continue the conversation when she and Bryce had all the information they needed. Then he left them alone to proceed as they saw fit.

Although naturally better with words than with numbers, Gillian was savvy enough to read a balance sheet and decipher the story inherent in the figures.

From what Stella inferred about their father's recent wild spending habits, she half expected to find the ranch hovering on the edge of bankruptcy. A thorough examination of the books reassured her that the situation wasn't nearly as dire as that.

Although her father had always been generous, in the past year her father had donated large sums to just about every charity imaginable and set up a healthy pension fund for Dustin and Bette. In addition he'd set up a renewable scholarship in his wife's name for high school graduates interested in pursuing a degree in agriculture. He'd also discovered eBay and was spending a small fortune on antique coins and collectibles. In spite of the healthy bite this all took out of his monthly living expenses, John's own needs appeared to be quite simple. Truthfully Gillian wished he would spend more of his hard-earned money on himself instead of everybody else.

After hours of scouring the books, Bryce leaned back in a red-tooled leather chair and announced, "Your sisters might not approve of what your father is doing with his expendable income, but it looks like everything is accounted for. Even taking into consideration any questionable expenses, the ranch appears to be doing well. I see no reason why it can't sustain itself for many years to come."

Gillian nodded in agreement.

"We should probably look into some of those charitable foundations," she suggested, "just to make sure they're legitimate. Maybe we can persuade him to focus his spending on those causes that have the greatest need and use their contributions most wisely."

When Bryce stood up and stretched, his tight-fitting jeans and dark turtleneck did little to hide his muscles from her feminine appraisal.

"Listen, Gill," he said, looking her straight in the eyes. "I need you to be honest with me. Are you or are you not on board with Rose and Stella's plan to sell the ranch and live off the profits?"

Although insulted by the question, Gillian did her best to respond in a level tone, knowing she hadn't given Bryce much reason to think she didn't agree with her sisters. "I just want what's best for my father."

Bryce looked at her skeptically. "It wouldn't take much to convince your father to sell out to a developer, and you'd never have to work again. You could be living the high life instead of slogging through day after dreary day of showing housing and putting up with unreasonable clients."

Gillian's eyes snapped with indignation as she leaped to her feet.

"Look, you don't have to tell me that selling this

ranch is the last thing he wants to do, but there's more to consider than just the books. I have to think about his health, too. It's all well and fine for you to stand here and accuse me of being an unfit daughter. None of this will matter to you once you're back home. I'm the one who'll be worried sick when I'm hundreds of miles away wondering whether he's fallen and broken a hip."

Unmoved by the emotional fervor her voice had taken, Bryce broke into her tirade with cold, hard logic.

"What about modern technological wonders like alert monitors?" he asked.

"They're wonderful if you live in a city," Gillian pointed out. "Are you forgetting how long it would take for help to get here even in ideal circumstances?"

"Home health care is always an option."

Gillian rolled her eyes. "Do you want to be the one who suggests that?"

A personal nurse wouldn't last more than a week with a man as fiercely independent and contrary as her father.

"What if, to save his pride, we were to call it 'house-keeping services'?" Bryce proposed. "Complete with a cook to make sure he eats right, too?"

It wasn't a bad idea. And Gillian would have given it more thought had not another modern technological wonder interrupted the discussion as Bryce reached for his cell phone. She noted how his facial expression immediately softened when he discovered Vi was the caller.

"It's good to hear your voice."

Gillian tried to make the hard lump forming in the pit of her stomach go away by telling herself that by all rights, she was indebted to this woman for letting Bryce come here at all. If she could only stop hating her for a minute, Gillian supposed she might actually like Vi under other circumstances.

"I'm fine," Bryce said. "Everything's fine, but until we get John's affairs settled and it's safe to travel, I'm just not sure how much longer I'm going to be stuck here."

Stuck here with her, he meant.

The saliva in Gillian's mouth congealed at his choice of words. Swallowing became impossible when he asked about Robbie.

The ugly truth was that Gillian felt far more threatened by that darling little boy than his mother. Seeing how Gillian had been the one to file for divorce, she knew how utterly unfair it would be to begrudge Bryce another woman's companionship. However, Robbie was an entirely different matter. The idea of him adopting a child to replace Bonnie left a steel blade protruding out of her back.

"Tell him I'll do my very best to get him to that

Nuggets game." There was only a short pause before he added, "I miss you, too."

Gillian made a beeline for the door, she didn't want to hear him tell another woman that he loved her. Besides it was hard not to resent how eager he was to return to Vi. She remembered how hard it used to be getting Bryce to take any time off from work to make time for Bonnie and her.

Having averaged over sixty hours a week at work herself over the past year, she had a better understanding now of the work ethic that had put such a strain on their marriage. It struck her as odd that Bryce hadn't so much as mentioned his business since embarking on this journey, let alone obsessing about it the way he used to. Although she couldn't quite put her finger on it, there were an awful lot of ways that he seemed different from the man she remembered. It wasn't just that he'd grown so hard toward her, either. He seemed more sure of himself, more comfortable in his own skin. Maybe it was because he'd finally made it to the top of his field that he seemed more relaxed and at peace with himself.

Safely away from his conversation with Vi, Gillian took the opportunity to call her sisters and leave messages for them letting them know that she'd arrived safely. She suspected that neither one of them would be happy to hear that she was snowed in for an indefinite length of time with their ex-brother-in-law, so she deliberately didn't mention it. Hoping to delay a confrontation with them until she had all the facts about their dad together, she made another call to the family doctor inquiring about her father's general health.

"He'll probably outlive us both," Dr. Schuler told her. "That's not to say that hiring someone to look after him isn't a good idea. And I'll run some tests for Alzheimer's if you still want me to."

Gillian thanked him before hanging up. She wondered how her sisters would feel about his prognosis or if they would insist on a second opinion.

The remainder of the day passed without a harsh word spoken between Bryce and her. Having accounted for the books, they set up conference calls with lawyers, bankers and home care agencies to try to come up with some way for John to remain at the ranch and allow those who loved him to rest easy.

When dinnertime finally rolled around, Gillian's brain was mush. Earlier Bryce had taken three big T-bones out of the freezer. While they were marinating, he scooped a path through the snow to the propane grill on the back deck. Gillian contributed to the meal by preparing a fresh salad and throwing some potatoes into the microwave. When her father finally emerged from his bedroom, he was greeted by the smell of his favorite dinner.

"It's been a long time since I've eaten so well," he said, savoring each and every bite over the clicking of his dentures.

Gillian was happy to see he had an appetite. He ate everything she put in front of him, making her wonder if he'd been eating little but what could conveniently be dumped out of a can and warmed up in a saucepan. She also noticed that his hands shook when he held out his plate for more. When he finally pushed himself away from the table, it was to announce that he was glad the books met with their approval.

"I really do want to discuss some business matters with you, but I'm feeling a little too tired and too full right now so, if you don't mind, I'll turn in early tonight and we can talk about it tomorrow."

"Sure, Dad." Gillian's head hurt from crunching numbers all day and trying to come up with a creative solution that would satisfy her sisters while still leaving her father's pride intact.

She walked him back to his room where Padre was waiting. The poor old thing was barely able to lift his head off his paws in greeting.

After safely helping her father into his recliner, Gillian took a hard look at the man who had always been her rock. Etched into John Baron's weathered face was a lifetime of hardship and love. Marred by age spots, the wrinkled hands that patted the top of

Padre's head were the same ones that had held her as an infant and provided sympathy at his granddaughter's funeral. She was suddenly flooded with love for the remarkable man who had built an empire on little more than sheer determination and hard work.

"Did I ever tell you what an amazing job you've done maintaining the ranch all these years and raising three kids all on your own after Mom died?"

Her father looked so perplexed by the compliment that Gillian regretted not having told him more often. She always assumed he knew how she felt.

"Don't you think it's time you allowed somebody else to take on the burdens of running this place?" she asked gently. "Have you given any thought at all to asking for a little help?"

"Once in a while," he admitted through a tired smile. "It's been a good life. I've been lucky to thoroughly enjoy what I do. If there's anything I regret, it's only that I don't have any grandchildren to pass my legacy on to."

Gillian knew that he didn't mean to be cruel, but those words cut like barbed wire. Didn't he know that there was nothing *she* would have liked more than to give him a grandchild? Bowing her head, she turned away to hide her pained expression.

"Night, night," she said, employing the same phrase he'd used to tuck her in at night until she'd become too old for such nonsense. The same sweet words she'd whispered to Bonnie every night for the short, precious time she'd been on the planet.

Fighting off a pervasive sense of melancholy, Gillian ambled back to the main part of the house where Bryce was engaged in a battle with a string of Christmas lights that appeared to be tangled beyond help. She'd almost forgotten that Christmas would be here in two days whether she was ready for it or not. It didn't appear as though they were going to get out of here tomorrow as originally planned. The last place she ever expected to be spending the holidays was in her girlhood home with her ex-husband, but all of a sudden that didn't sound nearly as awful as spending it all alone. Doubting there would ever be a better time to let go of any lingering animosity between them, she offered her services to the cause.

"What can I do to help?"

"You could pour me a stiff drink before I strangle myself with these lights," Bryce told her.

Gillian obliged by unearthing a bottle of fine Riesling from a full wine rack in the pantry. She poured a generous portion into two goblets and proposed a toast.

"To Christmas."

They clinked glasses and shared the taste of a

vintage year. Soon Gillian was digging a tree stand out of one of the boxes Bryce brought down from the attic earlier. Positioning it in the traditional place of honor in front of the big picture window, she helped him settle the tree inside and line it up. For her efforts she suffered the indignity of pine needles stuck in her hair. Bryce helped comb them out with his fingers.

When she felt his touch, Gillian had to remind herself to breathe. Embarrassed to be so utterly flummoxed by such a simple courtesy, she quickly gave her attention to a cluster of lights heaped in the middle of the floor. With an efficiency that made his business so successful, Bryce started unraveling one end and directed her to start the other. Some of the knots were more intricate than others, but it didn't take long for their patience to pay off. With all the arguing they'd being doing, Gillian had forgotten how well they worked together.

If only it were as simple to untangle our lives as a string of lights, she thought with a sigh.

After wrapping the tree with twinkling bulbs, they proceeded to unpack several dusty boxes of ornaments. Each evoked a special memory: some were given to Gillian as gifts, some she'd made as a child for her parents and some commemorated special events in her life. Those made of handblown glass were bona fide antiques and would fetch an impressive price at an antique shop. Those more sentimental in nature were priceless.

"Oh, no!" Gillian exclaimed, holding up a crystal snowflake that had broken in the box. A present from her mother shortly before her death, it was very dear to her.

"How could someone be so careless?" she wondered aloud.

Bryce's eyes clouded over as he seemed to consider the question on many levels. Coming to stand beside her, he explained, "Sometimes we simply forget to take care of the things most precious to us."

Gillian's defenses crumbled beneath that subtle apology. There were things she had failed to take proper care of, as well—like her husband's need to provide for his family and the baby she'd put down for a nap, never imagining the unthinkable could happen.

The damaged ornament slipped from her hand and shattered as it hit the floor.

"And sometimes," Bryce said, tipping her chin up so she was forced to look at him, "things happen that are out of our control, leaving us no choice but to accept them and move on."

The multicolored lights on the Christmas tree blurred in the reflection of Gillian's unshed tears.

"What if I can't?" she asked in a choked whisper.

Gathering her in his arms, he cradled her against

him as the emotion finally burst through the dam that had held everything back for so long.

"Go ahead and get it all out, sweetheart," Bryce urged softly.

"What's wrong with me?" she asked in between sobs. "Why can't I let go of the pain like you?"

"Maybe you're just still mad at God."

"Why shouldn't I be?" she demanded to know. "What kind of monster would take an innocent baby from her mother?"

"And her father..."

Gillian nodded. Having felt her baby's heart beat beneath her own for nine months, she tended to forget that tragedy touched both of them.

Bryce paused before attempting to answer the impossible question she'd put to him.

"I don't think God's a monster. He also gave us one another. I'm sorry that wasn't enough to get us through that terrible loss."

Gillian drew back angrily. "I don't need to hear any religious platitudes from the same man who placed the needs of his business over those of his wife and daughter."

"I did the best I could at the time," Bryce said, holding her against his heart. "You have to believe that."

Deep down, Gillian knew Bryce hurt as much as

she did and regretted her outburst. "I know," she conceded in a broken whisper. "We both did, but it wasn't good enough to save our baby."

Gillian fully expected Bryce to blame her as much as she blamed herself. However she tried spinning the events of the past, she was the one responsible for Bonnie's death. All the times she'd laid blame at Bryce's feet for not being there when she most needed him, she had really been railing at herself.

She never should have taken a nap while the baby was sleeping.

She shouldn't have panicked and wasted precious time before dialing 911.

She should have taken a course in infant CPR before ever taking Bonnie home from the hospital.

She should have found some way to keep her baby alive until help arrived.

Bryce's angry voice sliced through her guilt. "Stop looking for blame, Gill. It wasn't anybody's fault. Nobody holds you accountable—least of all me."

As he wiped the tears from her face, a sad smile played with the corners of Gillian's lips.

"How did I ever let you go?" she wanted to know.

"I didn't go willingly," he reminded her, then sighed and added philosophically, "but what's done is done. Beyond finally finding closure, there isn't much point in belaboring what's happened in the past."

When he bent down to deposit a platonic kiss on the tip of her nose, Gillian was seized by a fierceness of emotion. She lifted her head so that his lips met hers and poured her heart into a kiss that didn't just stop the world from spinning on its axis. It completely reversed its rotation.

He tasted of fine wine and pure redemption. Gillian dragged her fingers through the soft hair at his nape. She didn't know exactly what she was starting, and she didn't care. Incapable of rational thought, she had no grand scheme attached to her actions. The only thing she knew for sure was that she didn't want to face another night alone.

Nine

Gillian was no fool. She didn't expect whatever was going to happen next to alter anything between them permanently. She wasn't out to steal her man back from Vi, nor did she intend to demand any more from Bryce than he could offer. She just desperately needed him for the night.

One harmless body-and-soul-melting night.

Filling her lungs with his all too-familiar masculine scent, she felt a slow, steady tug in her belly. It reminded her how much she missed the feel of a man's skin hot against hers. Being with Bryce resurrected in Gillian the sensual being she'd thought long dead. She wanted to run her hands through the variegated strands of gold that were interspersed in his dark hair and lose herself in a bout of mindless sex.

Slipping trembling fingers beneath the weave of his shirt, she was relieved to find that her touch still could make him shiver. She was thrilled to feel his heart beating out a wild cadence against the palm of her hand.

Gillian doubted that Bryce had remained celibate since their divorce.

As she had. Although she'd dated since their divorce, Gillian hadn't met anyone for whom she'd been able to feel the same intense emotions Bryce evoked in her. Physically she wanted to be with a man, if anything to help her put Bryce behind her, but she hadn't been able to get her heart to listen to her head.

Shoving aside that thought, she told herself not to overthink her actions for once in her life. After all, this wasn't rocket science. She wanted this man. And needed him like never before.

She dismissed that "be careful playing with fire" look glittering in Bryce's eyes with a "Don't worry. I'm a big girl" look of her own. Anticipation thrummed through her entire being as she tilted her face toward his and claimed his lips an instant later with a possessiveness that belied her promise to give him up willingly later.

Gillian took her time exploring his sensual mouth, which insisted the present was the only thing worth living for. Giving herself completely over to that belief, she pressed herself against the long, hard length of his body and welcomed the responding pressure of his erection. Her pulse vibrated in her ears. Her head began to swirl. And sparks exploded behind her eyes.

It was impossible to get enough of each other.

They clung to each other beneath the twinkling Christmas lights and the watchful eyes of the angel topping the tree. Dropping her head into the safe hollow of Bryce's shoulder, Gillian felt truly at home for the first time in years.

Unfortunately that sense of security lasted only a moment before he took her firmly by both shoulders, pushed her away and put an end to any fleeting fantasy about picking up where they left off.

"I didn't cheat on you when we were married, and I'm not going to cheat on Vi when we're about to become husband and wife," he said, wiping the kiss from his lips with the back of his hand.

Blood roared in Gillian's ears and the heat of shame settled on her cheeks. She imagined Bryce was taking a good measure of enjoyment from seeing her so vulnerable and needy.

So hurt.

So utterly pathetic in light of his high-minded refusal to her no-strings-attached offer of sex.

Thoroughly humiliated, Gillian scrambled to find any words that might help put her degradation behind her. Covering her mouth with her hand, she took a step backward. Looking him in the eye was one of the hardest things she'd ever had to do.

"I'm sorry," she said. "About everything. For dragging you back into my family's problems, for embarrassing both of us just now, for being such a bad mother. But most of all for hurting you. I hope you can believe that."

Feeling his resolve chipping away, Bryce told himself that he couldn't afford to be entranced by those hypnotic eyes again, even if they were misting over with tears. Finding it impossible not to be moved by her beauty, he was amazed he'd ever found the strength to push her away at all. She was still as lovely as the day he'd taken her to his bed as an innocent bride. Only now her face was marked by a woman's rite of passage: the splendor of finding love, the transformation of a daughter into a wife and the unspeakable agony of losing an infant. It was a face no man could ever forget.

"You were a wonderful mother. This has nothing to do with that," he said gruffly, unable to stand the thought of her going through life thinking she wasn't.

Gillian gave her head a self-deprecating shake as she continued to back away.

"I certainly didn't feel like it at the time. I was so tired and cranky and out of sorts most days trying to juggle your demanding schedule with Bonnie's needs. Needs that always seemed to take priority over yours. And my own for that matter. Looking back, I'm sure I was impossible to live with. No wonder you don't want anything to do with me."

"A little hormonal maybe," he grudgingly agreed. "But not impossible."

At the time Bryce had deeply resented Gillian's lack of interest in his career, as well as her being too exhausted most nights to do little more in bed than promptly fall asleep. Looking back it was far easier to put into perspective what she must have been going through as a young mother.

"I'm sorry I wasn't more sensitive to *your* needs," Bryce said, remembering days when he was actually relieved to go to the office and leave her with the colicky baby. "Even though we were both overwhelmed and doing the best we could at the time, you'll never know how bad I felt about being out of town when…"

He was unable to finish the sentence. Images of his baby girl in her crib and his wife frantically doing everything in her power to breathe the soul back into her lifeless body left him feeling powerless. Guilt-ridden.

"I should have been there."

In light of his rejection to her advances, he was astonished when she offered him the last thing he ever expected from her. Absolution.

"It wouldn't have made any difference. It was wrong of me to blame you—it was just so much easier than blaming myself. That day, when I closed my eyes for such a short time after putting Bonnie down for a nap, it never occurred to me that that would be the last time...."

The crack in her voice matched the one that broke Bryce's heart in two. He put a finger to her lips to stop her from continuing.

"Enough," he said. "We can't go on beating ourselves up over this. Probably the only thing we should have done differently was have this conversation sooner."

They'd both been so wrapped up in their grief at the time that neither could break through the other's barriers. It wasn't long before they'd stopped talking about everything altogether.

"I know you're afraid to have more children, but there's no reason that you shouldn't," he said. "There's no evidence that SIDS is genetic. The doctors told you that you could have as many healthy, happy, beautiful children as you want to. And you should."

Gillian shook her head sadly. "I haven't had the same luck moving on with my life as you have."

"You will," Bryce told her with the same optimism that marked his business acumen.

She wished she could believe him. As good as it felt to clear the air between them and as much as she appreciated his kind words, she just couldn't see herself ever getting married again. The few dates she'd gone on after the divorce were mostly miserable setups by well-meaning friends attempting to play matchmaker. The strained conversations generated by such dates only served to convince Gillian that she wasn't ready to move on yet.

It was strange to think that she and Bryce might still be together had they only been able to talk like this before for surely it had been the lack of communication between them as much as Bonnie's death that had led to the demise of their marriage. In retrospect Gillian was sorry she hadn't taken more interest in his business when he'd been working so hard to make it a success. She wished she'd made more time for the two of them as a couple instead of focusing all her energies on the baby and being more a mother than a wife.

As much as she hated to put an end to this meaningful albeit painful exchange, Bryce had made himself perfectly clear about "saving" himself for Vi, leaving Gillian no other choice but to respect him for that. The last thing she wanted to do was ruin their temporary truce by accidentally saying the wrong thing.

Like how sorry she was for ever letting him go.

"I suppose we should call it a day," she said, moving toward the stairs.

"I'll come with you," Bryce called after her.

Still stinging from his earlier rebuke, Gillian refrained from mentioning how disappointed she was that they were sleeping in separate beds. With every step they took up those stairs, the poison of old bitterness drained from her body. It occurred to her that while she had no control over the past, how she lived the present was truly up to her. She could live each day as bitterly as Stella who had never gotten over the humiliation of her ex-husband's indiscretions. Or as lonely as Rose who was still pining for some mythical knight to come charging into her life astride a white horse. Or as a woman able to forgive herself and others for their mistakes.

She and Bryce paused at the landing to survey the scene below. A fire crackled in a hearth decorated with stockings, ornaments glittered amid shimmering Christmas lights and the smell of pine hung heavy in the air. A peaceful feeling settled over Gillian.

Standing on tiptoe, she ventured to place a chaste peck on Bryce's cheek. Marked by the stubble of a day's growth, it felt rough against her lips.

"I hope Vi knows how incredibly lucky she is," she said before turning and closing her bedroom door firmly behind her.

Ten

There was no pounding at the front door the next morning to alert anyone that the house was under assault. No sirens or alarms went off. The intruders simply opened the front door and walked in as if they owned the place.

"Surprise!" they hollered.

It wasn't long before the sound of tramping feet signaled that the invasion had come upstairs. The force with which the bedroom doors were flung open would lead one to think the Secret Service had arrived with a warrant for a deadly criminal. Gillian came to with a jerk. Standing in the doorway of her bedroom was her oldest sister Stella looking as if she had just swallowed a case of TNT.

"What are you doing here?" Gillian asked as she clamored out of bed and grabbed a robe.

The shriek down the hallway prevented Stella from answering. The two of them rushed to where Gillian's other sister Rose was cemented in the threshold of Bryce's bedroom, an expression of horror on her face. The exact same question that Gillian had just posed to Stella leaped out of her mouth.

"What are you doing in Dad's room?" she demanded of the naked man who was occupying her father's bed.

Suddenly grateful that her plan for seducing Bryce last night hadn't actually materialized, Gillian imagined their reaction to discovering her in bed with Bryce would probably register on the Richter scale.

Roused from a state of deep sleep, the man of the hour sat up, looking completely disoriented. He rubbed the exhaustion from his eyes as if to rid himself of a recurring nightmare. He then folded his hands behind his head, allowing the sheet to drop away from his torso and puddle around his waist.

"To what do I owe the honor of this intrusion?" he asked.

A blush the same shade as her name crept up Rose's neck and settled upon her plump cheeks. She looked everywhere but at Bryce's deliciously bare chest. Gillian wasn't so shy. Even on the brink of a family feud, it was impossible not to appreciate all of that masculine glory rumbling to life.

"What are you doing sleeping in here?" Stella asked.

Gillian thought Bryce made a better big, bad bear than poor Goldilocks as her sister continued pressing for answers.

"What have you done with him?"

More amused than insulted by the question, he had the audacity to chuckle. "Didn't you check the freezer before rushing up here?"

Gillian threw herself between him and her sisters when she saw the look of horror on their faces.

"He's moved into the downstairs bedroom off the den," she explained.

"I can't believe you had the gall to move poor Daddy out of his bedroom just so you could—"

Gillian hastened to interrupt before matters got any more out of hand.

"He made the decision all on his own long before we ever arrived. He says he can't handle the stairs anymore."

Although irritated at having to explain herself, she was at the same time relieved to discover she wasn't the only one in the family who hadn't been informed of her father's change in living quarters.

That simple revelation made her somehow feel less negligent as a daughter. For all her sisters' ranting about how worried they were about his welfare, they were just as clueless as she was about the daily goings-on of their father's life. Which made her question on what they were basing their assessments of his health.

"Thank God we got here before…"

Gillian wasn't a child, and Stella's dangling implication didn't sit well with her.

"Before what?"

"Before I could coerce you back into my bed," Bryce filled in, dropping all pretense of nicety. "It's hard to believe you two showed up today out of any real desire to spend Christmas Day as a family. I have a sneaking suspicion that what you're really concerned about is your own pocketbook, and that's something you'll have to take up with John, not me. So if you *ladies* would excuse me, I'd like to get dressed before continuing this conversation downstairs."

When the sisters refused to budge, he threw a bare leg out from under the covers as a prelude of what was to come, causing Rose to squeak and back out of the room as fast as she could. Stella was harder to persuade. Gathering her indignation about her like a robe, she informed Gillian, "If you have any sense of decency at all, you'll follow us!"

Although she knew Stella was right, Gillian was sorely tempted to see what Bryce was hiding under the covers. With a sigh, she smiled at him before turning and giving him his privacy.

It was hard, if not downright impossible, for Bryce not to savor the irony of the situation. He wouldn't trade the memory of the horrified expressions on the faces of his ex-sisters-in-law for anything. It was priceless. He harbored no illusion about ever convincing either Rose or Stella that he wasn't trying to orchestrate some licentious scene involving their little sister all the while trying to get his hooks into their daddy's money. He had as much hope of doing that as he had convincing Gillian that her sisters simply wanted to have their father committed so they could have free access to his fortune.

Bryce was happy that his obligation lay with John Baron instead of anyone else in the family. Considering how his own father had been so emotionally and physically distant so much of his life, Bryce supposed it was only natural that he would come to think of Gillian's dad as more than just a mentor and friend. His ex-father-in-law had been the only member of the Baron clan to support him during the terrible days when his marriage and his life were falling apart. If there was a hell on earth, surely it existed for those parents who have lost a child. Bryce would be forever in John Baron's debt for all he'd done to make the pain of that unspeakable grief a little more bearable.

He couldn't stand the thought of such a good man being mistreated by his own flesh and blood.

Recalling how Rose and Stella had taken every opportunity to imply his heavy work schedule into some kind of deliberate abandonment of Gillian and Bonnie, Bryce took his own sweet time showering and getting dressed before making his way downstairs. Angry voices—the same ones that had plagued him for years—ascended to greet him like steam rising from the depths of a devil's lair. Stepping into the kitchen, he interrupted a heated discussion with a simple question.

"How did the two of you get here? I didn't think the snow coach was running."

Not moved to civility by his attempt to be friendly, Stella snapped, "Same way you did, of course. Prehistorically."

Bryce didn't even try to suppress a grin as he glanced out the window to where two more gleaming snowmobiles were parked in the driveway. Everyone knew how much Stella and Rose despised anything to do with "roughing it." In fact, they'd both opted to attend private boarding schools as soon as they were through junior high whereas Gillian chose to finish high school in Jackson Hole proper after her mother was diagnosed with cancer. Virginia Baron passed away before her youngest daughter finished her freshman year of high school. While her sisters traveled after returning home for the funeral, Gillian remained home, helping her father through the anguish of losing his wife and assisting him with the daily operations of running the ranch. And had truly loved every minute of it. That Bryce's two prima donna ex-sisters-in-law would strap themselves on a snowmobile under such arduous conditions was proof enough of just how desperate they must be.

"Part of the trail was cleared late yesterday. It's barely passable now and the snow coaches won't be running until after Christmas," Rose explained. "The ride in was terrible. It's a wonder we made it at all."

"Which just goes to show how utterly ridiculous it is for Daddy to remain here, cut off from all civilization," Stella added with an indignant sniff.

She winced when Bryce joined them at the kitchen table after pouring himself a cup of coffee.

"Are you sure you didn't arrange for Daddy to move into the farthest corner of this house just so you could have some special time to sink your claws back into your Gillian and try to turn her against us—"

"Stop it!"

The same booming voice that had once ruled over a houseful of querulous teenage girls ended the conversation with an unquestioned air of authority. Shaking his head in disgust, John Baron stared at his contentious brood.

"Merry Christmas, Daddy!"

Stella and Rose jumped out of their chairs and rushed to envelop him in a hug. He reveled in their enthusiastic embrace before asking, "What are you two doing here? You can't be bothered to visit when the weather's good?"

If Bryce had any doubts about the old man's competence, they quickly evaporated as John proceeded to prove that he was perfectly capable of taking care of himself. Leaning back in his chair, he watched to see how Stella and Rose were going to attempt to convince the crafty, old codger that he wasn't in complete control of his faculties.

Rose responded with a hurt expression.

"We thought it would be a nice surprise to drop in on you for the holidays," Stella explained.

Harrumphing, John gave her a steely look.

"If I had wanted you two to join us here, I would have asked you. Frankly what I want to discuss with your sister and Bryce is none of your business."

"You can't possibly mean that!"

Her father's expression softened at the sight of Rose's tears.

"That's not to say that I'm not happy to have you girls all together for the holidays. I can't remember the last time we celebrated Christmas Day as a family. Actually, this probably will work out for the best after all. It's just that I wanted to run my ideas past Bryce and Gillian before involving the rest of you in my decision. And mind you, it is *my* decision."

The room grew jarringly quiet as he cleared his throat and turned to address his oldest daughters.

"Since you two are convinced that I'm incapable of remaining here on my own, and neither one of you have ever bothered to hide the fact that you want nothing to do with running this ranch, it is my intention to give it to Gillian and Bryce jointly."

Eleven

"And a Merry Christmas to you, too, Daddy!" Stella exclaimed angrily in reaction to that little bombshell.

Rose dragged the back of one arm across her puffy face and whimpered, "You can't possibly mean that."

Before Gillian could turn away in embarrassment, Stella pointed a bony finger in her face.

"You always were Daddy's little darling. I'll bet you've been planning this for years. Probably ever since you tied up with...with...that gold digger!"

She said it as if this were the worst name she could think of. Watching Stella lash out indiscriminately reminded Gillian of the time she'd accidentally disturbed a nest of rattlesnakes. She'd been shocked and scared at the time and was very careful when she retreated in case one of the snakes lashed out and bit her.

Unable to believe what she was hearing, she had to ask, "Do I need to remind you that Bryce and I are divorced? And you're the one who insisted I convince him to come here with me in the first place? Have you forgotten how strongly I objected to *that* suggestion?"

"That's right," Rose chimed in. "I warned you that it was a mistake to involve him, Stell."

"Like I had any choice in the matter," she retorted. "The codicil that Dad attached to the will makes it virtually impossible to do anything without Bryce's consent."

Reminded of their father's shocking decision in the matter, Rose decided to direct her fury at the only person in the room who appeared to be enjoying her histrionics.

"You're no longer a part of this family," she yelled at Bryce. "Truth be told, you never were."

Though a flicker of pain darkened Bryce's blue eyes, it was her father's reaction that most worried Gillian. His face was growing redder by the second, and a purple vein in his forehead throbbed threateningly. If her sisters truly were as concerned about his health as they claimed, they would deal with this situation calmly and not be pushing him to have a heart attack.

"I've had just about enough of this nonsense!" he roared. "Do I have to remind all of you that you're still in *my* house? I'm not dead yet! And I'm not about to let anybody put me in my grave until I'm good and ready to go there!"

Far from extinguishing the growing blaze of discord, his words seemed to merely throw gas on it.

"You're not being fair!" Stella yelled.

"If you think we won't fight you on this, you'd better think again," Rose added.

Gillian was glad when Bryce posed a question that put the "conversation" back on a more rational track.

"What stipulations are attached to the offer, John?"

The family stopped fighting long enough to hear the answer. Ignoring his daughters' angry expressions, John Baron took a deep breath before looking Bryce squarely in the eye.

"You and Gillian are to run the place together and let me live the rest of my days right here—on this ranch, in this house—for however long that might be."

A stunned silence fell over the room. Gillian cleared her throat uncomfortably.

"You do realize that Bryce and I are divorced and that we don't have any plans of getting back together, don't you?"

Obviously insulted by the implication that he was losing control of his faculties, her father said, "Whoever said anything about you two getting back together? All I said was that I'd like you to run the place. Living arrangements would be up to you— that's nobody else's business. Not mine. And damned sure not your sisters'."

Stella's eyes narrowed with contempt. "Is this about the need to bail out poor Bryce again? Has his business gone under? I warned you not to lend him any money the first time, Daddy, but since you wouldn't listen to me then, I don't expect you will now. I wish you'd just consider the past a valuable learning opportunity and accept that Bryce is never going to make anything of himself—with or without the backing of the Baron money."

Gillian hated that Stella couldn't let Bryce forget that he hadn't been born into the same kind of privileged circumstances they had. Both of her sisters acted as if working for a living was somehow beneath them and had always assumed that Bryce had only married her for their dad's money, which was insulting to both of them.

And as far from the truth as it could be. If anything, Bryce's insistence on building the business on his own had been a sticking point in their marriage. Over his protests, Gillian took the initiative herself and approached her father for the seed money to launch her husband's fledgling company. Bryce had been downright angry when she'd presented him with a signed blank check to finance his entrepreneurial dreams. It had taken all of her womanly finesse to coax him into accepting it as a loan.

John Baron raised a trembling hand and called for quiet. "I'll have you all know that Bryce paid back every penny of that a long time ago. That's a hell of a lot more than I can say about any money I've given anybody else in this room!"

The protests to that observation practically rattled the exposed beams overhead.

"How can you possibly turn your back on us in favor of *him?*" Stella demanded.

Having spent the better part of her marriage defending her sisters to Bryce—they were her sisters after all—Gillian was now embarrassed for them. The fact that they had stepped in to act as a mother for her early after Virginia had been diagnosed with cancer did not absolve them of such behavior. Their vitriolic reaction had her reexamining Bryce's claim that they'd deliberately worked to undermine their marriage. Although she knew that her and Bryce's problems as a couple were of their own making, looking back, she couldn't help but wonder if Rose and Stella may not have intentionally exacerbated them.

Perhaps that was part of the reason she hadn't kept in closer contact with them since the divorce. The thought of three single sisters, who were all mad at the world, hanging out together wasn't exactly Gillian's idea of a fresh start.

As Rose's and Stella's wailing increased in volume, their father took on a more conciliatory tone.

"That's not to say that I'd ever leave any of my girls out in the cold," he assured them. "Considering the financial strain it'll put on the ranch's operating expenses, a million dollars split evenly between Rose and Stella should take care of any objections that either of you might have to my proposal. Did I mention that Gill and Bryce can't sell the place until after I'm dead and gone—which I'm hoping won't be anytime soon? They can divide the ranch however they see fit when that happens, though."

The substantial sum named was enough to put a stop to his daughters' tears momentarily. Rose repeated the sum incredulously.

"A million dollars?"

Stella recovered more quickly. "Moon Cussers is worth ten times more than that!" she protested.

"Only on paper, honey," her father said, wisely shaking his head.

Having spent the last twenty-four hours poring over the ranch's books, Gillian considered that a fair assessment. Her background as a Realtor gave her a good grasp of the staggering figure mentioned.

"Making a ranch this size profitable isn't easy given changing times," she interjected. "It's only worth that extravagant amount you've got in your head if it's sold to a big-time developer. And we all know how Dad feels about that."

"Maybe we could find an environmentally-minded developer?" Rose timidly suggested.

Bryce laughed, but John's eyes took on a steely glint.

"That's my offer," he said in a tone that brooked no compromise. "Take it or leave it."

Gillian felt as if she were being pulled in two by opposing forces. She felt honor-bound to think of her father's best interests above everything else. Having never considered returning to the ranch on a permanent basis, she was surprised how strongly the idea pulled at her. Deep down a part of her did long to return to her home. She also wanted to ensure her father was well taken care of and knew that being here would make that task much easier.

Outside the wind was shaking snow off tree limbs, scattering it like diamonds. Inside, hope landed lightly on Gillian's shoulder. The thought of trying to patch things up with Bryce was tempting. Just being with him these past few days made it hard not to remember why she'd fallen in love with him in the first place.

Was it possible they could start all over again? Maybe even try to start another family?

Bryce had made a point of telling her that she'd been a wonderful mother and reminding her that there was no reason she shouldn't try to have another baby. They— What was she thinking? He'd proposed to another woman and was getting married.

Gillian stammered over the hammering of her heart, "This is too big a decision to make on the spur of the moment. Bryce and I both have our own careers and our own lives to get back to." *No matter how empty and lonely they might be....*

She watched Bryce swallow hard before taking up the cause.

"I can't tell you how much it means that you would entrust me with the ranch that you've spent your entire life building, John. That's not a decision to be made lightly."

Obviously as moved as Gillian was, he seemed to choose his next words carefully.

"But...the truth of the matter is that I'm no cowboy. I'd be completely out of my element trying to follow in your footsteps. As Gillian said, times are changing, and as much as I hate to admit it, the days of working ranches around here are numbered.

Taking that much cash out of your capital to appease your children could very well doom you to bankruptcy. If anything, instead of taking money out of the ranch, I'd recommend you pump more into it and take it in an entirely different direction."

Stella came unglued at that.

"So you not only want our inheritance but our million dollars, too!"

Gillian winced. "Apparently a million dollars is a pittance—until it threatens to disappear altogether," she said, shaking her head in disgust.

Rose appealed to her father on a purely emotional level.

"Can't you see what he's trying to do? He'll tear the entire family apart in no time at all for his own personal gain and ruin everything you've worked so hard for in the process."

"I don't need anybody's money," Bryce said contemptuously. "I'm in the process of selling that little business that you like to speak of so disparagingly. In a couple of months I'll be able to buy this ranch and ten more like it if I want to—I don't have any reason to steal your inheritance. But I'd sure like to repay your father for the faith he put in me when I needed it the most by giving him all the money he needs to run the ranch and put a halt to your cold, calculating proceedings to declare him incompetent."

Gillian thought she could almost hear her father's heart break when he heard Bryce's words. She caught him by the arm as he stumbled reaching for a chair.

"You'd really do that to me?" he asked his daughters, his voice barely audible.

"Of course not!" Rose said less than convincingly.

"H-how could you even think that?" Stella added.

Bryce hastened to assure his old friend. "As long as I have dual power of attorney, I won't allow that to happen. You have my word. And if anyone's foolish enough to try to push that through over my objections, I'll use my last dime to fight you in court."

As John Baron struggled to accept the thought of his own children's betrayal, Gillian tried wrapping her own mind around Bryce's news—he was going to be as outlandishly wealthy as he'd always promised her. And he'd done it on his own terms. Without her at his side.

Gillian couldn't help but admire him for that. In spite of the personal tragedy that had derailed their marriage, Bryce had never lost sight of his dream. She was only sorry she hadn't been there to share in his success.

"I'm proud of you," she said.

"Me, too. Damned proud," her father added.

His Adam's apple bobbed up and down as he struggled to keep his emotions under control.

"But that doesn't change my offer," John continued. "A young man as ambitious as you doesn't want to retire. What'll you do with yourself? You're not the type to be content filling your days with golf and endless travel. If you want to take this ranch in a new direction, I'd like to think I'm not so old that I can't change."

The brightness in her father's eyes told Gillian that he wanted Bryce to accept his offer not just for her sake but also for his own. The two of them shared a rare respect that existed well beyond their common interest in her.

"It's tempting," Bryce admitted. "But as Gillian pointed out, we've both got our own lives to live. I intend to relax and take a good long while off before making any decisions about what to do with the rest of my life. I've been thinking about starting up another business, one that allows a better balance between my professional and personal life. As much as I once loved your daughter and desperately wanted things to work out at one time, we could never heal our marriage when family members—" he glared at Rose and Stella "—kept tearing us apart. I've got to tell you, sir, I don't see that changing anytime soon."

Neither did Gillian. When her sisters didn't bother denying the charge, Bryce continued philosophically.

"There's a good woman waiting for me back in

Cheyenne, and I made a promise to a little boy I can't disappoint. I'm pretty sure the only thing more foolish than trying to start over with Gillian is denying myself the possibility of any future happiness with someone else."

The defeated look that settled into her father's features reminded Gillian of old Padre just waiting for someone to put him out of his misery. And made her wonder if he really hadn't intended for her and Bryce to reunite all along.

Twelve

Whether the tears stinging Gillian's eyes were from regret or resentment, she wasn't sure. Only one thing was certain—not only did Bryce not need her family's money nor want their most prized possession, the ranch, he didn't need or want *her*.

In spite of all the progress they'd made in resolving their differences, Gillian had to face the fact that he truly was over her. Having just assured everyone in the room that reconciliation wasn't in the cards, she wondered why she felt so betrayed. After all, she was the one who had initiated divorce in the first place. And she couldn't claim ignorance about Vi and her little boy being a part of Bryce's life before she had attempted to seduce him last night, either.

Gillian winced to see her father looking so defeated.

When had he gotten so old and frail? Who will watch out for him if not me?

Certainly neither Stella nor Rose. They looked so obviously relieved that Bryce wasn't interested in their father's money, Gillian couldn't help but feel ashamed of them.

Unlike her sisters, Gillian wouldn't simply tell her father whatever he wanted to hear in hopes of earning his favor. She would be there for him when he needed her—just as he'd been for her since the day she'd been born.

Lately she'd been battling a growing sense of dissatisfaction with putting in limitless hours at work just so she could avoid any kind of social life at all. Returning home was a poignant reminder of what was really important in her life, and it wasn't making a name for herself in an industry that measured people's worth by their credit rating. Nor making lots of money for some stranger to invest on her behalf because she was, quite frankly, too tired and busy to enjoy it.

A myriad of terrible images played in her head: her father falling, lying on the floor unable to reach the phone to call for help; sitting in a nursing home alone; his funeral on a cold and windy day.

Standing in the midst of her dysfunctional family and faced with the reality that Bryce wasn't about to rush to the rescue, it became suddenly clear to Gillian what had to be done.

"I'll do it," she said.

Rose looked perplexed. "Do what?"

"Move back home and help Dad take care of the ranch."

Bryce was shocked. He shook his head in disgust as Gillian's sisters halfheartedly tried to talk her out of giving up the career she'd worked so hard to establish. They were frustrated that their plans for immediately taking over their father's assets had fallen through, and Gillian's offer to take him completely out of the picture opened the door to further machinations on their part.

"Are you sure you want to do that?" Stella asked.

Bryce couldn't keep from adding his thoughts on the matter. "I suggest you think long and hard about giving up your professional life—"

"Just to sacrifice your own life for somebody who has already lived most of his," John finished, although clearly moved by the selflessness of his youngest daughter's decision. "You have no idea how much your offer means to me, but Bryce is right. That's too much to ask of one person alone."

Those words made Bryce feel suddenly small. He

hated to let down the old man. Although his immediate plans were to take a long, well-deserved rest pending the sale of his business, he couldn't deny that the thought of turning Moon Cussers into something extraordinary was intriguing.

When he looked at Gillian, he couldn't help but think of the night before. He'd never wanted to hurt her, but he could tell that she was taking his words to John hard despite the smile on her face.

"Nobody needs to feel like I'm giving up anything that I don't want to," she said. "The allure of a full-time career is fading, and this opportunity gives me a chance to do something meaningful with my life—like being where I'm needed most."

She turned to address her father specifically.

"There isn't any place I'd rather be than here with you, Dad. If you're willing to let me help you and the ranch without including Bryce in the package, I'll give notice as soon as I get back to Cheyenne and start putting things in order. But before I do, I want your assurance that you won't second-guess my decisions."

"You have my word," he promised. Tears clouded his eyes as he opened his arms to her.

Bryce had never heard the old man sob before. All at once he went from feeling pity for Gillian to feeling jealous of her. Once again he felt like an outsider looking in. His impending fortune meant little when compared to the love between Gillian and her father. He thought he would derive more satisfaction from breaking the news of his extraordinary success to the women who had helped destroy his marriage.

"This is wonderful news," Rose squeaked, rushing over to throw her arms around them both.

Bryce looked on skeptically as Stella joined in their family hug. As long as their inheritance remained intact for the time being, he doubted whether Gillian's sisters could care less about the sacrifice she was making on their behalf. After he was long gone, he supposed they would try to bully their sweet little sister into doing whatever they wanted.

He wasn't sure how successful they would be in that endeavor. Gillian wasn't the same naive little girl he'd married once upon a time nor the easy pushover Stella and Rose had manipulated in the past.

When he found it at last, Bryce's voice was rough around the edges. "I'll be leaving bright and early tomorrow, but I don't want you to think I'm abandoning you, John. I'll only be a phone call away. I'll continue to be involved in your affairs for as long as you want me to be."

Stella surprised him by assuming the unlikely role of peacemaker instead of taking exception to that remark as he would have expected.

"Now that everything's settled," she said, "what

do you say we have an old-fashioned Christmas like those we had when Mom was here? Rose and I brought along as many presents as we could pack on a snowmobile."

Rose's voice took on a nostalgic note. "A real Christmas dinner just like Mom used to make...."

"Turkey with all the trimmings," Stella continued.

"With pumpkin and pecan pie for dessert," Rose said excitedly.

"With fresh whipped cream..."

Listening to them reminisce reminded Bryce of all that had been missing from his own childhood. Accompanying his parents on a cruise now couldn't make up for all the sad holidays he'd spent as a kid, disappointed when Santa brought him socks, underwear and serviceable jeans instead of anything as extravagant as a new bike. Although he and his parents tried to get together on occasion, they would never be a real, loving family like the Barons, whose roots sunk so deeply into Red Rock Canyon that their blood was mixed into the soil for eternity. Despite his constant bickering with Stella and Rose, Bryce knew they loved Gillian and their father.

The next thing Bryce knew, he and John were being shooed out of the kitchen and into the living room with instructions to stay away while the women prepared a mouthwatering meal guaranteed to fulfill their every fantasy. Over the sounds of chitchat and laughter in the next room, the men relaxed in front of the television to watch a football game. Bryce had forgotten how much fun the Baron sisters could have when they all got together. They might be bossy, intrusive and opinionated, but they also shared a special bond that he couldn't help envying. He supposed it was only natural that Gillian's sisters felt threatened when she'd married a nobody from outside their tight circle of friends. A nobody with little more in his pockets at the time than dreams.

Dinner was a banquet that delighted all the senses at once. Since there hadn't been time to thaw and cook an entire turkey, a succulent ham decked with pineapple and drizzled with honey served as the main course. Cheesy scalloped potatoes, steamed asparagus topped with hollandaise sauce and flaky biscuits baked to a light, golden hue were presented on the floral blue china that Virginia Baron had saved for special occasions. For dessert, they had a decadent pecan pie piled high with whipped cream.

After shamelessly stuffing themselves, Gillian looked at her sisters. "I already mailed my Christmas presents to you. I hope you got them before you took off. If I'd known you were coming, I would have mailed them here instead."

Sheepishly Rose admitted to opening her gift the instant she'd received it rather than waiting for Christmas Day. "I love the cut-glass vase you sent me. It matches my pattern perfectly," she gushed.

Stella had gotten her present as well but, a stickler for tradition, she had waited to open it. She thanked Gillian in advance, then directed everyone to take a seat around the Christmas tree and presented her father with an exquisitely wrapped package. Inside was a gold Rolex.

"It's far too extravagant," John protested, confirming her assumption that it was just the kind of luxury he'd never buy for himself.

A snide remark popped into Bryce's mind about Stella using it to mark time until she tried collecting early on her inheritance again. He refrained, however, since there was no good reason to ruin the tentative truce they'd established at the holiest time of the year.

"Now I'm embarrassed to give you the flannel shirts I special ordered for you, Dad—even if you do desperately need some new ones," Gillian said, appreciatively eyeing the Rolex.

"Your coming to live here with me is the best present I could ever hope for," he assured her.

Something grabbed Bryce in the chest—hard—and refused let go of him. Until that very moment, he hadn't realized how deeply he longed to take back his old life the way Gillian was.

He drew a small nickel-plated, ivory-handled revolver out of his pocket and presented it to Gillian's father.

"I brought you something, too, John" he said. "Sorry I didn't get around to wrapping it."

The old man accepted the revolver reverently and examined it at length.

"A Colt dating back to the 1800s!" he exclaimed, reluctantly handing it back. "I'm afraid I can't accept something this expensive."

"You'll hurt my feelings if you don't," Bryce told him.

"Then thank you," he said, extending a hand in friendship. "It's the perfect piece to add to my collection."

Seeing the pride and happiness on his old friend's face was one of the best gifts Bryce could have received that Christmas.

Gillian swallowed against the emotion clogging her throat, wishing that her relationship with Bryce had been as uncomplicated as his with her father. She wished there was a way to hide the last present she had under the tree without drawing attention to the act. She didn't want her sisters reading anything more into that gift than was intended when she'd bought it as a token of appreciation for Bryce coming here with her on such short notice.

Rose got a funny look on her face as she withdrew the small, ornately wrapped package from under the tree and read the gift tag aloud. She passed it to Bryce with all the temerity of a spy handing over a package of Grade A plutonium.

He looked just as surprised. Beneath the foil wrapping was an expensive business card holder. Carved from elk antler, it boasted a brass insert upon which an image of a grizzly was etched.

"If you're going to be a bear…" Gillian said, recalling his old motto.

"You might as well be a grizzly," Bryce finished for her.

They exchanged a look that made everyone else disappear. The room grew hotter as they gazed at each other.

"I feel silly," she said. "Had I known you were selling your business, I never would have bought it," she explained feebly.

Bryce leaned in, his eyes never leaving hers. "I love it."

Those words were warmed by a gracious smile. Gillian could hear the thrum of blood rushing through her veins. Every nerve in her body was aware of the man sitting next to her.

"I'd better call Vi, wish her a happy Christmas Eve and assure her I'll do my damnedest to get home tomorrow," he said, rising to his feet and running for the safe haven of the next room.

Gillian felt torn between gratitude to the woman for loaning out her fiancée over the holidays and jealousy so ferocious it clawed at her guts. She pasted a false smile on her face only to realize that her family was either deliberately avoiding making eye contact with her, or studying her with expressions of pity.

When Bryce returned a little while later, he looked surprised to see Rose and Stella packing up their things.

"It was hard enough getting here in daylight. I hate to think about navigating the trail in the dark," Stella explained. "And I don't want to risk waiting around until another avalanche traps us here indefinitely."

Once her mind was made up, arguing with the woman was useless. So despite her father's insistence that they remain and Rose's suggestion that they at least wait until morning and leave with Bryce, they were soon saying their goodbyes. John kissed them farewell and asked them to keep in touch more often. Stella even managed a polite "Merry Christmas" to Bryce before heading to her snowmobile with all the determination of a general deploying her troops. Mumbling under her breath, Rose followed behind.

Gillian was honestly sorry to see them go. She

stood in the doorway a long time, watching their re-
treating figures cut a path through the snow. The roar
of their snowmobiles died away before her father
saw fit to close the door on the cold air that rushed
to fill the house with their absence.

Thirteen

Once they were all settled in the living room, John suggested a game of cards. They spent the next couple of hours filling the room with the sounds of good-natured ribbing that brought back childhood recollections for Gillian as crystalline as the snow that began falling softly outside.

"This is the best Christmas I can remember since your mother passed away," her father said at one point.

She agreed.

It was nice to laugh and enjoy familiar company again. To be sure, it had been too long since Gillian had asked herself what she wanted out of life—

beyond tamping down any memory that might bring back the pain she'd felt after Bonnie's death. Unfortunately, she'd also buried any memories with the power to heal the hurt, as well.

She knew Bryce thought she was crazy for giving up a successful career to return to a life she'd left so long ago. But the funny thing was she hadn't felt more certain about anything since Bonnie had died and left her so unsure about absolutely everything.

Gillian wasn't about to be dissuaded from that gut feeling by anything as mundane as logic. She'd listened to her head too much since that horrible day, and all she'd managed to do was forget how to live.

She leaned over the edge of the table to kiss her father on his roughened cheek. In spite of his deteriorating health, the hug she received in return was strong enough to crush her bones but luckily not the heart she'd so recently taken out of storage. She was still having trouble dismissing the nagging suspicion that her father had exaggerated his condition in hopes of bringing her back together with the son-in-law for whom he still cared so deeply.

Too bad it didn't work, she thought wistfully.

Returning her attention to the card game, she grinned when she noticed her hand. "Gin!" she yelled.

Slapping his cards down on the table, John glared at her.

"Do I really want somebody running this place who'd cheat her own father at cards?"

Since Bryce had flatly turned down her father's request to run his empire, Gillian wondered if he wasn't really worried about how she would manage a place of this size alone.

"I don't know. Do you?"

Her father's expression grew suddenly pensive as he gave the question some thought.

"Only if it's what you really want, Gillian. I don't want you giving up your life to move home. Taking care of an old coot like me isn't exactly the future your mother and I envisioned for our baby girl."

Gillian smiled as she attempted to explain her reasoning to everyone in the room. Including herself.

"Some of the dreams we have for our children are taken out of our hands," she said, fighting back a sense of melancholy. "And some are miraculously given back when we least expect it. I loved Bonnie fiercely, but I don't think she would have wanted me to tie myself to a stressful job and lock myself away in an empty apartment. Yes, I admit I was hesitant to come home, but it's been the smartest decision I've made since she passed. It's made me remember how important it is to hold on to the people we love for as long as we can."

Looking at Bryce through a sheen of tears, Gillian

wished she could make him understand how sorry she was about the part she'd played in everything that had gone wrong between them.

Her explanation seemed to satisfy her father, if not her ex-husband. "It's good to know that somebody loves me for more than money alone," he said.

Dropping her gaze, Gillian found she couldn't look her father in the eye. She felt terrible for the way her sisters had acted and hoped that, in time, she could help her family heal.

Turning to Bryce, he added, "The richer you become, you'll find the more that will mean to you."

That said, he excused himself from the game and shuffled down to his room, using the wall for leverage the entire way.

In the distance, the lonely refrain of a coyote's song echoed off the cliffs surrounding the ranch on three sides. The sound caused an unexpected sense of panic to well up in Bryce's chest at the thought of leaving Gillian and her father all alone to fend for themselves. Not the type given to "analysis paralysis," he rose impatiently to his feet, wishing there were some easy way to put his worries behind him.

"I'll be leaving first thing tomorrow morning. With your father's affairs in order and your mind made up about taking over the responsibility of the ranch, there's really no reason for me to hang around any longer."

"There's no hurry," Gillian said.

"There is if I want to make it back by midnight Christmas Day and I told Robbie that I'd take him to a ball game in Denver. I don't intend to break another promise to someone I love for as long as I live."

He was thinking about his promise to always be there for Gillian, the one he'd broken the day his baby had died and Gillian had been so alone she'd nearly gone out of her mind waiting for him to arrive.

Bryce pushed aside those heavy memories to focus on something more affirming. "Before I go, I have something for you, too."

"You didn't have to do that," Gillian protested.

She followed meekly as he led the way into the other room and sat her down in front of the Christmas tree. The look on her pretty face as she watched him rustling around in the tree's branches made Bryce glad that he had acted on impulse. With a flourish, he extracted a tiny envelope with her name neatly written on it. He shook off a couple of strands of tinsel that were clinging to his sweater before handing it to her. Inside she found a gilt business card with the name Carl Hartman embossed upon it. He was one of her favorite artists, a local who had made quite a name for himself on the prestigious Jackson

Hole art scene. The commission on one of his paintings alone was often as much as Gillian made selling a house in Cheyenne.

"Before our flight, I sent Carl a copy of the photograph of Bonnie in my bedroom and asked him to duplicate it in oil for you. He'll have it done in a couple of months."

His voice suddenly broke as he took her hand in his. "It's dedicated to all that we once shared, not everything we lost."

Seeing her dab at her eyes with the back of her hand, he could barely refrain from wrapping his arms around her. Seized by emotions beyond his control, he felt his heart trip over the possibility that they could finally let the past go and embrace it at the same time.

"You have no idea how much this means to me," Gillian said, truly touched by Bryce's thoughtful gift.

Not so long ago she questioned whether she could live with such a poignant image openly displayed in her home for fear that the memories evoked would incapacitate her. Today a ray of sunshine pierced the shroud of darkness that had been holding her hostage for so very long. She'd come full circle returning home and she was now able to let go of past hurts and wanted to share her newfound sense of redemption with the man she'd lashed out at during a time when they should have been offering each other comfort.

"I-it was wrong of me to blame you for not being there when Bonnie…"

Swallowing hard, Gillian steadied herself by laying a hand on Bryce's chest. The beat of his heart against her palm stirred old emotions.

"No one can predict SIDS," she said, quoting from the stacks of materials she'd waded through after the tragic turn of events that changed their lives. "You couldn't have possibly known what was going to happen any more than I could. No one could. Otherwise you would have been there. I know that nothing could have kept you away. I hope you can forgive me for ever insinuating otherwise."

Bryce sucked a breath into his lungs, breaking the silence that followed her apology.

"That you can ask *me* to forgive *you*…" His voice cracked like icicles driven into frozen ground by the force of their own weight. "I'm the one who desperately needs you to forgive me."

Gillian tilted her face toward the twinkling Christmas lights and blinked back the tears welling to the surface. Raw with need, she let him take her into his arms. Lust finally sheared away the last of his restraint as he muttered an unintelligible oath and claimed her mouth.

Hot, wild and wet, his kisses awakened a feral response in Gillian. Linking her arms around his neck, she offered herself to him as the final present under the tree. Although she could not hope to have him for more than one night, she silently vowed that if he would just give her one more chance, she would somehow find the courage to make her days worth-while, if not truly enchanted by a more lasting love, when he was gone.

Even if it meant sustaining herself on memories alone.

Seeing herself reflected in his eyes, which were blazing with desire, Gillian never felt more beauti-ful. She reveled in the warmth of his skin against her hands as she drew his sweater slowly over his head. A moment later she was resting her head against the wide expanse of his bare chest. Passion sizzled as they surrendered to their desires.

"Gillian," he murmured into her hair.

The huskiness of Bryce's voice was both rough and tender. She tore her jersey over her head, then stood still in the glowing light of the fireplace and allowed him to admire her breasts as she reached behind her back and divested herself of the scrap of lace that restrained them.

They discarded the rest of their clothes in a frenzy without regard to where they fell. Their urgency to be together defied the logic that compelled Bryce to take a condom from his wallet. Considering that they'd been unable to conceive a child for months after Bonnie's death, Gillian thought it a waste of time. He gave her no chance to voice any objections, though, and a moment later she was begging him to take her.

Drawing her to her knees on the carpet, he asked in a strangled voice, "Are you sure about this?"

Gillian didn't have the courage to ask him the same question.

"I want you in me now," she said instead.

That throaty command rendered foreplay unnecessary. Gillian pushed him onto his back, climbed on top of him and, without stopping to consider his impressive size, braced herself by clutching his shoulders and claiming him all at once.

Groaning, Bryce took her by the hips and guided her movements in a way that maximized his pleasure while simultaneously intensifying hers.

Throwing her head back, she gasped as their bodies, their souls became one. Gillian moaned. Called out Bryce's name. And said a little prayer to commit every loving detail of this night to memory.

Tangling his hands in her hair, Bryce drew her down to him and kissed her. Those slow, measured kisses matched the rhythm of his driving force. When she made the slightest move to change position, he merely tightened his grip.

"I'll let you go when I'm good and ready," he

growled, keeping the hot, delicious slickness of his mouth centered on hers.

He disentangled his fingers from her hair and focused on caressing the silky-smooth length of her body. Tenderly he dawdled over the small of her back before moving onto her rib cage and stopping to explore the swell of her breasts pressed against his chest. Gillian whimpered into the hollow of his collarbone.

Bryce would have none of it.

"I want you to look at the man who's making love to you," he commanded, thrusting into her with ragged, shuddering breaths.

Gillian did as she was told. Digging her fingernails into his shoulders, a moment later she crested on an orgasm that took her out of her body. Multicolored lights exploded behind her eyes as Bryce joined her someplace suspended between heaven and earth.

His whole body shuddered as he poured himself into her. Cherishing the beat of his heart beneath her own, Gillian held him tightly to keep him exactly where she wanted for as long as she wanted.

Chests heaving, they clung to each other beneath the glimmering Christmas lights and the watchful eyes of the angel standing guard atop the tree. Their tangled limbs and a blazing fire kept the cold away until they could no longer ignore that either a blanket or a change of rooms was necessary.

"Want to take a shower with me?" Bryce asked, rubbing away the shivers rising along her bare arms.

Having already enjoyed her sin so completely, Gillian saw no point in forgoing the pleasures of the flesh before the morning sun dictated that she had to. Surely there would be time for regrets and recriminations later.

She held out her hands. "Help me up."

Bryce pulled her to her feet as if she were made of nothing more than fluff. Together, they padded up the stairs naked to the master bathroom where he turned on the water and adjusted it to the right temperature before they both stepped inside.

Parts of Gillian that were sore from their lovemaking welcomed the gentle massage of water. Dizzy from the aftereffects, she leaned against Bryce's strong, hard body and willed the warm water to wash away her guilt.

Was there anything worse than discovering that she was still in love with the man she'd divorced?

Perhaps only the terrible knowledge that he no longer felt the same way about her.

Refusing to belabor that which she could not change, Gillian proceeded to soap Bryce's back with great tenderness. She rubbed shampoo into his hair and massaged his head gently with her fingernails, making him so content he was almost purring.

"Turnabout's fair play," he said, intent on returning the favor.

He proceeded to soap her breasts, sore from the demanding caresses they'd received earlier, only to inflict more sweet abuse upon them with his mouth, suckling her beneath the warm, running water. Gillian pressed her back against the wall, making no move to escape when he followed the brazen act by dropping to his knees in front of her. She gave in to more than just the guttural sounds welling up inside her and opened herself to everything he had to offer. The delicious pressure of his tongue made her explode into a million flickering fragments of light.

They had to have been in the shower a long time for the hot water heater gave out. Shutting off the tepid stream, Bryce helped Gillian out of the stall and offered to dry her off with a big, white fluffy towel.

"I can barely stand up," she admitted, grateful that he had the strength to carry her down the hall to his bedroom.

They spent the rest of the night in a sturdy hand-carved bed, wrapped in nothing more than clean sheets and each other's loving arms. Tomorrow Gillian knew that life would fall back into place as if nothing more than civil words had passed between them. But knowing she had a lifetime left to rue the past, she chose to enjoy this one magical night.

Sex with Bryce had always been wonderful, but by the end of their marriage, they'd deliberately turned their backs on each other in the bed they'd shared, unable to reach out to the other. After tonight Gillian didn't know how she could ever go back to sleeping alone.

Smiling past her tears, she was rewarded with an encore of kisses and caresses that resurrected something inside her that felt too much like hope.

Fourteen

"I could never stop loving you, no matter how hard I tried," Gillian whispered in the dark.

The words rocketed into Bryce's brain like a heat-seeking missile, destroying any preconceptions he might have had about the night being a farewell to the past before they finally went their own separate ways once and for all.

He couldn't quite wrap his mind around the possibility that Gillian still loved him.

Had never actually stopped loving him.

Moved by the raw emotion shimmering in her soft

violet eyes, his whole being cried out with the realization that he loved her, too.

But he could never admit it.

Studying her silhouette in the moonlight, he was certain that there wasn't a single molecule in her body that he didn't cherish. Awake or asleep Gillian was the most beautiful woman he'd ever known. That didn't mean there could ever be anything between them again, though. After the way their marriage had crumbled, he couldn't see how something permanent could be built out of the rubble.

One maddening little phrase kept repeating itself over and over in his head. *Too little, too late.*

In the silence following Gillian's sex-induced admission, Bryce heard her stop breathing. Reaching over to place his hand over her heart, he found her skin still damp from their lovemaking.

She directed her gaze to the base of his throat. "I'm so sorry I hurt you," she mumbled. "So damned sorry."

In response to the shudder that ran the length of her body, Bryce wrapped his arms tightly around her. He couldn't let her go like this, racing for the safety of her own bed, leaving him to suffer in the silence of what he could not bring himself to say.

"I'm also sorry for what I just told you," she added in a hoarse whisper. "Given where you are in your life right now, it was wrong of me."

Bryce could love her no less for gathering her pride about her like the sheet she drew over her breasts.

"No, you probably shouldn't have," he conceded. "Any more than I should have ever made love to you. For God's sake, Gillian, I'm *engaged* to another woman! Someone who put her trust in me when I promised that there was nothing left between you and me."

"Vi doesn't have to know." Her voice was flat.

For the second time in less than five minutes, Bryce couldn't believe his ears.

"Is that how little you think of me?" he demanded, letting her go roughly. "Do you really think I could marry another woman with a lie of that magnitude hanging over my head? We made a mistake, Gillian. You know that as well as I do, and Vi needs to know."

"The truth isn't going to absolve you, and it won't do anything but hurt her, either," Gillian said evenly in response to his rising voice. "Maybe it wasn't right, but we were two lonely people who hurt each other in the past and somehow managed to put that hurt behind them for a single night. That isn't the worst thing that could ever happen."

Bryce raked his fingers through his hair in exasperation. He wasn't proud of what he'd done and couldn't imagine living with the ugly lie for the rest of his life. But that wasn't to say that Gillian might not be right about there being no need to hurt Vi just to assuage his sense of guilt, either.

Gentle fingers stroked the lines of his jaw darkened by a day's growth of stubble. "If we ever hope to find happiness again, we have to forgive each other for being human," Gillian said soothingly.

Her unexpected kindness made Bryce feel worse than had she hurled hateful accusations in his face. Or threatened to tell Vi herself. At the same time, he knew he couldn't hide this from Vi. He already had one failed marriage; he didn't need to add another one to the list.

"That's easy for you to say," he said. "You aren't the one who betrayed your fiancée. You're not the one who has to face a little boy who's already started calling you Daddy."

Gillian couldn't bear to hear another word. She understood how a man's pride could get in the way of his heart, but when she was lying naked in bed with him, the last thing she wanted to hear about was another woman.

Or her darling, healthy child.

Considering their history, Gillian shouldn't have been so surprised to have Bryce take a great big bite out of her heart before offering it back to her on the silver platter she'd polished to a sheen with the last shreds of her pride. She couldn't believe she'd been so stupid as to expose her vulnerabilities to the very man she'd been doing her best to forget. She'd been a fool for thinking he could ever feel anything more for her than pure and simple lust.

Gillian rolled to the side of the bed and sat up, protectively wrapping her arms around herself.

"You're right. I don't have to face anyone but myself in the mirror. Unlike you, I haven't found anyone who's even come close to replacing the void in my life. The best I can do right now is cling to my family. So if you're looking for me to apologize for seducing you tonight, you might as well forget it!"

The hard note in her voice was intended to bring the conversation to a close, but Bryce snaked an arm around her waist and tried pulling her back into the warmth of his bed.

"It isn't exactly fair to say that you seduced me," he admitted.

That Gillian was unsuccessful in pulling away from his embrace wasn't from lack of trying. Both were panting hard by the time Bryce pinned her down with his superior strength. She groaned in protest when, in spite of her anger, desire once again flared in the pit of her belly.

"Would you stop fighting me for a minute and listen to what I have to say?"

At the moment, Gillian would have agreed to

anything just so long as he let her go. Forcing herself to lie still, she grudgingly consented to hear him out.

"I'd have to be blind not to notice how uncomfortable you get whenever the subject of Robbie comes up. I want you to know that I wasn't drawn to Vi just because I wanted to be a father to her little boy. Surely you know that nobody will ever replace Bonnie in my life. Nobody."

He repeated the word with such conviction that it was hard for her to doubt the depth of his sincerity. Gillian felt herself relax slightly in his arms.

"Just like nobody is ever going to be able to replace what we once had together. But as tempting as it might be to give our relationship another try, I just don't see us going down that path again. After all, what's really changed to make things turn out any different this time?"

Me! she longed to tell him. *I've changed. And I'd do anything to get you back.*

Pride warned her to remain quiet however. Indiscriminately throwing words like those around would just reopen wounds that were only now beginning to heal.

"Your sisters still don't trust me," Bryce reminded her. "Just the thought of us being alone sent them racing to our doorstep at the speed of light. I don't ever see an end to their meddling."

Neither did Gillian, but having grown up a whole lot over the past couple of years, she knew things would be different when it came to Bryce. Never again would she seek outside advice in matters of the heart.

"Whatever they might have told you," Bryce continued earnestly, "it's important that you know I don't think you any less a woman just because we didn't conceive another child together."

He released his grip on her but kept her pinned with a soul-searching gaze.

"Looking back, I think we both just tried too hard after we lost Bonnie. It all became so clinical. In bed. In our marriage. In what we allowed ourselves to say—and not to say—to each other."

Gillian lay perfectly still. If only they had somehow found the courage to have this conversation years ago, there was a good possibility they would still be married today.

"Sweetheart," Bryce said, seemingly oblivious to how that simple endearment moved her. "I can't stand the thought of you living the rest of your life under the assumption that God is punishing you for something either of us did or didn't do. I know it's hard to understand, but sometimes bad things happen to good people for no reason."

The back of Gillian's eyelids stung as she blinked back tears. Logically, it was easy enough to accept that she might never have children again and that that didn't mean she was somehow defective. Emotionally, however, that truth was harder to believe whenever somebody posed a thoughtless question about why she didn't just have another child to replace the one they'd lost. As if it was as easy as going to the pound to pick out a puppy after burying the family pet.

"I want you to know that I would gladly give up every minute spent building my career to buy back time with our precious little girl. I would toss away every cent I have for a second chance just to make things right between us."

"Shh…" she whispered, putting a finger to his lips, which were swollen from kissing her, and trying to stop the words pouring forth from the depth of his soul. They were solace to her wounded spirit, and she would carry those sweet words to her grave.

Gillian could no longer deny that Bryce was the one thing she wanted more than anything else in this world. More than house or home or security or even another child—although that longing would surely remain with her till the end of her days.

Although she knew better than to give herself over to wishful thinking, she decided that tomorrow was soon enough to face reality. Tonight she intended to rewrite destiny—if only in her mind.

Torn between desperately wanting this man and needing to let him go graciously, Gillian spent the rest of the evening committing to memory every loving detail of a night that would have to last her a lifetime: his musky, masculine scent; the salty taste of his skin; the ripple of muscles beneath her fingers; the curve of his lips brushing against her own; the texture of his hair; and the rise and fall of each and every breath he took.

At dawn when Gillian woke to the muted sound of Bryce's conversation with Vi on the phone in the next room, she was not at all surprised that it was followed shortly thereafter by the roar of a snowmobile pulling out of the driveway and heading in the direction of the distant horizon.

Fifteen

Since the ground was too hard to dig a grave by hand, Dusty used a backhoe to turn over a little piece of earth in the aspen grove behind the house. He looked relieved when Gillian thanked him for all his help and told him that she would take care of the rest herself.

"It's the least I can do for such a devoted companion," she explained.

Tamping down the last shovelful of dirt, she said her goodbyes to the one friend who'd never failed to protect her without thought to his own safety or to offer his love unconditionally. Claiming he could no longer bear the cold weather, her father shed his tears in private and watched out the window as his daughter got down on her knees in the snow to say a prayer that everyone she loved might someday go to heaven as easily as Padre had drifted away in his sleep.

Although she hadn't cried since Bryce had taken off without a backward glance, it was hard fighting back the sniffles on such a sad occasion. Nearby the river gurgled beneath layers of frozen ice, hinting of the spring thaw that was sure to come, although no one could predict exactly when. Thoughts of green shoots lying dormant under the snowpack renewed in her a sense of hope that had disappeared Christmas morning on the back of a snowmobile. If the world could miraculously manage to rebirth itself every year, Gillian liked to think that it wasn't altogether inconceivable to imagine the human spirit doing likewise.

To that end, she imagined Vi had forgiven Bryce for his little "indiscretion" on one condition—that he promise never speak to his ex-wife ever again.

It was not an altogether unreasonable request.

Still, thoughts of the happy couple all cozied up on a couch with Robbie playing happily at their feet were enough to make Gillian physically sick to her stomach. And unwelcome images of them in bed together kept coming between her and a good night's sleep. It was little wonder she felt so tired all the time. Or that she'd skipped a period.

It was easy enough to blame her fatigue and nausea on the pressure of quitting her job, packing up her things and moving back home all within such a short time frame. Not to mention the incredible amount of work involved in running a ranch the size of this one, especially when she was in the midst of taking it in an entirely different direction. One that included getting more help for Dusty and hiring an on-site caretaker to see to her father's daily needs so that she could attend to more pressing matters, such as laying the groundwork for Moon Cussers to become a premier destination spot for some of the finest trout fishing and hunting in the nation.

However, the following month, when she fainted in the barn and came to with hay sticking out of her hair, Gillian could no longer dismiss the sudden changes to her health as merely stress-related. She'd already dismissed the possibility of pregnancy. Since she'd been unable to conceive when she and Bryce had tried so hard to make a baby, it seemed highly improbable he would impregnate her when he'd used a condom.

Worried that some other medical cause was the root of her problems, Gillian was glad that she'd carried her insurance from work forward until her private coverage kicked in. She wondered if her sisters would appreciate the irony of her falling ill so soon after volunteering to nurse their father back to full health.

Picking herself up off the barn floor, she dusted herself off, thinking there was little reason to share her concerns with anyone else until she'd given a doctor a chance to run some tests.

Stepping out from under the shade of the barn, she paused, scarcely able to remember a time when the aspen trees had budded so soon. She hoped a wet snow didn't bend their supple limbs to the breaking point. If they showed but a little of her father's resiliency, they would probably be just fine. The instant she'd moved back home and assumed the burden of running the ranch, he seemed to shrug the years off his rounded shoulders.

Beneath a blue sky that had no beginning or end, Gillian suddenly was filled with an inexplicable sense that her own little girl might be sending a gift from beyond. Hopefully it was one that would make Gillian remember that miracles could happen and that she would have her own soon.

A little less than a week later, Gillian prepared for whatever the doctor had to tell her. Dr. Schuler greeted her with a great big smile as he stepped through the door.

"Happy news for Valentine's Day," he announced jovially. "You're going to have a baby."

Those words bounced off the office walls and reverberated through the decorative string of shiny red hearts taped to the front of his desk.

"I'm afraid that you've got your holidays mixed up," she said, giving her old family friend a look that let him know she didn't find his odd sense of humor a bit funny. "April Fools' Day is in two months."

His responding laughter did little to dispel her incredulity as he pulled out a pad and began writing prescriptions for prenatal care vitamins and supplements.

Still in shock, she wondered whether Bryce even realized the condom they'd used had been faulty. She doubted it. Likely he would be just as bowled over by the news of her pregnancy as she was. Nonetheless, Gillian didn't want to tell him the news until she was comfortable with it herself. What point was there in throwing everybody into a dither until the critical third month had passed and the threat of a miscarriage was greatly reduced anyway?

Bryce needed some crazy, pregnant woman hanging on to him like he needed a rock tied around his neck. Especially when the rock was his ex-wife. Besides, he was already committed to marrying someone else.

Gillian had no desire to bind him to her through a misplaced sense of duty or guilt, but knowing how passionate he felt about his own father's lackadaisical style of parenting, she doubted Bryce would ever willingly opt for absentee fathering himself. And that would jeopardize the wonderful life he was building with Vi and Robbie, neither of whom should be punished for her poor judgment.

If her father suspected anything out of the ordinary as the days passed, he kept it to himself. He'd been treading lightly around his daughter ever since, in a hormone-induced fit, she'd accused him of master-minding the entire drama at Christmas to get her back together with Bryce.

He didn't deny it.

And, much to her surprise, Gillian discovered that she was no longer able to hold it against him.

Later that month, Gillian found herself back in the kitchen mixing up yet another pan of brownies. Putting a hand to her back, she stretched with the languid luxury of a cat looking for a sunny spot to take a little nap. Lately she just couldn't get her fill of chocolate. Or sauerkraut. Or the view of the Tetons out the window. Or the funny feeling that crept up on her and left a goofy smile on her face at odd times throughout the day.

In spite of the latest curveball she'd been thrown, Gillian was so much happier than she'd been just a year ago. Make no mistake about it—life was no-where near as perfect it had been once upon a time before heartbreak turned it upside down, but it was immeasurably better than those horrendous days following her divorce.

Understandably it was even harder for her to let go of Bryce now than before. She hadn't realized how often he would slip uninvited into her thoughts. A pair of geese waddling down a frozen riverbank made her long for her own wandering gander. The sound of an elk bugling in the timber made her wish she had someone to share a similar revered courtship ritual. Stars on a cloudless night brought *his* eyes to mind. And just then, the sound of the front doorbell sent her imagination into overdrive with silly images of a blond Adonis waiting for her on the porch holding out a bouquet of roses and a great big diamond—

"Would you mind getting that?" her father called from the bathroom.

Slipping the pan into the oven, Gillian gave the timer a cursory glance before padding into the living room. She wiped her hands on her apron before throwing open the front door. The reality of finding Bryce standing on the front porch was very different than she'd imagined it.

He didn't have any roses.

And he wasn't smiling.

High altitude had nothing to do with how difficult

it was forcing air into her lungs. Singed by a smoldering gaze, Gillian realized that loving this man at
a distance was far safer than facing him up close and
personal. The floor swayed beneath her feet. Grab-
bing the nearest wall to steady herself, she swallowed hard and summoned all of her lost composure.

Her hand self-consciously went to her hair. Since her
new life didn't include a routine list of dates and the
livestock paid no mind to her appearance, she'd adopted
a simple look since moving back home. Her chic hairdo
was growing out, and she'd barely bothered to put on
a smidgen of lipstick and mascara earlier in the day.

Once Gillian managed to get her heart to start
beating again, she stammered, "What are you
doing here?"

"We need to talk."

Nodding mutely, she gestured for him to come
inside, then hid her shaking hands in the deep pockets
of her apron. She could think of no reason he would
be here giving her such a hard, searching look
unless…unless…

*Unless her father was up to his old tricks, and he'd
told Bryce that she was pregnant!*

But that was impossible. How could that cagey old
man have possibly guessed the truth? Had her insatiable
cravings tipped him off? Her need for a nap every day?
Or was it simple wishful thinking on his part?

In the time it took Bryce to divest himself of his heavy coat and take a seat on the couch, Gillian had worked herself into a terrible state wondering whether her father had somehow conned the information out of their longtime family physician. Whatever his suspicions, he had no right to meddle in her affairs.

Had he not chosen to lock himself in the bathroom, Gillian probably would have questioned him in front of a hostile eye witness.

"What do you want?" she asked, not bothering to sit down herself.

Bryce hadn't so much as cracked a smile since he'd arrived. His voice was as rough as his gaze was direct.

"I told Vi everything," he said.

Gillian's world skidded to a halt as she stood gaping at him in total disbelief. "Why in God's name would you do that?"

"Because it was the right thing to do, and you know it."

Her mind raced out of control as she imagined the worst-case scenarios coming from such an ill-advised confession.

"What did she say?"

"She was deeply hurt naturally. And she wanted to know if I still loved you."

It was the same question Gillian had been asking

herself ever since he'd driven away with her heart weeks ago. It was all she could do to refrain from demanding an answer herself.

"That's why I'm here," he explained evenly. "Because I couldn't look Vi in the eye and tell her that I'm *not* still in love with you. I'm here because since I left, nothing's been right. I'm more success- ful than I ever dreamed possible. I have more money than I can spend. And I'm miserable. I'm here because I want you to marry me."

When he finally smiled, Gillian blinked slowly as her heart performed a series of crazy acrobatic feats that would have left a cardiac surgeon shaking his head. Her knees failed her, and she sank down next to him on the couch.

The only thing stopping her from smothering him with kisses when he gathered her into his arms and crushed her to his chest was the terrible thought that his proposal might be motivated by news of her preg- nancy and not a genuine desire to marry her for herself.

Gillian couldn't answer him unless she knew the truth. No matter how painful it might be.

"Does this have anything to do with my father spilling the beans?" she demanded. Righteous in- dignation held her chin up and kept the waver out of her voice.

"Why? Has something happened to John? Or is

there some problem with the ranch?" Bryce looked so genuinely worried that her fury lost some, though not all, of its storm.

"I'm not some pathetic charity case in need of pity, and I'd appreciate you telling that to my father and the ever-understanding Vi, too, for that matter."

Bryce held up both hands in surrender as his concern turned to confusion.

"I haven't spoken to John since I left here. And, just for the record, Vi wasn't all that understanding. But she's not the kind of woman who'd marry a man just to give her son a father. Especially not when he's in love with someone else."

If ever sweeter words were uttered, Gillian had yet to hear them. He didn't know about the baby, and he wasn't asking her to marry him out of some misplaced sense of obligation.

That wonderful revelation posed another quandary, though. How was she going to break the news to Bryce that he was going to be a father? How would he react to her keeping that a secret from him?

"What does John have to do with my being here anyway?" Bryce asked, looking at her directly.

"Nothing," she began when the timer went off in the kitchen. Grateful for any excuse to gather her wits about her, Gillian jumped to her feet.

"My brownies!" she said by way of explanation.

Not so easily distracted, Bryce pulled her back into the seat beside him. "Whatever you have in the oven can wait."

Gillian closed her eyes against the sunshine filtering into the room through the lace curtains. She hoped her omission wouldn't make him reconsider wanting to put a ring upon her finger. Things were definitely more complicated than that long ago day when she'd come home bursting with news that she was pregnant with Bonnie.

"We're going to have a baby," she blurted out in a raspy voice.

Bryce's stunned reaction confirmed that this was the first he'd heard about it. The temperature in the room dropped several degrees by the time he found his voice.

"Were you ever going to tell me?" he asked.

Gillian nodded her head. "After the third month. Or after you married Vi. Whichever came first."

Bryce's hoarse laugh was without humor.

Gillian reached out to cup his face with trembling fingers and did her best to explain herself.

"I didn't want to force you into a relationship if you wanted to be with someone else. I didn't want you to feel honor bound to ruin what you have with Vi and that little boy who already thinks of you as a father."

"I'll still be his friend," Bryce said fiercely. "I'll always be his friend."

If he thought she was going to be so ignorant as to argue with such pure loyalty, he was mistaken. She certainly wasn't going to take that away from him. Gillian felt bad for Robbie—and for his mother, too.

Bryce looked so deeply into her eyes that Gillian could actually feel his soul connecting with hers.

"That said, there's something that you should understand about me. In my whole life I've loved only one woman and I never want to lose her again. I can't think of anything more exciting than starting a new life with you and the new baby on the way."

He emphasized the point by pulling Gillian to him for a kiss that devoured the sigh on her lips and left her begging for more.

"Do you want me to get down on my knees?" he asked.

Gillian shook her head.

Blissfully happy, she didn't require such formalities. Or ask for any guarantees. She understood better than most that one day did not automatically entitle a person to another. Yet, in spite of that terrible knowledge, she refused to be a prisoner of fear or blame ever again. Not everyone was lucky enough to get a second chance at love—a chance to make life as perfect as was possible on a crazy, imperfect planet.

"That won't be necessary," she said, smiling softly. "I'll marry you. Next year, next week, tomorrow or right now if you want."

"It wouldn't be soon enough."

Bryce lowered his mouth to kiss her again only to draw away in surprise when a loud voice from the other room interrupted. "What's burning out there?"

"I hope it's your ears," Gillian called out.

Bryce laughed. "I can hardly wait to see the expression on your father's face when he hears he's going to be a grandpa again."

Standing up, Bryce offered a hand to the woman whom he'd never been able to let out of his heart. Just as the past had hurt so many people, the future was certain to fill the emptiness in many more lives than just their own. Gillian slipped her hand into his as they went to tell her father the good news together.

"I hope he has the decency to act surprised," she said with a wry little laugh.

* * * * *

Turn the page for a sneak preview of

Bedded by the Billionaire
by Leanne Banks.

This exciting first story in the new
BILLIONAIRE'S CLUB
mini-series is available from
Mills & Boon® Desire™ in May 2009.

Bedded by the Billionaire

by

Leanne Banks

"I understand you're pregnant with my brother's child."

Lilli McCall instinctively put her hand over her swollen belly and studied Maximillian De Luca. She'd reluctantly allowed him and his associate into her small suburban Las Vegas apartment. Heaven knew, she'd had several unwelcome visitors since Tony De Luca had died two weeks ago.

She'd spotted the family resemblance between Tony and Max through the peephole of her door—the natural tanned complexion, similar bone structure. Only this man wasn't as pretty as Tony. Tony had been full of easy smiles and charm, and ultimately lies. This man's face was so hard she wondered if it would break into pieces if he smiled.

Tony had told her about his brother, Max. He'd frequently complained that his brother was cutthroat, even with his own family. He'd called him the man of steel, a steel mind and a steel heart.

Lilli had detached herself from Tony for good reasons. She wanted nothing to do with him, his friends or his family.

"Miss McCall?" Max prompted.

Taking a quick breath, she gave a slow nod, willing herself not to be intimidated by the tall man. "Yes, we got involved after my mother died, but things didn't work out between us," she said in a voice she knew was stilted, but she couldn't smooth it for the life of her.

"The details aren't necessary. As you know, my brother died in an automobile accident. He had no will and no provision for children, so—"

"I didn't expect anything from him," she interjected.

He paused, his gaze flickering over her in a considering way again. "Really," he said in a doubtful voice.

His tone jabbed at her. "Really," she said. "Tony was kind to me after my mother died, but it became clear to me that I didn't belong in his world."

"Why is that?"

"I—" She hesitated, her chest tightening as she remembered the fateful night that had made her break up with him for good. "We had different values. I wanted the baby brought up in a different environment."

His gaze fell to her pregnant belly. "You came to that decision a little late, didn't you?"

In more ways than he could know, she thought. "Yes, but I can focus on the baby or on my failures. Focusing on my failures isn't going to help me. So," she said, more than ready for him to leave, "since I wasn't expecting anything from Tony, you don't need to—"

"That's where we disagree," he said and nodded toward the man standing behind him. "Jim, could you give me the paperwork? Lilli, this is Jim Gregory. You may recognize him as someone who has knocked on your door a few times recently."

Lilli tore her gaze away from Max long enough to look at the older man and recognized him. "I apologize," she said. "I live by myself, so I'm not really comfortable opening the door to men I don't know."

"I understand," Jim said and she thought she saw a hint of compassion in the older man's eyes. "Here it is, Max," he said, producing some papers from a manila envelope, along with a pen.

Max took the papers and pen and handed them to Lilli. "It's a simple document. In exchange for one million dollars now and another million dollars if and when the child reaches the age of twenty-five, you agree to give up any rights to my brother's inheritance. If you should die or fail to raise the child in a responsible manner, you agree to relinquish custody of the child to a suitable guardian of my choice."

Lilli felt her jaw drop to the floor.

"It's all there," Max said. "Let me know if you have any questions."

Lilli stared blankly at the paper and felt her hands begin to shake with anger. Shoving the papers back at him, she stepped backward. "Are you nuts?"

"Should have known," Max said to Jim. "I told you she would want more money."

Stunned, Lilli continued to stare at him. "So you *are*

nuts," she said. "You didn't hear me earlier, did you? I didn't expect anything from Tony. I don't now. And I certainly don't expect anything from you. And if you think for one second that I would let someone I've never met choose who raises my child, you're totally crazy."

"That clause is just to protect the child in the event of your death or in case you develop any dangerous habits." He placed the agreement on top of her mother's marble-top table. "Read it. Sleep on it. I'll negotiate the amount within reason."

She snatched it up to give it back to him again.

He shook his head and held up his hand. "The drama is unnecessary. It costs a lot to raise a child. It will be difficult since you're doing it alone. Think about your child's needs. Do you really want to give up everything this money can buy for your child?" He paused while her heart pounded in her chest five beats. "I'll be in touch."

As soon as the two men left her apartment, Lilli flipped the dead bolt in place. Incensed and insulted, she paced into the den. Her pulse was racing in her ears, her nails digging into her palms as she clenched her hands together. Who in hell did he think he was, coming into her home and talking to her that way?

Granted, there were a few things that didn't put her in the best light, such as the fact that she'd even gotten involved with Tony in the first place, and the fact that she was unwed and pregnant. But everyone made mistakes. The solution was owning up to them and making the best of whatever choices have been made.

Although she hadn't intended to get pregnant by Tony, Lilli was determined to be the best mother she could be. Even with all the uncertainty and responsibility she was facing, from the moment she'd learned she was carrying a life inside her, she'd felt a little less lonely.

Lilli walked into the nursery she had begun to decorate and took a deep calming breath. She'd given the walls a fresh coat of paint and hung a puffy Noah's Ark wall hanging with removable animals. The crib was solid maple, and she'd already attached a mobile with friendly colorful butterflies and birds. With her next paycheck, she planned to buy soft crib sheets and blankets in blue for her little guy.

Pressing her hand to her belly again, she thought of Max De Luca. She'd never met a man like him. Arrogant, insulting, charm-free. At least to her. She couldn't deny, though, that in different circumstances he would have fascinated her. But lions had always fascinated her, too, and she knew better than to get into a den with one of them.